THE PROUD WAY

------ *SHIRLEY SEIFERT* ------

THE

PROUD

WAY

*We planted the switch or scion of a live oak tree; and now
it shades ninety feet in every direction.*

VARINA HOWELL DAVIS

PEOPLES BOOK CLUB

CHICAGO

To Adele

THE PROUD WAY

CHAPTER I

IT was a May morning—the year 1843. She—Varina Anne Banks Howell—was just short of seventeen years old. Spring was full in the throats of birds down Natchez way and the lushness of summer had already covered winter's scars. Near the house magnolia trees were opening their first white blossoms over garden beds blazing with color. Out on the river bluff, where forest giants frowned down on the tangle of bayou and ravine, bloom was chiefly the Cherokee rose, covering every exposed knoll, tumbling in drifts of white down the steep precipice. As she left the home clearing, Varina had plucked a bud from a hedgerow. It was opening its petals now against the warm mass of her dark hair close to one ear.

The western line following the river and the bluffs, the turn being marked by a double china tree . . .

So ran the warranty deed to The Briers, which she could chant from memory, if asked. Along the jagged edge of the bluffs, just safely back from the brink, a path, wide enough for two to walk abreast, had been opened and kept clear of undergrowth. The china trees spread neat umbrellas over their angle, but that was the end of orderliness. Behind the twin trees and Varina loomed virgin forest—oak and cedar and pine draped in moss, walnut and pecan where there was light enough for them to flourish. Below, a giddy depth below, an indescribable and seemingly unbroken mass of wild brush fell away on her left to an invisible bayou and before her to the river.

9

Except that a steamboat pushing up the river made it unlikely, Varina could have been the first white woman to walk these solitudes. She would have made a good settler's bride or daughter. She was tall and straight and strong in the way of one who had grown up knowing the feel of turf to the soles of her feet or who had been lifted from her cradle and set on the back of a horse. She had dressed herself for her morning's ramble in plain, starched gingham and stoutly cobbled shoes. She carried in one hand a stick of polished apple wood, stout enough for a prop and knobby enough for a cudgel if the need arose for either. So attired and so armed, she took joy in her aloneness. As she stopped to rest under the china trees, her free hand went out to the trunk of one in a simple gesture of possession. Her eyes, as she looked out over the ravine and the river and beyond, were alive with the same feeling. Black forest and giddy precipice and wildness had no terror for her. They were her own.

Her eyes saw farther and with more penetration than one would have expected of eyes their color. They were wide eyes of a soft leaf-brown and might have been dull except for keenness of vision, combined with a very alert intelligence. Her complexion was a clear, pale ivory. It gave her a minimum of trouble with sunburn and would wear well. Her face at sixteen kept much of childish roundness. For all her sturdy independence she had led up to now a well-guarded life. But there was strength in her features. Her nose had a straight, assertive line; and her mouth, full-lipped, subject to any number of changes of mood and feeling, had a curve betraying definite willfulness.

The willfulness was lost in a sudden smile. She was watching the steamboat. Below The Briers, the river began one of its notable great bends, interesting to view from above and a distance, but maddening to upstream navigation. The packet—a four-decker, from New Orleans, no doubt, and Natchez bound, of course—hugged the low Louisiana shore opposite, to escape the full strength of the whipping current, but was still having a time of it. It looked, Varina thought merrily, like a heavy dowager climbing a flight of steps and plagued by shortness of breath. It seemed to her that she could feel the panting of the engines; and presently, at a throaty blast from the steam whistle, the hard-packed clay of the bluff actually did vibrate. She laughed aloud at the distressful echo that filled her ears; then, as abruptly as before, her expression changed to the aliveness of speculation.

Company, the whistle meant—passengers aboard for The Briers. Every place of consequence on the river had its own landing, and the packets would stop to unload or take on cargo or mail or people. Atop the bluffs it didn't seem possible that the Howells could take advantage of such accommodation, but they could and did. From the carriage gates before the main house a steep but passable road wound down through the ravine to the water's edge. Right now at the stables horses were being hitched to some sort of conveyance to be sent down to the wharf. If she ran all the way, she might be in time to catch a ride in the same vehicle.

Wasting no more time on conjecture, Varina dropped her stick, gathered up her full skirts in two hands and raced back over the path. Halfway to the house, however, she stopped. She had better than a quarter-mile of ground still to cover, the morning was warming up, and she was amazed to find herself out of breath. That, she thought impatiently, was what came of wasting one's life in a seminary, where all one's exercise was dance steps or walking in a crocodile tail headed by a schoolmistress or games supervised against any real liveliness. A second and equally annoying result was an unexpected doubt of the suitability of gingham and brogans for receiving a visitor of importance. A year ago she would not have stopped to consider the point; but a year ago she would not have supposed possible what now she knew to be a fact—that at sixteen, just short of seventeen, she was no longer that bright, long-legged, pretty, but—well, rather unusual—Howell girl. She was, quite suddenly, and sometimes uncomfortably, a young lady.

Of course, the passenger arriving on the boat, if it was a passenger, might be just her father. He had been away when she returned from school a few days before and was still absent, looking over the family's Louisiana plantations. Her father would welcome her in any costume —his ewe lamb, his lovely eldest daughter. Still, it would be fun and proof of something to startle him. And there remained the possibility of an unknown visitor. Thoughts, speculation, dreams passed over her face like the light flickering through the dense trees as she hurried on.

A few minutes later she was letting down the bars to a gate set in a fence banked solidly with the white Cherokee roses. She went through the gate, closed it carefully, crossed a green, flowering pasture to another gate, a swinging one this time, set in a fence concealed by a more formal planting of lauri mundi shrub, and was at home.

She was too late now to ride to the river landing to meet the boat. Far down the road she could hear the scrunch of wheels and the restrained plunge of the horses that drew the carriage. It was the carriage, she felt certain, distinguishing by ear between its weight and the creaking of a dray or the rattle of a light gig, which would have been sufficient to receive her father alone. More active crashing through underbrush indicated, besides, a mounted escort. That would be Joe, the brother two years her senior. The slightly petulant curve to her mouth deepened to a near-pout, but it was only a fleeting and familiar protest against the disadvantage of having been born female, and her face cleared while she loitered at the gate.

There was no need now for running and the picture before her was too precious not to command a moment's respectful attention. Her eyelids drooped protectingly as she passed from forest gloom to open sunlight but not enough to hide again an unashamed, possessive gloating. How long, she wondered, would it take for her to unaccustom her vision to rows of prim, narrow brick houses on narrow streets, and know that she was here?

There were estates in Natchez and about with far handsomer gardens than those at The Briers. The wild here was too close to the cultivated not to intrude. Cedars, looking as old as time with their beards of moss, stalked among more amenable, glossy-leaved magnolias and made light of roses and lilies and sweet olive and pomegranate shrubbery; but growth everywhere was lush and the suggestion of disorder had its own charm. The house, as well, was not the stately mansion that the very wealthiest of planters now fancied, with spreading wings and a façade like a Greek temple. Broad and low and spacious, it, too, had the grace of unstudied charm. From where she stood, Varina had an oblique view of the long front gallery, of green shutters and small-paned windows, of the sweep of the hip roof, of a small frame and plaster schoolhouse just visible in the smother of trees. The last trace of petulance left her face. Her eyes misted.

"Sweet!"

Her lips shaped the word without sound and she hurried on. When she reached the front steps, she found that a search was on for her. The wide main door stood open. The whole house, in fact, was so protected by its deep galleries both to the north and the south and by trees, that all summer long, except for storms and in periods of violent heat, it stood open; and a call sounded in any part would echo its length and breadth. Varina's mother was calling her.

"Va-ree-na!"

The name, Varina often thought, was shaped for such ringing summons. The present tones were light, melodious as a bird's trilling, but insistent and compelling. They entreated and commanded anyone within earshot to heed their obvious will and do something about it. Certainly it was Varina's place to answer and only she would have had the courage or the inspiration to stand perfectly quiet for the pure deliciousness of hearing the sweet, searching cry:

"Va-ree-na!"

"Yore mamma say fix yoreself up nice."

Soft suggestion veiled the command but thinly. The open wild rose swam in a saucer of water on a marble-topped dresser. Green light, taking its color from tall bay trees and half-drawn shutters, came with an illusion of coolness through the windows of Varina's bedroom. A young mulatto woman, of strong, handsome features, marred somewhat by a disdainful expression which she thought the essence of propriety, was laying out a dress of flowered lawn on the bed. Her hands hovered over the light material and its ribbon ties; and anyone familiar with "For Sale" billings in the Natchez *Gazette* or *Courier* could have named her position at once:

". . . likely, a skilled seamstress and lady's maid . . ."

Varina, in fresh cambric chemise and multiple starched petticoats, taking down her hair before the bureau, was able with the help of the mirror to watch every elaborate movement the woman made; and her appraisal was more thorough.

"Yes, Melissa," she said placatingly.

Melissa was her mother's personal maid. About ten years older than Varina, she had received her first training in special service while the latter was a baby. This had given the slave a kind of title to the white child still in her crib and the bond had strengthened with the years. Varina on her part was as much attached to Melissa as Melissa was to her. Faraway in Philadelphia at school, she had missed the maid's exquisite care and her arbitrary, licensed scolding as much as any other feature of home; and she had no doubt now in her heart that Melissa had missed her. Nevertheless, Melissa at this moment was as seriously displeased with Varina as she had ever been in her life.

"Isn't it luck," Varina proceeded warily, "that I should be at home this time when Mr. Davis stopped off? I've missed him for two years running now."

"Luck!" Melissa snorted. "What you does is never luck. You plans it out to suit yoreself. Always!"

"Why, Melissa!" Then Varina saw a light. "Meliss', if I had just happened to be in Philadelphia still when Papa's letter came—the one I didn't get—and had waited in Trenton at Grandfather Governor Howell's until the folks came for me, would you have come with them?"

"Who else," Melissa demanded, "woulda waited on Miss Ma'gret, I'd like to know? Co'se, I'da gone, too."

"I'm so sorry," Varina said, with real contrition. "I hadn't thought about your being disappointed."

"Ev'ybody disappointed," Melissa told her. "Miss Ma'gret's terrible disappointed. She ain't been on a gran' trip since befo' you was borned. An' she's feelin' right frail since the new boy baby came. Yore papa disappointed, countin' on vistin' his folks in Jersey. But Ole Miss most disappointed of all. Looked like her best chance to git back to Virginny once mo' befo' she died. All they plans busted, it don' make much diff'ence about mine. Even," she concluded mournfully, "if I ain' ever been anywhere, let alone Niag'ra or Saratoga."

"Oh, Meliss'," Varina said again and with genuine feeling, "I am truly sorry. Some day, maybe . . ."

"How you talk!" Melissa interrupted. "You bust up big plans like that and who's goin' to pick up the pieces and put 'em together again? We'd even got a start on clo'es." She laid a black velvet ribbon sash on the bed beside the fluff of the skirt. "Who you goin' to trap aroun' here, I want to know?"

Varina laid hold of her heavy hair with both hands and shook it in a cloud around her face.

"Must I trap somebody?" she asked demurely, knowing the answer.

"You boun' to marry some time," Melissa told her. "But who? Ain't **nobody** aroun' here worth spreadin' much bait fo'."

"Why, Meliss', the nicest people in the world come from Mississippi, and most of them from Natchez."

"Nice enough," Melissa admitted grudgingly, "but they got sense, too. The young men awful perlite, but they marry as rich as they can and it don' hurt if the young ladies look out for themselves the same way. That's how we keep things goin' aroun' here."

"Then," Varina agreed, sighing, "Saratoga Springs or White Sulphur or Niagara would be the thing. Of course, you want to remember," she added slyly, "the very richest young men at those places are apt to be Yankees."

"All of 'em?" Melissa asked, aghast.

"Well, most. How would you like me to marry a Yankee and live up North the rest of my life—as far off as the State of Maine, maybe?"

"Miss V'rina," Melissa stood up straight and stiff as if she had been stabbed, "you ain' run fo' home to git away f'om the clutch of a Yankee, is you?"

"Maybe, I did."

There was no truth in the maybe; but, if it served for distraction, it was worth using. Melissa came over to the bureau and picked up a hairbrush. A minute later she was smoothing the long strands of Varina's hair, still scolding, but more respectfully.

"Full o' dust and smoke and wind snarls. Needs washin' and sunnin' an airin'. Tomorrer, if Mr. Davis don' stay over . . . he don', usually."

"Mr. Davis," Varina said dreamily, "is a rich man."

The hairbrush was still.

"You ain' goin' to work on him, I hope," Melissa said darkly into the mirror. "Mr. Davis ten years older than yore own papa—that much, anyhow."

"Very rich," Varina murmured, as if Melissa had not spoken. "Just about the richest man in Mississippi, I'm thinking."

The Midas touch, people said, describing Mr. Joseph Davis of Warren County. Money stuck to his fingers. Naturally she had no romantic notions about him. She had called him Uncle Joe all her life. Still, it was rather wonderful that he should be her father's closest friend. Two men more opposite in natures it would be hard to picture. Nobody had ever accussed William Burr Howell of the Midas touch. Sweet, affable, generous—he had friends wherever he went; but wealth

—real, hard wealth—was, as even Varina knew, more difficult to obtain and hold.

"Got twenty chil'ren hisself, big as you are," Melissa gloomed.

"Twenty?" Varina's eyes were wide. She knew that Joseph Davis was married. Naturally there would be some sort of family, but . . .

"I was just generally speakin'," Melissa said. The brush began to move again—long, thoughtful strokes. "Well, young or old, grampa or gran'child," she philosophized, "a man's somethin' to practise on."

"Silly!" Varina said, then impulsively, "Put it up, Melissa."

"All the way up? I kin try. Hold this tuck comb and the pins. Stiff as a horse's tail. Tomorrer mornin', first thing . . ."

Melissa's hands were gifted. The mass of hair went up into a braided coronet, not unbecoming. Melissa stood off to judge her work and Varina snatched the rose out of its saucer. She had to move fast. Melissa came at her with a rush.

"Miss V'rina, you ain't . . . that common, wild rose!"

The rose was in, against the shining braid.

"Papa's favorite flower," Varina said, sucking her finger where a thorn had pricked and managing a sweet, artless smile at the same time. It was a pleasing image that the mirror reflected. "Meliss', you are sure it was papa with Mr. Davis?"

"Co'se, I's sure. Is you forgot that big laugh so soon? Besides, I looked out the window." Angrily Melissa turned to the bed. "Common, trashy wild flower. Can't do nothin' about it now without tearin' ev'ything to pieces again. You are the beatin'es' child. Sit still now, if you kin, one mo' minute whiles I drops the skirt, then stan' up quick, so's you don' muss it befo' I git the tape tied."

The crisp lawn ballooned out over the full petticoats. The bodice, stayed with whalebone and shaped into points that came down over the fullness at the waist line, gave Varina's tall slenderness an illusion of delicacy.

"Looks all right, I reckon," Melissa sighed. "Guessed the measure pretty good." Then she considered Varina. "Green young . . . head's mostly eyes and topknot. Neck's got some hollers; but we'll have to draw in the stays if you fills out . . . they's a Legho'n bonnet goes with the dress."

The bonnet was a poke of smooth straw braid. A wreath of feather flowers surrounded the small, high crown. "Impo'ted," Melissa said—

made by humble, dusky fingers far away. Black velvet ribbons, meant for ties, looped gracefully over a shapely forearm. The hat was sweet against the sprigged lawn skirt.

"You could go out the back way," Melissa suggested, "and stroll aroun' the house carelesslike—that's how it was in the picture we studied."

"Or," Varina said, "I could go through the house and out the front door, as if I had a stroll in mind. . . ."

Sixteen, going on seventeen—innocent, trifling . . .

The studied picture failed somewhat of its full effect, through lack of proper audience. Varina's father and his guest were still in the former's office when Varina descended the stairs from her bedroom. Through open windows she could hear the clink of glasses, the dry, level tones of the visitor, and her father's richer ones, punctuated occasionally by a restrained big laugh. Joe Howell, her brother, would be there, too, Varina had no doubt, taking his glass of julep and looking as wise as he could, which wouldn't be too wise, considering his natural endowments and that he lacked only two years of being as "green young" as his sister. However, having been born a man, there he would be, just the same—the handsome, long-legged simpleton!

The staircase that Varina had descended opened on what was in fact part of the south or rear gallery. Here the arrangement differed from the broad, open veranda that extended from end to end across the front of the house. Wide, projecting wings walled in the south gallery to the east and the west, reducing its length to a mere sixty feet. In addition, about eight feet back from the outer row of posts, other columns, supporting wide arches, created the illusion of another wall and made of the more sheltered portion of the gallery a semi-enclosed, summer sitting room. The uncomfortable and odorous business of cooking went on in a kitchen which was a detached building, reached by its own passage from the gallery. From either extremity of the open veranda a flight of steps led down to a service yard, while from either end of the enclosed portion boxed-in stairways ascended to the rooms on the second floor. These included bedrooms in both wings, over special apartments below devoted to the use of Varina's parents and of her grandmother, and, over the center portions of the house, large double parlors with sliding doors, which could accommodate extra guests for sleeping or, in the winter season, were the scenes of social gatherings too large for the exquisite formal parlor on the first floor. What the closed stairways lost in grace by not being open flights they gained in protection, with doors above and below to shut off drafts in cold weather. After all, however brief and unpredictable his visits, winter did come to Mississippi.

In the summer sitting room servants were now setting a table for dinner. Varina passed them with a dreamy smile and went on through the empty hall to the front door, where she paused to reconnoiter. On the more shaded end of the north gallery, only her mother and her grandmother waited in a group of hospitable rocking chairs. Only? Varina posed a second on the threshold, light and uncertain and pretty as a butterfly, then, with unerring judgment, born of years of custom, went swiftly down the porch to curtsey first to her grandmother.

Granny Kempe was a formidable-appearing woman. She was, moreover, a formidable woman. She never forgot that she had been born a Graham of Prince William County, Virginia. The Natchez country was wilderness when she had left home to settle there with James Kempe, her lover and husband, an exile from Ireland and Ireland's wars. She brought slaves with her from Virginia, but there were hardships and privations from which neither they nor her position could save her. All her children except her first, now Varina's mother, had been born in the new land. Her home was hardly established when James Kempe, as captain of the Adams County Troop of Horse, had joined the rest of the Mississippi Dragoons to put down a bloody uprising of the Creeks; and the Indians were no sooner quiet than Andrew Jackson had marched by with his Tennessee riflemen to defend New Orleans against the British. A person would hardly expect an Irish gentleman to stay out of that fray. Twice, then, Margaret Graham had helped her husband belt on his sword and taken his goodbye kiss and watched him disappear down the forest trace, and then turned her mind, not to the dangers that loomed about her, but to the land James had planned to open in the young new year.

These days were gone now, with many that were grander and some that were sorrier; and she was the Widow Kempe, living in the home of her married daughter.

"And why not?" she would have said, had anyone questioned her position there, which no one ever did. "Was it not their child who

burned Kempton down around my ears? Where else was I to go
then?"

There was truth in the legend. On the outskirts of Natchez, the
charred ruin of what had been a proud house still stood, bearing witness. A charred ruin ... but here was no ruin. She who had been born
Margaret Graham sat on this warm day stiffly erect in her rocker,
buttoned uncompromisingly to her second chin in air-tight black taffeta.
One hand rested lightly on a silver-mounted cane. A cap of fine,
creamy old lace crowned her smoothly dressed gray hair. Two young
black girls stood, one to either side of her, waving large palm leaf fans.
She paid no attention to them unless their activity fell off. Then one
flicker of her eyelids had the fans going furiously. The black cane had
never touched the back of either girl, but there was always the possibility that it might.

"Very pretty," she said to Varina's curtsey. "Very pretty, indeed."

Her black eyes snapped. The man or woman didn't live, white or
black, young or old, who could deceive her. Varina knew this and
squirmed a little with the knowing, but all inside. There were those
who said she was the image of her grandmother. She wasn't really.
Except that her eyes and hair were darker than his, Varina resembled
her father; and even that darkness of coloring she might have had
from his family, his mother having been born a Burr, and all the Burrs
being dark. The resemblance between the old woman and the very
young one was, rather, a matter of will. More than a burned house
marked the tale of their relationship. They had clashed from the first,
the issue, barring the years in favor of the older woman, remaining
usually in doubt. Varina's curtsey this morning was deference. Her
"Thank you, Granny," was docile, but withholding.

"Let me see, darling."

With a warmer and wholly natural impulse, Varina turned to face
her mother's inspection. Here was another imperiousness—softer, but
just as insistent and even more potent. Margaret Howell was one of
those women born to rule because it is a pleasure to serve them. Back
in 1820, when she had been Varina's age and the Mississippi wilderness
was giving way before throngs of ardent, gifted young men who had
come to the new Southwest to seek their fortunes—or any other's avail-
able—her bright Irish coloring, her rose-leaf complexion, her blue eyes
with their dark lashes, her dark, curling hair and her sweetness had

been the toast of the Natchez countryside. Beautiful, rich, of proud lineage, she could have taken her pick of the young men; and one could imagine even now many a settled doctor or lawyer or planter, who had made sensible acceptance of defeat, lifting a glass in occasional silent homage to a dream he had lost.

Inevitably the field of choice had narrowed to two suitors. Here, according to the faintest and most subdued of rumors, had been the only instance when she who was to be Margaret Howell had come into open conflict with her contentious mother. The elder Margaret had preferred one young man, the younger another; and the younger had followed her heart. Who had been Granny Kempe's choice no one had ever said; and the Howell children had not ventured to inquire, curiosity implying a disloyalty to their father and a slight reflection on their mother. Only Varina, whose searching mind was harder to curb, had made certain shrewd speculations as to the identity of the rejected lover. These surmises, however, she had kept to herself, being as devoted as anyone else in the household to both her parents.

Margaret Howell in maturity was still a beautiful woman. Melissa's dark application of the term "frail" was a distortion. Fashioned on delicate lines, after the birth of each successive child people always said it seemed impossible that she could be the mother of such bouncing babies, and then waited for her to fade and pine, which she never did. The strength was not apparent, but it was there.

She looked quite herself today, Varina noted with thankfulness and some scorn of Melissa—fresh as a rose in a dress of light-weight plaid silk in tones of gray, with a fringed scarf exactly the color of her eyes thrown gracefully about her shoulders.

"Sweet," she said, smiling up at her tall daughter, her low, husky voice stirring a familiar shiver in Varina's breast. "Kiss me, darling. Where have you been all morning? Off on one of your ferocious rambles, Melissa said."

Her cheek was firm and just healthily warm under the touch of Varina's lips. She was not frail and she did not appear to be in any state of disappointment or displeasure. She seemed, rather, in exceptionally good spirits. Varina, thinking of all these things and at a loss, momentarily, for words that would cover the present pryings of her mind, found her attention distracted by the continued rumble of male voices from the far end of the house.

It seemed to her that the tone of that conversation had changed subtly. The clink of glass was stilled, and the occasional riffle of laughter. The talk would be serious, then—having to do with government or markets or credits—rich, meaty, men's talk. A flush of anger swept over her, dissolving all lightsomeness of mood. Here was fresh annoyance at having been born a woman. Down yonder this talk went on—about things that mattered. Up here, at the opposite end of the gallery, the women whose lives were deeply affected by the same debatable subjects, must be satisfied with rumbling echoes.

It wasn't as if they lacked comprehension. Granny Kempe had a mind to match any man's. Margaret Howell, for all her gentleness, had plenty of reasonable good sense. And she, Varina, was popularly accused of being especially endowed with intellect. In the schoolhouse adjacent to the office gable, before she had been sent East to acquire certain fol-de-rol graces, she had been given as stiff a grounding in the classics as any boy, and by the best of tutors. She had outstripped her brother Joe in the first year of their lessons. But all that would make no difference finally. Whether man's talk meant trouble or was merely a discussion of facts and figures, a woman must learn the gist of it indirectly, by subterfuge and inference, if at all. It was a wonder a woman's mind did not decay from disuse. It would have, except that she must keep her wits extra nimble.

Amusement again smoothed out Varina's annoyance. Joe, her brother, if the talk was too deep or no longer sauced with julep, would be in a mental state by now. Because he was named for Joseph Davis, he must try—and harder than any woman, not having a woman's practice—to make a favorable appearance before the older man. He might almost as well not try. Uncle Joe would see right through him. For that matter, their father, if the talk became too abstract, might lose his way in it and be mildly bewildered until he had time to absorb confusion in some healthier activity. Varina's lips sweetened at the passing thought of her father and the words she needed came.

"Thank you, Mamma," she said, "for the pretty dress and the love of a bonnet. And I'm sorry if I upset everybody's plans by coming home too soon."

Margaret Howell still held to her daughter's hand. She squeezed the fingers gently and a sparkle of mischief brightened her blue eyes.

"Thank Granny, darling. It was her idea."

"Granny . . ."

But, before Varina could say more, the men came out of William Howell's office; and Varina, again abandoning effect for natural impulse, raced the length of the gallery to fling herself into her father's arms.

The momentum of her onslaught would have upset a lesser man. William Burr Howell braced himself and took it standing. A good six feet and some inches tall, with considerable breadth of beam, he carried both height and breadth easily. In his younger days he had served his country with honor as an officer in the Marines; and the hardness gained then he kept now by spending as much of every day as possible in the saddle, overlooking plantations which he knew, without abashment, were his wife's inheritance. He just wasn't a man to bother his head about trifling circumstance. It, like the weather, was a thing to be met and dealt with as it came. You could neither hold it off nor alter it by worrying. Rejection of worry, more than any other one thing, it is probable, gave him his very open and likable nature.

He received Varina now with a mighty hug and the familiar big laugh. He snuggled her to him like a recovered lost pup, then kissed her heartily on both cheeks, so that it was an exceptionally rosy and happy face that she turned finally to her brother Joe, somewhat flushed himself for other reasons, and then to the guest of the day, whose presence had temporarily lost its exciting importance.

But only temporarily. Joseph Davis was not a man to content himself willingly with second place in anyone's considerations—certainly not in those of a child of sixteen. Moreover, right now something else had struck him. Instead of continuing down the porch to pay his *devoirs* to the older women, he had stopped to watch the meeting of father and daughter; and his expression, when Varina's eyes met his, was so compounded of wonder, question and compliment that it threw her sensibilities into a decided, though not unpleasing flutter. To cover confusion, she dropped him a low, elaborate curtsey.

"It's Varina, Joe," her father explained, with, one could have declared, a touch of impatience. "Our Winnie, if you can believe it."

"Varina," Joseph Davis said, the question in his eyes sharpening into something like speculation. "Varina . . . yes, I see now. Child, what a lovely creature you have come to be!"

The condescension of his approval produced something of a smart, to balance flattery. Nevertheless, the tribute was there; and Varina's senses were still in a flutter when she took her place, with the rest of the family, under the peacock feather fly brush at the dinner table.

She kept telling herself not to be silly, reminding herself that this was only Uncle Joe, who was always rather the visiting potentate when he stopped off at The Briers. Like many men who make their own fortunes, he was fairly proud of his wealth, and was inclined to make the most obvious display of its power where he felt that, otherwise, relative social rating was not in his favor. That was the case here. Granny Kempe could remember—and sometimes mischievously remarked on the fact—when he and several Davis brothers had been mere troopers in that same company of Adams County Horse which her splendid husband had captained. But mischief was all her reminder came to. Of all the family she had probably the sharpest appreciation of Joseph Davis's attainments.

Unless it was the Howell children. Their attitude toward their Uncle Joe hitherto had been healthily material. His visits, especially if he was on his way, as now, up the river from New Orleans to his home below Vicksburg in Warren County, were pleasantly associated with gifts and always with lively entertainment. Their grandmother was in high spirits while he was on the place. Their mother seemed rosier and prettier and sweeter than usual, their father gayer. The house oozed good food and drink. It rang with laughter and merry talk. Varina and Joe Howell would sit for hours, listening to tales of rare adventure. That their Uncle Joe had served in any capacity with the Adams County Dragoons recalled what was to them a golden era, when the woods about had teemed with Indians and, more awful still, real bandits.

By 1820, when their father had come out to Mississippi, a hero, barely existing on his retirement half-pay, the Indians were quiet, but outlawry still flourished. The abundance of crime, Uncle Joe declared, had been the lodestone that drew lawyers from every state in the Union, until in Natchez a whole row of buildings had to be erected adjacent to the Courthouse square, to accommodate them with offices. Lawyers' Row still stood, to prove it. Yes, that was true, their father said solemnly. No man in those days had thought of stirring from his lodging house unarmed. He would then bring out his Battle of the

Lakes pistols and demonstrate how he had belted them to his fine figure when he went courting.

When he went courting . . .

Their Uncle Joe probably was more than ten years older than their father, but he had been a bachelor still when the latter had come West. The two had beaued around together. Finally Uncle Joe had been best man at their parents' wedding, a bachelor still, his own marriage following several years later.

The relationship between the two men had gone deeper, one gathered, than casual friendship. Uncle Joe, already well established in law at both Natchez and Vicksburg, had been characteristically generous with patronage and advice, most of which, he declared, his young friend had handsomely disregarded.

"I even offered him a thousand acres at Davis Bend," Uncle Joe would say. "Best bottom land on the river, dirt cheap, teeming with fertility . . ."

"And alligators and malaria," their father would contribute.

"Unneighborly, uncharitable young rogue," Uncle Joe would continue. "I needed a few outside purchasers to carry the investment and I wanted to select my settlers; but neither love nor money would persuade the rascal to come in. He was smart enough, however, to pick the prettiest girl of those I took him to call upon down here. Well, you'd have been a richer man, Howell, if you'd bought in on my land; but I don't suppose you could have been happier."

Wealth—happiness—the difference in the natures of the two men had become more marked as the years went by, Varina thought now. Her father had preserved his rollicking, careless good humor as well as the hardness of his physique; Uncle Joe, who sat more in broad chairs on hotel verandas or on packet decks or on that mystery of mysteries, the Exchange, and who liked good food and drink a trifle better than the next man, had gathered extra poundage in a more centralized locality. It could not be said that he had a paunch. He was a tall man, too, and rode when he could find a horse to carry him. But his waistcoat did show a slight outward curve.

Contrasting temperament was even more pronounced in the two men's faces. Her father's showed no more trace of advancing years than it did of accumulating care. His cheeks were round and firm, his eyes bright; and not a thread of gray touched his abundant hair.

Uncle Joe had the bony head structure popularly attributed to the thinking man. Thinning gray hair accentuated this by elevating and widening the expanse of his forehead. Fine lines circled his eyes like the spokes of wheels, criss-crossing over the bridge of his prominent, slightly aquiline nose. These eyes, kindly enough in relaxed moments, and remarkable only because they were a very light blue, continued to study Varina throughout the meal—more openly and boldly, but perhaps no more intently, than she in turn speculated on him. The interchange was helped by their being seated opposite each other at the table.

It was not as long a dinner table as it was frequently, the only casual guests who had dropped in opportunely being Varina's Aunt Jennie Sprague and her Cousin Margaret, a girl close to Varina's age, but shyer and seeming younger. They had come out to see if possibly there were still any strawberries to be had at The Briers, they having eaten all theirs and expecting company of their own. The strawberries were gone at The Briers, too; but early blackberries were coming on. Blackberry roll, hot and luscious and waiting in the kitchen, perfumed the air at the rear of the house to the utter defeat of mere flower scents. A subdued clamor came in with the enticing smell. A handful of younger Spragues and Varina's small sisters—Maggie Howell, who would be forever that because of numerous older Margarets, and two-year-old Jane—were having their dinner in the schoolhouse in charge of the Howell nurse; and conversation seemed as lively there as at the main table.

The Spragues were in a twit over finding Varina at home. They were, they declared, never so surprised. They had understood . . .

"Surprised myself," William Howell said, "but not clear out of reason. Homesick, Puss?"

Varina, conscious every minute that she was under examination, made bolder answer than she might have under less provoking circumstances.

"Horribly, Papa. You know I hate the place."

"What place, may I ask?" Joseph Davis inquired.

"School," Varina answered politely. "Madame Greenland's **in Philadelphia**."

"Philadelphia? It seems a distance."

"I grew up in Jersey," William Howell reminded him.

"True." Joseph had not looked away from Varina. "You dislike school?"

"Not regular school," Varina said quickly. "This is a Young Ladies' Seminary."

"Oh?" He was still inquiring.

"It specializes in the more feminine arts. There is a French dancing master. He . . . reeks of pomade."

There was a shocked silence the length of the table.

"Pomatum," Granny Kempe corrected. "Gentlemen are not above using it, for correct grooming; or they were not, in my day. Your grandfather, I remember, among others."

Grandfather Kempe having died when Varina was in pinafores, she had no authority for disputing her grandmother's statement, if she had presumed.

"Monsieur uses pomade, Granny," she insisted. "A poor grade, I suspect. And . . . he does reek."

Down the table young Joe Howell snorted softly. Varina flashed him a dazzling smile. Margaret Sprague added a shy giggle and Varina frowned. That would be tribute to Joe, not to her wit, she understood. Joe was a handsome fellow; and he wouldn't, she thought, be caught dead with a hair dressing of pomade. Today being warm and he at ease in his home, he had not bothered even to put on a cravat. His soft white shirt was open at the throat. His skin was smooth and brown. His dark, curly hair was an unruly tangle. Planter folk left fussiness of dress to women. Her father and Uncle Joe were older examples. Both wore the loosest of alpaca coats and their wide, winged collars no tighter than need be. Irrelevantly—or so it seemed—a scrap of Melissa's talk drifted through Varina's memory. If and when she married, she decided then and there, her choice of husbands would be a planter.

"Please continue," Joseph Davis begged, amused at her prattle.

"And china painting," Varina said, thus encouraged. "Barrels of cups and plates and pitchers finally, with forget-me-nots and roses and birds—bluebirds, chiefly, because their pink breasts are so pretty. Or, if one chooses, one can spot up a length of satin ribbon or silk velvet."

"You are not especially proficient with a paint brush, I gather?"

"I daub," Varina told him. "So do most of the others, oh, but so elegantly! And willingly, because time spent that way excuses them from study."

"Then, some attention is given to cultivating the mind?"

"Yes, but . . ."

On the point of explaining that at Madame Greenland's the lessons laid out in the classics, whether Latin or Greek or English, were exercises she had mastered long ago under a real teacher, Varina hesitated. Until she had gone East to this seminary, to acquire the fol-derol graces, she had been rather proud of her capacity for learning; but at Madame Greenland's certain people, jealous, it might be, of her superior attainments, had tried to impress upon her that too much wisdom was not a woman's most potent charm. Women who paraded their mental gifts were eccentricities. For some reason Varina did not want the kindly disposed, but sharp examiner over the way to think of her as an eccentricity.

"I would not worry about Varina's mind," Granny Kempe interrupted. "It has been well taken care of. There is a wretched old man in Natchez . . ."

"Why, Mamma!" Margaret Howell said gently, before Varina could shape her hot protest. "How can you speak so? I am sure we never could have employed a tutor half so able or so devoted."

Her words were a cool, restraining hand on her daughter's impetuosity. Possessed of a fair, though controlled, intelligence herself, Margaret understood Varina's devotion to her favorite teacher. It was real devotion. For a minute, over the fragrance of blackberry roll, Varina could smell the dry paper of old books; and, over the talk here and the shrill Babel in the schoolhouse beyond, she could hear a cultured, persuasive voice, which some people also considered dry, explaining, exploring, guiding—a sage old man and a child . . .

"Education is all very well," Granny Kempe said, "but to stuff a girl's head with heathenish learning as if she were preparing for Oxford or Cambridge is outlandish, it seems to me. What's to come of it, finally?"

"Judge Winchester," William Howell explained to Joseph Davis. "You know him. We had trouble engaging a tutor for the children when they were small—Joe here and Varina; and he volunteered. Then he became interested and stayed on and—well, finally we forgot to look farther and he took over the schoolhouse."

The sharp eyes across the table asked Varina what she thought. Joseph Davis wanted to hear her say.

"He knows everything there is to know." The words were extravagant and, at the same time, inadequate. "He truly does," Varina insisted.

"Well, almost," Joseph conceded. "This is certainly his reputation at law. I've consulted him often. Cases and cases of books and he quotes from any of them without taking the volume off its shelf."

He did know Judge Winchester. Cases of books . . . but Joseph turned now to his namesake.

"Do you share your sister's enthusiasm for this very special tutor?"

"I think Uncle Judge is pretty fine," Joe answered loyally, "but Winnie is the brains of the family, sir."

"Is she, indeed?"

Was he amused or incredulous? William Howell changed the subject.

"What news do you bring of the family, Puss? I understood that Aunt Sally spent the winter in Trenton, to be near, if you needed her."

"I had Christmas in Trenton," Varina said, her throat dangerously tight. "Aunt Sally's a darling. She had a house full—from the school. She showed us the bridge where she and her friends scattered flowers before General Washington when he came that way as President. We read the poem Grandfather Governor Howell composed for the occasion:

> Welcome, Mighty Chief!
> Once more welcome to this grateful shore . . .

You know. There was a ball, too, at the Governor's Mansion and because Grandfather had been governor there, I led a cotillion and then we came back to Philadelphia and we had a box at the theater and I was quite happy. Really. I had no idea of not staying out the term until . . . one day, quite suddenly, it was spring. I saw a crocus. I heard a bird sing. And there were these people on their way to New Orleans. They stopped at the school for their daughter. . . ."

"Strangers," Granny Kempe said. "The man makes hats, I understand."

"His business in New Orleans was about straw," Varina said defiantly. "Straw from Mexico or South America. I forget. Oh, it doesn't matter about the Birnams, does it? It was just as I said, Papa. It was spring and something drew me back here. That's all, Papa."

She had spoken the truth. Home had drawn her, as a bayou could draw a tree, pulling its very roots out of the earth.

"Drew you, eh?" Uncle Joe repeated. "Hm. Natural instinct, surer than any judgment. And I, for one, am glad you felt the pull. Varina, are we to understand that you have abandoned the seminary for all time, that you plan to brighten Mississippi with your presence for now on?"

Varina was puzzled to know whether he was teasing or in earnest. She looked at him fully and frankly as she answered.

"I hope I can stay, now that I'm here."

"Good! Then, perhaps, one of these days you will honor me with a visit at Hurricane."

Varina could see afterward how everything since their encounter out front had led to this invitation; but at the time she was as startled as anyone else at the table, which was saying a good deal, everybody being struck speechless for a spell. Hurricane—the wild land, the alligator swamp. No, it couldn't be that now, if it was Uncle Joe's home.

"See if you don't think better of the place than your father did," Joseph said, reading her mind.

"That was a long time ago, Joe," William protested.

"I know. I had no idea how long until just now. Well, Varina?"

"Joseph," Margaret Howell said from her end of the table, "the child has just returned to us."

"I had no idea of taking her off under my arm right now." He was annoyed—slightly—not to the defeat of his intentions, however. "Summer coming on and the fevers. This fall or winter, I thought. Christmas is a good time. We usually have the house full then. I have a considerable family myself, Varina."

Twenty, Melissa had said, generally speaking. But he was not referring to his own children, as it happened; none of them being old enough to interest Varina. Apparently Varina's father had the same thought.

"I had the pleasure of meeting one of your nephews in New Orleans last winter," he said thoughtfully. "Another namesake."

"Tall?" Uncle Joe said. "With the Davis beak? Young Joseph— Isaac's oldest. The family lives near Hurricane, but on the mainland.

Yes, I had him in mind, among others. I think I can promise you lively entertainment, Varina, and, perhaps, a conquest or two. Well?"

A conquest? A trophy or trophies for her, and what for himself? Why did she think of that? Because he said in effect, "I know a young man who will fall in love with you on sight, if he should see you. I should like to arrange the meeting."

Why? Why did he want this?

"Varina," her mother said, "you haven't thanked Uncle Joe for his invitation."

"Or said yes . . . or no," he added.

Varina raised her eyes to his, met only the disturbing flattery of his examination, and lowered them, she hoped, becomingly.

"Thank you, Uncle Joe. I should like very much to visit you, if Mamma and Papa have no objections."

As a matter of fact, they had. At least, her father pretended to be displeased, but in a manner calculated only to whet her growing interest.

"Your Uncle Joe," he growled, "can be considerable of a busybody when he takes the notion."

Dinner was over. Everyone else in the household, from the honored guest to the humblest fly-chaser, was resting somewhere. At the close of the meal her father had put his arm warmly through hers and led her off alone to his office. For a private word, he said. She had no forebodings about the interview and was not alarmed by his growling. She thought again, and happily, what a big, comforting person her father was, with his ruffled hair and gentle eyes—her absolute ideal of a man. A pair of Joe's beagles were sleeping near the outer door when they entered the pleasantly cluttered room. The male opened soft, inquiring eyes; the bitch got halfway to her feet, but only in case someone might want to pat her.

"Down, Itsy," Varina said; and the hound dropped with a sigh.

Varina sniffed the familiar atmosphere greedily—horse, leather, dog, man, books, and some dust—deep pigeonholes that were never emptied, books undisturbed over years, especially her father's law books on the bottom shelf. He never opened them nowadays, and young Joe was reading his law in town. Above were ranked bound copies of *The National Intelligencer,* demonstrating the family's genteel Whig politics, which were further attested by a portrait of Henry Clay, hanging beside a bookcase, and, on another wall, a sketch some local artist had made of a Natchez procession during the late Harrison-Tyler campaign. That had been Varina's last winter at home. She remembered the torches and a party at The Briers, celebrating the election. There had been cider in barrels and a fruit cake with an iced cardboard roof, supposed to look like a log cabin—after a snow, presumably. Of course, the place of honor on the walls was left for a steel engraving of George Washington's second inaugural reception and ball. Richard Howell, Governor of New Jersey, and his wife, born Keziah Burr, were among the notables depicted. All these, and over the open desk a framed letter to William Howell, signed by Stephen Decatur, bidding farewell to a young companion at arms and wishing him well in a new country and new enterprise.

A sturdy chair with curving arms stood before the desk. It creaked as her father sat down. Varina considered briefly tapping his shoulder in warning and taking her accustomed place on his knee, then, out of regard for her dress and for reasons more subtle, took instead a chair some feet away. It was an error in judgment. Her father could look at her much more directly where she sat now.

"I suppose I don't need to tell you," he said, "that you have made quite an impression on our friend from upstate. I'd even go so far as to surmise that you are rather pleased with yourself in consequence."

Varina had the grace to blush. Then, at real trouble in her father's regard, she pouted.

"Well, naturally," she coaxed.

"Puss, are you going to turn out to be a sort of minx?"

"Meaning a sinner, Papa?"

"It amounts to that finally, I reckon. Daughter, it appears to me you have grown up very suddenly."

He had no idea how suddenly. It was enough to turn anyone giddy.

"Because I had Melissa put my hair up?" she suggested.

He considered her coronet of braids, the rose—faded by now, surely —and smiled; but the next minute he scowled as ferociously as ever.

"Varina, I must warn you, Uncle Joe is a sharp man. I don't know what scheme he has afoot in your case, but . . ."

He knew very well. He just disliked the idea so much that he wouldn't say. He thumbed the papers on his desk. They were a fresh copy of the *Intelligencer* from Washington, the *Picayune* from New Orleans, probably off the morning boat, and a much consulted *Merchants' and Planters' Almanac*.

"I certainly was surprised to be invited to his plantation," Varina said. "Must that be part of a scheme?"

"With Joe?" Her father looked up, still scowling, from the papers. "Certainly. He never makes a move of any sort without a reason."

"Dear me!" Varina sighed. "I don't know him very well after all. Do I?"

"Afraid not."

There they ran aground again on a shoal of implications, William unwilling to be more definite in his statements and Varina having the wit to know that it would add nothing to her father's peace of mind for her to say what she thought, which was, simply, that all this was more and more exciting and plainly there were advantages to growing up.

"This to-do about travel and marriage and the like!" William burst out finally. "Your mother and grandmother have had their heads together for months. What is the hurry, all of a sudden, I'd like to know?"

"I'm sure I can't say, Papa," Varina answered. "Such a thing never entered my head."

So it hadn't, up to the last hour or so.

"I should hope not!" William agreed. "That's what I told them. Well, you spoiled their fun, didn't you? I had to laugh when I heard. Then here comes . . ."

He pushed his papers around some more.

"Papa, I think Uncle Joe was teasing."

She thought nothing of the sort now.

"Do you, indeed? Well, I don't. Conquest, he said, didn't he? Offered you his nephew or offered his nephew you, I'm not clear which."

"But, Papa, I thought you liked young Mr. Davis."

"I've nothing against the young man. Personable, decent-appearing fellow. Mississippi's full of 'em. That's what I mean, Winnie. There's no hurry. You're in a position to take your pick. I'll help you when the time comes." bɔr

Oh! He wanted to select a husband for her. That was what irked him about his friend's interference.

"Tell me more about Uncle Joe's family," Varina begged.

He had mentioned "others."

"I don't know much more than you do," William said. "It's quite a tribe. He has a number of brothers and several sisters."

"Are they all married—with families?"

"I suppose so."

"Do you know Mrs. Davis?"

"I've not had the pleasure. She comes from away and is, I understand, something of an invalid, seldom leaving Hurricane."

Hurricane—Varina knew why the plantation was called that. There had been a storm. It had destroyed Uncle Joe's first building on the land and injured several people, killing a child, she believed. She wished now that she had paid more attention to the details.

"Tell me more about Hurricane," she begged now. "You've always just said it was an alligator swamp."

"Presumably they did something about the 'gators long ago," William said.

"You know what I mean, Papa. Warren County is well north of here. It seems strange that the land should be wild in just that way."

"Why, Winnie, I thought you knew your Mississippi. Our richest alluvial land, what we call the Delta, is above Vicksburg and extends clear to Memphis. In its natural state all that is sub-tropical jungle, given over to saurians, reptiles and marsh birds. At Vicksburg the bluffs and hills come close to the river and crowd out the swamps. Below, on our side of the river, alluvial land is found mostly in certain low pockets that the stream makes in its windings. Rodney, just above here, is an example. Davis Bend is another. The soil, formed by silt deposits, is by repute inexhaustibly deep and fertile. Being low, it is also fever-ridden and eternally subject to flood. Your Uncle Joe got his acreage for a song, gambled on developing it profitably and won. I saw the spot only once and wouldn't touch it. The Quitmans and Turners from here took a chance with him, and there were one or two others; but I understand they keep one foot on solid ground. Only a Davis would have the brashness to build right in the maw of the Old Man."

Varina sighed and her father laughed at her softly.

"Now, that's all I know," he concluded, "and it's probably far from a true picture at present. Mr. Davis will entertain you lavishly, I've no doubt; and you will enjoy the adventure. I wouldn't say a word against your going if he had not mentioned conquests. I do object to his setting snares for my daughter, no matter with whom he baits them —young Joseph or others. How do you feel about that?"

"I don't need to fall into the snares," Varina suggested.

"You are a minx," William decided. "You're going to give battle, eh? If I weren't your father, I'd enjoy watching. I'm not sure that the two of you aren't well matched. Well, I've warned you. Run along now and catch your nap. Mr. Davis wishes you to ride down to the boat this afternoon to see him off."

The packet would lie at its Natchez mooring until its top-ranking passenger finished his nap and had his afternoon julep, or longer, if he willed it. Varina coaxed up her father with a kiss and ran along. Just as she left the room, however, she was tripped by a passing thought. Suppose young Joseph turned out to be extraordinarily attractive. There would be a snare to consider!

Natchez Under the Hill and Natchez On the Hill, but the latter first, of course. To be a young lady in a charming frock with a becoming Leghorn bonnet and the heretofore hateful, added touch of a parasol, and to ride in an open carriage with a distinguished gentleman by one's side, with a velvet-collared black coachman sweating up front and a mounted escort—that was the way to see Natchez On the Hill. Varina was happily conscious both of the picture the carriage made and of the dear old town. Surely nowhere was there another like it.

The coachman this afternoon was mere decoration. Her father drove, because he liked to handle the matched blacks. Joe rode alongside, still perishing to be elsewhere, Varina surmised, but doing the honors handsomely meanwhile. He would compensate later with an all-night fox hunt or a cockfight. No, it would be something gentler this time. He had put on a ruffled shirt and a cravat, but not a hat. A beautiful young man, she thought again. It would be hard for any Davis to outshine him. He rode proudly, as became one of his traditions, not seeming to see or hear the squawking chickens or little colored children that scattered before their earlier progress. He was a trifle more aware of, though still fairly indifferent to, handkerchiefs

waved in greeting from other carriages or from doorsteps or curb-
stones as they drove into town.

Handkerchiefs fluttered, tall hats were raised, heads turned to follow
their passage.

"That was Varina Howell. It must have been. The Howell carriage, with Mr. Howell driving. When did she come home, I wonder?
Did you see who the gentleman was beside her?"

"Mr. Davis," would be the answer. "Mr. Joseph Davis of Warren
County. He came up by the New Orleans packet this morning. The
families are friends."

They drove over Front Street. The town climbed on uphill to the
right. To their left, the Esplanade spread a green carpet under neat
chinaberry trees for strollers who wanted a leisurely view of the river
panorama. Varina's heart sang. The Mall in London might be
grander and there were celebrated promenades in other cities; but nowhere else was there just this high road looking out over the greatest
of rivers. Her handkerchief was a constantly waving banner and her
eyes sparkled.

But the river could not be reached without descending the bluff. Beyond the Courthouse square, with Ellicott's Hill looming ahead, her
father drew the team far to the right, then turned them and the carriage at an acute angle down the precipitous road leading to the lower
town and the levee. Joseph Davis, acquainted as he was with the
topography, exclaimed sharply and took a firm grip on the strap at his
hand, but Varina only laughed. A person couldn't ride far in any
direction in Natchez without somebody cringing, thinking the next
minute would see him over the edge of a big or a little ditch. Long
years ago French and then Spanish governors had built a fort on the
bluffs because they were difficult of approach; so, when a town grew
up on the same site, its people had to make the best of the natural lay
of the land.

Usually there was small danger of accident. Certainly there was
none today. William Howell made the turn expertly and, with a just
audible rubbing of brake shoes, the carriage continued its stately progress down the hill. The road had been cut into the face of the hard-
packed clay bluff. Shanties and grogshops and miserable tenements
clung to it like tattered fringe. Scarecrow men and women of varying
shades stared at the carriage as it passed. Down at the river level there

were more people and more tenements—lodging houses and saloons and barnlike warehouses, all of them on stilts as a precaution against floods. Three years before this, a tornado had blown most of Natchez Under the Hill into the river. It looked neither better nor worse now for having been razed and rebuilt. A smell of decaying vegetables, animals, and fish pervaded the atmosphere, delicately tinged with rarer odors. The doors of most of the saloons stood open. Wild song and the stamping of feet and the screech of a fiddle or the whine of an accordion came through. From the steps of one a reeling, stubble-bearded giant made a threatening motion with a black bottle toward the gleaming carriage. In his unsteady condition he would hardly have struck his target had he thrown the bottle; but, as it happened, before he could carry out his threat, someone seized him by the belt from behind and he doubled up like a jackknife where he stood. His howl of animal rage followed the party down the street.

Joseph Davis pursed his lips and glanced sideways at Varina. Her eyes still sparkled, though hardly with merriment. She held her head up and looked over the filth of the street, over the levee, over the row of flatboats from upstream—source of half the brawls in the town under the hill—and held her attention to two dark-hulled, tall-masted ocean vessels moored to their special wharfboat.

"China, do you suppose?" she asked serenely. "It looks like they are moving chests of tea ashore."

"Tea and spice," her companion agreed. "I don't blame you for tilting your nose to catch their perfume. I shouldn't be surprised if our friend, Judge Winchester, were visiting aboard one of those ships. Isn't Salem his home port?"

Varina ignored the sally about her nose. She had noted the name in gold letters against the ship's black hull. Yes, the Judge very probably would be in the captain's cabin, inquiring about people and places he had known when he was young, which would be as near as he would ever come to returning to the land of his birth. There was another thing about Natchez. Almost everyone Varina knew came from away —Judge Winchester from Massachusetts, her father from New Jersey, her mother from Virginia, her grandfather from Ireland over the sea, General Quitman, who commanded the Mississippi militia, but very particularly the Natchez Fencibles, and was of Dutch parentage, from New York, the great Sergeant Prentiss—Mississippi's pride—from

Maine; and so on, beyond reckoning. The Davis tribe? She wondered. So many things to know, so many things still to be discovered. A woman's way, perhaps, of wandering the seven seas.

The New Orleans packet was tied up well down the levee, away from the brawl of bargemen. What cargo had been billed for the port of Natchez had been unloaded and stowed away. Chanting roustabouts in a long queue were now carrying aboard baskets of green vegetables and other perishable foods for the cook's pantry. A steward in striped waistcoat and brass buttons stood beside the mate, ordering the procession. The declining sun struck sparks from gilded fretwork and balls on the hurricane deck and from the gold lace of the captain's uniform. A golden light seemed to Varina's questing and dreaming eyes to wrap everything in radiance until even dust motes borrowed a sparkle.

"Ah, youth!" Joseph Davis said from the carriage step, smiling at her.

She returned his smile mistily. She did not leave the carriage. On the packet, languid ladies promenaded on the arms of frock-coated gentlemen. They were passengers, in the gold-laced captain's charge. On shore, this being Natchez Under the Hill, ladies remained in their conveyances, closely guarded by their male kin.

Joe Howell accompanied Joseph Davis and his luggage aboard the boat. There were gifts from The Briers for him and for the captain. The passengers' landing stage was pulled up. The line of black cargo loaders was pulled into the lower deck as cables were drawn from mooring posts. The packet backed and turned and backed again and nosed out into the channel. From old Fort Rosalie up on the hill cannon fired a parting salute. The throaty whistle of the packet answered.

"Well," William Howell said, "let's get back."

They took the ravine road home. The golden light bathed the familiar tangle of briers and trees. It dusted the gates and then the house as they arrived. On the front gallery Varina's mother and grandmother waited, as if there had been some anxiety about the safe return of the carriage.

CHAPTER II

THERE was more ice than usual in the upper river, the *Magnolia's*
captain said. The channel was blocked at St. Louis and was
threatening to close farther south than that. In consequence, the water
level all the way to the Gulf was low, even for midwinter. Mr. Davis
had advised him, by letter, not to atttempt a landing at Hurricane.
The mud flats beyond the wharf were likely to prove impassable for a
carriage and would offer treacherous bottom for the steamboat. They
would proceed, for that reason, upriver a piece to Diamond Head,
where soundings were deeper and more constant. That was where
passengers for Davis Bend were set ashore most of the time, anyhow.

Varina was disappointed at having missed a first view of Hurricane
from the river. The *Magnolia* had passed Davis Bend shortly after
daybreak, while she still slept in her stateroom. The packet had been
late in getting off from Natchez the day before and most of the sixteen-
hour journey had been made in the dark. However, her disappointment was quickly over. It was impossible to hold a sombre mood on
this bright morning. It seemed to her that there was a tingle of the
ice the captain mentioned in the air. It pinked her cheeks and red-
dened her lips. It gave color even to Judge Winchester's hollow,
ascetic face. Also, it rheumed his eyes a little, so that he had frequently
to turn aside and blow hard; but he didn't mind. He was enjoying the
fine weather as much as anyone, he declared, with the tenacity and
stubbornness of vigorous age.

And, of course, the brisk, cold air was just right for Varina's new full-skirted, tight-waisted coat of brown velveteen with its deep collar and cuffs of beaver, and for the modish velvet bonnet of the same color trimmed with a pair of scarlet bird's wings. Her bright cheeks and the bright feathers against the background of brown made her look as demure and saucy as a bird in new plumage; and that was how she felt, too. The new pokes were shortened above the ears. Hers were cold. She wondered if they could be as red as the end of the Judge's nose. She would have been more comfortable possibly in a quilted hood; but her ears could have frozen and fallen off before she would have considered changing.

The river unwound like molten silver. The low-lying, now almost barren Louisiana shore was etched in the same metallic hue by sun and the morning mist. The right, the Mississippi shore just here seemed as flat as the one opposite. The receding hills and bluffs were lost in a gray haze. The large, slow-moving packet was a gilded swan boat. It . . .

"You wouldn't change your mind, Miss Howell, and keep right on to Vicksburg?"

The *Magnolia* did not carry as many passengers at this season as at others. There were a few men, detained by business or other affairs at New Orleans, who began to be afraid that they wouldn't reach Memphis and their families by Christmas Day. There were travelers from Europe, lost in wonder and some dismay at the unfolding immensity of the United States of America. There was a company of actors, stranded, except for steamboat fare and their costume trunks, bound for Nashville eventually, which, for no reason that even they could give, together with Cincinnati, seemed to be a place of origin for Western theatrical troupes. Where they would eat Christmas dinner or whether they would eat on that blessed day depended on their finding a hall somewhere in which to give an impromptu benefit performance; and that, if successful, might be the beginning of a season. Varina did hope the benefit would be successful. There was a Jump Jim Crow singer who could also recite from *Othello*. He was by turns most amusing and tragic; and all had seemed so hungry at table last night and this morning!

The young man, however, who had just addressed her was someone very different. He was a student from Jefferson College near Natchez on his way home for Christmas vacation. He had appeared on deck this morning in what Varina was sure must be his best blue frock coat, open, in spite of the keen air, to display an embroidered waistcoat. Addressing her, he stood with his tall hat correctly in the crook of his arm and in such a position with reference to the wind that it blew his hair back from his face instead of forward like a bush. He was a mere boy—surely not six months her senior.

"My folks would admire to have you visit us," he pleaded. "My mother would make you welcome. I have three sisters, and I'm sure my father knows your father and you, Judge Winchester. Or you, Miss Howell, have, no doubt, other acquaintance in Vicksburg."

It seemed that, while going to school in Adams County, he had overlooked a treasure he should have discovered to his advantage much earlier. La-dee-dah, he certainly was young; but Varina smiled at him sweetly.

"You are very kind," she said, "but I am afraid I am engaged for the holidays."

"I could ride over to Diamond Place," he urged. "It is not far, not too far, at any rate."

Varina's smile, like the morning air, was now iced with cruelty.

"But I am only stopping at Diamond Place. It is Davis Bend where I am expected as a visitor. I hope to arrive there eventually."

"Oh!" The young man was visibly dashed. "Oh! Well, why in the world do you bury yourself in that place? Vicksburg is ever so much gayer."

The captain interfered, as was his privilege.

"The Davis plantations," he said, "are remote, in a sense—from some approaches occasionally inaccessible; but I doubt that Vicksburg society will be any gayer than that at Hurricane. From what I have seen of folks there and the way they live, I believe Miss Howell will do well to keep to her original engagement."

"I had never any thought of doing otherwise," Varina protested.

"That's right, my dear." The captain beamed on her approvingly. "You will find yourself the object of plenty of attention there, I am sure."

"That was what I feared," the young man said rashly; then, realizing his breach of perfect manners, stiffened. "I'm sorry if I spoke too impulsively, Captain . . . Judge Winchester, sir. Miss Va . . . Miss Howell, I shall hope to wait upon you another day . . . in Natchez, perhaps. If you will excuse me now, I shall go below. Diamond Head is the last landing we shall make before Vicksburg, I presume, Captain? Then I must be sure my kit is in order."

He backed off, still with the wind in the proper direction, wheeled and snapped his hat on his head in one instant, and marched away.

"Oh, dear," Varina said, "I'm afraid we've hurt his feelings."

"The wound is probably not mortal," the captain observed.

Then, he, too, had business on hand; and Varina found herself walking the deck alone with the Judge. Not that she minded. Dear Judge Winchester! Every year the debt she owed him seemed to multiply. For example, by offering his services as escort, he finally had made the present journey possible. When, in November, a letter had come from Joseph Davis, repeating his invitation for Varina to spend Christmas at the Hurricane plantation, and as much time after that as she could be content to give—a month, at least—the more serious objections to her going seemed to have been dispos... of in family council. The only questions raised were the assembling of a wardrobe and the choice of a chaperon.

Granny Kempe had declined ... serv... because of her rheumatism. Old joints, she said, did better i... ... ... nest at any time and surely in midwinter. Margaret Howell ... ...ked to leave home and her other children right at Christmas an... ... year she could not because her husband was expecting his beloved sister Sally for a visit. The same circumstance made William Howell unavailable as a guardian. He felt that he must be in New Orleans to receive his sister, who was coming by the ocean route. That left Joe Howell; but he was having a serious affair of the heart. For once, he had shown discretion in bestowing his attentions and the family hardly liked to press duty upon him. Surely there must be somebody. Aunt Jennie Sprague? That would mean Margaret must be included. And why not, pray?

Nobody said why not, but decision was postponed. Whereupon, the Judge stepped in. It mattered little, he said, where a bachelor of his years spent Christmas. He had business in Vicksburg and would be glad to see Varina safely to her destination. If the Howells would entrust her to his care?

So, here she was, aboard the *Magnolia,* with Melissa to wait upon her, and the Judge for duenna. He was perfect in the role. Aided by the good captain, he had thrown a wall of protection around Varina that would have been vexatious, except for the incense rising from his absolute devotion. Her father would have been much more casual in his attentions. Joe, for other delights, would have forgotten her much of the time; and some sparkle would have gone out of the adventure.

It was an adventure that already promised well. Varina thrilled to present perception and future anticipation. Just look at that sun, for example! A person could hardly believe it was December. Even Melissa was in better humor than usual. She was below now, locking trunks and talking. That, with variations, had been going on at The Briers ever since Uncle Joe's letter had come. Melissa's to-do alone for the journey would have suggested a Grand Tour. Varina could picture her clearly on the lower deck, seated on one of the trunks, herself dressed as modishly in remodeled silk as any high-stepping New Orleans quadroon, comparing families with others of her race in the best Natchez tradition. Before this, to a Natchez audience, she had made good meat for discourse out of the Kempes and the Howells. Now, in a burst of extravagance, she had added the Davises. Heaven only knew what she was claiming for them. One thing was certain. Her tales would not belittle the truth.

"Shall you be glad to see young Skilly or Skelly when you return to Natchez?" the Judge asked as he and Varina walked the deck in the sunshine.

"Scully, with a *c*," Varina said. "Mercy, I haven't got to where I am going yet. How can I tell about Natchez?"

"Fine!" the old man said. "Excellent!"

They turned, laughing, into the wind.

"Would you like to know really what I am thinking?" Varina asked when they reached the lee of the after deck.

"I would," the Judge admitted, "but I hardly presumed to inquire."

"Do you remember that story we read in September—our last reading in Tacitus?"

It had been a dreamy, languid summer, dull by some people's standards. In the low lands and in towns close to the river, cholera and yellow jack had not been as bad as in some years, but they were bad enough. Cholera reached for its victims as far north as St. Louis. There seemed some connection between the epidemic and travel; so, people who had high, healthy places in which to live, away from other folks, simply stayed at home. Margaret Sprague, whose mother claimed she looked delicate, had spent the hot months at The Briers; and Judge Winchester, for his own health's sake and to keep the young folks occupied, came and took over the schoolhouse again.

Lessons, for the most part, had been simple and general. On the warmest days there was only light reading. The judge had brought his shelf of Sir Walter Scott with him, and even little Maggie would leave her dolls or blocks or her slate and creaking pencil to listen to the stirring chapters.

"I do hope," Granny Kempe said, "she is not going to be another bluestocking."

But Granny, too, fell into the habit of having a chair placed for herself. Then little Maggie must sit on a low stool facing her and tug her skirt if she nodded. Joe Howell might be present. He would sit on the steps outside, laughing at the antics of pickaninnies on the cool brick cistern platforms, but giving at least half an ear to the reading. Because of the fever, he attended few cockfights at that season and the families remaining in town did little entertaining. He had with greater willingness taken a holiday from the law books. Sometimes, for diversion and more pleasing instruction, he rode with his father around the outlying plantations; but in midsummer there is little one can do about growing cotton except hope for the best and wait for the harvest; so William Howell himself was not above listening occasionally to a passage at arms.

"Those British were great fighters," he might say. "Sometimes I wonder we ever whipped them over here."

"The Scottish chieftains were the pick of the lot," Granny Kempe, born a Graham, would remind him. "And I've no doubt the Irish, who were close kin, were as doughty."

Lazily her son-in-law conceded the point. It was too warm for disagreement. Oh, drowsy, beautiful summer! The hum of bees, the subdued rattle of a pump chain, the dry, cultured tones of the Judge rounding a sentence in proper cadence. Cool lemonade and spiced cakes—sometimes to give the Judge refreshment and rest, Varina would take the book and read a while, and be pleased to find that all listened to her, too.

"You read very well, Puss," her father said. "I don't suppose you'd care to assist me through a dull column or two in the newspaper?

Either the news is badly reported or I am to blame, but I go to sleep trying to read the stuff to myself—I go to sleep every time."

Care? Varina was enchanted. So, through the columns of the *National Intelligencer,* the New Orleans *Picayune* and the Natchez *Courier,* she came to know the names of parties and their leaders and a little about political issues.

"I declare," her father would say restlessly, "sometimes I have to agree with Joe Davis. The tariff is going to choke the life out of the South if something isn't done about it. Well, don't bother your head about it, baby. Mr. Clay will take care of it better than I could. Let's not have any more speeches today, Winnie. What is the news?"

"Judge Porter, the *Courier* says, is some improved. He intends now to recover and retain his seat."

She spoke with some triumph and righteousness. Judge Porter was the senior Senator from Mississippi, now gravely ill at his home in Natchez. It had seemed to her shockingly unkind of his friends to appear more concerned about his successor in office than in his own suffering. You would have thought the vacancy in danger of being filled by a piney-woods Democrat.

"He'll be all right if he outlasts the hot weather," William said. "But is everything on the subject of death and destruction?"

"No. Here's a piece about Queen Victoria. Listen:

"At the late visit of Queen Victoria and Prince Albert to Cambridge, England, Sir Walter Raleigh seems to have been enacted all over again. On her setting forth unexpectedly on foot from King's Chapel, to go to Trinity College, there was a deficiency of crimson cloth for her to walk upon. The undergraduates immediately pulled off their gowns and threw them down before her Majesty, over which, smiling graciously, she made her way."

Varina laid the paper down with a sigh.

"Don't you love the young Queen?" she said.

"Eh?" William said, as if his attention had wandered. "Who? Victoria? Yes, indeed. She does very well, for a woman. She's made few serious blunders in the six years she has been on the throne. Of course, she has a good husband to help her. Prince Albert—some hold his nationality against him. They figure all Germans to be Hessians, but I think he will prove a good consort. He will steady her hand, when it needs steadying."

Varina objected in her heart to her father's grudging praise. Victoria had chosen Albert, had she not? How had she chosen? Why had she chosen him? Because he would help her rule her people or because he would be the husband she wanted? How had she known?

England's Victoria was only one of a parade of queens. It was a rich, satisfying summer, bearing out Varina's contention that the best of her education had been acquired under devoted, expert tutelage at home. Sometimes she felt like a blade of corn, growing taller by the hour because of grand association. There were Sir Walter Scott's proud women and there were others of a dimmer, farther era. Almost every day Varina and Judge Winchester had a quiet hour or two to themselves; and those quiet times, first, because it gave the judge pleasure, and secondly, because she enjoyed the lessons herself, they devoted to what were called the "classics."

"Agrippina?" the Judge guessed promptly this nippy morning on the *Magnolia*, steaming upriver to the most joyful of Christmases.

Agrippina, yes. That brave young creature, sailing home over the Mediterranean, carrying the ashes of her husband, the idol of the Roman armies, too much their idol for his safety, considering the jealousy of a corrupt and fearful tyrant, his stepfather, the great Tiberius. Agrippina had been so sure that the death of young Germanicus had been foully planned and foully executed that she had gathered his ashes in a silver urn and, with her own heart crumbling to dust, had carried them home to accuse Tiberius of the murder. Without order or sanction and to no avail, since, having spoken her heart, she, too, would die.

"Child, child!" Judge Winchester had said that summer morning when they read the story. "It all happened a thousand years and more ago."

He had closed the book in apprehension and dismay. Varina, her eyes brimming with hot tears of admiration and shared sorrow, shook her head. Things and people like that could not perish. They were part of the world forever.

"That awful old man!" she said, meaning Tiberius. "That awful, cruel old man!"

And this morning . . .

"I woke up dreaming of her," she said. "I suppose it was just the boat."

"The boat, certainly," the Judge agreed. "What a dream that must have been! Well, you will forget her presently and all other sadness, I am sure."

Yes, for a little while, and then remember. But the captain waited for them up forward, with news.

"We are approaching Diamond Head," he told them. "I have sent word to your stateroom, Miss Howell; but you will have time to join me in a small collation, if you will honor me, before we land."

Diamond Head stood up from the river at a height to protect the flat land behind it like a natural levee embankment, but it was not a bluff like those at Natchez or those now visible farther up the river. When the *Magnolia* rounded the point, the landing and a wide space of shore around it were in full view. A scattering of people waited on and beyond the wharf. There was a wagon for Varina's trunks; there was a light, open carriage. A young lady in a long-skirted riding habit and with a green plume trailing from a small riding hat, was having trouble, or so it seemed, controlling a bright chestnut horse; and who was she, Varina wondered. Another saddle horse, for a man, stood near the carriage. A dozen hands reached for the hawsers flung ashore from the boiler deck as the *Magnolia* slid into shore and a half-dozen other volunteers scattered before the warning order of the mate in charge of the landing stage.

The breeze died down. Varina felt that she would surely suffocate and opened her coat. It was much warmer on shore than on the river. A pretty, dark-haired little creature in bright silk and shawl and bonnet stood on the step of the carriage and waved, then left it and ran toward the boat, calling to a tall man behind her to hurry.

"Here she is!" she said; and, before Varina and the judge set foot on land, both her hands were out in welcome.

"Miss Howell? I would have known you anywhere from Papa's description. He admires you intensely, but I suppose you know. I am Florida Davis. McCaleb now. This is Mr. McCaleb, my husband. You will call me Floss, won't you? And shall I say Varina? Judge Winchester? How are you, sir? You won't remember me, but I remember you. Papa took me to court in Vicksburg one time. It was years ago and I was a little bit of a thing."

She was a little bit of a thing now and busy as a bug. Her talk scurried on any number of legs through Varina's first impressions. It was almost too much talk, as if with it she covered her true feelings.

"Dwight, will you look at Mary Bradford. That colt's not more than half-broken and she will insist on riding him. She can't steady him long enough to dismount and show her manners, and she won't be helped. No, darling, it's no use your trying. Just be sure, if you will, that Miss Howell's boxes get off the boat and all that stuff Papa ordered. But you will, of course. Is that your maid, Miss . . . I mean, Varina? Will she be content to ride to the house in the Dearborn? The carriage is very small. What is her name? Melissa? Robert, you be very attentive to Melissa. Do everything the way she wants. Judge Winchester you surely aren't making ready to go back to the boat? We thought you would stay the night, at least, at Diamond Place. We'll arrange to see you to Vicksburg in the morning."

On the warm shore the Judge's eyes had ceased to water. They twinkled slyly as he thanked Mrs. McCaleb for her hospitable invitation but said he would have to forego the pleasure of staying the night. He was expected in Vicksburg.

"Besides," he said, "who but me is to keep that young man yonder from throwing himself into the dark waters?"

"Is there a young man already?"

There! Something had been said to Florida McCaleb, to make her uncertain, watchful in her attitude toward Varina. She would show her manners, as she said, but liking was another, truer feeling.

"A schoolboy from Natchez," Varina said, as carelessly as possible. "The Judge is making a joke."

"Are you, Judge? Really? No, I think I see the young man. Would he be that tall figure in the blue coat on the top deck? He does look unhappy. How can you make light of his misery?"

The Judge gave up waiting for the chatter to cease and took Varina's hands in his to tell her good-bye. Varina clung to him in a sudden access of affection. His going seemed more of a severance than had her departure from Natchez. The landing at Diamond Head ceased to be a bright picture of brisk movement and took on an ominous sort of desolation.

"Don't go," she begged, shyly, but desperately. "Do stay."

"That's what I think," Florida added. "It seems so unwelcoming."

"Nonsense," the Judge said to Varina, and to Florida, "Thank you, my dear." Then to Varina again, "Have a gay, good time, child. Break as many hearts as you will but don't lose your own. Remember, you belong to us in Natchez."

It was his way of putting his love around her before these strangers. It was all Varina could do not to run after him as he turned and walked stiffly back to the landing stage, escorted by Mr. McCaleb. Something inside her hurt woefuly as he bowed his farewell to the latter and, again stiffly upright, disappeared into the boat.

Florida McCaleb was still talking.

"Was it cold on the boat? It was sharp here last night, but won't you lay aside your cloak now? It is lovely, but I should think you might perish . . ."

They were in the carriage at last. It helped Varina to turn her back on the river and the departing boat. As the carriage rolled away down a sandy, yellow road, a length of green velveteen brushed the mudguard nearest her. A clear, imperious voice spoke over her head.

"Be still a minute, Floss. I've run some of the Satan out of this brute and maybe he'll let me say a word. I am Mary Bradford, Miss Howell, in case Floss hasn't told you; and I'm most happy . . ."

The green plume and the snug little hat, directly from a late fashion plate, had listed far to one side, carrying with them out of line a mass of bright brown hair. Dishevelment, however, could not spoil a mold of features pure and exquisite as if some ancient sculptor had chiseled them from marble; and the physical effort of controlling the wild young horse, who seemed to have some Satan in him still, was visible only in firm hands in leather gloves upon the reins. Mary Bradford spoke with absolute composure.

"I am one of the clan." Blue eyes, deep-set, looked directly into Varina's. Blue eyes, Varina decided, must be a Davis feature. Florida McCaleb had them, too. "Flossie's papa is my Uncle Joe and I repeat, I am most happy—excuse me. We're off. I'll see you later at the house."

She disappeared in a swirl of velveteen and flying hoofs and dust. Varina laughed at the manner of her going. She laughed because contact, however brief, with this vivid person had brought back the unclouded joyousness of the day.

"Mary Bradford's mother," Florida explained, "is Papa's sister. They spend part of every year at Hurricane. Mamma . . ." she hesitated, frowning.

"She's lovely," Varina said. "And I'd like to try that horse."

"Would you?" Floss questioned. "I doubt that Papa or Jeff knew she rode him over here. They surely would have stopped her. He's just broken to the saddle. As to Mary, everybody likes her. She begins it, I think, by liking everybody herself—without question."

This was a fairly complete estimate of Mary Bradford. The two girls were close to Varina in age—Mary a few months older and Florida as much younger; but of the two, the younger had a much more complex nature. Mary Bradford was open and frank in mind, affections and speech; Florida McCaleb, for all her volatile chatter, was a dark, secret small person. Varina, unwilling to have any part of her holiday spoiled at its very beginning, soon decided that a fancied spitefulness in her speech was just that—fancy—or, at the most, part of a disposition common to pretty, little women, who had been pampered to death.

At this time she could not help thinking of Florida McCaleb as pampered. Diamond Place, her present home, was an estate in its own right, centered about a house which was already classically beautiful and would be handsome when wings were added to accommodate the family that the McCalebs hoped for. Inside, the house was furnished with a luxury that spoke to Varina of Joseph Davis's wealth, lavished, she thought, upon a favored child—the eldest of the still purely theoretical twenty. Later she discovered that most of the lavishing had been done by Florida's mother, another person of fabulous means.

What impressed Varina even more than the appointments of the house was Florida's manner there. As she stepped over the threshold, she seemed to gain stature. She had still to reach her seventeenth birthday, but she directed with unquestioned authority a household of slaves, her guests and her husband. The latter, still a young man, though indefinitely Florida's senior, and a member of a family at least as well-established as his wife's, seemed to find her airs alternately amusing and charming. He was, Varina thought, with an odd impulse of covetousness, about the most devoted husband a person could imagine.

Impressions, observations, experience crowded upon one another the balance of what was, on the whole, a most satisfactory day. Varina went to bed that evening at once so tired and so rested that she sank into oblivion before she plumbed the depth of down that received her. When she awoke, it was the middle of another sunny morning and Melissa waited to help her into her second-best dress.

"Ah-h!" Varina yawned, then sat up with a bounce. "Oh! But I was to go for a ride with Mary Bradford early . . ."

"Early," Melissa informed her, "was two-three hours ago. Miss Mary went by her lonesome. Miss Floss said to let you sleep. You were tuckered and you'd ride enough when you got to Hurricane."

"Did Mary go off without me?" Varina pouted.

"Miss Floss sent her," Melissa said. "Miss Floss her own self had to go see some sick folks in the quarters. She sot me here to watch ovah you. She'll be back directly, but you can have your breakfast when you is ready and amuse yoreself how you will meantime. She say, maybe if she ain't back too soon, you might like to walk out in the garden or come to meet her. What come ovah you, anyhow? You ain't nevah been one to lay in bed all mo'ning. You sick now—way off here?"

"No, of course not."

"What, then?"

Varina did not attempt to explain her deep sleep. She shook her head to remove the remnants of drowsiness that remained.

"Meliss', I think I'm going to have a wonderful time," she yawned.

"It's startin' off all right," Melissa granted. "Is you gittin' up now?"

Varina slipped out of bed and stretched.

"Yes," she said, "I think I will. I'll wash and dress and have a bite to eat and then, perhaps, I shall walk in the garden."

"Airs," Melissa commented. "What you puttin' on foh? This ain't yore house."

No; but, somehow, Varina was still half-lost in a dream when she finished breakfast and stepped out into the garden. Her mood was right for enchantment and so was the setting. Even at this season, with the leaves off most of the trees, holly and other shrubs and green grass provided a verdant expanse, surrounded by the usual high hedge, screening off the more utilitarian portions of the estate. Beyond the hedge she could hear the tinkle of a sheep's bell and, farther away, the excited barking of a dog.

Sunshine came down in a golden shower. A light square of Kashmir that she had wrapped around her head on leaving the house dropped to her shoulders. In a sheltered corner she saw roses blooming and, on all sides, white and red camellia buds unfolding. It had been days since she had plucked a flower for her hair. She started toward the nearest camellia bush, but halfway to it stopped, her keen ear detecting above the sheep's bell and the barking of the dog, the light, rapid beat of a horse's canter.

She thought it would be Mary Bradford returning, and stood still, half-vexed, half-eager. Then caution called to mind the antics of the spirited chestnut colt and she stepped aside into the partial screening of a sweet olive shrub. There was that to consider afterward—she was, in a measure, hidden as the rider broke through the hedge in the wide opening made by the drive.

The rider was not Mary Bradford. It was a man and a horse. A man and a horse—the image was indivisible. A gray horse with black hoofs and black stockings and a flowing, dark tail. A tall man in black —boots, trousers, coat, carelessly knotted cravat and soft hat—so easy in the saddle, in spite of a remarkable erectness of posture, that his movements and those of the horse flowed together inseparably. She who rode better than any woman she knew—far better than Mary Bradford, for example—conceded matchless horsemanship at once to the stranger.

Otherwise—well, of course, she was half-hidden by the sweet olive tree. He rode up to within a few feet of her before he saw her and, with an imperceptible movement of his hands, reined in the beautiful, deceptively docile gray horse.

"Well, hello!" he said. "I got here finally, didn't I? Where is everybody? I thought, perhaps, you had given me up and I might meet you on the road. . . . Oh, I beg your pardon."

He swept off his hat, then held it to shade his eyes from the sun as he stared at her. He dismounted. On the ground he was taller than he had looked on the horse. He was taller than Varina by a good many inches. Involuntarily she took a half-step backward and was angry at herself for the confused, abashed movement.

Hands reached out to take the reins of the horse. Where had the Negro come from? The stranger dropped the leather into the hands without a glance sideways. Assuming that it was quite natural someone should appear out of nowhere to wait on him. Haughty—Varina had never seen such simple, sure haughtiness.

"I don't know you, do I?" He took another step toward her and still held his hat to shade his eyes. His voice had a peculiar timbre. It was musical, almost sweet. It would have seemed delicate, effeminate, except that there was plenty of manly resonance behind it. Mercy, yes, and decision, and authority.

"I thought you were Mary. I . . . would you mind very much—my time is short—no, of course not. I'll go myself."

He strode past her and toward the house.

"Well, I never!" Varina thought. "Well, I surely never did!"

The pretty, new rose-colored merino with its corded stitching, the dainty, embroidered Kashmir scarf, her sweet spirit of receptiveness, her airs, as Melissa had said—and he brushed her off as if she had been a bluebottle fly. He went right on to the house without a backward glance; no—just short of the steps he turned and made a piece of a bow.

"I do beg your pardon," he said placatingly.

Varina inclined her head, smiled faintly, and turned her back on him. She went on to the camellias, chose a bloom that deepened the color in her pretty dress, thrust it into her hair, found a path that led out of the garden—she had no idea where—and followed it.

What else could she have done? Was she to run to the house after him, begging for a presentation? When she wasn't even curious as to his identity? Oh, but she was curious! She found herself halted again, this time by sudden perception. The eyes he had shaded from the sun were a familiar blue, deep-set under a broad, high forehead. The forehead, all the haughty features, had a chiseled, sharp perfection. Obviously he was a Davis. Could he be the very one Uncle Joe had planned for her to meet and know . . . and win? Young Joseph Davis? She decided not. Young Joseph would be somewhere near her in age. This man was not an old man exactly, but neither was he young. He was remote from her in that particular as in others—about the remotest person, she concluded, with a fresh access of anger, she had ever seen.

She continued along the path and brought up at a cluster of field hands' cabins.

"Missy lookin' for somebuddy?"

"Miss Floss," Varina said. "Did she come this way?"

"She come, Missy, but she gone, too, by now. Back to the house by anurr path."

"Thank you. I'll look for her there."

With no acceleration, Varina turned and retraced her steps. The weeds along the path brushed dust over her skirt. No matter. Cleaning it would give Melissa something to do besides gossiping in quarters. Then, just before she stepped into the garden, she stopped and shook off all she could herself.

To no purpose. The garden was empty. The stranger and the gray horse had vanished. He had said his time was short. On the front gallery Mary Bradford and Florida McCaleb met her with reproaches and effusive explanations.

"Varina, where on earth did you go? We called, but we couldn't make you hear. You missed Jefferson. He couldn't wait. He had business in Vicksburg."

Right then began, it seemed to Varina, a sort of din that rang in her ears all the rest of her visit. Jefferson, Mosser Jefferson, Jeff, Moss' Jeff. He was Uncle Joe's youngest brother. That made him Florida's and Mary's uncle. There, he was old! His nieces laughed at the notion. They called him Jeff—admiring, fondly—Florida with an air of "We know him, you don't." He was their favorite kinsman. He was the favorite of the family, of every branch of the family, of every plantation connected with it—Jefferson, Jeff, Moss' Jeff.

Mary Bradford considered Varina under level, inquiring eyebrows. "He seemed to think he had offended you. Did he? He does have at times a sort of oblivious manner."

Oblivious? Varina still smarted from being unnoticed.

"His thoughts are faraway much of the time," Florida sighed, again with that air of special knowing.

"It doesn't matter," Varina said. "Does he live at Hurricane?"

Yes, but on his own plantation, mostly. He had his own house, his own housekeeper, his own servants. No mention was made of family; but, no doubt, there was one. Increasingly, and provokingly, there was a solitary cast to her image of the horseman riding through the hedge and pulling up in the path before her, and there was hushed withdrawal in the way the girls spoke; but all that proved nothing. Up to within the last half-year, Joseph Davis had been a man with no visible domestic ties. Now they were multiplying at a confusing, if not alarming, rate.

With dignity Varina said she was sorry she had missed meeting Mr. Jefferson Davis. She had not considered that the stranger might be a member of the family. She had supposed he was looking for Mr. McCaleb. She was especially sorry because, if she had known anyone would be riding to Vicksburg she would have liked to have a letter posted to her mother. She had promised to write every day while she was away, but had tumbled into bed the night before, never thinking.

Her words were rueful, but all her rue was not about the omitted letter. A queer sense of loss rankled in her heart. Perhaps the feeling did not go so deep as a rankle. It was more like an itch. It would be gone, she hoped, presently.

"You know," Mary Bradford said, "we're forgetting the most important thing. Jeff stopped, Varina, to bring a letter from Uncle Joe."

"Papa wrote," Floss took over the explanation, "to say that the carriage will be here in the morning to take you all down to Hurricane."

"I'm riding Sultan," Mary said. "Jeff said I could—if I would promise to rest him until then and hold him to a walk. So, you can have my place in the carriage, Floss."

"I won't be going just tomorrow," a spark flashed from Florida's eyes and her mouth set oddly.

"Floss?" Mary said uncertainly.

"We'll be down later, Dwight and I. We did want to spend Christmas here; but, if Papa says come, of course we will. Papa," she explained to Varina, still with that strained look about the mouth, "can't tolerate having any of us away from Hurricane at Christmas. It would be treasonable, I suppose. . . . Do write your letter, Varina. We'll see that it gets posted. Your mother will be aching to hear."

> Dear Mamma:
> This morning Uncle Joe sent word by his younger brother—did you know he had one . . .

Varina began her letter after supper that evening, but did not make much progress. Again Melissa was packing. And grumbling like a buzz-fly that wanted out.

"You wanted to travel," Varina reminded her. "Well, that's how it is when you do."

"I hope we'll git where we're goin' finally," Melissa retorted.

"Maybe you won't like it when we do," Varina suggested.

"Maybe you won't, either. What, then?"

What, then? Varina considered.

"Lay out my riding habit for tomorrow, Melissa," she said presently, as the first result of thought. "Pack all the dresses."

Melissa sat back on her heels.

"Your new blue habit?" she objected. "And the hat with the plume?"

"Certainly. I didn't bring any other, did I?"

"Time you git anywhere, you won't have a stitch bran' new to show."

"Oh, yes. We don't intend to stay forever, you know. Anyhow, I've decided to ride to Hurricane tomorrow."

"Mr. Davis pintedly said he was sendin' a kerridge. In his letter."

"It will take the carriage and a dray, besides," Varina informed her, "to carry you and all the other *impedimenta*."

"'Pediment,' " Melissa said darkly. "You don't know what that word means. Where you goin' to git this horse you goin' to ride?"

"Don't be silly. If there is one thing the Davises have more of than another, it is horses. There will be a horse for me if I want one."

Melissa yielded with ominous abruptness.

"Reckon they will be," she grumbled, "if you wills it so. Some day . . ."

She did not complete the prophecy.

CHAPTER III

". . . all in the blue, unclouded weather . . ."

SHE could never think of the day without recalling the unmarred brilliance of the sky. On the river, the *Magnolia*'s captain had said the fine weather would hold another week or ten days. He said it with the assurance of one who knew the elements, squinting at the sun and sniffing the wind as he spoke. He had not promised that each day would be finer than the one before while the weather held. This one was perfect. The air of the early morning had been laced with frost. Now, at noon, after their journey from Hurricane the horses in the drive at Diamond Place stamped restlessly, as if they had just been led from their stalls and couldn't wait to be off again.

". . . we rode over the rustling leaves . . ."

There was a mount for Varina. Florida McCaleb, in Varina's room while she dressed, saw the new riding habit spread out and said, "How did you know?"

"I willed it that way." Mischievously Varina turned Melissa's reproaches to suit her needs.

The new horse was a filly—a dark bay with a mane like heavy silk floss, and a flowing tail. She wore her sidesaddle as a lady would a fashionable bonnet but she accepted Varina with a small show of restiveness, not liking too well the long skirt of the new habit.

"She ain't carried a lady much, Young Miss," the groom who had led her said, "but she's tractable. Mr. Jefferson gentled her himself."

That would, of course, be the ultimate in recommendation.

The McCalebs stood, in final token of hospitality, in the drive to watch the cavalcade get off.

"Tell Mamma, Mary," Floss said, "that we'll be along tomorrow. So she won't fret. Good-bye, Varina. It has been such a pleasure, entertaining you. Mary, you will remember what Jeff said about the horse? Good-bye, Melissa . . . William, Isaiah. You all be good now, will you?"

"Be careful," Dwight McCaleb echoed, his arm through his small wife's. "Do be careful, girls."

"*. . . over the rustling leaves, through the thick trees . . .*"

Trees hung over the road most of the way. Bare of branch though they were in general, they created a world of solitude. The roadbed showed signs of use, but today it seemed set apart for the small procession bound for Hurricane. No other traveler appeared on it. The leaves underfoot were oak and walnut and sweet gum and persimmon and pecan, with here and there in more barren stretches the softer carpeting of pine needles. Melissa rode in solitary state in the carriage among Varina's *"impedimenta."* That had been Joseph Davis's word in his letter of instructions to Diamond Place, but Varina had appropriated it. Melissa was determined that somebody in the family should maintain position in the eyes of the Davis people. The carriage was a stately, high-swung affair. It rocked where the road was washed. Melissa would have been more comfortable up front with the coachman, and she would have seen more of the countryside; but she remained inside all the way.

The horses that drew the carriage and the equally loaded light wagon were bays, a brighter shade than Glory and heavier, but proud steppers, too. Those hitched in a team to the wagon had the head-tossing freshness of colts. They might have made mischief except for the swaying carriage that blocked the way ahead of them. As it was, the parade was stately enough. Varina, riding well in advance with Mary Bradford and trailed at a respectful distance by the young groom, Isaiah, looked back and found the spectacle an excuse for consuming laughter. She turned to Mary for sympathy, thought she met an answering sparkle in that delightful harum-scarum's blue eyes, and forgot on the instant the latter's promise to hold the red colt to a walk.

"Race?" she challenged.

"Don't . . ." Mary protested . . . too late.

Varina had already shaken the reins along Glory's neck and the touch was all the encouragement the filly needed. She broke almost immediately into a gallop. Varina thought ruefully of her new habit before she did of Mary's certain fall from grace, but even that much repentance was only momentary. Never in her life before had she experienced such smooth swiftness of motion. The filly seemed to spread wings rather than to run. She stretched out, dropping close to the ground to find her best speed. If the blue velvet skirt had been six inches longer it must have swept the dust of the road. That was all its hazard or Varina's.

They passed Mary Bradford on the big chestnut and left them behind in the first instant. In less time after that than it takes to report it they passed beyond earshot of the party and were really alone on a strange highway. In her exhilaration Varina let the filly run the better part of a mile before she drew her down, ruefully, to a walk, thrilling, however, to her instant obedience, her "tractability." Varina considered turning back then, but on hearing a crashing off in the woods, thought better of the impulse and waited. A minute later Mary Bradford, thoroughly disheveled and outspokenly angry, rode out from among the trees.

"Varina Howell!" she exploded. "If I thought you had done this on purpose, I'd never forgive you . . . never!"

Only then Varina remembered Mary's promise. She was, for a minute, honestly contrite, and said so.

"I forgot," she said. "I truly did. I only thought what a fine morning it was for a run."

Some of Mary's anger melted before the honesty of the explanation, but not all of it. Seeing Varina, sitting cool and beautiful, not a feather out of place, on the quiet filly, she made futile efforts to right her hair and her hat; and her blue eyes glittered with unshed tears.

"Part of my mad," she admitted, half-laughing, half-sobbing, "is because I can't hold this animal even when I try. He's such a hare-brained fool, besides. When he runs, he despises anything like a road and just takes off across country."

"I am so sorry!" Varina said; but she was a trifle less so than before. Some day, she thought again, she would ride Sultan. With the least encouragement, she would have offered to change horses now.

"But I hate most of all," Mary said, having no idea of Varina's new impulse, "for Jeff to hear of this. He's bound to think . . ."

"For pity's sake," Varina snapped, "I'll tell him. I'll tell him I was to blame, too. I'm not afraid of him."

Before she could say more, Isaiah, the groom, rode up. If he comprehended the sort of words that excitement had brewed between the two girls, discreetly he gave no sign.

"You all right, Miss Mary?" he inquired. "Moss' Jeff's goin' to have to take that Sultan hoss in hand now, if it ain't too late. Best walk him slow for a spell. He's all a-froth."

"So am I," Mary said.

The groan of the carriage was now audible and the procession started forward again, the pace sober enough to satisfy anybody.

"*. . . all in the blue, unclouded weather, over the rustling leaves . . .*"

"It isn't," Mary said presently, "that I am afraid of Jeff or what he will say. It's just that, when he gives his word, he holds to it forever and naturally he expects others to do the same."

"You are afraid of him," Varina insisted. "That's being afraid."

"You don't like him," Mary said, hotly in his defense now. "Why? Is it something we've said?"

Varina made a face.

" 'Moss' Jeff,' " she quoted. "He's quite the most important member of the family, it seems."

"You wouldn't speak that way," Mary reproached, "if you knew him."

"But that's the strange part," Varina mused. "As often as Uncle Joe has visited at our house, I've never heard the name mentioned."

"It's not too strange," Mary said. "I suppose nothing brought his name up. He's rather a recluse, you see. I don't suppose, in the eight years he has lived at Davis Bend, he's been farther away than Old Greenville or Vicksburg and that not more than once or twice a year."

Recluse? There was a cold, repellent word. But he hadn't looked a recluse, riding through the gap in the hedge.

"The only reason it is strange that Uncle Joe didn't mention him," Mary went on, forgetting anger in perplexity, "is that he is so fond of him. Uncle Joe is fonder of Jefferson than anyone else in the world. Fonder of him than of his own children. Surely fonder of him than any of his other brothers and sisters."

Or of his brothers' and sisters' children? Varina wondered.

"Uncle Joe seems much older than Mr. Jefferson," she said, just to keep Mary interested. "They don't look like brothers."

"He is much older," Mary said. "There are ten brothers and sisters. Uncle Joe is the oldest, Jeff the youngest. It's all in the great Bible at Woodville. The family home is there. Some day you must know Grandmother Davis. She's wonderful. Everything that is best in us we draw from her. . . ."

But Varina was not interested in the more ancient members of the tribe.

"How much older did you say Uncle Joe is?" she asked.

"Twenty-four years," Mary said.

Twenty-four years—why should that make the sky seem brighter? Why should that give an entirely new aspect to a man on a tall gray horse?

"I suppose," Mary continued, "to a stranger that would make him seem more like a son than a brother to Uncle Joe. Jefferson was still in school when Grandfather Davis died and Uncle Joe became the head of the family. In a sense they are rather like father and son; but, do you know, I think the relationship is something closer than that, if possible. The special closeness began, I understand, when Jefferson left the Army and came back to Mississippi to live."

"He was a soldier?" Varina was more startled than surprised. This was the first bit that sounded real. Now she understood the stiffly erect back, the punctilious bow.

"Yes, and a rather fine one, I imagine." Oh, naturally! "He served on the frontier and loved it. Sometimes I think he grieves as much for the loss of those brave times as for any other thing. I do believe, if there ever was another war, he'd drop everything and go back to being a soldier again. Sometimes I could almost wish it would happen."

"Then why did he leave?"

Varina was not curious. Simply, it seemed such a preposterous thing to do—to leave a career so suitable. In a uniform, mounted, ordering people about!

"He left the Army to marry."

"Oh!" Mary's solemn tone left no other comment to Varina.

"There were parental objections."

To the Army, Varina was to understand, not to Mr. Jefferson Davis. Mary drew a long, sighing breath.

"And then . . . she died."

The sudden, tragic turn of the story shocked Varina out of small personal assumptions—what Melissa, too truthfully, called "airs."

"Right away?" She sounded as awed as Mary Bradford.

"Within three months. So, now you see," Mary said passionately. "He gave up everything to marry her and she died." As if that were the end of the world.

"At Hurricane?" Varina asked.

"No. They came to Hurricane after the wedding. Jeff hadn't a house ready. Uncle Joe gave him a thousand acres of land to open and he worked at that into the hot weather. She took ill of the fever. They started for the seacoast in July, but at St. Francisville, where Uncle Benjamin and Aunt Anna live—they are a brother and sister and both married Smiths—she died. She is buried on Aunt Anna's plantation at Bayou Sara."

Not . . . at . . . Hurricane. Not . . . at . . . Hurricane. The horses' hoofs beat a slow, soft rhythm on the little-traveled road. Not . . . at . . . Hurricane.

"When did all this happen?" was Varina's next question. It seemed to her that Mary had said, but she couldn't remember.

"Eight years ago."

Yes, that was it. *"In all the eight years he has lived at Davis Bend, he's never been farther away than Greenville or Vicksburg . . ."*

"I never saw her," Mary continued, lost in her peculiar sad contemplation. "I wasn't at Hurricane when Jeff brought her home. We live in Louisiana, too—Mother and I—I think Floss told you. But we were there when he returned alone the following spring. You see, he was desperately ill himself and all but died. He traveled all winter with his body-servant, James Pemberton. You'll see James if you ever visit Jeff's place. He used to follow Jeff like a shadow, but he's getting older now and hardly leaves Brierfield."

Brierfield—it was the first time that Varina had heard the name. Its similarity to The Briers made her turn in quick inquiry.

"Jeff's plantation," Mary repeated. "The land was all wild when he took it. That's the way folks spoke of it—the brier field; so he just went on calling it that. When he returned, he went right on with clearing the land and planting, as if he had not lost his wife. And, with James to help him, he built a house. When it was done, he moved in; and he has lived there ever since—alone. That's what I meant when I said that, once he gave his word or pledge, it was forever. So, now, perhaps, you see."

Varina did not see at all. A proud, haughty, terribly self-assured man —probably opinionated—and now obstinate, as well, it seemed. And she was supposed to find him charming in a melancholy, romantic way? She did not find him so in the least. Eight years alone, and he still brooded over a woman whom by this time he could hardly remember? It was the weirdest tale she had ever heard.

But she did want to be friends with Mary Bradford. She liked Mary, who in brighter moods could be rare fun. She sensed Mary's important position in the domestic picture at Hurricane. Besides just liking her, she thought she might need to be friends with her if she was to have the gay, triumphant holiday she contemplated. She was still contemplating it. She did not propose to have it spoiled by anyone, alive or dead. She turned her most dazzling smile on Mary.

"Thank you," she said sweetly, "for explaining about the family. You must help me whenever I get confused about anyone. And I am sorry that I made Sultan bolt with you. I surely do mean to explain my part in that."

"*. . . through the thick trees, to Hurricane.*"

The trees thinned finally as they crossed a flat strip of land overgrown with wild cane and stiff marsh grass. Field hands were at work beside the road, hacking at the growth. There was a glimpse of water and the dull booming of giant bullfrogs filled their ears. The water was the river, Mary said. In time of flood, Davis Bend was practically an island. The flat stretch of land was more an isthmus than anything else. Varina thought of her father's description—an alligator swamp. It surely was wild land.

Then the trees began again. Over yonder to the left, Mary said, General Quitman had a plantation; and beyond him and on the mainland across the inlet, his relatives-in-law, the Turners, owned places. Brierfield, Jeff's place, was beyond the Quitman and Turner holdings on the peninsula—southwest. Varina saw only the trees. The drive went on for miles under ever-increasing shadow and gloom. The road at times seemed to feel its way among the tree roots. Armlike branches had been cut back to furnish head room. There were areas where the sun could not come through and here the damp chill was of night air held close, as in a deep cellar. The growth was not new or strange to Varina; only its lushness was overpowering. Tree and vine and creeper seemed to drink deep of some root elixir. Occasionally a causeway or a mossy wooden bridge carried the road over a reaching inlet of brown backwater. She shivered once or twice, as if in a chill. The effect of Mary's ghost legend, perhaps. But she had said nothing of a ghost, really. The horses, fortunately, showed no reluctance about proceeding. They had scented the home stables and were pulling hard to reach them.

The opening, as might be expected, came with startling abruptness. The veils of moss and the darkness seemed to part and there were brick pillars marking an open gate and sunshine and grass and flowers and a house. It was a big house. Size was its first visible attribute, and then solidity. The storm that had given the place its name might have been to blame for that. The central and main portion, for all the invitation of surrounding galleries, seemed to rise like a square, battlemented tower. It was supported on the right by a long wing; and to the left, though apart, were other buildings—more and more and more of them; but those one took in more slowly and later. In this first moment there was only the main house.

Galleries shaded the first two stories. The pillars were uncommonly strong. The brick walls behind them looked uncommonly solid; the windows were narrow and spaced widely apart. The third story seemed to have been added some time after the main building had been completed. Its gables had an odd, cut-off, foreign look. Peaked dormer windows stood out like individual spires. A strange house, not beautiful, not ugly, not forbidding, but surely self-contained. Boldly different . . .

Ready hands reached out for Glory's bridle. Joseph Davis came down the steps to lift Varina from the saddle. He held her at arm's length on the ground, admiring most satisfactorily plumes, blue habit, bright cheeks, bright lips, then caught her to him and kissed her in hearty welcome.

She clung to him in a burst of released emotion.

"I thought to my soul I'd never get here," she cried.

His answering laugh was rich with satisfaction.

"But here you are at last," he said, "my girl!"

CHAPTER IV

EXCEPT for the warmth of this welcome, Varina's spirits might have been a little more dashed by her first impression of Hurricane. Certainly there was no indication so far of the gayety everyone had promised or of a house full of young and interesting people. Only the master of Hurricane waited to receive her. Behind him, in the doorway, against the dark of a hall, hovered a black major-domo in striped waistcoat, blue frock coat and trousers and many brass buttons. That was the extent, apparently, of the reception.

However, Joseph's welcome was an earnest of better things to come. The air with which he led her across the brick paving of the gallery to the open fanlighted door was impressive. The house was hers, he said, and all that belonged to it.

"Mary," he commanded, inside the wide hall, "will you do the honors upstairs. Please see that Varina is settled comfortably in a room to her taste. Solomon will send up the luggage and a bit of refreshment when you are ready."

Solomon closed the door on Joseph and the two girls. His smile illuminated much of the lower hall. Mary Bradford stood with her hand on the polished balustrade, looking up a steep stairway.

"You can have a room on the second floor, I suppose that means," she said. "Those are our state bedrooms. Personally, I prefer the attic."

There was that in her attitude which weighed something still in the balance. Varina said at once and gaily that, if Mary preferred the third floor, so would she, she was sure. The view from the windows there ought to be fine.

"Superb," Mary agreed.

"Of course, there are the extra steps," Joseph reminded her.

"Pshaw!" Varina said. "Only Melissa will fuss about them, and she'd be bound to fuss about something."

As she hurried up the stairs after Mary, she felt Joseph's approval following her—black Solomon's, too, for that matter. The rapidity of her heartbeat, when they reached the top floor, was not due to the exertion of climbing.

There were four rooms in what Mary called the "attic"—two to the front of the house and two to the rear. Mary Bradford's was the one on the northeast corner; and, for one night, Varina in solitary dignity, had the northwest one to herself.

"The rooms downstairs are much grander," Mary said again.

These were grand enough, spacious, furnished with the usual dark walnut pieces and other touches familiar to Varina—trundle beds under the canopied four-posters, cradles in dim corners, dolls sitting about in miniature rockers, like small, awe-struck visitors. And the view, as Mary had promised, was superb. While she waited for her luggage and Melissa, Varina went from dormer to dormer, looking out.

There was, first, the river, wrapping the peninsula in a great coil. Her river—just as she could stand under the china trees at The Briers, watching it for hours, so she could look out on it here and never find the scene empty or monotonous. It was a shrunken river now. She noted the distance between the levee embankments and the water— the mud flats; but she knew the river's power never dwindled to the vanishing point. The ice would give way up North or rains would come and it would fill its banks and lash out where it would for more room.

She saluted the Old Man gravely and almost reluctantly drew her gaze back to the nearer surroundings of the house—the trees, through which she had ridden that afternoon, and formal garden plots, out of which flashed the white and pink and rosy red of camellias, and here and there a bit of marble—a bench, a statue or a fountain. When she spoke of the extent of the planting, Mary took her to the rooms at the rear of the house, to show her the pergolas, arbors and beds of an area devoted exclusively to roses. To either side of the rose garden and beyond, fruit trees had been planted. They were literally uncountable.

"Uncle Joe will want to show you the rose garden personally," Mary said. "He's very proud of it, but you'll have to ride through the orchard. It runs to acres. He never hears of a variety of fruit or nut that he doesn't plant a specimen; and almost all of them thrive."

There it was again—that feeling of lush fertility, a jungle tamed to serve man's needs—or a man's ambition. Vaguely oppressed by her whimsical thought, Varina went back to her room and to Mary's to look at the side buildings on the estate. Of the wing to the right of the entrance, she could see little but the roof and a covered passageway leading to the addition. The buildings on the other side were more detached. There was a stone stable, of arena-like proportions, with a carriage house under the same roof. It dwindled off finally into several smaller stables of wood construction. She located the outdoor kitchen and a dairy house behind it. Still farther away, a road led to clustered small houses, overhung by trees. The quarters, she supposed. They made a village in themselves, if so. She turned from the window, accusingly.

"It's not just a plantation," she said. "It's a barony—a kingdom. And my father called it an alligator swamp!"

"There are alligators still," Mary informed her, "down Jeff's way."

Varina turned back to the window; and now, beyond the quarters, beyond a stretch of wild cane and some land that might be fields, beyond a far, indeterminate space of woods, she saw a roof and chimneys barely emerging from the cover of trees. She pointed the house out to Mary.

"You've good eyes," the latter said. "Most people wouldn't see it. It's several miles away as the crow flies, more by road. That's Jeff's house—the one I told you about, coming over. That's Brierfield."

The quiet of Varina's reception carried over through the evening; but, subtly, it seemed to her, the atmosphere changed as the hours passed. It was not so much quiet as quiescent, waiting. She tried to match her mood to that of the house and waited, too, brightly expectant, but subdued.

Supper was served informally in the "ladies' parlor," behind the main drawing room to the right of the great hall that ran through the house from front to rear. As the girls descended the stairway, Joseph

Davis again waited to receive them. He caught an arm of each under his and led them through the drawing room to the small parlor. Varina had a quick impression of thick carpeting, of green damask upholstery against rubbed mahogany, of a many-prismed chandelier, and a richly carved pianoforte; but these were things to pass in favor of a bright fire burning in the farther room and a gracious woman with dark, graying hair, in changeable taffeta silk, presiding over a table bright with silver pieces and crystal.

"Tell me, Sister," Joseph said to this lady, "could I bring you fairer armfuls of flowers than these?"

"No, indeed," the lady answered. "Considering that I raised one and you chose the other, both are, naturally, perfection."

The bright silk rustled. A bright laugh rustled with it. Sister—then, this was not Mrs. Davis. No, anyone could see at a second glance that it was not. A healthy padding of flesh disguised but could not conceal an increasingly familiar bony structure of brow and cheek and nose; and here again were those deep-set eyes, now gray, now blue, as they reflected light and color. An iridescent woman in iridescent silk. Not Mrs. Davis, but Amanda Bradford, Mary's mother, Miss Amanda or Miss 'Manda to the plantations and environs. Not the mistress of Hurricane in title, but very much its mistress most of the time in fact. She greeted Varina and Mary alike with a warm hug and a hearty kiss.

"Sorry I wasn't here to welcome you two," she said cheerfully. "I had a case of sore throat in the quarters. I wanted to 'tend to it myself, to make sure we weren't in for a round of measles or chickenpox or worse over Christmas. Bless the Lord, it was only a bad sore throat and a cough. Young Hagar's oldest boy," she said, just as briskly, in a sort of report to Joseph. "He'll be all right in a day or two. I left medicine. Young Hagar's smart enough to give it to him."

"Where was Aunt Rhina?" Joseph asked.

"She was there, you may be sure. With her full bag of tricks and that vile pipe she says Moss' Jeff gave her eight-ten years ago, when he was first home from fightin' the Indians and she cain' lay it down for his sake. Did he give it to her, do you remember?"

"I don't know. I asked him one time and he said he might have. He didn't remember."

"No. No, I reckon he wouldn't. Well, you might ask him to find her a new one some day. You could have cut the air in that cabin with a knife. The boy's eyes were popping and Young Hagar was wailing and Aunt Rhina was rocking and smoking like a volcano. I put her out the door."

"She'll put a spell on you now," Joseph warned, his eyes twinkling.

"She would if she dared," Miss Amanda retorted. "In ten minutes I had the boy breathing better."

"But what's to keep her out?" Joseph asked. "Young Hagar won't dare."

"I dare. I told her if I heard of her setting foot in that cabin before Kizziarch was up and running around as well as ever, there'd be no tobacco for her on Christmas morning. I know a few conjuring tricks myself and they work when I put my mind to it."

"A tower of strength," Varina thought. "If ever I need . . ."

"Awfullest old nuisance I ever saw." Miss 'Manda eased the stress of her experience with general complaint. "We could hardly make up our minds to put up with her except that she was a Davis before any of us were. She never fails to remind me that she came out of Georgia into Kaintuck with Papa and Mamma long before anybody'd heard tell of me."

She laughed in rich enjoyment. A tower of strength.

"And she knows certain secrets in the use of simples," Joseph added, "that keep our hands from dying off every fever season."

"Yes," Miss Amanda agreed, "though I never put any stock in her claim that, if she had been consulted . . . but we won't go into that. The chief thing is that her daughter, Rhina Number Two, is the best cook the world ever saw. Do you like honey with your waffle, Varina? Are you hungry, darling?"

"Starved," Varina accepted a ladleful of thick, golden syrup as a bite of short pastry melted down her throat.

"Good. The bees are the two Rhinas' special care."

"Hadn't you better tell Jefferson about your tobacco threat?" Joseph asked.

"Hm! Maybe," Miss Amanda said. "She'll have a long tale ready for him the minute he lights. When do you look for him back?"

"Some time tomorrow—or perhaps still this evening. There's nothing to keep him in Vicksburg, really."

"I suppose," Miss Amanda commented thoughtfully, "he understands that there isn't the slightest chance of his being elected to office."

"He hasn't consented yet to put his name up," Joseph told her.

"Well, personally, I don't see why he'd go out of his way to do so."

Varina hadn't the slightest idea what they could be discussing, though naturally she understood whom; but she liked the sound of their talk. She sat on, demurely quiet, letting it fall like pleasant rain on her thirsty young ears. Cut glass and delicate china and silver twinkled in the light of the flames and presently of candles, lighted by deft hands that came like a genii's out of blobs of shadow.

It is a barony, a kingdom, she thought, because of the talk ranging far and wide, and yet staying at home, because of the richness and plenty and, somehow, the power. It might be very satisfying to rule over such a place as queen—or queen presumptive. She wondered, dreamily, about the invalid who was its present mistress, whose place Miss Amanda filled so capably, yet all the while insisting that she was only helping out. Once, during supper, Miss Amanda said something about migraine and the effect of wind upon it and a new medicine for sleep which, she feared, was too strong; but her brother turned her query aside with a frown; and she went on, obligingly, to other topics.

A quiet, almost a dull evening, except for Varina's eager anticipations. Supper over, she was quick to accept Joseph's offer to show her something of the house while Mary and her mother caught up on the happenings of a three days' separation. There was deference and a hint of the confidential in his manner of making the suggestion.

"Now, if you like, my dear," as if he, too, had waited for this moment. Again they passed quickly through the formal drawing room.

"You will see enough of this, I think, in the natural course of events," was his dismissal of the richness here. "My rooms are across the hall."

Solomon, the major-domo, went ahead with an oil lamp and a taper for lighting candles.

"I dislike lamps," Joseph said. "They smell abominably and I'm not sure but they are a greater fire risk than candles; but they give a good light and are easier to carry about. Go right on to the library, Solomon."

The finality with which he put kerosene lamps in their place startled Varina. His tone was so reminiscent of another's:

"Would you mind . . . my time is short . . ."

Joseph and Jefferson Davis, though twenty-four years apart in age, were brothers, she could see now. However, in another second she had disposed of her comparison as neatly as Joseph had of the lamps. One might expect a man to be an autocrat in his own household, particularly a man of Joseph Davis's achievements.

His rooms were three, occupying the east side of the lower floor. His bedroom, to the front, was remarkable only for the simple austerity of its appointments. The library was another matter. Varina's fingers curled and uncurled at the array of books. The walls were lined with them. Space had been left above and between the rows of shelves only to accommodate the portraits of the first ten presidents of the United States, beginning with George Washington and ending with Mr. Tyler, now in office. At Varina's exclamation of pleasure and her greedy hands, Joseph laughed.

"Please feel welcome," he said, "to borrow any volume you fancy. You will find almost anything here—romance, poetry, history—what you will. However, if at any time you should choose to delight an old man with your company and conversation, you are likely to find me holed-in back here."

That was why he had brought her to this part of the house—to show her his throne room, the Hurricane office. It was a larger room than her father's office at The Briers, furnished similarly with broad, plain chairs and a crammed desk but, in addition, with a bare pine table, large enough to serve as a store counter. On the hearth a log fire slumbered. Besides the door through which they had entered the room, another led, Joseph said, to a store closet. He did not open it that evening, but Varina saw later that the closet filled all the space under the main stairway.

It was a larger office than the one at The Briers and, she saw at once, more important. No one could help feeling that business transacted here had far-reaching significance. How significant it was and how far it reached, Varina would not have believed at the time, if she had been told. One wall was pratically covered by a map of the central part of the North American continent, showing, besides the boundaries of the United States, a strip of Canada to the north and Spanish America to the south and the west. Joseph made no explanation of the map other than to call her attention to various spots marked with purple ink, to show where members or connections of the family lived—

Vicksburg, Davis Bend, Woodville, and, over the border in Louisiana, St. Francisville and Bayou Sara.

Bayou Sara . . .

"She is buried on Aunt Anna's plantation at Bayou Sara."

"Now, with your permisson," Joseph said gallantly, and ringed in Natchez.

Again Varina was startled. She had not given her permission. Embarrassed by her objection to what might have been a simple gesture of hospitality, she turned away from the map, to study the portraits in the office. These were two in number, the first of a chubby, handsome boy. Young Joseph, at last? But how young! The portrait must have been made some time ago. Young, yes, but something about the winsome set of the mouth that drew her.

"Our Jefferson," Joseph said, scattering her thoughts like leaves before a wind. "You saw him briefly at Diamond Place, I understand. The youngest of the family and our favorite, as you probably have guessed."

Indeed! Varina would have turned again, but the appeal of the boyish features still held her attention. It was then, she realized afterward, that a mad idea first crossed her mind—so mad that she would have nothing to do with it. Resolutely she turned her back on the smiling boy and asked about the second portrait. Nothing winsome about the lantern-jawed, wild-eyed image in that frame.

"Mr. Calhoun of South Carolina," Joseph said; and that was Varina's first warning that the conservative policies of Henry Clay had no place in this house. "Another favorite; but, if you are interested in portraits, I'd like to show you more of the family. We'll visit the music room next, Solomon."

They went out a rear door, over a paved gallery and through the covered passage leading to the west wing. While Solomon held the lamp, Joseph unlocked and threw open a heavy, paneled oak door. They stepped into what was more a hall than a room, running the full length of the wing—forty-three feet, Joseph said with some pride. The floor was paved with red brick, like the passage and the galleries outside. A long refectory table occupied the center of the room, flanked by side tables and massive sideboards. A cavernous fireplace filled the end wall opposite the entrance. Dinner was always served here, Joseph said, and other meals as well, when the family was of any size.

But his business and Varina's this evening was in the room above, reached by flights of stairs from either end of the dining hall. It was a room fully as large as the one below, but in a more lightsome mood. The plastered walls were a soft cream in color; the upholstery of chairs and the curtains draping the tall windows were in shades of rose. The polished floor was bare of carpeting; and the furniture, except for a piano, less handsome but more used than the one in the drawing room, was light and sparse enough to be moved easily against the walls, leaving the center of the room empty for games and dancing. A fireplace duplicated the one below. Its depth and the deep embrasures of the small-paned windows were the only reminders here of the generally heavy structure of the building.

"I hope you will have many gay times up here," Joseph said. "It is ballroom, music room, fun room by turns. The young folk, you see, can raise all the din they like without disturbing anyone in the house who wishes not to hear. And now, Solomon, our father's portrait."

Varina, having fetish ancestors of her own, was not too surprised at Joseph's tone of solemnity. Personally, she was disappointed at his parading an older instead of a younger generation. "More of the family" had meant that to her. Joseph, however, remained oblivious of her choice of interest. His solemnity deepened, as Solomon applied his taper to candles in sconces on either side of the picture in question.

"Hold the lamp higher, Solomon," he fussed. "There's a shadow. There! That's better."

A face came out of the darkness of the painted background with the suddenness of an apparition, though otherwise there was no ghostliness about the image. It was a strong face, gaunt, solidly real.

"Ole Mosser," the Negro said shakily.

Joseph, who up to this time had kept Varina's arm tucked under his, released it, and stepped back.

"Old Master, indeed," he said. "His name was Samuel, child." As if it might be important for her to know. "Our father—as good and godly a man as ever lived. Soldier, farmer, patriot, patriarch—you must get Aunt Rhina to tell of the family wanderings. It is a stirring story, at least to us. Our father, you see, had this vision of a promised land and set out with his flocks and his herds and his men servants and his maid servants in search of it . . ."

A visionary? Fruitlessly Varina scanned the gaunt features for any trace of the raptness that belong to a seer. A good and a godly man, perhaps ... she shivered with some sudden vague apprehension. These godly men of another day had had wills of iron.

"Welsh," Joseph said. "The name originally was David. The shepherd king, you know."

Yes, and a singer of songs—a poet. Varina shivered again. What came over people when they talked of ancestors? Here was a good and godly man, but hard, she could have sworn, unyielding in his rectitude.

"A wonderful figure on a horse," Joseph added. "Jefferson draws that from him, at least."

At least? Mary Brádford had hinted at a fearful rectitude there.

"Welsh," Joseph went on. "The family followed William Penn to America. They settled first on a grant of land from him. Part of the holding was in Pennsylvania as it is now, part in Maryland—old Pencader Hundred."

Familiar words turned the path of Varina's reflections.

"But I've heard Papa speak of Pencader Hundred—it was Papa or Aunt Sally."

"The Howells," Joseph informed her, "worshiped in the same congregation. I happen to know."

But how? Or why? Why had he troubled himself to make this discovery?

"Your grandmother on your father's side was of Penn's faith, I understand."

His study had been thorough. Now, as usual, when it was too late, Varina perceived the significance of the warning her father had tried to give her in his office at The Briers that warm, sunny and suddenly far-off day in May. If he had received support from anyone, including herself, he would have opposed outright her accepting his friend's invitation to spend any time at all at Hurricane. He knew the invitation had not been given lightly. He had sensed and feared the purpose that Joseph Davis might have in mind. But it was in keeping with his comfortable geniality that, unsupported, he had not made too vigorous opposition. He had said in effect, "Your Uncle Joe is a shrewd man, child, more clever than you think." He had intimated that she might not be a match for this Uncle Joe in wits, but then he had thought she might be, after all. What he had failed to say had been, "The man is hard, Winnie, ruthless when he goes after something." This was the quality that, bit by bit, and unwillingly, she had come to realize here in this battlemented castle, but never so clearly as right now. It was a quality she would do well to respect or even fear. Wits she could match with anyone, she thought. Hardness might be another matter.

"You resemble your father, don't you?" she said uncertainly.

He smiled warmly.

"It pleases me extravagantly," he acknowledged, "to be told that. I am his first-born son. You see, in modern times a man is not given a biblical patriarch's years in which to achieve his life's purpose. He must, of necessity, hand on his wish and his will to another—a son, if he is so blessed. If not . . ." The smile left his face. Its genial lines stiffened. In the half-light and the shadow the resemblance to the gaunt countenance on the wall was startling. A good and godly man, but unyielding . . . and then he changed back.

"That's enough for one evening," he said, "your first at Hurricane. We'll take a look at Old Miss another time, Solomon. She hangs just opposite our father, Varina; but another day. Amanda and Mary will have had ample time for their gossip and will be wondering what has become of us. You may snuff the candles, Solomon, and lead on with the lamp."

But Varina's eyes were wide and watching now. As Solomon led on with the lamp, the light swept briefly over the opposite painting and she had a glimpse of a face so purely and exquisitely beautiful that involuntarily she put out a hand to check Joseph. She dropped it, then, without touching him. As he had suggested, her discoveries for one evening had been ample and to spare.

She awoke the next morning to a twitter that she mistook, while still half-asleep, for birds, but found to be children's smothered titters and speculations, instead. The door of her room stood ajar and around the edge of it appeared four heads—one a girl's, smothered in yellow curls, one a boy's—blue eyes and dark hair in a square, Dutch cut— and two heads, male and female, distinctly African. For a minute she thought she was back at The Briers.

"Shoo!" she said, and the heads vanished in a cascade of delighted laughter. A sharp word and a slap silenced the fun. A girl, just grown, cocoa-brown and neat as new paint in starched gingham and white apron and cap, came through the still open door.

"Did those chil'ren wake you?" she asked. "I'll tell . . ."

Varina covered dismay with a yawn. She was not at home. She was in a strange room in a strange house, in the center of an enormous, unrecognizable bed.

"Yes—no!" she decided, yawned and stretched again; then, "Who are you?"

"My name's Betsy," the girl said. "I belong here. Will you be pleased to have your breakfast now?"

"Where's my girl?" Varina demanded. "Melissa?"

"She down in the clothes yard washing out some things."

"Visiting," Varina said severely.

"No'm, yes'm." The comely brown face drooped. "I said I'd be pleased to take keer of you and wait on you this mornin'. I'd be pleased to fetch yore breakfast when you is ready." The droop became a near-pout. "Rhina Number Two's my mammy. I's learnin' to be a lady's maid. I's learnin' jest . . ."

Varina cheered the girl and herself with a dazzling smile.

"Of course you can bring my breakfast, Betsy," she said. "After I've washed . . ."

"I is for a fact jest learnin'," the pout vanished in a smile wider than Varina's. "Would you like a little more light? I'll open the shutters."

The area of a dormer brightened, but not emphatically, as blinds were flung back.

"Is it cloudy?" Varina asked.

"No'm, not exactly. The sun's tryin' to come through, but the mist's right thick. It's fixin' to turn colder or warmer, one or the other. That's what ails the chil'ren. They're bustin' to git outside and go explorin', but they ain' allowed till the mists melt."

"Who are the children?" Varina asked.

"They belong to Moss' William Stamps and Miss Lucinda," Betsy informed her. "They come up las' night from Woodville, with their young ones and a parcel o' Miss Anna's from Loosiana."

Varina remembered now. The carriage had arrived while she and Joseph had been in the west wing. The occupants had been dead tired, Miss Amanda reported, saying something about a broken strap, and she had put them all directly to bed, without bothering to call her brother, who could greet them in the morning.

"They'll be rollin' in right along now," Betsy surmised. "There, then!"

She threw back the final shutter, rendering the room lighter, but chillier in consequence. She considered that herself and shivered.

"I'll fetch some real hot water," she decided. "You just stay tucked up in bed till I get back. I won't be a minute, and if those chil'ren bother, you shoo them again. They know better. Their mammies would skin 'em—white and black alike—if they heard."

Nibbling her breakfast a half-hour later, Varina decided that what ailed the children possibly ailed her, too. She herself was busting to get outside and go exploring. She finished a last crumb of biscuit and pushed her tray aside. As she moved audibly, a rustle in the hall told her that the children still kept watch.

They proved to be charming guides, sharing with the rest of the family a prompt assumption of possessiveness, tempered by exquisite manners. The boy with the cloudy blue eyes and the Dutch haircut was named Joe; and his sister, with the yellow curls, was a Lucy. Varina took pains to establish their names in her memory, but might have saved herself the effort if she had known that, before the week was out, she would know a Joseph of every age from five to twenty-five and almost the same number of Lucys. By then it seemed to her that the patriarch Samuel had been blessed too abundantly with sons and daughters. She made shift to keep their names straight because all, except the youngest—Jefferson—had been given strong, simple ones, either biblical or classical—Joseph, Benjamin, Isaac, Anna, Amanda; but after that confusion was doubled and redoubled by a distressing family habit of repeating these titles indiscriminately and forever among the children.

However, this morning there were only these two sprites. The mists had lifted, while Varina was breakfasting, enough to turn the house and its surroundings into an island of golden sunshine. The children were enchanted to show her about, she being a stranger and they knowing the place by right of birth and custom.

"This is the way to the kitchen, Miss V'rina. Wouldn't you like to see the kitchen, please? Sometimes, if Rhina Number Two isn't busy . . . but I 'spect she is this morning, making plum pudding, it's likely."

The fragrance of dark molasses and spice seasoned the misty air. It doubled in pungency as a door at the head of a short flight of steps opened. The frame was sized just to fit Rhina Number Two.

"Then you 'spect wrong, lil ole man," the cook chuckled. "What kind o' plum pudding would that be if I wait till two days befo' Chris'-mas to make it? Howdy, chil'ren. Howdy, Young Miss."

She had come out, Varina perceived at once, to take a good look at the special young lady guest. Having had her look, she had bestowed a title: Young Miss. It had its own significance, Varina knew. The cook was the second slave who, undirected, had so addressed her.

"Good morning, Rhina," she said. "It surely is a delicious something or other you're making."

Her manner was sweetly ingratiating, but nothing to the coaxing innocence of small Joe.

"Rhina," his tone dripped honey, "it couldn't possibly be 'lasses jumbles, could it? Hot?"

"You got a nose like a beagle houn'," Rhina told him. "Hot, but not too hot, I reckon."

She disappeared into the kitchen and came back with three warm, fruity drop cakes balanced on a pink palm and a plump forearm.

"Mind yore manners now, lil folk," she admonished. "Young Miss, would you favor trying a bite of Rhina's bakin'?"

Her eyes, the lids half-lowered in deference, searched Varina's face. They measured Varina's slender grace and youthfulness.

"Would I?" Varina met the examination by ignoring it. She selected a jumble and bit into it. "Mmm!" She licked the sweet crumbs from her lips. "Rhina, I'm glad I came."

Rhina gave the children their jumbles but continued to study Varina.

"You stay glad, Young Miss," she said, in soft approval of what she saw. "You come see Rhina again—whenever you fancy or need any-thing. Ole Hurricane proud to have and do for you."

"Thank you, Rhina." Nobody present, or expected, could have given Varina a more important endorsement. Being accepted at the front door of a plantation was like leaving one's card on a tray and going off again, if the back door didn't open. "Thank you, Rhina, I will. Maybe you'll show me how you make the jumbles."

"Can you stir up a cake, Young Miss?"

"I surely can. I'll prove it to you."

"You hear that, Lil Lucy? Young Miss hold her head so high and proud . . ."

"I hear." A small hand tugged at Varina's. "Thank you, Rhina, for the jumble. Cousin V'rina, aren't you dying to see the puppies in the barn?"

"Perishing," Varina said.

And it was then, with those small fingers pulling at hers, that the sound of light hoofbeats came out of the mist. It muffled the sound and, at the same time, brought it closer. The rhythm of hoofs beat on her eardrums and then on her heart, but was lost in another minute in the yelp of a boy:

"Uncle Jeff! I'll bet anything it's Uncle Jeff."

He broke and ran—around the house, down the front drive. He faded into the mist. Varina's free hand went to her throat, to hush a futile cry. A man on a galloping horse who had been known to overlook a young woman in a bright, rose-colored gown might not see a small boy in his path.

The man on the horse appeared mistily. He leaned from the saddle and caught the child, crying, "Jump!" The boy sprang and rode safely on the pommel. Doors and windows opened. Heads came out. Young people and old came running.

"Jeff! Uncle Jeff! Moss' Jeff!"

"It's Moss' Jeff, sure enough!" Rhina Number Two waddled down the steps from her kitchen to join the welcoming throng.

It was always so when he came riding home. A Douglas home from the wars, a Bruce who had won or lost a kingdom but held his pride whatever the cast of the die. Nearly always there was a child on the saddle, to make him look more than ever the warrior returned. Eager hands this morning, as always, reached out to take his horse if he should choose to dismount. He called greetings to the house, lifting his hat. He shook his head at the boys from the stable. He would ride on.

After he had dropped the boy. He brought his horse to a halt, and with an admonitory word and half a slap, set the child down on the drive. Small Joe was exalted and frightened, both. His eyes misted and his chin quivered.

"Ah-ah!" Moss' Jeff warned.

The child stiffened and, half-laughing, half-crying, saluted his uncle. Moss' Jeff returned the salute and rode on. The small girl's hand still pulled at Varina's fingers.

"It's Uncle Jeff, Cousin V'rina. Don't you want to speak to him? Cousin V'rina?"

Varina did not want to speak to him. She would not move an inch in his direction.

"You go," she said.

"No," Lucy decided, all in one second. "I'll hold my head proud and and high, too; but . . . we could take just a step or two and he might see us."

Reluctantly, helplessly, Varina took a step forward. The gray horse again was brought to a halt. This time the reins were tossed into waiting hands. He could always say afterward just who had held his horse on any occasion, though at the time he never seemed to notice. He dismounted. Hat in hand, he came over the sparkling grass toward Varina and little Lucy. His face was radiant, smiling. Somebody had admonished him about his manners.

"How do you do?" he said warmly. "How fine to see you here! I hoped . . . but hardly supposed I should—like this. I stopped at Diamond Place over night, but heard that you and Mary had gone on. Did you have a pleasant journey?"

The cries of greeting were hushed. Everything seemed to go quiet, waiting on Varina's answer. When she gave it, the words came high and thin to her ears, filled suddenly with a curious ringing.

"Thank you, yes. Your Glory gave me a truly glorious ride."

She must tell him about racing Sultan, but later.

"Did she, indeed? I must reward the young lady fittingly. And you must ride with me some day. Will you?"

"I should enjoy that very much."

"We were just about going to the stables," little Lucy said desperately.

"You were what?" The brightness went out of his face, leaving it stern and cold.

"To see the new puppies."

"You wouldn't! Joe, come here. You know you are not allowed to visit the stables without one of us present. Did you forget?"

"Yes, sir, I forgot; but I would have remembered, before I really went in, I think."

"You surely would not have taken Miss Howell, our guest."

The McCalebs had informed him of her name.

"No, sir. I . . . hope not."

"I hope not, indeed. It is because of one or two of the horses, you understand," he explained to Varina, his face still cold. "I cannot put the responsibility on the grooms. I shall be pleased to show the stables to you myself . . . and the puppies."

He smiled, bowed, remounted and rode on. Down the road people kept popping out of doors or hedgerows to greet him.

"Moss' Jeff . . . howdy, Moss' Jeff . . . Chris'mas gif', Moss' Jeff!"

"You're early, you rascal. See you day after tomorrow."

Down the road, into the mist again, the chorus following. Well, really! Varina thought, but had no words beyond that for the spectacle or her emotions.

CHAPTER V

Dear Mother,
This morning Uncle Joe sent word by his younger brother—did you
know he had one . . .

THE letter Varina had commenced to write at Diamond Place lay
unfinished, scarcely begun, on top of a bureau drawer devoted to
ribbons and other furbelows and stared at Varina accusingly every
time she came to her room to make a change or simple addition to her
costume, which was a dozen times a day, at least. She wondered why
she didn't tear up the sheet and start a new letter, except that in her
contemplations the new ones all began in the same vein and were
always on the same subject. This sentence already set down was her
only proof that she had thought of writing earlier, before things had
begun to happen so swiftly in succession that she seemed to have no
time to record them.

So swiftly, indeed! Why, then, must she write about only one person? Why not, for example, compose a description of young Joseph
Davis, the nephew about whom her family had been fully as curious
as she had been, and was, alas, no longer so.

He had proved to be, as Varina's father had foretold, a most agreeable young man. He arrived horseback later in that same morning
that brought Mr. Jefferson home from Vicksburg. He rode unex-
ceptionably well. He was tall, handsome and about the age of Joe
Howell, or very little older. Properly and responsibly he rode beside
a carriage conveying his father, Mr. Isaac Davis, and his mother,

known generally as Miss or Sister Susanna, and his two young sisters.

They were a charming family—typically charming—high-spirited, fresh-faced, outspoken, with a touch of the autocratic, but under fair control. As their carriage rolled to a stop in the drive, Miss Susanna was helped out first. She embraced everyone within arm's reach, then at once stated her mind and disposition.

"Well, Joe, here we are and happy to be here; but, I warn you, the first cloud will send us scurrying home to the mainland."

Mr. Isaac, it developed, was the brother on whom Joseph had relied most to help him open the wild land on Davis Bend. Mr. Isaac and his wife and two small sons had been living on the plantation when the storm had struck which razed the first house and outbuildings. The older boy was pinned under the wreckage and died later of his injuries. Mr. Isaac, caught by one foot under the same heavy timber, had been lamed for life. He was still, however, the farmer of the family, resembling Samuel, the Elder, more than any other son, though considerably mellower, it seemed, perhaps through long years of tempering the sharpness of his wife, who wore her scars on her spirit.

As for young Joseph, while his mother was in the middle of her first sentence, he saw Varina; and there was the conquest made. He had no eyes for anyone else at Hurricane from that instant, and no words, right then, except to beg for a presentation. The presentation made, like his mother, he at once made his position clear.

"I declare, Miss Howell, I had no idea this pleasure was in store for me."

It was too easy. It was flattering to bowl a handsome young man over like that, but it was not exciting, except for the bridling of his mother. Miss Susanna was understandably devoted to her one remaining son and did not accept Varina without question. None of the Davis women did, for that matter. That put Varina on her mettle and helped some.

But not enough. Young Joseph Davis, she decided captiously, was too young. He reminded her of Mr. Scully on the boat. He was much more like that chubby-faced portrait in Uncle Joe's office than was the original of the likeness. And there she was at the business of comparison, perhaps because the next time she saw young Joseph, he was with Mr. Jefferson Davis.

All that day people kept arriving at Hurricane and the confusion multiplied. To escape to herself, but more to round out an impression left tormentingly incomplete the evening before, Varina ran off to the music room after dinner. This being the ritual hour for naps, she thought she would find nobody else stirring. At the head of the steps, however, she put her ear to the door to reconnoiter; then, hearing no movement, no voices, she opened it and was inside before she realized her miscalculation.

Jefferson and his nephew were measuring for a projected Christmas tree and had merely stopped discussion, to study a point. They saw her and came toward her at once, young Joseph in surprised and eager welcome, the other more slowly, but graciously enough.

She could not escape. She did not particularly wish to escape. She wished only that she might invent a reason, other than the one she had, for being where she was. However, her wits refused, for once, to help her and she could only blunder out the truth, as becomingly as possible.

"Uncle Joe was showing me about last night," she said, addressing her explanation to Jefferson. "We looked at your father's portrait and then he carried me off before I could have a good look at your mother. She seemed so lovely that I wanted another opportunity . . ."

She couldn't have chosen her words better.

"I declare," young Joseph said, "I never heard a young lady say anything sweeter. Come right along. Jeff and I are proud to do the honors."

They stood, one on either side of her as she looked or tried to look at the painting. Afterward, she remembered the two men much better than the woman on the wall.

"A handsome young lady, don't you think?" Young Joe asked ingenuously.

Beautiful, in a still, proud way, but not young. Her complexion, as reproduced, was fair and smooth, her hair was brown, her eyes were bright; but they were knowing eyes. Without answering young Joseph, Varina appealed to Jefferson. He smiled—or half-smiled—at her unspoken question.

"She wouldn't sit for a portrait," he said, "while she was young enough to be vain of her beauty. She didn't mind being vain of her years. She was seventy when the picture was made."

"And still a raring beauty," young Joe insisted. "Don't you think so, Miss Howell?"

"She is lovely," Varina said honestly, troubled, however, by the wise eyes that seemed to look through her and, worse, beyond her.

Still, it was the men she recalled, reviewing the incident, the older man in particular. Young Joseph, for all his ebullience and insistence on being noticed, would slip and recede into the background, while the other stood out sharp and clear and . . . oh, what a bother!

> I do not know whether this Mr. Jefferson Davis is young or old. He looks both at times . . .

If she couldn't dismiss him from her thoughts, she might as well put it all down on paper.

> But I believe he is old, for from what I hear . . .

Mrs. Joseph Davis, Uncle Joe's invalid wife, told her explicitly and exactly how old Jefferson Davis was.

The McCalebs drove over from Diamond Place in the late afternoon of that helter-skelter day and Florida took Varina in to see her mother almost at once.

"Mamma has been waiting for someone to bring you in," Floss said. "She has had one of her worst headaches and hasn't felt like coming downstairs, but naturally she is interested in meeting you. Aren't you anxious to know Mamma?"

Varina was curious, at least. She could hardly pass from the third floor of the house to the first, or the other way around, several times a day without taking note of a room on the second floor, toward the front of the house, the door of which was always closed when she went by. From other rooms on the same floor would come a rush of busy talk or other sounds of cheerful occupancy, but this one room might have been sealed.

It was to this closed door that Florida McCaleb led Varina now. She knocked lightly and, without waiting for a response, entered.

To the end of her life, whenever Varina thought of Mrs. Eliza Davis's bedroom, she felt a smothering sensation. Partly this was due to a burdensome richness of furnishing. It was a large room, with four windows. Like all the windows at Hurricane, these were narrow, with small, thick panes, set in deep casements; but they would have let in light, if uncovered. Over the glass, however, hung lengths of heavy Brussels lace and from poles on silver mountings hung draw curtains, besides, of crimson brocade.

Varina could hardly keep her hands off the cords that drew the draperies aside or would draw them aside, if permission was given. The room needed light. The furniture was dark and ponderous. All wall space, not given to windows, seemed filled with chests—low, carved chests with lids, tall highboys, armoires—all of dark, polished wood, heavily, ornately carved. The poster bed with tester that jutted out into the room was extraordinarily wide. Vines twined about the posts. Individual pieces like any of those in the room, except the low chests—Mrs. Davis's ancestors had been Dutch merchantmen—Varina had seen often, but never so many crowded into one room, unless the occasion was a sale.

The room needed air. The atmosphere was close and burdened with a mingling of scents—orris root, cologne, oil of wintergreen. Finally, through a multiplicity of other impressions, all repellent on first contact to Varina, came the picture of the titular mistress of Hurricane— Eliza van Benthuysen Davis.

She was an invalid. The nature of her invalidism was and remained obscure, largely because examination into its cause or possible cure had not been very thorough. Chronic invalidism was a rather common phenomenon of the day. It might be due to personal unhappiness or some organic disorder, neglected because it was not understood. Varina, young and not unaccustomed to similar cases, was more interested in the personality of the sufferer than in the reasons for her state of health.

"My, oh, my, what a big girl you are!" was her greeting to Varina. "You are taller even than Mary Bradford, I think."

There was a slight, foreign intonation to her speech. It was so slight and so subtle as almost to escape notice; but it was there and so was also an equally subtle hint of malice in her words. They not only emphasized Varina's height, but they asked for attention to her own smallness of stature. Well, Mrs. Davis was small of stature still. In her youth she might have been, like her daughter Florida, petite in other ways. Of that dainty smallness there remained now white hands, covered with jeweled rings, and exquisitely tiny feet in beaded slippers. Otherwise, she was plump as the cushions among which she rested and in much the same inert way. Her pallor was that of confinement. Her brown hair under a rosette of lace had no gray in it. Her brown eyes were bright, almost glassy.

"Are all the Howells so tall . . . and Junoesque?" she asked next.

Varina, aware of tones and undertones, was slightly at a loss for words to reply, or would have been except for careful schooling in manners.

"My father's people are tall."

"And your mother?"

"Mamma is not especially tall—not especially one way or the other." But sweet and beautiful and dear! The oppressiveness of the present encounter brought Varina the sharpest pain of loneliness that she had experienced since leaving Natchez. If only her mother had consented to chaperon her on this visit! It seemed to Varina on reflection that she had quite positively refused.

"Darling, it isn't necessary. I'll send Melissa. Joseph will see that you are surrounded by every other sort of protection. He promised."

"But vigorously healthy, I presume?" The plaintive, insistent questioning continued.

"Mamma is quite well usually, thank you."

That brought forth a curiously defiant assertion.

"I, as you see, am an invalid, confined for the most part to my room." She dared someone to say that she didn't look like one who suffered. For a fact, she did not look so. The speech might have been made by a frail creature from one of Jane Austen's novels. Smelling salts, a wisp of handkerchief ever ready, a couch with warm shawls, were according to tradition; but Eliza van Benthuysen was too substantial for a Jane Austen figure. Either that, or Varina had formed the wrong image of those vaporing ladies.

"I am sorry you are not well," Varina said politely; but she was more uncomfortable, really, than sorry.

"It is of no consequence." The wisp of handkerchief was dabbed on the bright brown eyes. "It is the outrageous climate, of course. Natchez, I trust, is a healthier locality."

"Natchez On the Hill is considered quite healthy, ma'am."

"Then take my advice and stay there." Varina jumped. The words stung. "Why risk your youth and beauty in these fever-ridden swamps? It is the mists, you see. We have them summer and winter.

I thought I knew what mists were. My people are from New York; but I lived as a girl with relatives in Charleston. . . ."

There was a second daughter, named Caroline—a wild, pretty creature, riding, by preference, half-broken colts across country, her hair streaming in the wind. She came down the next day with an uncle and aunt from Vicksburg. Florida . . . Caroline . . .

"The fogs in from the salt sea," the mother said now, "are nothing, compared to these inland vapors. They breed fever in summer and chill one to the marrow in winter. There was that pretty creature Jefferson brought here when he was a gay, young man. For that matter, look at Jefferson himself. Are you acquainted with Mr. Jefferson Davis as well as with my husband, Miss Howell? Young Jeff?"

"Now, Mamma," Florida said, "you're as fond as anybody of Jefferson."

"Indeed, I am, dear child. The most charming fellow in the world. What is it the poet says about Orpheus? He could charm the damned . . . but it's ridiculous to cling to the superstition of his being still a young man. As if time had stopped for him and gone on for the rest of us. He's as old as I am, you know. He certainly is. I know, if you don't. I came out here a bride in 1827. I was twenty. Jefferson was still at West Point. When he finished, he spent most of his furlough here. He had then no attachments of the heart and was pleased to be attentive to his brother's wife. We compared ages. I was born in February and he in June of the same year. There is that much in his favor, but no more. My migraines cast discredit upon Hurricane and are a source of annoyance, but for some reason Jefferson's neuralgia is pardoned. The mists have nothing to do wtih his ailment. That is caused, we are told, by the pneumonia he all but died of in Wisconsin. . . ."

Neuralgia? Young men, to be sure, were seldom troubled by its pains. It would have been hard to imagine young Joseph Davis with a headache, and yet . . .

> He impresses me as a remarkable kind of man, but of uncertain temper, and has a way of taking for granted that everybody agrees with him when he expresses an opinion, which offends me. Would you believe it—he is refined and cultivated; and yet, he is a Democrat.

It was the dinner hour of the day before Christmas and Varina was due to receive her second warning of political difference. All morning one of those discussions with which she was both familiar and unfamiliar had been in progress in Joseph Davis's office. It had been well attended. Three Davis brothers besides Joseph and Jefferson had participated. They were, in order of seniority, two planters—Mr. Samuel Davis from near Vicksburg and Mr. Isaac Davis—and Dr. Benjamin Davis, a ruddy, jolly brother from St. Francisville, Louisiana. William Stamps, Dwight McCaleb and young Joseph also were present; and, hearing that Jefferson had returned from Vicksburg, General Quitman and several men from the Turner plantations had ridden over to see what news he had brought, if any. What that news might be the ladies of the household, as usual, were likely to hear indirectly, if at all. At the call to dinner, the men came trooping in company over to the west wing, full of talk that told nothing.

General Quitman led the way with Joseph Davis. The general was a small man, compared to the Davis brothers, but as stiffly erect as the stiffest of them, and very conscious of his position as commander of the state militia. He was as much surprised to see Varina as she was surprised and pleased to see him. He clicked his heels and bowed over her hand in greeting.

"I know this young lady well," he said. "Her brother is one of my Natchez company. Alas, if I ever have the honor to lead the Fencibles into battle, I am afraid he will be the first to fall. Not through clumsiness or cowardice, just exposure. Six feet, seven inches tall, you see. Frederick the Great would have had him in his Grenadiers. A fine fellow, a credit to his family and his state. One of those we shall have to consider, Jefferson, or, better, convert to our way of thinking. The fathers will be hard to dissuade from old allegiance. It is the sons we must hope to win."

"I am aware that the Whigs are firmly entrenched in Mississippi, John; but it is a party doomed to defeat both in the South and the North because of its refusal to face issues fearlessly."

That was the way he said it, his assurance something worse than his choice of words. What did he mean by the Whigs being afraid to face issues? Varina, as loyal a Whig as ever grew up in ignorance, was wearing at the very time, and proudly, the emblem of her party; and he was looking directly at it. It was a gold collar pin or brooch, representing a money safe with a watchdog chained to it. It had come into fashion during the Harrison campaign, when a much more serious issue than log cabins and hard cider had been the restoration of the National Bank, which Andrew Jackson and his successor, Van Buren, had scuttled. The Democrats, according to the Whigs, if allowed to continue in office, would eventually scuttle the United States Treasury. Wherefore, the noble Whigs must guard it with their very lives.

The complete details of Democratic demagoguery and rascality and Whig nobility and integrity, like all profound subjects left to masculine debate, Varina comprehended with feminine vagueness, sharpened by natural curiosity and keenness of perception, but dulled, to compensate, by equally natural loyalties. All the respectable folk she knew were Whigs and all the young ladies wore gold watchdogs. Down around Natchez, Democrats for the most part were river pirates on one hand and poor whites from the sandhills and pine barrens on the other. Even in Philadelphia she had felt something of the same distinction in caste. Was the situation reversed in Warren County? Had this surprise been reserved for a rude joke?

As dinner progressed, it seemed to her that the watchdog brooch increased in brilliancy and size. That morning she had found herself agreeing with Melissa's precautions against wearing the new off her best clothes prematurely and had chosen the simplest frock she had brought with her—a sober, Quakerish affair of homespun which had seemed to call for some bright bauble to fasten the ruching at the throat of the plain bodice. Now the bauble obscured the frock.

Joseph Davis, seeing her confusion bordering on bad temper, took her arm protectingly in his.

"Shall we call a truce on politics?" he suggested, or, rather, commanded, looking at all his brothers, but the youngest, in particular. "Varina is my special Christmas guest, and I don't purpose to have her fun spoiled by deep and solemn discussions of any issues, national, local or domestic."

Did he not, really?

However, for the present, he exerted himself to show her much personal attention and Varina responded by entering as brightly as she could into the gay talk of the younger people near the head of the table. Many of them were on holiday from school and there was considerable exchange of reports.

"I presume you have finished school, Miss Howell," young Joseph said, quite willing to forego politics in her favor and undismayed, apparently, by her affiliations.

"Just finished," Varina informed him. "I spent last Christmas in Trenton, New Jersey, if you can believe it."

"Varina's father comes from New Jersey," Joseph, Senior, added, and, that his namesake might know to whom he was offering his homage, "her Grandfather Howell was for a number of years governor of that state."

Young Joe was impressed briefly into silence, others not so much so. "Did you go to school in New Jersey, Miss Varina?"

"In Philadelphia," Varina answered. "Madame Greenland's Day and Boarding School."

"It is, I understand," Joseph again amplified, "a very special young ladies' seminary. You must get Varina to tell you of the dancing master."

"I'll do better than tell about him," Varina promised. "I'll give you all a lesson this evening in the music room."

"With or without pomatum?" Joseph teased.

"Without, I am afraid. I don't believe even Rhina Number Two could supply the ingredients for Monsieur's hair oil."

"You'd be surprised, Miss Howell," young Joseph had recovered his speech, "at what we might supply in the way of refinement, even here in the backwoods."

Varina smiled at him sweetly, if vaguely. Why would he continually remind her of Mr. Scully on the boat? Why was she vexed by his efforts to make himself agreeable? No doubt it was because his youngest uncle, two places removed from him at the table, was paying her no attention at all. Mr. Jefferson Davis was not concerned over his brother's special guest, her schooling or her ornaments. He would bow his head courteously now and again to listen to some remark made by the sister or sister-in-law at either elbow; but his real interest was, plainly, in the rag-tag of discussion the men had brought over from the Hurricane office. This had lost coherence in the flood of family and social converse, but scraps of it bobbed persistently to the surface. Somebody mentioned Seargent Prentiss and Varina herself dropped all pretense of politeness to listen.

Seargent Prentiss was the political idol of Mississippi, of Natchez, in particular, and a Whig to the marrow of his bones. That fall

Varina's father had taken her, as one of a party of young folk, to a rally, to hear Prentiss speak. It was November. Cotton was coming in from the back country. The great Prentiss was in Natchez visiting his wife's people, the Williamses of Longwood. He stood on a cotton wagon in Cotton Square to make his speech and all Natchez and most of Adams County stood to listen. Varina wished now that she could remember all or anything of what he had said. She recalled his pale, exalted face, the smooth flow of beautiful words; but there had been too many people present, too much excitement, she had been too much impressed with the fact of being on the scene herself, to single out one memorable phrase of the speaker.

She did remember a remark her father had made afterward.

"Sounds as good as ever, Puss. Rings as true."

Had he added or implied a reservation? Could the politics of the South or of Mississippi have changed in the two years she had been away at school? She didn't really believe so; nevertheless, she was sharply aware now, with a perception not born on the instant, of some strong undertow in the present muted discussion as, under cover of gay trivialities, she listened to the weightier talk at the table and under demurely lowered lashes watched the faces of the men who participated.

All the men, not one or two or three.

They were worthy of her consideration—these men of the cotton-growing South, her own country. Handsome, vigorous in mind and body, sure of themselves and their birthright. Men who, after long hours in the saddle or the dusty courtroom or banking office, could wear ruffled shirts and silken manners to the dinner table; and the table might be the pine boards of a barren inn or the polished mahogany of a manor house; but they were gentlemen either way. They had a gentlemen's code. It had never been written down. It had grown over the years. An outsider could never master it altogether. Perhaps those who lived by it did not understand it fully themselves. It was simply there, fixed and unalterable. They were men difficult to know completely, however open and unaffected their surface. They were impossible to convince of error even when they were in error. Among themselves differences often could be settled only with pistols and bloodshed. Imagine, for example, daring to differ with Mr. Jefferson Davis.

Mr. Jefferson, Moss' Jeff—with so many others present she could take a more leisurely view of him. Not that she discovered in her scrutiny of the chiseled sharpness of his features anything new. The image was already clear enough in her mind to disturb her unwarrantably. It was as beautiful a face, she decided again, as a man could possess without loss of strength. There was no loss of strength here. There was a raptness, a lack of worldliness, too much refinement of spirit, perhaps, too much of pure intellect for rough, daily usage; but here was the reason she could not be satisfied with a conquest of young Joseph Davis. She did not know it then, but from this time forward she would note in all other men's faces too much of yielding softness, too much of common coarseness, something of dross that would make her turn away, remembering this one.

It was a proud face—proud and still, with tremendous dignity and reserve; or, was that only the habitually withdrawn look? His dress was neat to the point of fastidiousness, but not fussy. He wore a high collar; but, thanks to his almost ascetic leanness, it did not seem uncomfortable. Besides, in place of the usual rigid stock, he had folded a black silk handkerchief, then brought it from front to rear, crossed it and brought it back front again, tying the corners in a soft knot. The effect was soft, original—it had even a certain dash.

The shoulders of his coat fitted unusually well. No, it was the set of the man's shoulders under the coat. They would neither invite nor tolerate wrinkles—goodness, she hoped she was not staring. He gave her such a look just then out of his deep eyes.

Such a look, indeed! Not seeing her, really. He turned immediately to listen gravely to something General Quitman was saying. What would a young lady have to do, to make him look at her just once with undivided attention, to make him, in short, as aware of her as she was aware of him?

It was then that an idea took full shape in Varina's mind which certainly was not born all in one instant. Here, she thought, would be a conquest that any woman might be proud to achieve. Here would be sport to challenge all her ingenuity and persistence. If she could come off the winner, what a joke on Uncle Joe and his plans! What a joke on the whole delightful, but rather cocksure Davis family!

"Child," Joseph teased, "you haven't spoken a word in fully five minutes."

She turned to him a face merry with mischief.

"Granny would say you ought to be thankful to have me quiet, but also you should be on your guard."

"Why on guard?"

"Gracious, didn't you ever hear Grandmother Kempe tell how I set fire to Kempton Hall?"

"No, by Jove! Did you, and were you quiet then?"

"If I hadn't been so quiet, it wouldn't have happened, or so I've been told."

There! With all at that end of the table, Mr. Jefferson was looking at her now.

"You didn't really ever set fire to a house?" he questioned.

"Yes, I did." Her heart chirruped wickedly.

"Tell us."

"Oh, I couldn't—not now. Not here. I was a very naughty child—obstinate, willful . . ."

"Were you, indeed?"

"Granny says I was."

"I must hear the story, to judge."

I shall never like him as well as I do Uncle Joe. Everybody on the place bows down to him . . .

Dwight McCaleb said to her after dinner, "Well, what do you think now of the handsome younger brother?"

"Do you mean Mr. Jefferson?" she asked. "Gracious, I haven't known him long enough to form an opinion."

Of course, he meant Mr. Jefferson.

That evening in the music room the Christmas tree for which Jefferson and young Joseph had taken the measurements was set up; and everyone, except the smallest children, took a hand in trimming it with candles and gilded nuts and oranges and wrapped bonbons and tinsel angels with isinglass stomachs filled with candy confetti. When the candles were lighted, the children were called in. They waited in a mass outside the door. Hurricane was now running over with guests. A few of the young men had to be accommodated temporarily by Jefferson Davis in his lonely, remote house. Mary Bradford had moved in with Varina and soon afterward a trundle bed had been made up for a couple of small girls who promised to be as good as gold if they were allowed to sleep in Cousin Mary's and Cousin Varina's room.

Miss Amanda said she couldn't remember a Christmas when so nearly everybody had been able to come and she wished their mother down at Woodville, spending Christmas quietly with Sister Anna, could see.

Or that they might have gone to Woodville instead of spending Christmas here, someone asked. Mercy, no, Miss Amanda said. The Poplars was the sweetest spot on earth and home, but it would never accommodate a crowd like this one. The house had always been too small even for one family. As fast as each boy had grown up, he had moved out, to make room. Joseph, the eldest, to this day couldn't claim a bed there as his own, because when the family left Kentucky he had stayed behind to finish his law studies and when that was done, there wasn't a chink open for him at Woodville.

That was quite true, Joseph lamented. However, he said, in his young days that had seemed to be a young man's lot. If he wanted to be sure of a house to live in he had best hustle forth and provide one. And, if anyone wanted to know, Jefferson had been cast forth about the earliest. He had been only seven when the family had bundled him off to school—too far to come home for any holidays.

"Uncle Jeff, tell us about the time . . . Uncle Jeff!"

Varina did not need to raise her voice in petition. The children made clamor enough. This was their part of the evening; and she could sit back, listening to their pleasant babel and, undisturbed, watch the most popular member of the family move about his duties. On some impulse, best understood by himself, he had laid aside graver cares to devote himself to the evening's fun. He managed, notwithstanding, to remain rather gravely aloof, after all. He had superintended the lighting of the candles on the tree; and now, as Joseph called attention to him, he was fitting a wet sponge to a long pole and marshaling other assistants with other sponges to snuff the candles when they burned down or to douse the first sign of flame in the tree.

It all made a pleasing picture—the press of people, the happy children, the dark tree with its twinkling lights, the tall man—like Saul, head and shoulders above the multitude—deeply intent on his simple responsibility. The room became suffocatingly warm. He halted his patrol finally to direct someone to open a window. Soft, cool air stole in, bringing a sound of string music and singing, mellowed by distance. Christmas had begun in the quarters, too. In the morning every scrap of help on the place would be at the door, expecting donations;

but tonight the fun was of the black folks' own making and none that could be spared was asked to stay at the post of duty. For a week, help would be fairly unreliable.

"Tell us, Uncle Jeff, about going away to school when you were seven."

He doused a taper with a lively hissing of his sponge.

"Well," he said, "it was like this. Your grandfather had certain ideas about education and Woodville was a small place, though the capital of the state in those days. Perhaps its being the capital had something to do with my being sent away. Your grandfather did not think too highly of professional politicians and their hangers-on."

Did his eyes catch a reflection of the candles or was he amused over the idea? Did he realize the general reputation of the party of his choice?

"The truth is," Uncle Joe put in, "Father thought your Uncle Jeff's mind merited special instruction."

"The very truth," Miss Amanda corrected, "was that he was Mamma's pet and Papa didn't want him to grow up tied to her apron strings."

Fancy that! The twinkle became a mellow, chuckling laugh.

"Oh, don't tell us about the school," some younger Joe protested. "Tell us about going there—riding horseback over the Trace and the Indian stands and Andrew Jackson."

"But if you know it all in advance . . ."

"Tell it, anyhow," the boy insisted. "It always sounds different." Gay shouts and a pelting of bright bonbon papers. "I mean, I hear something new each time and the little ones haven't heard it at all. Please, Uncle Jeff."

"All right. Let me go around the tree once more and collect my notes. All things considered, I'd like this to be a good telling. Of course," he spread his coat tails and sat down on the arm of Miss Amanda's chair, still keeping an eye on the tree, "I can't hope not to disappoint you after what you've been led to expect. To begin with, there's this matter of riding horseback. There was another boy, you know. His name was Howell Hinds. I don't suppose, Miss Varina, there was any connection."

Varina, startled by the sudden direct address, said she supposed not.

She had never heard of Howell Hinds. Was he the son of Colonel Hinds of the Dragoons?

"Yes. Colonel Hinds, you see, was in command of our party. The boy, Howell, and I shared a pony and, since Howell, being nine, was the older, he rode in front most of the way. Once in a while the Colonel out of pity would take me up with him and then I rode, I thought, in commanding style. The Colonel had a big, black horse and was himself a fine figure of a man. It was the summer after the battle of New Orleans and he still wore his uniform. It seemed safer, traveling the Trace. The supposition was that any outlaw or Indian would recognize him on sight and abandon at once any idea of molesting us."

"Don't forget the sword, Uncle Jeff."

"Oh yes, the sword. It was a cavalry saber, presented to the Colonel by his Dragoons. The first one of its kind I ever laid hands on. The Colonel was good enough to let Howell and me play with it. Like the pony, we had to share the adventure. It took the two of us to lift the sword."

"The wonder is," some woman said out of the shadows, "that you didn't cut off a leg."

"It is a wonder," Jefferson agreed, "but we didn't. Do you want to hear about the Trace now? We followed it into Tennessee. It was a clear trail then, as now, but much wilder, much less traveled. The only people we met were pack and wagon trains. I remember the bells on the horses and wagons. The horses were belled so that, if they broke their tethers and got away, they could be traced. The wagons were belled against thieving savages. The Indians coveted the bells as much as any part of the cargo and inevitably they were always overheard at their pilfering.

"The traders gave us no trouble, nor did Indians, perhaps because Colonel Hinds posted a guard each night. We camped in the open for the most part, spreading blankets from tree to tree for shelter. We spent only one night on the whole journey really at an Indian stand. That was a night it stormed. The stands were nothing but rude log cabins and not too clean. Indian half-breeds kept them. They are not by nature very fastidious housekeepers and their transient guests were not in the habit of washing themselves or their clothes as much as they might, considering the abundance of fresh water along the way.

Well, it seemed much pleasanter out of doors than in, if you comprehend."

"We understand, Jeff." Miss Amanda said. "Don't distress yourself with the particulars."

This, Varina was thinking, rather than marks of years, made Jefferson Davis seem a man approaching the state of being old. He had lived through so much varied experience, of which so far she had heard only the vaguest hints.

"Thank you, ma'am," he said. "I will go on to pleasanter topics. The journey, as you can see, was full of adventure, and it ended magnificently with a visit of three days at the home of General Jackson."

A kind of sigh went through the room.

"I must remember to tell Granny Kempe," Varina thought, sighing with the other children.

"I can see now," Jefferson continued in a minute, "that Colonel Hinds had planned his route the way he did because it passed near The Hermitage. At the time it seemed to me a sudden provision of Providence that the house turned up on our path. I all but fell off the rear of the pony when the Colonel turned in his saddle one afternoon and said, how would we like to visit the hero of New Orleans. Howell and I were fairly speechless for a day and a half."

"Tell us what Old Hickory was like, Uncle Jeff. Tell us now. Why do you always stop to think?"

Yes, why? And of what did he think in those brooding pauses?

"Old Hickory?" he said. "Why, he was like the best you've heard of him. I believe that to be true of most great men. They are nearer the best of popular report than the worst. The things I remember are things some people wouldn't expect in a backwoodsman or a fighting soldier; but, in view of later experience, I'd say they only make a good soldier a better one. I remember how he said grace at table—humbly, devoutly—and then how he fell to on the victuals and told us to do the same.

"I remember how he took us over his handsome house, taking great pride in it, and then how with even greater zest he took us into the woods where he was cutting timber and taught us how to use a cross-cut saw and an axe. He said a house was a fine place for resting, but the outdoors had it beaten in most other ways. He ran foot races with us—and beat us—then showed us why, teaching us to save our strength and our wind, as he did. He joined in our play like another boy; but here's something. He never would let us wrestle. About that, he talked strangely for a fighting man. He said, 'Keep your hands off each other and you'll never come to blows. That's where trouble always begins. The fellow who lays on hands first is the one who starts it.' He was right, when you think it out. Of course, he could fight—in defense of self and property and principle, but never because he wanted to."

"Was Mrs. Jackson at home?" someone asked.

"Aunt Rachel? Yes, indeed. We boys left there with all our stockings darned fresh and our buttons in good order. She saw to that."

"Does she smoke—I mean, did she smoke a pipe, Jeff?"

"I don't know." The candles were all out now, but he made a circle of the tree, to be sure. "I don't know," he said again. "I never saw her do so. A person should tell about another only what he can say on oath that he actually saw with his own eyes. Suppose she did smoke a pipe? What, then? The best of her was not that. The best . . ." he was directly in front of Varina now. "Why, child," he said abruptly, "what big eyes you have!"

Varina flushed to the roots of her hair. His light comment hurt sensibilities she had hardly known she possessed. They were not those of a child.

"Were you really only seven years old?" she asked.

"So young," he told her, and tried to placate her with one of his best smiles, "that at St. Thomas's—the school I was making for—one of the Brothers took me into his room for fear the bigger boys would browbeat me."

"Mamma was so put out," Miss Amanda told. "The only time I ever saw her angry with Papa. He had sent Jeff off without consulting her; so she made him send for Jeff to come home, the first time he could arrange an escort."

"Did you come by Andrew Jackson's and the Trace again, Uncle Jeff?"

"No. I came by steamboat. In 1817 that was equally wonderful and even more fearful. Nowadays they name steamboats for flowers—Miss Varina travels on the *Magnolia*, for example. In those days they were named for volcanoes. Mine was the *Aetna*. There were two others on the river that year—the *Vesuvius* and the *Volcano*. And, all these perils notwithstanding, four years later I was back in Kentucky again at school—Transylvania, this time."

He pronounced the name Kentucky as if other reminiscence gave it value.

"It is a beautiful place?" Varina asked, appropriately, she thought. "I have seen something of it from the Ohio and have heard that it is nice."

Not to be compared with the state of Mississippi, of course.

"It is beautiful land," he answered gravely, but had now forgotten her again as suddenly as he had noticed her. "My birthplace, and I have other attachments. In the spring of the year, parts of Kentucky come close to being Paradise. A beautiful land, of gracious, kindly, brave people; and," he snapped off sentimental reminiscence sharply, almost curtly, "amazing in the production of horses. Exceptional pasturage—that's the reason."

"Yes," Miss Amanda said, "and that's enough of tales for tonight. Exciting as it all is, some of us are nodding. Shall we have some music, then? A couple of Christmas hymns, and then to bed?"

She played the piano. Florida McCaleb was the better musician, but Miss Amanda had a fine spanking touch for general use. Everyone sang heartily, Varina with the rest, to cover a burn in her heart and another on her cheeks. Plainly it had been a blunder to invite Mr. Jefferson to dwell on the subject of Kentucky.

> *"So now is come our joyfullest feast;*
> *Let every man be jolly."*

How dreadful to have to pick and choose one's words! Was it always like this? How dreadful and how silly! For the good of everyone somebody ought to unseat His Highness.

> *"Each room with ivy leaves is dressed . . ."*

It was warmer than ever in the room. To cool her burning cheeks, she pushed the nearest casement farther open and leaned out. Oh, lovely night! A million stars winked at her from above. On earth little lights picked out the Negroes' houses. The music from inside the room rushed out to meet cadences, jubilant and mournful, from the quarters. A hand touched her elbow and she jumped; but it was only the one she had been told to call Aunt Lucy.

"Come back inside, darling. You'll take your death out there. The little ones have gone to bed and we're waiting up for that dancing lesson."

"French style, Miss Howell. You promised."

Dance? Oh, yes, she had said she would show them how Monsieur taught at Madame Greenland's. That would be fun and fun was what she had come here to enjoy.

"I am overcome," she said, drawing her shoulders high and pretending reluctance, "but if you insist, and if Madame at the pianoforte can oblige with a polka . . ."

"Madame," Miss Amanda protested, "would much prefer to join in the dance. Besides, she is very unsure about playing a polka. Would a galop do?"

"A galop? No!" Varina said. "The dance is for the refinement."

"A waltz, maybe?"

"Later. We shall begin with a polka or a gavotte, if you like."

"Go 'way, Aunt 'Manda," Florida McCaleb said. "I'll play. How's this?"

"*Magnifique!*" Varina listened raptly. "Excellent. Now, if the young gentlemen will choose partners and step into line . . ."

"Miss Howell, will you honor me?"

"No, no, I am not the partner. I give the instruction only. In line, please. I shall station myself a little to one side, but in front. So that you may see how I do."

"I am not the partner, either," Miss Amanda said. "I want plenty of room and I want to lead, so that I'll be sure to see how Monsieur does. Maybe," she hinted, "he will occasionally want to take my hand for a measure or two."

It was great fun. Varina pulled down a bang of hair, smacked it back into place with the palm of her hand, feeling sure that it would fall forward at frequent intervals, as it obliged her by doing. She fussed at the cuffs she didn't have on her wrists and made elegant curves of her hands.

"And now, *mesdemoiselles—et messieurs*—we shall proceed. Monsieur will take Mademoiselle by the hand. Ah, no! No, no! You do not pull her where she does not wish to go. You have the honor and the pleasure. You will hold the hand high and respectfully. Mademoiselle, only the tips of the fingers, please. So! Let me look at you now. Yes, that is better. No, not the music yet, Miss Floss, please. The elbows are not right. Ah, the elbows! It cannot be estimate how important is the bend of one's elbow, the curve of one's wrist."

"Look at mine, Monsieur," Miss Amanda implored. "I am all elbows."

"They are beyond compare, Madame," Varina said through the bang, "but it is for me to say, not you. I judge the elbows. Very well. We will point the toes, so. Miss Floss, if you please. One, two, three, hop; one, two, three, hop! Observe me, please. Put the grace into it. At Fontainebleau, at Versailles . . ."

It was a riot of fun. Varina was breathless, the bang entirely out of control. Miss Amanda said in another quarter of an hour she would have split her best silk.

A riot of fun. Two brothers stood in the shadow of a betinseled cedar tree, looking on. Two brothers, alike and yet, very different, the one sleek, benevolent, commanding where he seemed only to observe, the other young enough to have been the first man's son, taller by an inch or two, more finely drawn, a man whose spirit ruled his flesh and would do so inexorably until he died. Now and again, as they watched, they exchanged smiling comment. They found her antics amusing? Much she cared!

Everybody here bows down . . .

"Varina," Mary Bradford asked sleepily from the high bed, "what are you writing?"

"I'm trying to write to Mamma," Varina sighed. She drew her wrapper more snugly about her shoulders and adjusted the book she had propped around the candle to shade the light from the rest of the room and throw it on the paper. "I never seem to find time."

"But what can you think to say at this time of night?"

"Nothing." Varina blew out the candle, took down the book and laid it across her paper. It was not lack of something to say that defeated her. It was the confusion of too much. She groped her way to the bed and crawled under the comforter with another sigh and a small shiver. There was a singing in her ears. She hoped she hadn't taken cold. Surely she wouldn't just now.

Yet he is most agreeable and has a peculiarly sweet voice and a winning manner ...

"Chris'mas gif'! Chris'mas gif', Moss' Joe. Thank you kindly, Miss 'Manda. Thank you, Young Miss. Bless you forever!"

They came to the Hurricane office on Christmas morning, one and two and three at a time. They carried largesse away in baskets, in their hands; or sometimes their grandchildren toted it for them. They hobbled with the help of canes, they ran and danced; they went off, invoking blessings and praying, or laughing and shouting. Even to Varina, who had seen plantation hands gather before, the procession seemed endless. Each slave must be greeted by name and his health and needs inquired into, and checked on a ledger. Some must be presented to the visitors helping with the distribution and handling of the gifts. Or the visitors were presented to the slaves.

"Uncle Rob, this young lady is Miss Varina Howell, from Natchez. Her grandpa knew George Washington. So did her grandma, both grandmas, I hear. Old Rob has had more than one Christmas gift from the General at Mount Vernon, Varina."

It seemed quite possible. Never had Varina seen anyone so active who looked so ancient.

"I was driver for fiel' hands back home in Virginny, Young Miss," the old man said with dignity, "neighborin' the Washin'ton lands. We visited back an' fo'th. That was befo' Ole Mosser pick me up and brung me West, then give me to Moss' Joe, fo' which I is eternally thankful. He and Moss' Jeff take fine care of the ole man. Plenty o' bacon and molasses and coffee. I nevah want fo' a thing. Thank you kindly, Moss' Joe, in the name o' the Lawd. Rhina'll be along directly."

"Rhina?" Joseph said. "I was going to send her things to her. They told me her rheumatism was bad."

"It was bad, Moss' Joe," the old man chuckled. "Miss 'Manda spoke sharp to her and hurt her feelings clear down to the marrow; but she ain' goin' to sulk pas' Chris'mas. She'll be 'long."

Along came Old Rhina, then. She peered out of a witch's face at Varina, with eyes almost as bright and keen as Rhina Number Two's, and much bolder.

"Glad to see you so spry," Joseph said, twinkling. "I gave Uncle Rob your vittles and Miss Varina will measure off enough of that cochineal flannel for the two of you. See that you divide with him now. He feels the cold as much as you do, remember."

"I'll see to all dat, Moss' Joe. Ole Rob kin have his half o' de flannel, but I'll bang him ovah the head with a stick o' firewood, do I ketch him settin' in my new rockin' cheer Moss' Jeff give me."

"Jefferson give you a rocking chair?"

"He did that. He stored it up fo' me. A fine rockin' cheer, split-bottomed, but stout. If somebody now is a min' to give me some piece goods an' a sparin' o' brown cotton or goose feathers, to keep my ol' bones f'om pokin' thu' . . ."

"Get along," Joseph said. "One of these days you'll be begging St. Peter to open the gate of Heaven wider so that you can come through without squeezing. Be content with your flannel today."

"Yassah, I is. I kin see it's mighty fine flannel."

"Special cochineal dye, I tell you."

"What that?"

"Miss Varina will explain."

"It's a bug," Varina said. "Bright red and from the tropics. That's why the flannel is warm and good for aching."

"Do tell."

"And this is Benjamin Montgomery, Varina, our storekeeper. I think our supplies will just about reach, Ben, but with little to spare. We'll have to do some bookkeeping and ordering right off."

The supplies, however, seemed to Varina also to be without end. All but perishables came out of the closet opening from the office. She never came to an end of the inventory of the contents. There were shoes, garden tools, pieces of harness, even saddles and bridles. There were dress lengths of linsey and calico. There was a rack of guns, with boxes of shells below it. These were for the slaves who were good hunters, but, of course, were given out only by the master on special occasions. There were pocket knives, nails, screws, shears, shirting, stockings, hats, and the prized red flannel. A son of Ben Montgomery, named Thornton, helped with the plantation ledger on the desk. Another son, younger, the Isaiah who had brought the saddle horse for Varina to Diamond Place, burrowed into the store closet for the gifts, seldom coming up with the wrong thing, either in size or definition. If Varina had had no further opportunity to observe the Montgomerys than this morning allowed, she would have perceived their rating in the plantation hierarchy, not only from their quiet manners, their comparative literacy of speech, but by the fact that Joseph and all the household conceded them the right to a surname. Only outstanding slaves carried this mark of respect through the changing vicissitudes of ownership.

It seemed to her she had heard of another slave of this class at Davis Bend—a man belonging to Jefferson Davis. Mary Bradford had called him by name, but she had forgotten what that name was.

These and other impressions and observations, most of them bright, and more, rich with friendliness and mutual trust, stored themselves in her receptive mind through the morning, as she took her turn with Miss Amanda, Miss Lucy, Mary Bradford, Florida McCaleb and other women of the house, standing beside Joseph, the master, lending grace to his generous giving. Possibly her perceptions, always acute enough, were more acute than usual, her senses more readily startled. She knew, for example, the second when someone entered the room who had not been there before, though she did not see him come through the door. She knew him before Joseph hailed him.

"Hello, Jeff. All done down your way?"

"Long ago. I haven't the string of retainers you have, even counting those who pay their respects to both of us."

Surely his was the pleasantest voice she had ever heard. It could have been the singing in her ears that she had feared might be a cold.

"Yes," Joseph said dryly, "the limitations of rheumatism are peculiar."

But she couldn't stand there, listening to the cadences of a bodiless voice, no matter how musical, and give no sign. She turned and, without her seeking his attention, he was looking at her, even with a certain expectancy. Young Joseph Davis had come up from Brierfield with him. He had a covered basket on his arm.

"Chris'mas gif', Moss' Jeff," she said on impulse.

Expectancy became delight.

"How did you know the basket was for you?" he asked. "The young stranger within our gates?"

And how could she keep any feeling of spite if he was going to speak to her now so sweetly? Nothing more graceful had been said to her that day, not even Joseph's greeting, bestowed at breakfast with a fatherly kiss and a gift he had for her. It was a miniature of her mother, made when she was a girl. The year of her marriage, Joseph said. She and Varina's father had given it to him when he stood best man at their wedding.

"It has always been one of my treasures," he kept his arm around Varina, and looked over her shoulder at the delicate, lovely face, "but I had a feeling that you might like to have it now. I was tempted to give it to you in its original frame, but that showed twenty years of handling too plainly. After all . . ."

"Isn't she a beauty?" Varina sighed, hardly hearing what he said. "I don't look much like her, I'm afraid."

"Not like her, sweet, but you remind me of her. She had a sparkling wit, too, and a merry laugh, and a tender heart. She would never willingly hurt anyone."

"But I . . ." Varina began in protest.

"The tenderness of your heart has still to be proved. It is there, I am sure."

Perhaps he was right. Surely her heart felt tender now as, with a complete lack of bright or fitting words, she put out her hands to receive the basket. As young Joseph gave it to her and something stirred under the cover, his eyes had a shine of fun along with adoration.

"Careful!" he warned. "It's alive."

Varina turned back the wrappings on a kitten, black and tawny, about three weeks old. It had been fed. It had had a sleep. It was ready now for play. She set the basket on the first piece of furniture handy—Joseph's desk, and with a gasp, picked the kitten up and tucked it into her neck. Tears started in her eyes. They were due to the flimsy softness of the live thing in her hands. Surely that was all the reason.

Others in the room had varying emotions. Young Joseph lost his heart all over again, to see Varina so subdued and gentle. Joseph, Senior, raised his eyebrows in amused question. The women for a bit were too surprised and shocked to speak. Then one of them found a way of expressing her dismay in practical terms.

"Jeff, a live kitten?"

"Certainly alive," he said. So, he had a will, too? "I'd hardly present a young lady with a stuffed cat."

"It's one of Marshy's," Young Joseph said in support. "Therefore, it has beautiful manners. Marshy attends to that."

Jefferson shrugged his shoulders.

"Manners," he agreed, "but I do not guarantee the moral heritage. There seems to be a trace of Persian . . ."

"Jefferson, you can be too whimsical!" This was Miss Susanna. "Who ever heard tell of a tortoise-shell Persian?"

"Varina," now it was Miss Amanda, "you are being made part of a conspiracy. Jeff has been determined for years to present Hurricane with a cat."

"Oh, no!" he protested. "I'll agree I prefer cats to mice and you do have mice up here, I understand, but in this instance nothing was farther from my mind than that old argument. Miss Varina, do believe me . . ."

Varina found it safer to take the cat out of her neck and look at it rather than at him.

"She's precious," she said, with a slight catch in her voice.

"She's a he," Jefferson corrected, "in case you contemplate a christening."

"He's just what I wanted."

Varina had to look at him directly now. Was he being perverse, to annoy his sisters, or did he have his lighter, gayer moments? His eyes sparkled for some reason.

"I thought it an appropriate gift," he said, "quite within the requirements of good taste, if not good sense. If problems arise as to care and training, I am sure you will find willing help."

"I'll take care of him myself," Varina said. "I'll keep him always."

"I tried to tell him as we came over, the pleasant prospect that lay ahead of him," young Joseph sighed.

"Still," Jefferson insisted, "there will be problems. Food, for one. We could discuss that now with Rhina Number Two, if you would care to do so."

"Jefferson," Miss Amanda objected, "Rhina has both hands full with her Christmas dinner."

"She'll set us out a saucer of milk," Jefferson said confidently.

She did, of course, for him. Her eyes were only bright with question on Varina.

"The stable's another good temporary shelter," Jefferson said, gravely restraining the small animal from walking into the saucer as it fed. "Cats take to stables naturally; and, speaking of stables, would you enjoy riding over the land with me for a guide, this afternoon? I haven't made my rounds for several days now."

"Oh, Jeff!" young Joseph groaned. "I was going to ask Miss Howell."

"Seniority, old man," Jefferson said and turned the warmth of his persuasive smile on his nephew. "You'll grant me plenty of that, won't you?"

CHAPTER VI

. . . he has a winning way . . .

"You looks a lady," Melissa said, eying Varina this way and that, "but the kind of eatin' goes on here ev'y day I don' see how you kin help bustin' out o' what you got in a week at the most."

"I'm going riding with Mr. Jefferson Davis this afternoon," Varina said, half-singing with pride of so much accomplishment. "It will probably be a long ride and we'll gallop some and the plum pudding won't matter, then."

"Mmm!" Melissa said. "Mr. Jefferson Davis is a fine figure of a man, but . . ."

"But what?" Varina asked.

"Nothin'."

"Mmm!" Varina said in her turn. "I wish I needn't bother with a hat. It's warm as April out of doors, and if we should gallop . . ."

"You pin on the hat," Melissa admonished, "to 'mind you not to do any gallopin'. Mr. Jefferson Davis rides awful fast horses. They don' come too big or too wild for him, 'cordin' to what I hear."

"Pooh! I rode one of his fast ones coming down from Diamond Place. She was easy as a rocking chair. I never was thrown by a horse in my life. You know that."

"You kin be yit," Melissa warned. "Pin on the hat now like the lady you was borned to be."

The young lady walked sedately enough, presently, over a clean,

soft scattering of tanbark; but the little girl who loved better than anything to run out from the big house with a lump of sugar or a bit of
apple for a favorite horse danced with delight under the modish velvet
and sparkled in the leaf-brown eyes. The little girl was very happy;
but then, so was the young lady. The stables smelled of sweet hay and
clean straw and the tanbark, as much as they did of leather and horses.
The kitten slept in its basket by the door, a delighted black boy in
charge. The long blue skirt of the new riding habit was held out of
the way of her booted feet by a loop of matching ribbon over her
gloved wrist. There was a feel of rightness about walking through the
subdued light of the stable beside this tall, erect, gentle-mannered,
though still easily distracted man who had politely offered his service
as a guide.

The horses were munching their Christmas oats.

"Do you think they know?" Varina asked.

"They are quite aware of the oats," he answered.

"And of you."

It was true. Heads were raised as he approached. Jaws might still
grind at the grain, but sensitive ears pricked forward and soft eyes
rolled. He spoke to each horse by name and Varina said the names
silently to herself after him, learning most of them that day. This
seemed to her important.

There was Black Oliver, sire to the filly, Glory, that she had ridden.

"You fancied Glory, I think you said."

"She was perfect."

"Isaiah, you saddled Glory for Miss Howell? Good. From now on
she is to be kept for Miss Howell's use whenever she wants to ride."

"Yes, Mist' Jefferson."

Isaiah Montgomery, Ben Montgomery's son. The Montgomerys had
schooling as well as a surname.

"Oliver comes to Mississippi by way of Canada." Long, sensitive,
strong fingers parted the jet-colored mane. The horse lowered its head
to the feed box and raised it, munching quietly, accepting the touch.
"He was a colt when I saw him. Belonged to a Hudson's Bay man.
The British know their horses. Oddly enough, I won him in a race."
His hand was still. Even the horse waited. "Amusements are few,"
he said thoughtfully, "for a young man far from home and friends,
serving at a frontier post."

"Was it when you were in the Army?" Varina asked, with cautious respect.

"Fort Crawford, Wisconsin." Dark forests temporarily replaced the stable. They were strange forests to her, remote and cold; and he was there and Black Oliver, a skittish colt; but she was not there. "Trouble arose with the Indians over lands," he continued. "In the spring I was detailed to bring down prisoners to Jefferson Barracks at St. Louis."

On a later day he named the most illustrious of the prisoners, a chieftain, called Black Hawk; but it was another who repeated for her the tribute the smoldering Indian had paid to the young lieutenant who delivered him to his jailers:

"We came to Jefferson Barracks in a steamboat, under the charge of a young war chief, who treated us with much kindness. He is a good and brave young chief. On our way down we called at Galena. The people crowded on the boat to see us, but the war chief would not permit them to enter the place where we were, knowing what his own feelings would have been. . . ."

It was a soldier friend in later years who laid the balm of those proud words on a heart sore with much enduring; but all "Moss' Jeff" said to her that Christmas day was,

"I was detailed to bring prisoners to Jefferson Barracks at St. Louis. I stabled the colt there. I could have sold him. He was beginning to show his speed. I've always been glad that I refused all offers."

His hand rested on Black Oliver's shoulder; then they went on, she beside him, perhaps just a little at his heels, because that was the way people did walk with him. As they went along, her mood became more and more quiet. The gay rattle of talk she had for others was not the same when she was with him. Never the same, even when willfully she spread it about to cover inward disturbance.

There was the big gray horse he had ridden through Diamond Place on his way to Vicksburg. The name was Medley; but, when Varina laughed at that, she was told gravely that this was the animal that made the stables forbidden territory to children and women without suitable escort.

"He has an uncertain temper," Jefferson said. "At least, he killed a boy last spring. Some said, 'Shoot him. He is not safe to have about.' But I don't know all the circumstances. I didn't know the boy. He was new to the place. I don't know what he did. Medley was never vicious before that. He's a big brute and hard to handle, but he was never mean. So I spared him. Perhaps unwisely. They say that once an animal kills he is not safe. You will remember?"

This was not a question. It was a command, sharp and sudden.

"Yes," Varina said, meek as a thumb-sucking pickaninny. "Poor thing!"

"Yes, poor thing," Jefferson agreed. The stallion had a big head and powerful shoulders. He was a homely horse, compared to others in the stables; but the master's hand was as caressing on him as on Black Oliver, as unafraid, as sure, as fond, though with a difference. "I am the only one who rides him now. I do, however, quite often. There are times when I prefer him."

The black hours, which all men know, when the demons of unrest and loneliness and defeat and despair and futile regret are out in force. He and Gray Medley rode out those hours together. Had he ridden to Vicksburg that day in such a mood and, for that reason, been unaware of Varina in the garden at Diamond Place?

"And now, that sugar you brought from the table would be appreciated, I am sure."

How did he know of the lumps wrapped in a handkerchief in the small bag attached to her belt?

"In fact, I believe something of the sort is expected."

They stood now before another large horse, red, with no particular history except that he was a good horse, fast and strong, whose eyes had failed. The Davises had bought him from a racing stable, not because he was going blind, but because his record for speed was what it was and his blood lines were good. His racing name was Highland Henry; and, of course, having been a race horse, he was used to being pampered. All the ladies who rode or visited the stables just to look at the horses fed him cake or sugar. By now he had learned to distinguish the swish of a skirt.

They went into his stall and Varina fed him the sugar, all but the lump she kept for Glory. She put her arm around Highland Henry's neck and told him she was sorry about his eyes and he said he didn't mind too much. His health in general was good and not every horse could spend his declining years in such pleasant surroundings. Moreover, he had his memories and they were gayer and brighter, he was sure, than those of some of the other plugs in the stable.

"You see," Jefferson said. "I told you he was pampered. All the ladies take on over him like that."

"He likes it," Varina said.

"I am sure he must."

There was a Western horse—dun-colored, with black legs, mane and tail. A wild horse of the plains—a Comanche captive. He had still a toss to his head and a snort that spoke of freedom; and the stable became briefly a treeless desert, the color of Old Duke's hide. Cottonwood leaves rattled about an adobe fort on the edge of a shrunken river.

"Fort Gibson, Indian Territory," Jefferson Davis named it that afternoon; and, on another day, in another connection, he said, "You cannot know a man's true nature unless you meet him at a waterhole." Out of such meager threads a woman's searching mind must weave the full tale of a year of exile. Only, Varina did not know then how thirstily she would go searching.

The Comanche horse was fast, too. All the horses were fast. Why must his horses run so? Because time dragged? The shining hours, the beautiful days? What an idea!

All the horses were fast, but one. That was a flea-bitten gray, a distant cousin of Gray Medley, perhaps, but surely a poor relation. Its name was derisive—Old Speck. It was Joseph Davis's horse, his choice of mounts for riding over the estate where a carriage or a gig wouldn't take him. Spirit in a horse didn't matter to him, just safety and endurance; and there was the difference between the two brothers—in years and in character.

"But you will think that we have only old plugs in our stables," Jefferson said.

No, there was Glory; and there was the chestnut colt Mary Bradford had ridden. Varina faltered in her speech and halted. She had forgotten all about her promise to Mary.

"Yes," Jefferson continued without noticing, "one of Highland Henry's sons—we thought the best; but he seems to have a hard mouth or he doesn't share his father's preference for skirts. Mary will ride him and she can't seem to hold him."

"Please," Varina begged; and then, all her small triumph of being where she was evaporating, she made her tardy report. As it turned out, she needn't have troubled herself.

"Thank you," Jefferson said. "That's the first I have heard of that run. Just the same, I thought I would try him today, having the afternoon. If you don't mind. . . ."

"Why should I?" Varina asked, but found that she did mind. She had hoped he would ride the big gray, to bring reality out of mists and musing.

"I want some day to match another with Glory," he said absently. "I'll show you."

They left the main stable for another, almost as large, reserved, Varina learned, for blooded mares. The one Jefferson had in mind was in a padlocked box stall. She stood with her head out the barn window, sniffing the air and the sunshine, disdaining gifts that were bought with captivity. Born proud, anyone would have said, knowing horses or not. She was a gray horse and tall, for what could a Davis do on a pony? But there her resemblance to big Medley ended. She had a silver mane and tail and a slate-colored muzzle. She had small, sensitive ears, and slender legs that gave no hint of their tireless endurance.

"Arabian," Jefferson said. "As pure as they come. Joe gave her to me."

Then he spoke to the mare.

"Haidee?"

One fine ear pricked forward. He said the name again, then took a key from his pocket and fitted it to the padlock. The statuesque head at the far window turned a little.

"Haidee, my girl! Whoa, now. So-o!"

He was inside the stall. He had owned the mare only a few weeks, Varina discovered. If Haidee had been disposed to kick and bite . . . but she was too proud for such a display. She turned her beautiful head a bit farther, but only in curiosity. She kept her air of dainty disdain, and Moss' Jeff forced his attentions no farther.

He stood by the door of her stall and talked to her softly.

"I know I promised you a run this afternoon. I know you want out. I know. The sun and the grass and the sky and the water—all strange until you get the feel of things here. I know. Come, my beauty, come. I won't have you disappointed altogether. Come now."

Finally the mare came. She turned a half-inch at a time, but she turned. The man she would call master talked on in a steady flow of soothing cajolery and moved a little closer.

"You know me, beauty. I'm Moss' Jeff, your friend. Come."

Finally his hand was on the bridle, not suddenly, but surely. Haidee drew back, but it was only a feint. The next instant she dropped her head and was ready to follow. Jefferson led her from the stall. He and Varina and the gray Arabian went back over the soft, clean litter of the floor; only it was really he and the gray Arabian and Varina, she being a lagging third of the picture. Once more she found her presence ignored, forgotten. If she had obeyed an impulse to slip out of the stable door that was behind them, it would have been some time before she was missed.

"Now, really . . ."

It helped her feelings but little to admit that Haidee was the most beautiful horse in the world. She was that, surely. Out in the sun her silver perfection was breath-taking. A man could hardly be blamed for taking pride in her—if that pride and devotion hadn't excluded all others. He made such a ceremony of giving her bridle to a stableboy. There was always that boy!

"Walk her a few times, Moses," he ordered, "then turn her into the small paddock alone. I'll give her a run when I come in."

"After I've disposed of this nuisance of a girl," he meant. "Guest of my brother, but he likes to nap after dinner; and so, I said I'd take her around. After all, I must show her some politeness, I suppose."

That, no doubt, was how the afternoon had been arranged. Joseph had asked Jefferson if he didn't want to perform this service. He, Joseph, at his age and on Old Speck wouldn't be much fun to her youth and liveliness; and it should be one of the owners who showed her the plantations. If Jefferson had nothing better to do . . .

Jefferson absently, not giving the matter much thought, had said he would be glad to oblige his brother, if Joe thought Miss Howell would take any pleasure from his company. Joe thought she would. She was a child in years, but quite mature mentally. It might be well to give her occasionally stronger fare in the way of entertainment than the antics of the young men who were her actual contemporaries. Something of the sort might have been their conversation while they stood beside the Christmas tree the evening before, smiling indulgently at her instruction in the dance.

Coming back to the present, Jefferson watched the boy lead the silver Arabian away, then turned to help Varina mount the waiting filly. She accepted his help as absently as, she thought, he gave it. Glory seemed to meet her spring into the saddle halfway. Mr. Jefferson seemed of a mind to comment on the ease of her mounting, but said nothing, after all; merely occupied himself briefly with testing her stirrup and the saddle girth, then, just as lightly, lifted himself to a seat on the big chestnut. Varina waited hopefully for Sultan to jump or rear or bolt, but he did none of those things. Their departure from the stableyard was a model of sedate propriety.

For that matter, the first part of the ride was extremely sedate. Dimly Varina was aware of the respectful attitudes of the stableboys as they departed. Dimly she perceived buildings and trees and paths. Afterward she could have drawn a fair chart of all that she saw, but at the time external objects meant little to her. She was too conscious of herself and of the tall, reserved man who rode beside her to be aware of much else. Here, she perceived more clearly than ever, was a conquest well worth someone's while, but she was beginning to doubt that it could be achieved by a mere girl, like herself. It was humiliating to concede defeat so early. She was not sure she did concede it, but she saw how defeat might be in store for her if she did not abandon her wayward impulse.

That she herself might be falling in love with Jefferson Davis she did not for a moment dream. If anyone had said to her, "You are already more than half in love with him. When you are all the way in love—and that's not far off, my girl—you'll never rest quietly in your bed again for wanting his love in return for yours so freely given. His love, his whole heart, mind you, not half of it, not cold ashes fanned to glowing embers, but a hot, consuming fire, to match your own flame—" if anybody had said that to her that Christmas afternoon, she would have been shocked, incredulous and more chagrined than ever.

"Of what are you dreaming?"

The question startled her.

"Oh! I'm so sorry. I didn't mean to be inattentive. What did you say, please?"

"I asked of what you were dreaming. You were, you know."

She blushed.

"I mean, before that what did you say?"

"Before that for ten minutes I hadn't said a word."

"Oh! . . . Oh!" The most superior man, really. "The orchard is lovely, isn't it? Everything Uncle Joe does is magnificent."

"The orchard will be lovely indeed in the early spring. That may come sooner than we think. If the warm weather holds, I shouldn't be surprised to see a few peach trees or pear trees burst into bloom in a week or two."

"They will be frostbitten for their pains," she said, which was just what anyone else would have said to the same statement. Back through the years she could hear people saying it seventeen times over.

"They will be, indeed." His eyes shone. He smiled. Such a sweet expression for a man—except . . . was he laughing at her? Again?

"Would you be interested in seeing our quarters, I wonder?"

"Yes, if you please." She tilted her chin haughtily.

But she paid closer attention now. She was not going to be accused again of dreaming. So they rode into the slave hamlet, for that was what it amounted to—a village entire within itself, though part of the estate. It was a theory of the brothers—and theories grew at Davis Bend as lush as vegetation—that the Negroes were happier living their own community life, in a sort of supervised independence. Varina came to know, when all things here were more familiar, that Joseph Davis's local pride was the production of the fields, then his garden of roses and shrubs and his fruitful orchard; but Jefferson, after the cultivation of the fields—he was the better planter of the two—prized most the two libraries, his own and the one at Hurricane, his fine, fast horses, and the life on the plantations. He would spend hours, listening with absorbed attention to a hand's tale of injustice or ailment. He might laugh at the tale afterward up at the big house. He was all gravity at the time of hearing. That was why every black being on the place, young or old, adored him. Well, so did the white folks, to be sure.

This afternoon, as he and Varina rode through the lanes that separated the whitewashed log houses, he became lost in a passionate fervor. It was, once more, a thing in which Varina had no personal part; but, if she pretended to pay attention to what he said and what she saw, she had to realize something of his intensity. She knew instinctively, besides, that in these quarters she was looking at a model settlement of its kind.

Each house was set on its own plot of ground. Each had its biblical fig tree and nearly all had other trees, planted for shade and fruit. Each had its own vegetable garden. Most had chicken yards and a pigsty and in a far corner or two she saw mule sheds. Jefferson quoted solemnly:

"Before anything else be done, every overseer and manager is required to produce a generous harvest of food for man and beast that cultivate the land. Hogs must be fattened on the corn, mules grow strong on oats and hay, and man be fed by all the kindly fruits of the earth."

Varina looked at him in quick surprise, half-expecting the sharp refinement of his features to change to the rigid forthrightness of the patriarch, Samuel Davis.

"Was that a saying of your father?" she asked.

"No." Surely his smile was personal for her. "Just a thing I read in an old book on plantations." Then, quizzically, "What do you know about our father?"

She blushed again. It was not his question that made her uncomfortable. It was his deep eyes. Did he think her silly or impertinent or something of a curiosity?

"Just what Uncle Joe told me when he showed me his portrait," she said.

"Yes, I remember now. Well, did he tell you, for example, that father was responsible for my devotion to scholastic pursuits?"

"He didn't mention your devotion. Are you devoted to such things?"

"Absolutely. It goes back to a day when I was twelve. I had a disagreement with my schoolmaster in Woodville. So I packed up my books and quit. I told my father I was through with school. He said that was all right with him if that was my choice. I must understand, however, that he was a poor man with much land to care for and he could support no idlers. If I didn't want to work at my books I would have to work in the fields. Well, I was sure I didn't want to go back to school, so out into the fields I went." He looked at her, the same quizzical something or other in his expression. "It was September."

"You didn't!" Varina said in horror. "You didn't pick cotton—right with the field hands. You never did!"

"You didn't know my father. I surely did just that." He flashed at her now his bright, warm smile. "For two long, wretched days I worked in the fields as a common laborer. Then the rebellion was over. On the third day I returned to the Academy and after that I was fairly avid and constant in my pursuit of learning."

He could look back upon the episode now as amusing. He had told it, thinking it might amuse Varina. She repudiated the whole idea.

"No!" she said again in horror, and again, "No!"

"But I assure you, yes," he insisted gaily. "A couple of times later on in life when youthful exuberance threatened me with disgrace, I believe what saved me was my recollection of that experience."

But . . . it was hot in Mississippi at the beginning of the cotton harvest. If you drove out in a carriage while the sun was high, the heat beat through a parasol or rose up in waves from the road to slap you in the face and knock the breath from you. If you rode a horse down the rows of stalks set with bursting seed pods, the heat was not that of fire, not searing, but a smother of light dancing with dust motes. Ahead of you or to one side a dozen or more hands were hidden among the stalks, because the first cotton bolls ripened low and a picker had to bend double to catch them. When the pickers stood up for a minute's rest, you couldn't tell man from woman because all wore ragged hats to keep their heads cool and all made the same motion of rubbing chafed shoulders or aching backs. If you noticed such things and were troubled, people said:

"Oh, they don't mind. They were born under an equatorial sun, remember. They are better off here than they ever were in the jungle."

It was reasonable to suppose this was true. A field hand who was well housed and well fed lived often to a ripe old age and he might not have done so in his native Africa because of tribal wars and the horror of savage captivity; and, of course, his extremely hard labor during cotton harvest was only for a few months out of the year; but it was agreed to by everybody that a white man could not endure it. There would be no vast cotton plantations, the kind that made fortunes for their owners, if white hands had to gather the harvest. These facts were so plain, so generally understood, that Jefferson Davis had no difficulty in comprehending Varina's unqualified horror.

"It wasn't the sweat I minded," he said more seriously, "or even the labor. I was strong for my years. 'A stout lad,' everyone says."

No, it would not be the sweat and the toil. There were other things; and, if you were not born knowing what those other things were, how could they be explained to you? But the sweat and the toil were degradation enough. The tall man on the chestnut horse was strong in a supple, wiry, disciplined way; but, if Varina had not seen the portrait of him as a boy in Joseph's office, she could hardly have realized him as 'stout,' meaning apple-cheeked and ruddy with health. And, if he had been that kind of boy, why, all the more reason . . .

"Your father," she said, but respectfully, "was a hard man."

"He was what you might call just," Jefferson corrected. "A man of stern principle, but unfailing wisdom and rightness. As a family, we owe everything to his good judgment. I can see that now."

Yes. From two days' humbling toil in the field to this—a man in hand-turned boots and fine black cloth and linen shirt and black silk stock, at once careless and fastidious, riding a blooded horse down the lane of a slave hamlet, doing the honors of an estate to a young lady in velvet and plumes on a second blooded horse, and two dozen or more other blooded horses ready for any other guest who might choose to ride abroad that fair afternoon. Shyly and respectfully still, Varina told her fancy about Hurricane being a sort of principality.

Jefferson was more shocked at that than he had been at her comment on his father.

"Child," he said, "that's what our enemies, our bitterest critics, say of us. They say we live in a feudal aristocracy, complete with castles and serfs. I thought you were one of us."

He looked at her searchingly, but still with indulgence. She smiled uncertainly in answer. She was "one of us." She had not meant to be critical. She didn't mind being a feudal aristocrat. It was a lovely way to live, but how was she to say so properly to this strange man, so typically a feudal aristocrat, too, but one who rode off to Vicksburg on business having to do with a political party composed largely of poor folk from the sandhills?

"I mean, I had no idea what it would be like up here. I knew Uncle Joe had this land and that it was very rich and productive, but . . ."

"It is rich land. There is none richer anywhere than the alluvial land built by our river." She thrilled to the possessive fondness of his tone. "One of us," indeed. Then he, too, seemed to need to search for the right words. "The richness of the land is God's gift and the river's; the bringing of it to full productivity is the sum of man's own efforts. It is a task the same as any other, with unusual hazard, however, as to its outcome. If a man succeeds in drawing the richness from the earth, his responsibilities multiply rather than lessen. The ownership of land, and of wealth, is a grave responsibility. You know that."

She knew; and yet . . .   .

"The responsibility for the happiness and well-being of these human chattels is the gravest burden of all."

They stopped continually as they rode along to reply to soft, affectionate greetings.

"Evenin', Moss' Jeff. Evenin', Young Miss. Mighty fine day to be takin' the air. Git up out o' the road, B'diah. You want to be trompled? Moss' Joe give you plenty o' yard space to play in. Git out o' the way o' those high-steppin' horses. Git out o' the way o' yore Moss' Jeff now."

Moss' Jeff . . . Moss' Jeff . . . Moss' Jeff. Even when for a few minutes there was nobody, remembered cries followed as they rode along. They did not lessen at all what Moss' Jeff called feudal aspects. They went far toward restoring Varina's poise, shaken by her discomfiture at the stables.

"We are grateful to them for the work of their hands, for their loyalty and devotion. We aim to make return to them in care and protection. Within the reach of their abilities we give them what amounts to their freedom—a better freedom than they might enjoy if turned out into an unthinking, uncaring world."

He meant what he said in all sincerity. He studied all these things in his mind constantly. He pored over the opinions of others. Long, rainy days he spent in reading and long, lonely hours at night by light of candles when he should be sparing his fine eyes, because he wanted to be sure he was right. He could not bear to be wrong. He chose his words for Varina carefully today and she must have heard them, for she remembered them all forever; but at the time she felt mostly the drugging sweetness of his clear voice, without dreaming how many others might listen to it some day or where.

"We know we are dependent on them as much as they are dependent on us and we make acknowledgment in all suitable ways."

There had been green peas on the Christmas dinner table. Part had been raised by the gardener for the big house, the rest in the quarters. All the surplus of the cabin patches was traded in at a store kept by Benjamin Montgomery, who sold it then to the big house or to neighboring plantations. Did Varina remember Ben? She must see his store presently. Ben had come to them with a fair common school education. The store was his own idea. He had worked it up from a small money loan Joe had given him, just to see what he could do. He carried on a respectable business not only at Hurricane but also with the Turner and Quitman plantations. Jefferson knew, because he had helped audit the books. Ben attended to gathering and shipping the fruit from Joe's orchard. He was bargaining now with Joe for the purchase of next summer's harvest. It was fun to hear the two of them go on. Joe would have to advance Ben the money and then Ben would pay Joe the purchase price after he had sold the fruit on the market. Joe was pretending to hold Ben off, but he was really all for the proposition.

Would anybody say Ben Montgomery could do better elsewhere? Ben had two fine sons. Did she recall them—Thornton and Isaiah? Their mother was dead. Ben had raised the boys. And very strictly. They had learned to earn their keep with their hands first; then he had asked for and obtained the privilege of teaching them to read and write and figure. A model family. There was no sum of money that represented their value to the plantations. And, of course, there were others.

The quarters had its own meeting house. Uncle Rob was the preacher. Once in a great while, one of the Davis men would read a psalm or a funeral service, but usually not. This was the servants' own community. They had their own court of law. There someone had often to interfere, to save a good hand from too severe judgment at the hands of his righteous fellows. Moss' Jeff chuckled.

The words trickled through Varina's ears. He was not speaking in defense of the institution of slavery. If challenged, he would have said there was nothing to defend. The thing was. It always had been. He could quote the Scriptures to prove his point:

"When the low and vulgar son of Noah, who laughed at his father's exposure, sunk by debasing himself and his lineage by a connection with an inferior race of men, he doomed his descendants to perpetual slavery."

If Varina, or another, had ventured to point out to him that few slaves in the South lived so well as those at Davis Bend, he would have demanded why not? It was right and it was profitable, too, to manage things the Davis way. He loved administering the plantations and did the most of it. If this was not all his pleasure nowadays, it was the greater part of it. As a matter of fact, only one question occurred to Varina:

"Why, when you lead such an ideal existence here, everything at your command and just as you would have it, do you ride off to Vicksburg on any kind of business?"

It was too bold a question for her to raise, of course. She said, instead,

"I wish Papa could see. When I asked him about Hurricane, he said all he could remember was swamp and alligators."

She waited for him to laugh or show indignation. He did neither.

"That must have been before Joe opened any of the land. It was a good description, I believe. Perhaps I can show you something of the way it was then."

That was why they rode out of the quarters past the gin and the compress and the isolated, lonely seeming homes of two white hands—the ginwright and another—to look at the wild land. She had asked in a way to see it. But, before they left the quarters, they changed horses.

"I think," Moss' Jeff said, "it's the skirt or the sidesaddle that this fellow doesn't want. He responds readily enough to the bit. I must ride with Mary some day soon to make sure."

"Would you like me to try him today?" Varina offered.

"Why, that is most kind of you."

It wasn't kindness. She wanted to ride Sultan. She had ever since she had first seen Mary struggling to hold him; and with Varina, a want unsatisfied did not die. It only grew stronger.

"Sure you're not afraid?" Jefferson asked.

She tossed her plumes and said to him as she had to Melissa,

"No horse ever threw me."

He dismounted. As he did so, the usual boy sprang up from nowhere to help lift the saddles. Jefferson put Varina on the chestnut's back, watching not her but Sultan, his strong, nervous hand ready to seize the bridle.

Sultan did not rear. He tossed his head, but stood.

"Good," Jefferson said again. "Watch him."

Then he mounted Glory and they rode off to look at the wild land. And Varina watched Sultan now, because she needed to. He did not like the exchange of riders. She could feel his restlessness. She was still not afraid, but she knew she must be ready if he should try to shake her off. But he gave no sign of that. They rode right to the edge of the wild land and there was still only that quiver of restlessness.

She and Jefferson sat on their horses, looking at the wild land. It was a canebrake, limitless from where they viewed it; and the canes grew taller than any she had ever seen. A gray desolation at this season spread over it. Varina looked up at the sky to be sure that the sun still shone. The sky showed no trace of clouds, but the brightness seemed now all behind them.

Varina had never seen land wild in just the way this land was wild. The land she knew was made of brown clay and loam bluffs that pitched off sharply into ravines, with snaky bayous in their depths. The Louisiana flats across the river from The Briers she had viewed only from a boat on the water or, more often, from her high lookout on the bluff path. This was marshland, like what she had seen of Louisiana. A cart road opened into the canebrake. Its bed was dry, occasionally piled with dust; but even the ruts in the dusty road gave evidence that recurrently water rose in the canebrake, covering all or part of it—rose and receded, rose and receded, leaving each time a new coat of fertile slime out of which sprang more tangled growth.

The growth was sword-bladed cane and stiff, tall grasses and brush and bramble and vine, and willows in the slashes. There were patches of timber, showing the white, ghost branches of cottonwoods on the rim, then darkening off into moss-hung cypress and oak and magnolia. And always there was the cart road, exploring the tangle, leading where? She thought she could guess.

It was a road showing signs of use. The ridged dust had been lined by wheels very lately. Sultan knew where the road led. He tossed his head impatiently, quivered again, then with no more warning, was off. Varina had not touched him. She had not spoken to him; but the cry that followed her in flight could have come from her own guilty heart. She had harbored an impulse to explore the road and Sultan had taken his command from that.

At first the run was exciting only. Sultan's gait had not the easy stretch of Glory's, but it was a smooth enough gallop. Varina was in no danger of being thrown. She was in no danger at all unless some tree thrust a low branch across the way. She leaned to the right across the saddle and the shoulders of the horse, so that her head was lower.

There, it was as low surely as the head of a man on the seat of a wagon. Yes, except for her plumes. She must make out to lean still more.

They swept through the patch of forest and were in the heart of the cane again. And now the narrow track began to turn and wind. It dipped suddenly and there was a ditch to cross. So far, Sultan fortunately had shown no desire to abandon the narrow track. His heels scarcely touched the water as he took the ditch.

"Whoa! Whoa, Sultan. Easy, boy!"

Repentance, as usual, came too late. She was not so much frightened as dismayed. She had never ridden through a canebrake without a guide, even a small canebrake; but she knew enough about them to be wary. If only Sultan knew as much! The road turned this way and that and there must be a reason for the turning. The cart tracks were still visible for as much of the path as she could see; but a plodding mule or dray horse is not a fresh and galloping colt. And now, besides turning and twisting, the road crept steadily downward.

"Whoa, Sultan! Easy, boy! Easy!"

There was entreaty in her command. The colt snorted and slackened his pace a little, but not enough, not soon enough. Dark water appeared ahead, and more trees. Leaning low along Sultan's neck, Varina could not see how much water. She could not judge its depth or flow.

It was a slough, and slack, but deep enough. Sultan stumbled as he plunged into it. Varina forgot the trees, held his head up, helped him to regain his footing. With a fearful splashing he crossed the ford and climbed out. The cart road began to rise again and he was through with running. Varina could pretend that she had brought him under control, but the truth was Sultan had had his fun and had stopped of his own accord.

There was a lighter splashing behind them. A dark horse and rider swept past and a few yards farther on turned to wait.

To Varina it was like riding straight toward the Last Judgment to advance those few yards that separated her from Moss' Jeff. He sat straight as a ramrod on Glory. His face was white with controlled emotion. It looked more than ever as if it had been chiseled out of stone. His eyes burned deep in their sockets, like candles in a wall niche. It was like riding toward the Last Judgment, but she had to go forward. Her own face turned white and her eyes burned and she set her teeth on the inside of her lower lip so that it wouldn't tremble and rode on, then faced him and waited.

Anything he might have said in anger or reproach would have been justified and such words would have been easier for her to counter; but what anger the man felt he kept under matchless control.

"I shall never forgive myself for letting you ride the horse," he said stiffly.

She could only shake her head at him in dumb denial. She could manage Sultan. She was sure of that still.

"You might have been killed—injured badly, at the very least."

She shook her head again. There had been no danger to her. The horse might have fallen and broken a leg. Then he would have had to be killed, but she would have jumped free in the fall and escaped whole. She was sure of that, too.

"As it is, you have ruined your beautiful dress."

"Oh!" The gasp broke her hold on her lip. She looked down. Sure enough, the water and mud of the slough had splashed and splattered the blue velvet skirt well up from the hem. She thought of Melissa. She thought of the fearful cost, imposts and all, of Lyons velvet. She thought of her preening majesty a short while before when she walked through the stable at Hurricane, the unsullied extra length of skirt held up by a loop of ribbon over her arm.

"Oh!" she said again and looked up to find the white tension melted from the stern face of Jefferson Davis. For a second she thought he might laugh; but, when he spoke again, it was still with restrained anger.

"You'll have to come on to the house now," he said. "There will be someone can repair some of the damage."

There was a clearing just ahead. Through the trees Varina could see the corner of a house. It would be the place called Brierfield.

Brierfield was a small house as such places went. The wonder was that Varina could see so much as its roof even from the top floor at Hurricane, because it was only a story and a half high and was set in the center of a grove of live oaks. It looked as if the oaks had been cut out to make room for the house, but this was not the case. When Joseph Davis had first given his brother Jefferson the Brierfield acres, there had been only a scattered growth of trees among the cane. The masses of shade had been of the young master's planning and planting. Anyone who did not know the fertility of Mississippi marshlands might have found it hard to believe that in less than ten years he could have achieved the appearance of a natural forest, but Jefferson Davis knew. He had willed a forest into being and here, sure enough, was his design complete—or nearly.

It was easier to believe that he had planned and built the house. On Varina's first close view it startled her with its strangeness, and there was never a time when she was not amazed by this or that about it— the width of the doors, the set of the windows, the material of its walls, the absence of ornament; and yet, in some daring, original fashion, it was beautiful. It was the kind of house one might expect to be built by a man who knotted a black silk handkerchief about his collar and called it a cravat and, moreover, made of it a cravat—not modish but having an air more striking than mere fashion.

Jefferson Davis had not aimed, like his older brother, to build a castle. He had built, for comfort and seclusion, a place of retreat. The basic plan was simple and familiar—a square house divided through the middle by a central hall—a plan he might have carried over in his mind from the house in which he had been born in pioneer Kentucky—a double-pen house, with a breeze way.

The walls were of a rough cat and clay plaster on a framework of cypress. The plaster, with heavy, exposed roof beams, and brick paving to all the galleries, was a thing he had borrowed from Spanish houses he had seen, built on oases in the Western deserts, though he would explain, when his architecture was questioned, that plaster was a favorite wall finish with French settlers, too. The pitch of the gabled roof, coming down to cover the galleries, was true French in style.

The house was of no particular school. It was Mr. Jefferson Davis, really. It opened wide doors in mannerly welcome; but it stood apart, secluded behind masses of trees. It had grace, with its broad, paved galleries; but it had a stiffness, too. The windows were set high and had solid board shutters. Where he had lived in the years preceding his building of a house, at military posts, windows had been a weakness on the point of defense. He was a soldier, turned planter to win and care for the woman of his heart. And then she had died. He had built his house to hold and cherish a love that was denied him. Had the woman lived, had she stood by while the house was being built, she might have said, "Could we do this or that, dear, for instance?" Or, he might have thought of changes, considering her comfort. But she was away and forever. He built the house then to hold his bitter loneliness, perversely unwilling to bow his head to unkind fortune.

And there it was. Varina sat on the chestnut horse, Sultan, looking at the house, startled, surprised, awkward because of her recent discomfiture, a little ashamed, but not to a purifying extent. She had not thought of turning the horse and fleeing for the shelter of Hurricane. She waited, to see what might happen next.

A dignified mulatto man came around the corner of the house. Yes, she could see in that direction cabins lost in the encircling trees. For the Brierfield house servants, no doubt. The mulatto man was dressed in the cloth of a privileged servant. He had broad shoulders and quite gray hair. He came up to the horses.

"Yes, James?" Jefferson said; and there was affectionate reliance in the quiet greeting. "Where is everyone?"

"The young gentlemen took guns and went off hunting, Mr. Jeff. They said something about rooting out Old Man Alligator, but I assured them he was tight asleep in some deep hole and wouldn't come out yet a while. I reckon then they settled their minds on rabbits. The boys took out after them a spell back with the dogs."

"Is Maria at home?"

"Yes, sir. She's around in back somewhere."

"Will you call her, please, James? Miss Howell had the misfortune to splash her dress as we forded the slough. We came the back way. It is a very nice dress and I hope we can repair the damage."

"Yes, sir."

The man turned his quiet, waiting look upon Varina.

"This is James Pemberton," Jefferson said, presenting him, "my faithful friend and companion at arms from way back."

"Good evening, James," Varina said.

That was her first meeting with James Pemberton. He was Moss' Jeff's particular man. There was a letter, written by Samuel Davis to his youngest son shortly before Samuel's death: "I have left your servant James . . ."; but the title was more than a matter of written request. James Pemberton belonged to Jefferson Davis. Anyone could have told that who ever saw them together. His speech was the speech

of gentlemen because he had waited upon gentlemen all his life; and
his back was broad to carry burdens, for, perhaps, the same reason.
He was a broad back, then, and capable, willing hands, and a grizzled
head disappearing around the corner of the house in a simple act of
obedience; and Jefferson was helping her down from Sultan to the
brick paving of the gallery, but taking his time about it until Maria
should appear and establish the necessary proprieties.

When Maria did appear, they were established in full and on the instant. Maria was a woman little older than Melissa, but butter-plump
and settled and matronly in her clean calico dress and white apron
and headkerchief. Gold rings hung from her ears below the kerchief.
Gold lights sparkled in her eyes as she laid able hands on the velvet
skirt. She ah-ed in dismay over the spots.

"It's just mud, I think," Varina said hopefully.

"Just mud, Miss," Maria agreed, "but the sooner we gets it dry and
flicks it off the better."

"Have you a fire going?" Jefferson asked.

"Yes, sir. I got a hot fire in my kitchen and James put a new log
in the sittin' room jes' now."

"Perhaps we had better go to the kitchen," Varina said, still shy
and confused. "There's a good deal of mud to get off. There's no use
in taking it into the house."

"Please do not stop to consider our bachelors' hall," Jefferson begged.
"It has been well baptized with mud before this. I think Miss Howell
will be more comfortable in the house, Maria."

Well, she wasn't—not exactly. Jefferson stepped across the porch and
opened a barnlike front door. Varina summoned what dignity she
could muster and entered the wide, bare hall.

It was bare in the sense that, even more obviously inside than outside, the house lacked ornament. There were none of the bits of things
even the tidiest of women would have had about on chest or table or
mantelpiece. She was shown from the hall into the sitting room. It
extended, without partition, the full depth of one side of the house.
There was no parlor—just the sitting room.

Because of the high windows and the deep galleries and the near-
ness of the trees the light inside the house was dim. The rooms would
have seemed dark in any case. The furniture was dark and heavy—
hand-rubbed walnut and oak, cushioned, if at all, in leather. The smell

of leather pervaded the air—the leather of upholstery, of boots, of harness. Tobacco blended with the leather smell, and Bourbon whiskey, and dog, and horse. Everything was picked up clean, but the smell remained. A stout smell that in no way offended Varina's sense of the fastidious; but, because it filled a house instead of part of a house, it troubled her.

Maria pulled one of the cushioned chairs to the edge of a brick hearth.

"No," Varina said, "I'll stand, thank you. I can turn around then and the mud will dry faster."

But it was only the wide, circular sweep of the skirt, the part that hung down modestly over her foot in the stirrup while she rode, which had received the splash. She could very well sit down and did so the next minute, so that Maria could spread the breadth of velvet over another chair.

"Pshaw!" Varina said impatiently. "That much would have dried on the way back to Hurricane."

"Moss' Jeff wouldn't want to take you home with mud on yore dress," the Negress explained. "Ev'ybody say, 'Whar you bin with Young Miss? Whar you fin' that deep ditch to run the hosses thu'?'"

"Yes," Varina sighed. "I suppose. Some probably will, anyhow."

"Not many, Young Miss. I'll fix you up so they won't. See, yere's a spot's plumb dry already."

She manipulated the area in question so as to crack the surface of the mud, then, with the friction of her fingers and the occasional peck of a circumspect fingernail, removed it. Another gentle rubbing brought up the nap.

"Mighty fine mater'l," she marveled.

"Lyons velvet," Varina admitted.

"Yes'm." Pink-tipped brown fingers caressed the surface, reluctant to let the stuff fall. Suddenly the kerchiefed head dropped and a plump brown cheek was laid on the velvet.

"It feels so good," Maria pleaded, then sat up with a sigh to match Varina's. "I don' git to touch stuff like this very much," she apologized. "I don' git even to see many young ladies down this way."

"Not even the family?" Varina was startled by the admission more than by Maria's respect for the velvet.

"Oh, the fam'ly come sometimes," Maria said. "Miss 'Manda and now an' agin, Miss Mary or Miss Lucy; but even they don' come much. Ain' much to come fo' less they want Moss' Jeff and cain' fin' nobuddy to send. Miss 'Manda used to come down a lot to see how Moss' Jeff gittin' along. Ain' no sense to that. I keeps the house jes the way he wants it."

"I'm sure you do," Varina agreed, sitting back in the chair and letting go a little. Goodness knew how long it would be before Maria would get all the mud off if she worked as admiringly over every spot as she did over the first one.

Varina leaned back. Before her was a simple brick fireplace with a slab of wood for mantel. Above the mantel, spikes had been driven into the plaster to make a gun-rack. Above the gun-rack a scabbarded sword hung by tasseled cords. The guns had been borrowed for the afternoon's hunting and were gone. The sword had the wall space to itself.

An officer's sword. The scabbard showed marks of wear.

"Ef you've a mind to take off yore hat," Maria suggested, "you could res' better."

"No," Varina said. "I—we mustn't stay that long. Besides, I told my maid to pin the hat on tight and I'm sure she did. If I tried to take it off, I'd probably take my hair down with it."

"Yes'm. I could pin it up agin fo' you ef you did."

"No, thank you, Maria," Varina repeated. "I'm not tired, really."

"No'm." Maria was not one to give in easily herself. "It's sech pretty black hair," she said, with an emphasis on the *black*.

"It's a horse's tail," Varina quoted.

She brought her eyes down from the sword, but kept them above the level of the Negress's unctuous flattery. Bookshelves flanked the chimney. Open bookshelves and closed bookcases filled all the wall space not taken up by chests or cabinets. There must be as many books here as in Joseph Davis's library at Hurricane. Not so many tall, bound volumes of periodicals, but more that might be novels or histories or books of poetry. She reached for a volume on the shelf nearest her.

It was a small book, bound in calfskin. The title had been rubbed away. She opened it and forgot the matter of title in studying a signature. The script was fine and exact as engraving. The characters were small but legible. It was the handwriting of a scholar, it struck her, someone who would want to crowd as many words as possible on a

age, paper being hard to come by. Every line would be straight,
every word to itself. . . .

"Kin you read what it say?" Maria asked.

"Yes, of course."

"Yes'm. Then, would you, please, ma'am, read somethin' fo' me?"

Before Varina could stop her or even guess her purpose, the woman
ose from her knees and crossed the room to a closed bookcase. She
came back with a volume of poetry which Varina recognized at once.
A copy of the same book had been given to her mother on some
Christmas or another and it lay frequently on a marble-topped table
n the best parlor at The Briers. It was bound in blue morocco with a
garland of leaves and the title embossed in gold on the cover:

The Ladies' Wreath.

"That's the outside," Maria said. "What do it say inside?"

Varina opened the book, and closed it immediately.

"You shouldn't have brought me this, Maria. You shouldn't have
asked."

"Yes'm, I's obliged to ask. I's obliged to know. He sit there an'
lon' open that book, jes' hold it."

"Mr. Jefferson?"

"Moss' Jeff, yes'm. Then I's 'bliged to know what it is he won't look
t."

Yes, and now Varina was obliged to know something, but couldn't
ask as boldly. Did he treasure the book still? After all these years?
She had thought what she had heard might be a tale, no longer as
rue as it once had been—just a thing people liked to keep true through
elling.

"Put the book away, Maria," she said. "It's only a name."

"Her name, Young Miss?"

"I don't know. I suppose it is. I never heard her name."

"Miss Sarah, Young Miss?"

"Then it is her name, if that is what you called her."

"Yes'm, I call her that. Mos' ev'ybody do. Moss' Jeff call her so and
hen she tell him that ain' the name she goes by with her folks and he
knows it right well. Is that other name written down in the book,
Young Miss?"

"Knox?" Varina said. It was all there.

"Knocks," Maria muttered. "What kind of name is that?"

"It's a very sweet name," Varina said. "Do put the book away, Maria, please."

"Knocks!" Maria fussed, back on her knees, rubbing the velvet skirt. "And she sech a mite to look at!"

Knox, she called herself. Sarah Knox Taylor. She was small. Perhaps Jefferson had given her the book before their marriage. Then afterward, had he read from it to her? By this fire? No. She had died before the house was built. He had built it, anyhow, for her and her books. Poetry. *The Ladies' Wreath.* A little thing. Sarah Knox, only she preferred to be called Knox.

Maria still rubbed and scratched and smoothed the velvet. When she raised her eyes they were ponds, rather than pools of wistfulness, of eloquence she couldn't speak.

"Can I help you with that skirt?" Varina offered.

"No'm, I'll make out."

Someone knocked on the door. It was James Pemberton with a glass of sherry on a tray. The horses were ready whenever Miss Howell wished to leave.

"I'll come at once," Varina said.

She stood to sip the sherry. Maria drew the long folds of the habit out in order and looped the ribbon over Varina's arm.

"So tall and straight and fine—and healthy!" she said in soft adulation. "Miss Sarah was puny little thing. Anybody could a tol' she wouldn' last. I was to wait on her. That's how come I wait on Moss' Jeff now. I cooks fo' him and I keeps his house. I ain' complainin'. Nobuddy treats his people finer than Moss' Jeff. 'Ef it suits you, Maria,' he say, askin' you to do yore bounden duty; but it's lonesome. Plantin' season ain' so bad. Moss' Jeff's a turrible drivin' man then. It's between times that's lonesome. Young folks don' come down this way much. Nevah a fine young lady like you. I don' reckon you'll evah come back agin?"

"I don't know," Varina said uncertainly and soberly, then in a spirit of defiance, "I might."

"Might you?" Maria asked hopefully. "How you goin' to manage that, Young Miss?"

Varina had expected to find her saddle on Glory when she came out, but it was still on the chestnut. The horses had also received a grooming. There was no trace of mud on their coats.

"You handle Sultan very well," Jefferson said casually.

That left Varina no way of apologizing for what had happened, and an apology might not have been sincere. She was not feeling altogether repentant and she still believed she had merely allowed Sultan to have his way about running. Well, there would be no repetition of the episode. She would let Mary have her big horse now and she would be content with Glory. She hoped she would be content.

They rode back to Hurricane by a different route—a second narrow road that skirted the slough. It ran through trees and canebrake and a corner of cleared land. Frogs chattered and grumbled and groaned in the swamp and there was the occasional cry of a marsh bird. Humanly, it seemed to Varina, everything was ominously quiet.

"The cane is the tallest I ever saw," she said finally, to make talk.

"Thirty feet in places," Jefferson informed her briefly.

"How do you ever get rid of it?"

"The usual way. We cut it and burn it."

Their eyes met and just as quickly turned away.

"That's all there is to it," Jefferson said smoothly. "I remember the first planting here. We worked like demons cutting the cane. Then we took sharp sticks and punched holes and dropped the seed. It sprouted almost overnight. Of course, after such crude clearing we had to keep hands in the fields throughout the growing season, chopping cane sprouts."

He remembered the first planting. He remembered . . .

"Did you have a good crop?" Varina asked.

"I can't say. I wasn't here for the harvest. I believe the books showed a profit."

Too late again to say, "Sorry." Of course, he had been away. Varina studied Sultan's ears and forward-reaching head. It seemed to her that they rode for miles in this uncomfortable speechlessness, the air teeming with subjects for thought and conversation, but all of them forbidden. The buildings of Hurricane were in sight—the low cabins, the stables, the towering house—when Jefferson turned to her at last and, with a kind of forgiving indulgence in his regard—or so she interpreted it—asked her if she remembered promising him at the dinner table the day before that at some more proper time she would tell him how she had once upon a time burned her grandparents' house to the ground.

"Oh, that!" Varina pouted. He was making talk now. "You wouldn't be really interested in that old story."

"But I would," he insisted. "I've thought about it a lot."

"Really?"

"Truly."

This time as their eyes met, they held a flashing second longer. Varina turned her head first.

"Well," she said, studying Sultan's ears again and fighting down a flutter in her heart that threatened to rise into her throat and choke her, "it was like this. I was six years old and we were spending Christmas at Kempton—children and grandchildren, just like here. Somebody gave me a child's broom. Naturally I was possessed to sweep with it."

"Naturally," he agreed. "Isn't that the purpose of a broom?"

"But you don't understand. I like to sweep."

"Do you, really?"

"Yes. I can't see a broom without my hands itching to lay hold of the handle. Swinging a broom is such a grand, free motion. If I'm cross or out of sorts or things haven't gone to suit me, and I can have a broom and some actual litter to sweep away, it helps wonderfully. It . . . well, that's how it is with me."

She peeped at her companion around the edge of a plume. He had that absorbed, contemplative look on his face now. He wasn't interested. He wasn't listening. Oh, but he was!

"You don't mean to say you indulge in dark days?"

"Yes." If this was going to be a confessional it had as well be a good one. "You see, I want to have things or do things that nobody thinks I should and that is very vexatious, but it doesn't help much just to be vexed. I don't care what Granny Kempe says, it is better to do something; only, Granny thinks I want to do such awful things. She doesn't approve of me mostly."

"Doesn't she? Why in the world not?"

"I'm afraid I can't explain," Varina said. "I reckon you'd have to know Granny, to understand."

"I shall hope some day to have that pleasure."

The politest man, when he tried. And would it be a pleasure, or not?

"Granny has her own ideas of how a lady should feel and behave," Varina continued. "She's Virginian, you see, and pretty high and mighty about some things. I think, too, there was a time when, to make things livable around her, she had to do a speck of sweeping and, maybe, even take soft soap and scrub. Granny would expect a true lady to do either or both rather than be defeated by hard circumstance, but she wouldn't expect a lady to enjoy such menial tasks. She was furious to think that anyone should have given a white child in her family a broom—even a play broom; and she was angrier still when I preferred it to anything else I had received. She said for me to let the thing alone, let it alone now. My mother said, 'Not here, Varina. You'll raise a dust. Later, darling.' But Granny was snorting mad."

"Such a time ago and you remember so well?" Jefferson said.

"Oh, perfectly. If Granny had left it to Mamma to coax me up, nothing would have happened. Mamma's wonderful at coaxing. She said, 'When we're back home, Varina, we'll find a spot. Maybe you can sweep the schoolroom after lessons.' Granny said, 'The idea! If you're short of hands at The Briers, Margaret, I can make out to spare a girl or two.' Mamma said, 'We'll stand the broom over here, darlin', where you can see it, but don't touch it, darlin', will you, please?' Granny said, "Will she, please? She'd better not.' So, there was the broom where I could see it, but I mustn't touch it. And Granny going on like that. It had red and green stripes on the handle. By and by it was dinnertime and everybody went out to the dining room. The children went last and I was last of all. I took a long look at the broom. I was sure it would be gone when I came back into the room where it was. I thought, if I could just make one stroke with it, I wouldn't feel so bad. So, I did. There were nutshells on the hearth. I swept them into the ashes. It didn't take a minute and I felt ever so relieved. Then I heard someone coming after me. I didn't have time to put the broom back where it had stood, so, quick as a flash, I just stuck it into the closet by the fireplace and skipped out."

"Um-um!" Jefferson Davis said. "Don't tell me what happened. Just tell me when."

"We were almost through dinner. Somebody said, 'I smell smoke.'

But it was too late then. The timbers were afire clear up to the roof."

"Did the house burn completely?"

"Everything but the bricks of the chimney. Granny said, 'We'll let it stand.' And there it stands to this day and will to the end of time, I reckon, to show everybody, to point the tale: 'This is the house Varina Howell set fire to when she was only six, burned it down around her grandmother's ears.' That was and is and will be my punishment."

"You poor child!"

"Why do you say that?" Varina demanded suspiciously.

"Because I know how you must feel."

Did he, indeed?

"Well," Varina said, "I was terribly sorry, of course, about everything that was lost. All Granny's lovely furniture and Grandfather Kempe's military coat and his flute—he played the flute—and everybody's Christmas, including my own; but . . . I still like to sweep."

They were at the steps of Hurricane now. Jefferson Davis swung himself off Glory and came around to lift her down from the chestnut. His face was alight with laughter. How could she be sorry about Kempton then?

But he didn't help her down at once. He stood, with his hand on Sultan's shoulder, the flesh of the horse alive to his touch, the beast's handsome head turned in proud inquiry; and that troublesome flutter afflicted Varina's heart again. Foolish heart, she was hurt again the next minute.

"How old are you now, Varina Howell?" he asked.

How could she know that her youth was a knife in his heart, which he thought could never feel pain again? She believed that he was accusing her of being not much more than six right then.

"I shall be eighteen my next birthday," she informed him.

"Eighteen," he said, contemplatively. "Mary Bradford's age."

"Oh, no!" she said. "I'm several months younger than Mary."

"Well, that makes it even worse. Miss Varina, I have to thank you for a most exhilarating afternoon."

What did he imply by *exhilarating*?

"I am sure, Mr. Davis, the pleasure has been mine."

"Come, then."

He lifted her to the ground. He really lifted her and she was no mite. His arms were iron. A strong man in every way. Strong, vital, unspent . . .

"My kitten!" Varina said, rather wildly. "I almost forgot him."

"I'll send him up to the house," Jefferson offered.

"No. He's mine. I'll not have him feel neglected."

And she was off at a run for the stable.

CHAPTER VII

"No!"
Varina awoke in the night with the cry of protest on her lips. She was afraid at first that she might have given voice to it; but Mary slept quietly in a snuggled bunch on her side of the great bed and the two children allotted to the room were equally undisturbed. Melissa on her pallet at the door didn't stir. Only Varina was awake.

She was wide awake. It was as if in the depths of weary slumber she had fought the whole matter out to a conclusion. The situation was absurd. It was unreal. It was intolerable. At least, she was not disposed to endure it. This had not been the design in anyone's mind when Uncle Joe had asked her up the river to spend Christmas at Hurricane. With each passing day Varina was more sure that he had hoped he might make a match between her and his nephew, young Joseph. But it made no difference what Uncle Joe's scheme had been or how she had planned to meet it. At Hurricane she had met a man who—well, it mattered just as little whether he was young or old, great or small, whether she liked him or sometimes violently did not. Having met him, she could never content herself with another.

Young Joseph Davis? The idea! All Varina's breeding, all her education, all her training, such as it had been, to meet life's problems, had been centered around the idea that somewhere in the world, her world preferably, there was a man whose destiny waited on her destiny for the proper completion of both. When she met him, either by accident or design, there would follow in appropriate order love, courtship, a wedding, marriage. She would be Mrs. Somebody-or-other. She would have a row of babies. In the fullness of time she would be Granny Whatever, with a cane and two black girls to fan her; and so, with exciting variations or placid dullness, the story of Varina Howell, from cradle to monument, would play itself out. Finis.

Well, here was the man. Jefferson Davis, Esquire, of Brierfield and Hurricane Plantations, Davis Bend—post office interchangeably Palmyra, Warrenton or Diamond Head, Mississippi, below Vicksburg. She knew he was the man whose destiny waited on hers as surely as she knew her own identity. It didn't matter whether he was young or old. Most of his years, the rich, full years, were ahead, and she had a part in them. As a matter of fact, in the circle of society in which she moved, a distinguished marriage more often than not amounted to a girl's capturing the fancy of a man considerably older than herself, whose position and fortune were established beyond question. But the thing had passed beyond her whim to capture Jefferson Davis's fancy. He had captured hers when he had first ridden around the barrier of a hedge, out of the nothing of distance into the reality of here and now—and she had drawn back, like a skittish filly, putting on a dozen silly airs of shyness and proudness and hard-to-catch. If she hadn't known then that this was so, she knew it now. All the doubts and questionings and impulses of the past few days were resolved into clear perception of the truth in this black hour of night, when she lay in bed in this thick, stout house, surrounded by every sort of care and protection that her manner of living could assemble.

Well, then, if all this were true, and she knew it was true, would she be likely to admit, willingly or unwillingly, the existence of an impassable barrier? No!

No! That was the cry of body and spirit that had wakened her in the dead of night. No!

Still, the barrier was there. How broad and high it was, how real or unreal, how nearly impregnable, she could not say, until she made examination or tried its strength; but she would not be defeated by it. She just would not, and that was settled. If she was sure that some day she would find herself on the far side of that barrier, if that was what she wanted with all her heart, there was no use in wasting more time and thought on that. And she did not.

What she had to consider, then, was how to achieve a break-through. She lay awake most of what remained of that night and many an hour of other nights pondering that. Night was the best time for thinking. She was more alone, more unobserved when surrounded by trusting companions sound asleep than at any time during the day, when she could be sure always of someone's eyes upon her—the candid eyes of children, the somewhat more discreet and veiled, but shrewd and judging eyes of older folk, the humble, respectful, watching eyes of servants. She had no doubt that she was at present the most talked-of and most speculated-upon person at Hurricane. If she hadn't perceived that herself, Melissa's fuss would have told her. Melissa, if possible, grew more irritable with each passing day. She had been more upset by the work that Maria had done on the spots on Varina's riding habit than if Varina had returned unabashed and defiantly muddy. Where and who and how and when and what for, she had demanded, until Varina had lost her temper and boxed her ears. Varina had cried then and said she was sorry, but would Melissa please try to remember how alone she was and how far from home and everybody who could help her or advise her?

"Green young, like I say," Melissa told her, startled by the slap because it had been a long time since she had received one, but mollified by Varina's repentance or something else. "An' they's always somebody you could ask; on'y you never do."

Possibly Melissa was right, but who in this case would the somebody be? Varina had no idea—at least, not yet. The first thing she had to do, she thought, was to look fearlessly, with no la-dee-da delicate shrinking, at the stuff of which this barrier was made. Was it real or unreal? How much of it was the fiction and guesswork of loving friends and kinfolk? If that was the most of it, the work of demolishing the barrier should not be too difficult. In the end reality dissolved unreality as the midday sun came through the morning mists. Patience, the inestimable advantage of being alive and present . . .

But, suppose family gossip was merely a protecting veil about something raw and painful and desperately real, after all—the undying devotion of a man, obviously capable of great constancy, to the memory of one woman—a woman long cherished, however briefly held. What, then?

"How you goin' to manage, Young Miss? How . . ."

The answer lay in the characters of the two people involved. She must know them better. Particularly she must know the woman better.

Varina scowled in the darkness. She did not want to know the woman better. She did not want to admit her having existed. But that wouldn't do. That was balking. Balking was the way of mules, of badly broken horses. It invited punishment and suffering. It never won a race.

There had been this woman. Sarah Knox Taylor. She had been a little thing. Puny, Maria at Brierfield had said. A person would know she couldn't last.

A little thing. *The Ladies' Wreath* . . .

"You're so tall and straight and fine," Maria had said to her, Varina, thinking, no doubt, of the other one. And she had felt so good, being tall, walking beside Mr. Jefferson Davis, who was tall like a bamboo cane.

"Jeff says you handled Sultan superbly. . . ."

That was Mary Bradford, afterward, rushing upstairs generously to give her the compliment. Well, then, she was tall and capable. She would carry her head high and be tall and see what came of it.

Sarah Knox Taylor. That was all Varina knew now—a name that acknowledged smallness because the owner wished to be called Knox, reaching for dignity so. Her smallness and a pretty name, written in a rounded, girlish hand in a book of poetry. It was too much not to know more. She needed to know more. She would know more—much more. Now, when people talked, she would not withdraw into the shyness of a stranger. She would lower her eyes and be busy with her hands; but her thirsting ears would gather every drop of distilled information.

About her and about him—Moss' Jeff. For what did she know of him so far? He was a rider out of the mist. He was a legend himself in this house, or nearly that. He was a boyish fellow who gave a young lady a cuddly kitten on Christmas morning. He was a chivalrous gentleman doing the honors of his brother's estate, doing them handsomely, showing her with reserved feeling, masked under great politeness, his own harsher way of living. He loved horses. He loved

and honored his Brother Joe. Had he room in his heart for other love?
Or was he content to say that had been and gone?
No!

"How you goin' to manage, Young Miss? How . . ."

Every late afternoon and every evening after supper at Hurricane
the ladies of the house, particularly those old enough to enjoy a good
bit of quiet sitting, gathered in the ladies' parlor. There a great flashing of needles and a greater clacking of tongues went on. As someone
said, it was a large family, and a month of Sundays would hardly give
them time to catch up on all the news of everybody and everything.

Sometimes there were callers to be entertained with wine and plum
cake passed around. On her better days Mrs. Joseph Davis lent the
glitter of her jet and jewelry and the soft sighing of her plaintive,
poking, slightly or frankly malicious speech to the fireside picture. The
regulars, however, were the various sisters and sisters-in-law. There
were always four or five of them present and Varina now, as often as
she could without exciting suspicion or provoking question, unobtrusively joined them.

Miss Lucinda, who was Mrs. William Stamps of Woodville, was
involved in the crocheting of a spread she called a "throw," made of
multi-colored bright yarns. Varina, sitting on a low stool, her hat off
and her dark hair tumbled from a canter, trailing her riding crop over
the carpet to lure her kitten into play, said she thought she might sit
still long enough to learn to do something as pretty as that, a square
at a time. Miss Lucinda said she doubted that—yet a while. It was
old ladies' fancywork. Some day she'd show Varina, maybe, if Varina
was around where she was. Meanwhile, she'd be obliged if after supper
some evening Varina would help her wind some skeins of yarn into
balls. That is, if she wasn't engaged for charades or some other fun
in the music room. The children—and some who weren't exactly
children any more—had come to depend on her to lead their fun.

Varina said she enjoyed the fun in the music room as much as anyone; but maybe just tonight, having had a wild canter indeed that
afternoon—she and young Mr. Joseph Davis and the tomboy Caroline
had pretended they were running a fox to earth—she would prefer to
sit and hold yarn. The colors were certainly lovely. What was Miss
Lucinda going to do with the throw when she had it finished?

"Give it away, I reckon," Miss Lucinda said. "How would you like it for a wedding present?"

"I wasn't hinting exactly," Varina said, rising and picking up her kitten; then added pensively, "Suppose I didn't have a wedding? Suppose I never got married?"

"Oh, dear, listen!" everybody said at once. "In Mississippi? Where there are still ten bachelors to every pretty girl? And you . . ."

"You must go with me some day to call on Aunt Rhina," Miss Amanda said. "She'll tell your fortune."

"I should want her to be feeling friendly when she does," Varina demurred.

"Oh, Rhina and I made our peace long ago. Now, don't let me forget."

Bright talk, parti-colored, like the gay throw. It was made in small pieces and you put them together according to your own whims. It was after dinner now and Varina sat patiently holding the bright yarn. She had on her pretty rose-colored dress; and the kitten, full of his own victuals, had curled up in the folds of the skirt where they swept the floor, and slept, snoring.

"Your kitten's too fat, V'rina. He'll be having fits first thing you know. . . . We'll take him with us, darling, when we call on Aunt Rhina. She doses them with copperas. . . . What kind of cat do you suppose he's going to turn out to be? His hair is long but I still maintain I never heard of a Persian cat with tortoise-shell markings. . . . I'm bound to agree with Jeff that his mother hasn't too much character. She spends too much time in the quarters—and not her own quarters, either. . . . Sh! Sister Aurelia, do be careful. Did you see the kitty's mother when you were at Brierfield Christmas Day, Varina?"

So, everybody knew where she had been, after all.

"No," Varina said. "I reckon she wasn't around."

No use to say, "I wasn't there very long." They probably knew how long. And it would have been bad to admit, "I didn't think."

"You can drive over with me some day," Miss Amanda said, "and we'll look in on Marshy if she's anywhere around. I haven't been to Brierfield in some time now and I like to go at intervals. James Pemberton is a marvel of reliability and Maria's a good girl, but they both do better for remembering I'm here."

"How are the roads over that way now, Sister?"

"Pshaw, we never consider roads when the river's this low," Miss Amanda said. "Half the bayous and sloughs are dry."

"It's not like that spring when Jeff left his niggers chopping cotton," Miss Lucy from Vicksburg said, "and raced off to Kentucky to marry poor little Knox Taylor. The river was all out over everything clear up into June. We didn't begin to dry out before July. It's no wonder they both took the fever. I thought we'd all drown before we were through."

"Some day," Miss Susanna said—she was young Joseph's mother and the one who feared Hurricane, "some of us will drown. The spring rains will come on top of the February thaw and that old river will cut this land into a mess of good-for-nothing islands and those who don't take warning in time will be like so many rabbits on a piece of driftwood."

As usual, the family laughed at her doleful prophecy.

"When that happens," Miss Amanda said, "Jeff won't raise any more ring-streaked and striped Persian kittens. The only tortoise-shell tom I know in these parts belong to the Turners."

"Good gracious, 'Manda," Miss Lucinda objected, "you don't think . . . over all that swamp land?"

"It's love," Miss Aurelia sighed. She was the wife of the jolly doctor brother—Benjamin Davis. "Love laughs at miles as well as locksmiths."

"But, in the case of a cat, won't cross water. That's what I meant."

"Sh, Aurelia! 'Manda, I declare! In front this sweet young girl, shame on both of you!"

That's how the talk was. Hit and miss, like the throw of yarn, and mostly miss; but, if you sat still as a mouse and twice as demure, ever so often out came something important, like that bit about the wedding in Kentucky. So, that was why everybody shuddered when a stranger mentioned the blue grass state.

"Speaking of floods and freshets," Miss Lucinda went on now, "Sister Anna had visitors this autumn at Bayou Sara—you'd never guess who."

Bayou Sara . . .

"Colonel Taylor and his wife."

"Lucinda—not Jeff's Colonel?" See, someone might even ask the question in Varina's mind.

"Colonel Zachary Taylor himself. He owns land near Rodney."

"Rodney?" Miss Aurelia said. "Isn't that where they've had the most trouble with high water lately? You don't suppose Jeff—or Brother Joe—recommended the purchase, do you? From what I hear . . ."

"Well, I hope not," Lucinda said. "Colonel Taylor said he had made only a couple of real crops and he never knows whether he's going to plant the next one in Mississippi or Louisiana."

Rodney, a short distance above Natchez on the river. Varina remembered her father's mentioning it as an example of low alluvial land in a pocket made by the winding river outside the rampart of the Mississippi bluffs. Colonel Zachary Taylor had a plantation there? And he had been the father of Knox Taylor? Then, he had been the one to object to Jefferson Davis as a son-in-law. Colonel Taylor, the Indian fighter? Why? Sit still, Varina; only sit still and listen.

"I don't think the Colonel and Jefferson correspond or ever did," Miss Lucinda said. "Everybody's talking cotton nowadays and river land. Colonel Taylor was transferred from the North some time ago. His military headquarters are at Baton Rouge now. The government, I hear, is concentrating troops on the Southern border. It has something to do with Texas, I believe. Anna gathered from the Taylors' talk that the Colonel bought this land, hoping to retire soon from the Army. But he says, the way things have gone, he'll probably have to die in harness."

"Oh!"

It was a general exhalation, followed by a hiatus which Miss Lucinda was confidently expected to fill. When she did not speak up as promptly as she might, the hiatus exploded into direct question.

"What is he like? Did Anna say?"

"Yes." Miss Lucinda had waited on purpose. "He's a sweet old bear, she said. And his wife is sweet, too—a motherly body. Anna invited them in, of course, and made them welcome in every way she could. All the time she was wondering why they had come. I mean, she knew why and they knew she knew why, but who would speak of it first? Finally Mrs. Taylor said, 'Dear Mrs. Smith, would it trouble you too much to show us where our dear girl lies? I understand the place is here.' So, Anna took them and showed them. It's a sweet spot. Anna and Luther tend it as if it were one of their own buried there. Anna said it was a bright day but there was a wind sighing through the pine trees. Colonel Taylor blew his nose hard several times. Finally he said, 'I'm a soldier, Mrs. Smith, a fighting man. If a man's worth anything as a soldier, he has to make decisions and then abide by them, right or wrong, win or lose.'"

"Oh!" Miss Amanda said. She loved her brother Jefferson more intensely, if possible, than the others did. "Then he admits he could have been wrong, now that it is too late?"

"I don't know," Lucinda said. "I . . ."

"Do you mean," Susanna Davis demanded, "that he never forgave that poor child while she was alive to know it?"

"I don't know," Miss Lucinda said again. "Anna said she couldn't feel spiteful toward him that day. He seemed so broken up. Mrs. Taylor kept patting his arm and saying, 'There, Papa, don't. She knows. Our angel knows. Everything's all right now.'"

"Well," Miss Amanda said, "it's a blessing Anna received them instead of me. I'd have felt obliged to give that old man a piece of my mind one way or another. I hope Anna let him know that the wretched business came near to being the death of Jeff as well as of his daughter."

Varina held her breath.

"I'll never forget," Miss Aurelia said, "the day Jeff brought her to Bayou Sara. They had to carry her on a litter from the boat landing to the house. Jeff walked, but it was only will power that made him able. Luther Smith took one look at the two of them and sent a boy riding hard with word for Benjamin to meet them at the house. Then Luther put Jeff on his horse and walked by him to keep him from falling off. Jeff said, clenching his teeth to keep them from chattering, 'I'm afraid Mrs. Davis is quite ill.' All the time he was burning like a fiery furnace himself and shaking with chill. But he wouldn't give in. Anna put Knox to bed and Jeff sat by her until Benjamin came and by main force and strong medicine got him out of the room. Benjamin saw what was going to happen. He came home to supper and to fetch me to stay with Anna. He said, 'She won't last the night, 'Relia.' I said to him, 'What about Jeff?' He said, 'God's will be done. He has a strong constitution. He's one of us.'"

"Yes, but he's never been as strong since as he was before," Miss Amanda declared. "He had worked himself to the bone in the spring putting in a crop and trying to forget how he hated to leave the Army. It was on his mind all the time."

That was the kind of piece Varina would take to her room to study, trying to see everything as it was—the plantation house at Bayou Sara that historic evening. Would it be a great, stout house like this? No, more likely it was a farmhouse, like The Briers; but that didn't matter. The rooms were large. The beds were large. Sarah Knox Taylor—Davis—a little thing, wasted with fever, lay in a wide, strange bed in a strange house. If she awoke in the night, she wouldn't know where she was. She wouldn't know the frightened Negro maid set to watch her or even the white woman in the room or Dr. Benjamin, his pleasant, ruddy face grave with anxiety, his strong fingers on her fluttering pulse. She awakened once right after they brought her to the house, but her young husband was near by then. She saw only him and dropped off with a sigh into unconsciousness. But when she awoke in the night, he lay in another room. It could have been miles off, so long as she could not see him. And all around her was strange; and she cried out in her fear.

She must have cried out. Jefferson Davis lay in another room, deep in narcotized sleep; but he heard her. She died in his arms, the sisters said.

Afterward Varina learned that Sarah Knox had not cried out. It was sadder than that, but everything had to come to her in pieces, to be set together. It was another evening—a gay one—in the music room. Miss Amanda was busy elsewhere; Florida McCaleb was with her mother, who was having a bad night; and the young folks felt like singing.

"You play, don't you, Miss Varina?" young Joseph Davis entreated.

"Surely I do," Varina told him. "Can you imagine a young lady attending fashionable school in Philadelphia without doing exercises on the pianoforte? Besides, there was my grandfather who played the flute. Of course, I play—if you can find simple music. I've neglected my practicing lately."

She had never been too faithful at it. There had seemed always some more interesting activity—or, at least, more vitalizing—waiting. Now she thought with some regret, which was in itself evidence of change creeping over her, that it would be pleasant to sit down at the piano like Miss Amanda and play accompaniments for people to sing and dance by. She thought—and this was Varina unchanged—if she put her mind to it, she could do it. Oh, not so well as Florida McCaleb, so that people hushed and listened. That was a special accomplishment. But she could do as well as Miss Amanda, who was not musical, only spirited and willing.

There was sheet music in two cabinets against the wall near the piano. Varina and Mary Bradford opened one and Varina took out an armful of music to examine it. She felt encouraged by the frayed edges of the pieces. They had been well handled and some would surely be familiar. However, she had hardly got her hands on them when Mary took the whole armful from her.

"Those old things!" she said in a queer, startled way. "Let's look in the other cupboard."

"But why?" Varina protested, not sure she would be so fortunate if she tried her luck a second time.

"Sh!" Mary squeezed her elbow. "Tell you later."

Consequently, Varina's left hand stumbled occasionally over the chords of *"Frère Jacques."* Her thoughts were more on the music Mary had put away than on that before her. But she didn't stumble too badly. The albums from the second cabinet were well within the scope of Varina's abilities. Moreover, her chorus was a gay, carefree group. They laughed over her more obvious mistakes and drowned out the others. Varina thumped away vigorously. Presently she sang a line or two.

> *"What's this dull town to me?*
> *Robin's not here . . ."*

Jefferson Davis had not visited Hurricane in days. Some of the Christmas guests had gone now, leaving Brierfield with only one tenant besides its master—young Joseph. He spent all his waking hours at the big house. What kept the other away?

> *"What was't I wished to see . . ."*

The singers gathered close to the piano and closer. Varina had not thought there were so many. Perhaps a few who had not been there in the beginning, hearing the fun, had joined the others. Who had opened a window?

"Cousin Varina, do you know . . . Cousin V'rina, please play . . . Cousin Varina, Miss Varina, please . . ."

Varina worked her arms like wings, pushing with her elbows to make the singers stand back and give her room. She didn't believe there was a window open, after all. She could hardly breathe. What was wrong with that music in the first cabinet? She had glimpsed only the title of the first piece. Whose music was it? As if she didn't know.

"Cousin Varina, will you play charades with us this evening? You didn't come up here last night after supper at all. You stayed downstairs and just sat and talked. It's much more fun when you or Uncle Jeff play with us. You have such wonderful ideas; but he's busy all the time now, talking to Uncle Joe or General Quitman or reading or arguing. Politics, I suppose. Cousin V'rina, will you come this evening? Promise."

"Sh! Yes," Varina said. "Yes, yes. I promise. Run along now. It's almost suppertime. What kind of trash are you? Would you eat without washing? Shoo!"

That disposed of the children. There remained Joseph Davis, the younger.

"Miss Varina," all his heart was in his deep-set Davis eyes, "to find that you have another accomplishment!"

"You have no idea!" Varina smiled, to soften the mockery of her retort.

"I know," he sighed. "Miss Varina, I never get to see you alone, it seems like. I must speak out before Mary. When will you ride with me—just with me?"

"Why, Mr. Davis, I didn't know that was what you wanted. I'd be delighted any time. Tomorrow or . . ."

"Tomorrow?" Blood rushed to his fine, earnest young face. "Is it a promise?"

"It's a promise." Would he never go? "Unless something interferes."

"I'll hold you to your word, Miss Varina."

"Varina, how can you lead him on so?" Mary Bradford reproached when he had finally left. "He's sick in love with you. He's writing a poem. Aunt Susanna says she knows he doesn't sleep."

"How sweet!" Varina began gathering up the music. "Now tell me," she asked, "what was wrong with the stuff in that other cabinet?"

"It belonged to Jefferson's dead wife," Mary said, with the usual hush. "I can't imagine how. . . ."

His wife. Varina had suspected as much. Here came that smothering breathlessness again. She turned to the second cabinet, her arms full of music books.

"Did she sing?" she asked.

Did she? Exquisitely? *Miss Varina, to find that you have still another accomplishment!* Oh, fiddle-de-dee!

"I suppose so," Mary said. "Yes, I know she did. But you'd think her music would have been put away. Anybody could take it out and play the pieces, not knowing."

How did Mary Bradford know? Varina sat on a hassock before her cabinet, very precisely laying away childish albums bound in pasteboard. She hummed a line of song:

What's this dull town to me . . .

Was it politics that kept him away? Just politics?

"Maybe somebody here thinks playing the music would be a good thing. Ghosts are not pleasant daily companions for the living."

"You don't know what you are saying, Varina Howell!" Mary Bradford was horrified. "Only a stranger could look at it that way. You just don't know. To hear, accidentally, a bar of that first song might be enough to drive Jeff fairly out of his head. It was her favorite song of all. That's how I knew the music was hers."

Varina could see the sheet as plainly as if Mary had held it before her. "Fairy Bells" . . .

"Fairy Bells" . . . *A Ladies' Wreath* . . . a man would go lonely all his days for that?

"She sang it that night," Mary said.

"What night?" Varina asked willfully.

"You know. The night she died."

So, once she had opened the Pandora box of memories, Varina had the story more clearly with each passing day.

Sarah Knox had not awakened that night to a consciousness of the strangeness about her. Life had slipped away in a dream. If she saw at all the earnest, watchful ones near her bed—a man or a woman with high, narrow forehead and deep-set eyes and sharp, clear line of nose and cheek and chin, which were Davis features on all the family whether flesh was spare or plentiful, young or old—she must have thought the face was that of her young lover and husband; and so, she did not cry out. She sang to him instead. A song that he liked, perhaps, as well as she, a song, at least, that he would know as hers. And that was the sound he had heard in his drugged sleep beyond thick walls.

And so she had died. In his arms, not knowing; but he would know always. Or, so they said.

The song was one that Varina had never heard, to know it by name. She thought it didn't matter. She thought then that some day she would steal off to the music room and finger it through, just to follow the melody, which might, after all, prove to be familiar. However, as young Joseph Davis said, it was hard to find a moment when she could be alone. He was a good one to make that remark. One ride did not satisfy him. He begged for another and another; and Varina indulged him twice, for the exhilaration of the gallop. With their horses at a walk, he proved troublesome.

"You are *distraite*, Miss Varina," he complained on the second ride. "You have something or someone else on your mind."

Certainly she had. She put him off after that and one day even declined to share a general migration to the Turner plantations, saying she had letters she must write, and immediately after dinner stole off to the music room. She opened the door stealthily, because she had a stealthy feeling; and then, at the crack, she stood still, startled into immobility. Someone was at the piano. The touch was so light, the air so old-fashioned, that she could almost have been mistaken. In another second, however, she drew a long breath as much in relief as disappointment.

Florida McCaleb sat at the piano, fingering a piece hesitatingly for her. She stood up as Varina pushed the door farther ajar.

"Hello," she said, "are you restless, too? It must be the wind. An east wind does give a body the fidgets. We are working around to a change in the weather, I imagine. Come in, if you don't mind how I amuse myself."

Varina hesitated, although she had long ago decided that what she had once fancied was a dislike for her on Florida's part was merely the result of an estrangement between Florida and her father. The estrangement might have been accentuated by Joseph Davis's unconcealed admiration of Varina, but it had its roots in something deeper. This was the invalidism of Florida's mother. There was a mystery worth exploring, if Varina had not been occupied by a quest more pertinent to herself.

"Come," Florida repeated, "and hear this quaint music I've stumbled upon. It's some old stuff that Aunt 'Manda or somebody put in my cabinet—where I used to keep my music when I lived here. When I married Dwight McCaleb and moved to Diamond Place, I took everything I owned that was movable—even my dolls, if you can believe it. Dwight used to say, to tease me, that he could see where he'd never be rid of me for so much as a single day. I had left nothing here to come back to. Except Mamma. Poor Mamma . . . do come listen to this song, Varina. It's kind of sweet. I'm sure I've heard it before—maybe on a music box."

It was that kind of tinkling air.

"Varina," Floss said next, "what ails you? You look as if you'd seen a ghost."

"It's like that," Varina told her. "Don't you really know whose music you are playing?"

"No." But the small hands were still on the keyboard. "Not . . . it couldn't be . . . not hers . . . Jefferson's wife?"

Varina nodded.

"How do you know?"

"Mary Bradford told me. She said this song 'Fairy Bells' was the one she—Mrs. Davis—sang in delirium the night she died."

"Well, I never heard that. I surely never did."

In anger and bewilderment Floss looked more nearly a Davis than Varina had ever seen her look before. Her blue eyes had sparks in them. Streaks of color came and went in her white cheeks.

"I always understood," she said, "that everything of hers had been carried to Brierfield—everything."

"Still," she conceded seconds later, "I suppose something like the music might have been overlooked. Jeff could hardly have borne to open all the boxes and check their contents. On the other hand," sparks flashed in her eyes again, "it was not by accident that the music was put out again. Somebody—it could have been Aunt 'Manda. She has always acted as if she would like to blot out the whole story. To her it was the kind of thing that should never have happened to Jefferson Davis. He has always been her favorite."

Hers and that proud woman's, whose wise eyes looked over the young things at the piano—whose favorite was he not? A little of her first objection flamed in Varina. It was not enough. It would never be enough to protect her.

"Aunt 'Manda never stops to think that Jeff must have married somebody about that time and if the poor thing had lived, he would be a successful planter now—like Uncle Isaac, interested only in cotton and horses, contented, but a little dull."

No, he would never have been dull.

"Or like Papa—something of the gentle despot—I think you must have seen by now that Papa is something of despot . . ."

Nor like Uncle Joe. Yes, Varina had observed the despotism.

"Or," Florida continued, "that if he had stayed in the Army, she wouldn't be seeing him more than once in a lifetime. He'd have been promoted by now to be a major or a colonel—perhaps to a cavalry command out West; or he might have settled in Texas. Some of his friends from West Point have done so. There is one he corresponds with still. His name is Johnston—Albert Sidney Johnston."

All the while Florida knotted her brows over the problem of the music.

"Botheration!" she said finally. "If it wasn't Aunt 'Manda, then who? It wasn't accident, I'm sure. But I can't ask. That is . . . help me put the music away, Varina, will you? You'll not breathe this to a soul, will you? *Merci, mille fois,* darling. Now I must get back to Mamma. She's better today, but she hates an east wind. Would you care to come with me—just for distraction? That's what a person like her needs sometimes."

Varina went with Florida, willing to be a distraction and having, besides, a more selfish end in view. The noisy, happy house party at Hurricane was now facing complete disintegration. When the clan had first assembled, few of the visitors had contemplated staying beyond New Year's Day; but, when that happy holiday came it was, "Surely you can stay till the end of the week?" And most of the guests acknowledged reluctance about going by, "Well, maybe that long; but we must leave on Sunday, at the latest." Sunday now was close at

hand; and for Saturday evening, by way of final celebration, Mary
Bradford and Varina had chosen teams and had promised something
exceptional in the way of charades—the young people's favorite entertainment. Varina suspected that Mary was raiding outlying plantations
for accessories today and the thought occurred to her that Mrs. Eliza
Davis might lend her a few treasures from her chests if she, Varina,
could summon boldness enough to ask for them.

When she and Florida arrived at Mrs. Davis's room and were invited
to enter, it did look as if Varina might have chosen or been lucky
enough to be awarded an auspicious moment for her request. The invalid was up on her feet. She stood before a mirror, framed in heavy
gold leaf, which reflected almost the whole of her bedroom, and was
engaged in trying on a succession of embroidered shawls. She was
feeling quite well for herself, she said in response to Varina's respectful inquiry, except for the horrid wind. She had contemplated a drive
earlier. It had been a long time since she had indulged in a ride about
the more civilized portions of the estate. But then this wind had risen.
There was nothing like an east wind to fray a person's nerves, she
thought; and she had decided to stay out of it.

" 'When the wind is from East, 'tis neither good for man nor beast,' "
she quoted. "Oh, I don't think it portends a storm—at least not immediately," she continued in her soft, pettish, complaining way. "It
will likely wait to make travel difficult for those who came and must
go by carriage. It will blow around, and keep everybody on tenter-
hooks right up to Sunday. Then it will storm probably and everybody
will say, 'I told you so,' and spend four or five days more regretting
indecision—as if they all didn't know the climate and its possibilities."

Varina admired the shawls extravagantly and finally asked to be
allowed to try one. Preening before the heavily framed mirror, she was
startled a little at her own reflection. It seemed to her she had changed
immeasurably since spring. Then, meeting Mrs. Davis's bright, prob-
ing eyes in the glass, she blushed, and stammered out her request for
costume accessories.

"Am I invited to the entertainment?" the invalid asked.

"Oh, surely," Varina said. "Will you come?"

"If I'm able," Mrs. Davis sighed, and took a bottle of smelling salts
from Florida, who knew just when to have the bottle in her hand. "I
have my good days and my bad. Ah-h-h!" She inhaled deeply. "This

is a good day for me; but the chests must wait, my dear. I have something else in mind for the afternoon. Having been defrauded of my drive, I shall spend the hour instead in the ladies' parlor, I think. I shall take a spool of linen thread and my tatting shuttle and descend —and condescend—to listen to dear Sister Lucinda Stamps continue her report of the visit of the Taylors to Louisiana. I am sure she can't have finished with the tale. She has been doling it out in stingy bits to make it last over her visit. Have you heard any of it, Florida? Oh, you should. Varina sits there all ears. Yes, you do, my dear, I've seen you."

Varina asked meekly if there was any reason why she shouldn't hear what was said.

"Mercy, no, dear! Especially not if you are at all interested in the subject. It's all very illuminating—especially the way Sister Amanda spits and sputters. Dear Amanda! She has never forgiven Colonel Taylor because he objected to Jefferson as a son-in-law. She won't let the thing rest at the Colonel's own statement that he, having been a soldier all his days, did not wish any of his daughters to marry army men, which they each and all proceeded promptly to do. Amanda takes the Colonel's objections to Jefferson still as a personal offense, admitting, if she only knew it, that there might be other reasons."

"Now, Mamma," Florida coaxed.

Mrs. Davis patted her daughter's cheek and smiled wickedly at Varina. "All ears again?" her too-bright eyes seemed to ask.

"The incomparable Jefferson," she prattled on, "was never the angel of purity those foolish women insist on making him out to be. His life since his return to Brierfield has been without stain, but everybody agrees that is most unnatural. As a boy, I understand, he was quite spirited, even a trifle wild. After Mr. Davis, my husband, hurried him into West Point, he narrowly escaped dismissal twice. That by his own account. So, why should one believe that he was not one of the gayest young officers in those forest outposts in the North, where he served most of the time. From the day of his graduation he had his body-servant. He had money when there was anything to be bought with money. He had elegant uniforms. There are boxes of them still at Brierfield, gathering mold."

Varina jumped. Her skin prickled. She should have recognized the early symptoms of a fresh impulse and been on her guard. Uniforms

—could she manage to borrow some of the military trappings? How? Why, for that matter, if she didn't want the past recalled? Wasn't there enough and too much of that? Still her skin prickled.

"And boots," Mrs. Davis continued. "He will never wear out his supply of custom-built boots. And horses. And a family—they adored him those days, too—loading down every boat that ascended the Mississippi with such delicacies as could make the journey and probably many that could not. Why, of course, this Colonel Taylor, who is, by reputation, a man of rough ways, looked on him as nothing but a young officer dandy, a shining example of the dancing, singing, flirting, drinking West Pointer."

"But, Mamma," Floss objected, "Jeff admires Colonel Taylor. He won't let Papa or anyone else criticize the man."

"The soldier in him, precious. Colonel Taylor challenged him in every way he could. He gave him the harshest assignments, exposed him to death over and over, and finally exiled him to the Indian Territory. Ah, me! That did it. The Colonel may be a good Indian fighter, as Jefferson declares he is; but he is no strategist."

Mrs. Davis made a final selection of a pale saffron shawl. It might have been expected to turn her sallow, but did not. It brought to life rather, what color remained in her hair and, with a pair of twinkling ear drops, gave a greenish light to her eyes.

"No strategist," she repeated. "The clandestine meetings at Fort Crawford in Wisconsin—after Jefferson was forbidden the Taylor house—the business of intermediaries, notes, gifts and pledges, were nothing compared to the greater separation. There could have been no other result. In no time at all Jefferson was riding north and Knox Taylor was taking the first boat downriver after the ice gave way in the spring."

To meet in Kentucky—land of fine, generous people, beautiful women and blooded horses.

"Did they elope?" Varina asked.

"Sh! Never murmur such a thing in this house." Mrs. Davis turned reluctantly from the mirror. "How little you know Jefferson, child, if you think that in any straits he would allow the breath of ill repute to rest on a woman he cared for! They were married quite properly at the home of Knox Taylor's uncle. She was surrounded by family, only not her mother and father, naturally. At the last minute she did have their blessing. There would have been no point in Jefferson's resigning his commission except that it forced Colonel Taylor to abide by his word that he had no objection to Jefferson other than that he was an army officer. So finally he sent the blessing he would have done well to give earlier, for if the two had married while Jefferson was still in uniform, the end of the story might have been very different. As it was ... well, you know what happened."

Yes, Varina knew. How much she knew now, and still, how little! "What was she like?" she asked.

"Sarah Knox? She was a pretty little thing. She had brown hair ... light brown. The wind blew it into tangled curls and she fussed, but she laughed, too. She had a merry laugh. And blue eyes. They should have had a picture made of themselves in their wedding clothes, but they waited ... too long. They arrived here, dressed in their best. I'd never seen Jeff out of uniform. He looked so strange in the new, tight breeches held in place over his boots by straps under the instep, in his white brocaded waistcoat and long-tailed black coat. He looked taller than he really was and younger, because he was so solemn and devoted. She made him look taller, too. She hardly reached to his shoulder. Her traveling dress was blue, buttoned severely to her chin and then softened by a jabot of lace. She had a little hat that matched the dress, with a blue feather on it. Her eyes were the color of the feather ... poor, pretty little thing!"

Mrs. Davis reached up unexpectedly and tweaked Varina's ear.

"Prettier than you, my dear," she purred. "Very different. Pretty, I say, not handsome. A lady by nature and gentle breeding, but not a fine lady. Not proud. Just sweet. She had a spirit and a will of her own, to match that of her father. She had demonstrated that; and yet, there was something she lacked. Was it stamina? Or was it wisdom?"

Oh, wisdom! What had wisdom to do with love?

"And now, my dears, will you come with me to the parlor and hear first-hand, Sister Lucinda's afternoon tidbit? What do your suppose has brought the old story to life like this? Is it Lucinda's gossip or is it Mr. Davis's insistence that Jefferson give the forlorn cause of the Democrats in Warren County the unexpected benefit of a champion from the land-owning gentry? Mr. Davis would never expose himself to the rigors of a political hustings; but ... well, certainly there is something. Will you come, my dears, but quickly? I have spent myself talking to you until I am in need of a glass of Amanda's sherry and shall only hold my tatting in my hands for pretense."

Varina thought that she would not go to the ladies' parlor that day. She had heard enough. Her head ached.

She went instead to her room to look up her kitten, which she had now christened Paladin. Of course, the kitten wasn't there. As usual, she had taken the basket to the barn before dinner and had not thought to call for it afterward.

She went down to the stables. Young Thornton Montgomery met her at the main door.

"Would you wish a horse to ride, Young Miss?" he asked.

She remembered then that the choice mounts had all gone with the party for the Turner plantation. She could hardly ask Thornton to saddle one of the forbidden stallions. She thought fleetingly of going to the mares' barn to look at the gray Arabian, then restlessly decided against that.

"No," she said. "I just came for kitty."

Back in the house, she stopped in the hall to smooth her hair. The wind had roughened it. She could not call the tangles pretty.

Green young . . . she smoothed the strands and reset a couple of pins. *All eyes and bones* . . . she pinched her cheeks to make them bloom. She could hear the chatter in the small parlor. Faintly, but it drew her. She crossed the drawing room reluctantly, slipped through the door, and as unobtrusively as possible took a hassock and freed her cat.

"Well, according to Anna," Lucinda Stamps was saying defiantly, "that is what she said in her letter: 'Do not make yourself uneasy about me, dear mother. I am not afraid. The place is quite healthy.'"

"Poor thing!" Mrs. Eliza Davis said, her tatting, sure enough, idle in her lap. "That amounted to a confession of fear."

"Nonsense!" Miss Amanda said. "She was in no danger so long as she stayed up here at the house and took reasonable precautions. If she had kept away from the swamps or out of the morning and evening mists, she would not have taken the fever. Or, if they had been willing to leave when they were advised to. I am sure when Joe gave Jefferson the Brierfield acreage he never dreamed that the place would prove fatal to him or to his bride."

There was soft silence.

"Sister," Susanna Davis began then, in a kind of desperate deter-

mination; but Mrs. Eliza Davis had been shaping a retort simultaneously and her words took precedence.

"It would be difficult," she said, "to judge the depth or the extravagance of my husband's devotion to this land; but . . . how many entire
summers has he, or have you, Amanda, spent at Davis Bend?"

The silence took possession for another moment.

"I don't know, dear Eliza, what you mean to imply," Miss Amanda
said starchily. But she did know.

"Why, nothing," her sister-in-law answered, "except that Davis Bend
is anything but healthy. The place is not fit really for human habita-
tion—not white human, at any rate. The source of its fertility breeds
its venom. The brier field, as we called it long ago, was the richest
and the unhealthiest part of all. Now, if you will excuse me? Florida,
will you carry my reticule? Varina, I will thank you for your strong
young arm. You might like to look at what I have in my chests, perhaps, now."

Varina hated being dragged from the ladies' parlor at this point.
Mrs. Eliza Davis was beating a strategic retreat, but Varina wanted to
hear more clearly the outburst that followed her departure. Her im-
plication had been clear enough. She had accused Joseph Davis, her
husband, of giving his youngest brother the most fever-ridden and
unprepossessing part of the peninsula for his inheritance. Why? To
try him, as Colonel Taylor had tried him in the Army? Going farther,
had Joseph hoped in this way to wreck a marriage he did not favor?
Hadn't he favored it? Why that? Instead of being elated by the suggestion, Varina was repelled. An uneasiness that had been wakened
in her on her first evening at Hurricane came to life again. What sort
of man was Mr. Joseph Davis really? If she had asked her father now,
could he or would he have told her?

A dozen questions confused her so that she made a fumbling business of examining the treasures in Mrs. Davis's chests and finally, mentioning her headache again, begged to be excused until another day
and ran back to the parlor—to rescue her kitten, she said. The sudden
hush that greeted her return told her that truly she had missed all she
wanted to hear. She picked up Paladin and left, feeling all the sisters'
eyes watching her with renewed question and pondering.

When she reached her room at last, restlessly seeking comfort wherever she might find it, Melissa was there, going over her clothes.

"You makes more tatters and picks up more dust and brush," she grumbled; then she took a good look at her young mistress and laid her work aside. "Where you been now?" she demanded.

Varina's hands went to her hair.

"Nowhere in particular. It's this horrible wind. Melissa, have you time to give my hair a good brushing?"

"Is I got . . . co'se I have. I got what's left of the day. Set down here. Wait. I'll loosen up those stays."

"The hair first," Varina begged. "I feel every pin."

Melissa's hands were quick, sure, and gentle. She freed the shell pins and drew the hair down gently between her palms. The long, black . . . horse's tail!

"I'm goin' to brush it good now I got a chance," she scolded, but soothingly. "First though, I'm goin' to loose the stays. Then I'm goin' to sop a cloth in witch hazel extrack and you can hold it on yore eyes while I brush."

The sopped cloth stung, then was deliciously cool.

"Miss Ma'gret packed the bottle in yore beauty box," Melissa said. "She likes it if she feels a headache comin' on."

"It isn't a headache, really," Varina confessed. "I never have headaches."

"I knows you don' and you ain' goin' to, if Miss Ma'gret or I kin help it. I brought you up yere whole and healthy and so I'm going to take you back—if I has my way 'bout it."

Who or what would keep her from having her way? She was a wonder with a hairbrush. Slowly Varina relaxed.

"Mist' Jeff'son Davis been sick mo'n three days now with a headache."

Varina jerked to attention.

"Alligator-huntin' in Jan'ary!" Melissa sniffed.

"Oh, so that . . . did they get the alligator, Meliss'?"

"Mist' Jeff'son did, not the young harum-scarums. Alligator kill a calf. Young Mr. Joseph and the boys went out huntin' it. Slick ol' 'gator. Flip his tail and slide into a deep hole out o' sight. 'Did you mark the hole?' Mist' Jeff say. Yes, they mark the hole but you couldn' even see the 'gator at the bottom of it. Mist' Jeff say, 'I'll git 'em.' He put on his boots and take a long pole and his gun and set out. He come to the hole. Ol' 'gator down there eyin' him but not showin' hisself. Mist' Jeff take his pole, push it down the hole, way, way down. Ol' 'gator snap his teeth on it and hol' fast, still a laffin' to hisself. Mist' Jeff say, 'Ah!' Then he lay his gun barrel longside the pole and, bang, he shoot that 'gator's tongue plum' thru his tail. Monst'ous big 'gator, they tell me. Monst'ous smart man shoot him like that, but it's jes' the kind o' doings to bring on neuralgia."

"He is subject to neuralgia, I understand."

"Kinda. His man, Mist' Jeems Pemb'ton, say he had a spell o' bein' snowblind one time when he was soldierin' up Nawth and anurr time he come near to dyin' o' pneumonia. Since then it seem like too much wind or water or sun kinda settles in his eyes."

Not his eyes! Please, not his eyes! Deep, brilliant, laughing, thoughtful, inscrutable . . . how could she know their many expressions having looked into them only a few times? Was there anyone down at that lonely house who would know enough to sop a cloth in witch hazel?

"What do you think of James Pemberton, Melissa?"

Melissa pondered that for several sweeps of the brush.

"What I thinks o' him ain' what counts," she decided. "It's what Mist' Jeems Pemb'ton thinks o' hisself. He is the uppities' cullud man I ever see anywhere. He's the boss o' Mist' Jeff. He's the boss o' Brierfield plantation. He's the boss o' Davis Ben'. If he warn't a niggah underneath his airs, he'd make out to be President and boss the whole country."

So, he had put on airs with Melissa! Varina held back a smile.

"Mr. Jefferson sets much store by him," she suggested.

"Yes'm. Likely that's what make him so uppity. Man can' belong to proud man like Mist' Jeff'son without feeling kinda impo'tant."

"Are you enjoying yourself here, Melissa?"

Melissa considered that.

"I is and I ain'," she said finally. "Now, then. You feelin' better?"

"Much better. I'll be all right now, I'm sure."

"I'll turn back the bed," Melissa said. "An' you slip outa that dress."

"Oh, Meliss', I can't go to bed now. It's almost suppertime. Everybody will be coming home and we're planning charades."

"You could stay away one evenin'. It makes a nice appearance."

"It makes a false one, or would in my case. Somebody might get the idea that I am delicate. I'm not. I never could be. So, why pretend?"

"I don' know," Melissa said. "You so ve'y polite jes' now: 'Melissa, do you have time to brush my hair?' I got kinda skeered you might be comin' down with somethin'. But I reckon not, if you're goin' to play charades again. You ask me how I am enjoyin' myself. Are you havin' as much fun as you reckoned on?"

"I is," Varina echoed, "and I ain't."

A smile played around her lips and simultaneously a tear bubbled up under the sopped cloth.

"Of course, I am having fun," she said with determination and wiped the tear away. "It's all wonderful."

Mr. Jefferson was ill—with neuralgia. That had been all his reason for staying away from Hurricane. Why hadn't someone said—young Joseph, for example? Probably because Mr. Jefferson didn't want his illness fussed about.

Neuralgia . . . *How old are you, Miss Varina? Eighteen? So young and I am old . . . I suffer with neuralgia if I take a deep chill . . . old.*

But he hadn't said that, really. Perhaps he hadn't thought it. Because it wasn't true. He wasn't old. There was no longer anything like old and young between them.

Neuralgia . . . she missed him.

"A penny for your thoughts, Miss Varina," Young Joseph bid in a dance figure that evening.

She shook her head at him. He wouldn't want to hear her thoughts.

The next morning the wind had lulled. It was still in an easterly quarter and that boded no good ultimately, but meanwhile there was pleasant respite. Joseph Davis, Senior, indulged himself in a long walk through his garden; and Varina joined him. She had heard a horrid thing said of him the day before. She wanted not to believe it, if unbelief were possible.

"Radiant creature!" Joseph greeted her as she came around the corner of the house, with the very small kitten making dashes at the hem of her skirt as if the garment were alive and elusive. "Fresh as the morning and twice as lovely!"

He broke off a pale pink camellia bud and gave it to her. She fastened it in the heavy knot of her hair.

"I believe," he said in grave judgment, "I like your hair dressed low better than high."

"Thank you," Varina said. "I rather do myself. I am so tall! There is no use in adding inches."

"You speak in a tone of grievance, my dear. There was a day when to be tall was a requisite of queens and goddesses."

"An ancient day?" she questioned. "Times and tastes change."

"Not really," he assured her. "With people of discrimination classic standards always prevail. And now, are you off afield or have you truly come to give me the pleasure of your company?"

"Something like that." She laughed. "If I am not in the way. I've waited to see the garden until you were free to show it to me."

"Have you, indeed, my lovely flatterer? Then, come. The gardener is making rose cuttings. The bushes need trimming and he hates to waste a twig. We'll follow him about. You must see the roses and, by all means, you must see and know Mr. O'Connor."

John O'Connor, the gardener, was the other white workman on the plantations besides Mr. Perkins, the ginwright. Varina remembered their homes in an individual clearing between the quarters at Hurricane and Brierfield; and Mr. Perkins had a family and lived in his house, but what time John O'Connor found to visit his, one could not imagine. Mr. Perkins had a taste for reading and "between times" borrowed books from the libraries at both big houses and took them home to study. John O'Connor knew no season for idleness. He hovered in all weathers close to beds and borders and shrubbery thickets in the garden that was his in joint ownership with the master of Hurricane.

He was a wizened, weathered little Irishman with the elusive and illusive qualities of a leprechaun. He appeared in a turn of the path as Joseph Davis finished speaking. He touched his cap when he was presented and gave to Varina, ready cut, a long-stemmed rosebud just loosening the edges of petals so purely white as to seem faintly tinged with green.

"If you will put it in a deep vase with plenty of water, it will open fully," he assured her, following the rose with his care even as he gave it away.

"It's lovely," Varina said and thanked him. "Have you these in bloom now?"

"Mr. O'Connor has roses blooming the year round in one way or another," Joseph said.

"Yes, but the young lady is right," the gardener protested. "This is an off-season. Only the warm weather we are having has brought the bushes into bud; and I'd as lief," he squinted at a sky dappled with cloud patches, "they'd stay in tight bud a while. Especially the white ones. Naught blights like a white flower in frost or rain, it seems like."

Then he was gone; and Varina, holding the rose stem, thoughtfully denuded of thorns, lightly in one hand, was walking alone with Joseph Davis between flowering camellias on the one side and massed holly trees, bright with berries, on the other. John O'Connor could well be busy keeping all in check. The growth, though tamed with shears and knife, was as lush here as in the canebrakes.

"I can smell the richness of the soil," Varina said.

"Can you?" Joseph was as pleased as if she had offered him personal tribute. "You have a discerning nose. Do you find the richness oppressive?"

"A little," she confessed, "because I wonder . . ."

"You wonder how long it would take for all this to revert to the wild state? A year would destroy all seemliness. Five years would bring back the jungle."

He spoke almost angrily, as if somebody or something had threatened him with loss.

"It won't happen," Varina said. "You wouldn't allow it to happen. It is all too beautiful."

"I pray God that it won't happen," he said, "but you are mistaken if you think it can't."

Again his words were defiant more than they were prophetic. His safety, his comfortable affluence had been threatened. Perhaps a person could not build up so much treasure on earth without knowing doubt and fear. No, the threat had been made by some definite person or force. It was not a mere acknowledgment of man's impotence. She could not say again, "You won't let it happen," because from his tone he meant to do what he could toward prevention. He was angry, defiant, and cold and hard all at once.

Soberly Varina followed him through an arch draped in smilax and stepped suddenly into the rose garden. And there was the leprechaun squatting beside a rosebush, doing delicate surgery with a pruning knife and shears. In a path near by stood a two-wheeled cart, half-filled with discarded brush. On the ground beside John O'Connor a basket, lined with moss, received the cuttings he chose to save. A black boy of perhaps twelve years crawled about the cart on all fours, playing with Varina's kitten between jobs of light hauling.

The simple peace of the picture, in contrast to Joseph Davis's harsh defiance, pierced Varina's perceptions with the force of real pain. The kitten made a sideways jump at the boy, back arched and tail high; and the boy rolled on the ground and laughed. The sound was a chain of silver bells ringing.

"Better get up off that damp ground, Kizzy," Joseph said. "You'll be having another bad throat."

Bad throat? This must be the boy who'd been ill the day of Varina's arrival, the one Miss Amanda had dosed. Kizzy, Hagar's son. A boy and a little, weathered man who asked no more of life than that he should be allowed to spend it in this garden of opulence.

For it was an opulent garden. Varina made no attempt to estimate its size or the number of beds in various shapes intersected by broad paths, broken by pieces of sculptured marble. The ground was damp, in spite of the stretch of fine weather. The smell of the earth was richest here, where it had been kept crumbled and clean of weeds. The bushes were in bright leaf, as if unkind winds had never touched them; and on most of them buds, like tapers, reached up to the sun for light.

Kizzy, the colored boy—the full name was Kizziarch—rolled out of the path and stood up, shyly smiling; and the leprechaun laid his shears on the cart and touched his cap again.

"It is nothing now, Miss," he said modestly, reading her thoughts, "to what it will be in a month or two. Last April I had a thousand bushes in full bloom at one time."

A thousand . . . Varina could not picture so many. With parted lips she looked over the green expanse, then brought her examination back to the smaller picture close by—the weathered little man in blue cotton jeans, the cart, and the boy. Thoughtfully she inhaled the rank, sweet smell of the earth.

"You know," she said, "I believe I might like to garden. I believe I would even be good at it."

She had never given the matter thought before, accepting tree and bush and flower with gratification and without question. Now, stirred by a new impulse, she stooped and gathered up a handful of the black soil. It went to bits in her fingers and sifted through, leaving some grime and stain on the delicate lining of her hand. She made a rueful face at the marks, shrugged her shoulders and laughed, a feeling persisting . . .

"Women are good at gardening," the leprechaun said, "if they turn their hand to it. The most of them, that is."

The worthy ones, his bright, respectful eyes suggested.

"The fruiting earth shares her secrets with her daughters, you mean, John?" Joseph said. "You're right, as usual." Varina wondered why she blushed. It was a kinship with the earth she had felt. "What are you doing with the cuttings?"

"I promised Mrs. Turner some," the gardener said. "She's opening a new plot. With your permission, that is, sir."

"Good heavens, yes. Give her all she'll take. It seems to me I saw signs yesterday of your invading my peach orchard. Eh?"

"That is for those new varieties we are having up from New Orleans, sir. They being untried as yet. If the bed seems too far out of bounds, I will find another place for it."

Joseph winked at Varina, his evil humor, if it had been one, soothed out of existence by the spell of the garden.

"Leave the bed just where it is, John. I merely wanted you to know I noticed it. Will you have cuttings to spare for Miss Howell to take home with her when she goes, though I hate to contemplate that day?"

"I'll select and pack them myself, sir. Where do you live, Miss?"

"Out from Natchez," Varina told him.

"Ah! I had thought I might have the pleasure of setting them for you; but Natchez is too far."

Since he had gone to work at Hurircane, Varina learned, John O'Connor had not traveled farther than on benevolent work missions to neighboring plantations; and he did not go that far often. Varina had a moment of panic. Home with a bundle of rose cuttings? Nobody could say how many. Pledged to grow them? "I'll have to get Mamma to help me. No, I must do it myself. There is land enough and we have hands, too, to help with the digging."

All the while she knew that it was not at The Briers she would want to plant rose cuttings from the Hurricane garden. There was rich, dank earth in another quarter that could be brought into bloom.

"Excuse me, Mr. Davis, I see Mr. Jefferson on the back gallery. Would he be looking for you, maybe?"

She had not conjured up his presence, surely . . . or had she? She tried to wait passively while Kizzy at a word from Joseph ran to say where they were. She tried to keep her heart out of her eyes as she watched him come striding down the paths. Ah, dear! He had as much grace walking as riding. It might have been such an ungainly, loose-jointed length of limb. The back might have bent, the shoulders might have bowed a little; but they never did. They never would. He had a fine, free step. He carried his head high, his shoulders back. Having learned the way of that, it was the only way for him.

He wore a hat this morning, a soft hat with a wide brim. He swept it off as he approached, then held it between his eyes and the sun. His eyes were deeper in their sockets today. He seemed pale. Was it the neuralgia? Or other pain? Varina's throat felt queerly tight. His first words touched a sensitive spot on her conscience.

"I see you have made another conquest," he said, indicating the rose in her hand. "Are you fond of roses?"

"Yes, I am."

Would he remember that she had barely glanced at garden or orchard on Christmas afternoon when they rode that way? It was possible. A light flashed in his tired eyes. In view of the wide-brimmed hat, it could not have been a reflection of the sun. He went on to talk of roses.

"The Glory of France is my favorite, I think," he said. "Are any of those opening yet, John?"

The leprechaun's eyes were bright and observant as he replied in the negative.

"But soon, I think, John."

He held a tight, green bud lightly in his finger tips and released it. Then it was he who led the way through the garden. If anything, he was more familiar with its plan and its variety of planting than either his brother Joseph or the gardener. The excursion ended in a hot debate between him and John O'Connor over the proper season for making rose cuttings. Was it better to take them from a plant in the high tide of growth and development or when it rested, semi-dormant?

Varina thought the two would be at each other's throats and wondered that Joseph Davis did not interfere. He shook his head at her look of startled inquiry. "It is nothing," he meant to imply.

Nothing? John O'Connor's last speech came out a half-strangled cry.

"Who are you to be telling me what you have from this authority and that?" he demanded. "You, who have never marked off a rood of land down yonder on which to prove your theories? Will you be showing me a garden of your own planting some day, then . . . and when?"

Jefferson Davis was nearer to laying hands on Mr. O'Connor then than at any time before in the argument. He was furiously angry, and then,

"*Touché,*" he said, with a twist of his mouth.

Animation left him. His body stiffened. His face paled. His eyes were gray then, not blue. It was one of the times when he seemed— well, if not old, certainly not young; and a moment before, self-forgetful, he had seemed very young.

"You're right," he said curtly to John O'Connor.

The latter stiffened, too, but did not yield his point. "You cannot grow anything with words and just logic," his stubborn, outthrust jaw maintained.

Varina thought the tightness in her throat would choke her.

"You're right," Jefferson said again, not quite so sharply, but still rather stiffly. "I am not sure that flowers would flourish at Brierfield, no matter how I tended them." Then he saw Varina. At least, he looked at her, and came back part of the way from whatever black thoughts John O'Connor's taunt had pricked in him. "A rose garden," he said, with a movement suggesting a bow, and a thin smile over the bitterness on his mouth, "to do well, must have sunlight, and a lady to walk its paths, to lend it loveliness."

CHAPTER VIII

THE scene in the rose garden gave Varina but little illumination as to Joseph Davis's capacity for dark as well as benevolent design. He knew his brother Jefferson well—that she had understood before. However, he knew him, she saw now, not only from past experience, but from continued study and observation. Joseph Davis was a man who studied people. Why? Because he found them interesting? Or the better to use them for his own purposes? If the latter were true, then it was eminently possible that, when the time came, he would use them, friend or foe, ruthlessly. That followed.

But how did that affect her and the heartache that was the most of her profit so far from indulging in a whim to win the favor of one well out of the range of the usual feminine blandishments? She did not know the answer to that, either, except that she was sure a new romantic attachment was not part of her Uncle Joe's plans for his handsome younger brother. Those plans, she thought she discovered, lay in quite a different field.

"Varina, child, are you at liberty? Would you lend the brightness of your presence and particularly of your eyes to a chore of reading? I am a lazy man by nature and disinclined at this late day to change, and someone has piled a heap of periodicals and mail on my desk. Jeff would do better to rest his eyes a spell longer. Would you find the task too tedious?"

She would not find it tedious at all. An electric spark of recognition

touched her nerve centers. This was closer than she had ever hoped
to come to being admitted to the brothers' more intimate councils.

"I'm on my way this minute, Uncle Joe. As soon as I dispose of
Paladin."

"Bring him with you, child, and come on."

So she gathered another picture and one she studied, perhaps, more
than any other—the two brothers together in Joseph Davis's office at
the end of a working day. They had been out most of the afternoon,
Joseph on Old Speck, Jefferson on Old Duke, the dun-colored Plains
horse, giving him gentle exercise, holding him down to the flea-bitten
gray's pace. It was their habit to make a round of the plantations together on afternoons when both were at home and the weather was
suitable and more urgent business did not demand the attention of
either one. Most of their plans for the improvement and partition of
the land were made from the saddle and on the spot. They had been
out together this afternoon and had returned, to find that Dwight Mc-
Caleb had ridden down from Diamond Place to see his pretty wife—
he would stay with her now until they returned together on Sunday—
and to fetch a wagonload of mail. Varina had letters herself from The
Briers, and a packet of brightly wrapped Philadelphia sweetmeats that
her Aunt Sally had sent her. But, of course, the bulk of the mail was
for the master of Hurricane.

Jefferson Davis was sorting the papers when Varina entered with
Joseph.

"This is really too bad," he said deprecatingly. "I am sure you could
pass the time more pleasantly."

"But not more profitably," Joseph said. "Will you take a chair by
this west window, child? And shall we get on with the reading, to
make the most of the light?"

He placed a copy of the *National Intelligencer* in her hands. Varina
looked from the Whig sheet to both men in question.

"But I thought . . ." she said, rather hopefully, it must be admitted
They laughed at her expression.

"We have not changed our politics, I'm afraid," Jefferson said. "We
read the views of our adversaries only to fortify our arguments in
opposition. It is much more invigorating than to listen to endless repetition of our own thoughts by those who agree with us."

Varina properly made no answer beyond opening the paper rather starchily. Finding that neither man paid any attention to this slight gesture of defiance, she gave her shoulders an impatient shake and settled down to the reading, glad to have the form and, she would have supposed, the content of the news familiar.

She was amazed then to discover that world affairs, which had seemed fairly humdrum when she left Natchez, had in a few weeks assumed alarming aspects. Either that was true or the brothers Davis were ready to make controversy out of any incident. Joseph, in particular, would turn the light of his personal reflection on an item and it would stand out immediately in bold, scarehead type. He did this, Varina soon observed, not for the pleasure of airing his own views, but to draw opinion and comment from Jefferson, who never lacked for ideas of his own and had greater eloquence with which to express them. Joseph, having set him off, would sink back into his chair, consider the level of toddy in his glass, reach over from time to time to refill it from a pitcher handy on his desk, and with about the same frequency slip in a sly, provocative comment. One glass of toddy, Varina noticed, lasted Jefferson through the evening. Most of the time it stood forgotten on the mantel. Joseph, on the other hand, emptied the pitcher.

Varina watched and listened at first with wonder, with curiosity, with question, and then, when she saw how Joseph led his brother on, with growing uneasiness and resentment. Didn't Jefferson realize how he was, in a manner, being put through his paces, drilled and redrilled on set exercises? Or, didn't he care? It was, in truth, a dazzling show, if only . . .

For example, the first news item Varina read had to do with Texas. That, of course, in Mississippi had been a live and burning subject ever since General Quitman had led a band of Fencibles over the border to help Sam Houston avenge the dead of the Alamo; but the subject really mattered little. On the same page there was an account of the sufferings of settlers traveling a new route to Oregon, known as the Fort Hall Trail.

"What do you think," Joseph asked, "of this man Frémont?"

Varina could have listened the balance of the evening to Jefferson's comment, and even longer to the observations and speculations of one who had himself spent hard years on another frontier. There was a ringing in her ears that was delight in the cadences of Jefferson's singularly musical, pleasing voice. There was delight in her mind over his ability to bring the wilderness and its dangers into this snug, safe room. Then suddenly her delight was lost in bewilderment. Somehow Oregon had become part of the Texas question and both were part of a problem called national expansion and territorial rights; and the firelight glowed in the eyes of the man on the hearth and his bright, clear talk was argument; and she, who had once thought she would give anything to be allowed to listen to the good, rich talk of men on subjects of real importance, found herself closing her ears to fervor, trying to distill only the drawing sweetness of Jefferson's voice.

It was a drawing, compelling sweetness. Mrs. Eliza Davis had once compared him to Orpheus, who could almost bring back the dead to life; but Joseph was not grooming his beloved younger brother to work among the dead. He had work for him in the land of the living.

Listening, listening, Varina thought of Seargent Prentiss. Was it heresy to believe that the impassioned man in this darkening room could have all the great Prentiss's power and something more? She considered a meeting of the two on the same platform and drew away, her skin prickling with a first premonition of disaster. Disaster for whom? She could not or she would not say.

Her musings were interrupted by Joseph Davis's dry tones.

"Read on, child. The light gets no better."

The light got no better and Varina's heart no quieter. Something pulsated in this room with its graying shadows and its slumbering fire of logs, in the coming twilight outside, that was more significant, that was beyond the reach of the words she read from the rustling paper. She doubted that the words in the paper would tell her what that thing was. She must listen more closely to what the brothers said.

She read on.

There had been rioting in the settlement of a Mormon congregation at a place called Nauvoo, in Illinois. It seemed indelicate to linger near people who practised polygamy and were said to steal their wives. Varina hurried on to the next paragraph, which dealt with a debate at Washington over the reception to be accorded to representatives of the new Republic of Haiti, if Haiti should send them to the National Capital. They would be black, of course.

There was no oratory now, but the reading halted. No oratory . . the brothers faced each other in serious, sober thought; and Varina

with a start recognized the nature, at least in part, of the threat which
Joseph Davis felt hung over his kingdom. His was a fear known to
every man of great possessions in the South, a fear acknowledged in
so many words by none: "Our blacks. Suppose this idea of revolt
should spread. Suppose someone should come in from the outside
and incite them to violence. They outnumber us . . . by how many?
God knows. We'd have to make a census."

But, since this fear was so general and so inadmissible, why did
Joseph want to sound Jefferson out on this point? Surely he knew
what Jefferson would think as well as he knew his own mind. No,
he was not asking Jefferson now for an opinion. He was reminding
him of a danger they both shared. Some day, in the near or distant
future, he would call for action.

Yes, that was it. There was some service Joseph planned to ask of
his gifted brother. Perhaps he had already named it to Jefferson. To
Varina the service was still indefinable, though imbued, she was certain, with peril. The latter, of course, would not hold Jefferson back
if he made up his mind to face the task.

Varina read on, stumbling now and again, not because of the fading
light, but because of her preoccupation, and so fell presently into a
speech by a Mr. Slidell, Member of Congress from Louisiana, urging
the repeal of a tariff law. As she might have expected, her reading
was interrupted by a spontaneous outburst from both men. The South
had always fought protective tariff.

Varina listened now in a kind of numbed wonder. Jefferson's eloquence leaped like a flame now to this side, now to that, of the favorite topic. Joseph had little fanning to do here. He listened, too,
and greedily, Varina thought. She herself could not fail to be thrilled
by Jefferson's sharp, caustic comment and even more by the obvious
scope of his reading and his retentive memory. He quoted authority
after authority until even Joseph chided him, still with the effect of
prodding.

"John Randolph of Virginia is dead, my boy," he said drily, "and
some think Mr. Calhoun of South Carolina is equally so, politically
speaking."

"Impossible!" Jefferson fairly worshiped John C. Calhoun, it seemed.

"Not impossible at all," Joseph told him. "After a number of years
one man's views and oratory grow monotonous, especially if they have

failed to score a victory. Then it is time for another, younger man. . . ."

Without noise or sputter, he added his fuel to the blaze. Jefferson looked at him with strangely glittering eyes, then away and out the window behind Varina into darkening space. He tipped his head back and began to speak. The words, the marvelously well molded phrases came smoothly and easily from some inexhaustible well of opinion.

"What is good for the nation is good for all the nation, if it is to be written into our national law. If a thing is good for one section and not good for another, then jurisdiction in that particular belongs to a section. . . . A planter must sell the fruits of his labor where best he can. He should be free to buy also to his best advantage. . . . The market price should be established in free competition. Consider the spectacle of a planter being compelled to sell his cotton on the open market but being forced to buy goods woven from it at a price dictated. . . . Finally there is nothing in the Constitution . . ."

"God bless my soul!" Joseph said abruptly from his chair. "The light's entirely gone."

"It has been gone for some time, I believe." Jefferson shook himself, looked at Varina and smiled; but his face was still pale with his great earnestness.

"But where is Solomon to light the candles?" Joseph fumed.

"I's here, Moss' Joe. Right here. 'Scuse me, but it sound so fine, I didn' like to bus' in."

"Well, bust in now and do your duty. Varina, are you writing?"

"Yes," she said. "When I couldn't see to read, I moved over to the table." A pad of paper had drawn her. "Like Solomon," she finished lamely, "it sounded fine to me too, so I wrote it down as I could."

"In the dark?"

"It is never altogether dark to me," she said. "I can always see a little."

"You have such eyes?"

There was wistfulness in the question. It would be as near as Jefferson Davis would come to complaint or even to acknowledging a weakness. His eyes were a physical weakness. They could not endure strong light or other exposure. And the strain of long hours of reading and study—most of his communion with the world through eight years in what amounted to a hermit's cell, no matter how well-furnished—had not strengthened them.

Dear Lord, did one come to loving through knowing and sharing pain?

"Let me see what you have written," Joseph commanded.

Varina surrendered the paper unwillingly, though she had not, of course, written the words for her own keeping. Joseph read and raised his eyebrows.

"To the dot," he said.

"But heresy," Jefferson quizzed gently, "to one of your upbringing?"

"I don't know," Varina said, confused now about that.

"But what an idea you've given us!" Joseph said, still reading. "Jeff does his best composing on his feet. You'd look far, my boy, before you'd find a more able amanuensis."

So, now he thought he would use her.

"I would not think of asking or accepting such a sacrifice," Jefferson declared.

"I would be most happy to help in any way."

This was Varina Howell speaking, Varina Howell, who had declared she would not bow down like everybody else on the place.

Would she not, indeed?

She thought, "If I could reach his heart, if I could make him look at me just once with longing and desire, instead of amused indulgence, I might break the spell."

She did not know whether the spell was good or evil, simply that it was of another's plotting. She needed no further warning as to Joseph Davis's astuteness or stubborn prowess as an adversary. She knew her only chance of coming off victorious in an encounter with him was to strike at him in an unexpected quarter. She was sure he would be the last member of the family to think of his brother Jefferson as vulnerable to a second woman's allurements.

If, indeed, he were vulnerable. The barrier seemed twice as formidable as it had been before.

How you goin' to manage, Young Miss?

She was so green young, she had so few resources! Nonsense, Varina Howell! You've aged ten years in two weeks. Use your wits!

She thought of the planned charades. If she could secure one of his uniforms, if young Joseph would wear it for the privilege of a romantic scene with her . . . How would she get it? Jefferson mustn't know.

"Va-ree-na!"

Varina jumped, but it was not her conscience screaming a warning. It was Miss Amanda at the foot of the attic steps, calling.

"Varina, if you and Mary can do without a few petticoats—down to just the demands of modesty, I think I can fit the two of you into the seat of the wagonette with me. I'm driving my rounds today and should be delighted to have your charming company."

In spite of discarded petticoats, the three of them crowded the seat of the light wagon to capacity.

"I don't think giggling helps," Miss Amanda said, with pretended severity. "Settle down now. There!"

She took the lines into capable, gloved hands and slapped them knowingly over the backs of the horses—the same team of well-fed bays that had drawn the carriage from Diamond Head.

"That storm," she said, casting an eye at the sky—everyone did these days—"is going to hold off until it amounts to something."

Kizziarch rolled his eyes at them from the tail of the wagon.

"Kizzy," Miss Amanda said, "is to keep the horses from noticing too much difference when I take on my real load. Those bundles in back aren't a circumstance. I've got a list a yard long that Rhina Number Two wants me to fill at the store. Kizzy has it, rather. Kizzy's going to hop out with it presently and run ahead, because we are going to visit Aunt Rhina first and Kizzy is keeping clear of her these days. She might, she just might put a spell on him and bring back his sore throat so that she could try curing him again. And we don't want to risk that. Do we, Kizzy?"

"No'm." Kizzy's smile wrapped itself around his face. "No, ma'am!"

The horses clopped along.

"Speaking of groceries," Miss Amanda said after two minutes of silence, "seems to me our Rhina knew enough ways of cooking without your bringing her some new notions from Natchez—you and that maid of yours—what's her name? Melissa—yes. I never had a girl named that and I keep forgetting."

"I like to fool around a kitchen sometimes," Varina said, "and Rhina has been good to my kitten."

"Yes—well, she's possessed to try your formula for tipsy balls now. Melissa said she'd help. Melissa makes herself right useful in many ways. She sewed up Aunt Rhina's red flannel. It's in one of those bundles."

"That was good of Melissa," Varina agreed demurely.

"Yes, it was. I'm sure she did it of her own accord. You didn't tell her to. Well, anyhow, Rhina will be glad to have the new flannels if it turns cold; and maybe this will be an auspicious day for having fortunes told. Here you are, Kizzy. Jump. Tell Ben I'll be along. If there's anything on the list he doesn't have, we'll see about getting it."

Old Aunt Rhina's cabin smelled of smoke—wood and tobacco—of pot liquor and liniment, and a general sealed mustiness. The Negress had drawn her rocking chair close to the hearth so that her gaitered feet rested all but in the embers. She made a half-hearted movement toward rising when she saw who her visitors were.

"Sit still," Miss Amanda said. "We won't stay long. Is the rheumatism bad again?"

Aunt Rhina looked up with eyes veiled like a droopy fowl's.

"It's bad," she admitted. "But it ain' as bad as it's goin' to be directly. I'll make out, though."

"I'm sure you will," Miss Amanda agreed. "Especially when you pull on your new flannels. I brought them—yours and Uncle Rob's." She dropped the two bundles on the bed.

"Gi' um here, so's I kin feel um," Aunt Rhina demanded.

"No. You'll have to wait. I forget now which bundle is yours and which is Uncle Rob's. You wouldn't want to open his by mistake and embarrass these young ladies. Where is Uncle Rob?"

"Pokin' 'roun' summeres. He ain' trubbled with misery like I is. He figger, I reckon, if he keep hoppin' fas' enough, ol' age ain' goin' to ketch um." The veiled eyes scrutinized the visitors one at a time. "I knowed I was goin' to git company," she went on. "I read it in the ashes this mawnin'." The old eyes came to rest on Varina. "Ol' Rhina read lots o' things in the ashes an' smoke. I learned it from my mammy who belong to Ol' Moss' Sam'l way back in Geo'gia and she had it f'om her mammy. She Gullah niggah. She know all de Gullah conjure."

The eyes swept briefly over Miss Amanda, then came back to Varina. Varina felt a slight crawling up her spine, but Miss Amanda lost none of her cheerfulness.

"We didn't come here to be scared out of our lives, Aunt Rhina. I thought maybe you'd like to see these pretty girls and read the cards for them."

"Rhina don' fool with no cyards. You know that. She read the stars and the moon and the smoke and the ashes. I got a message fo' you, Young Miss, if you want to hear it."

"Oh, pshaw!" Miss Amanda objected. "It's half the fun to watch you at your art of divination."

"What dat?"

"Your hocus-pocus poking around. You know."

"Well, say so, then. You got as many big words as Moss' Joe and Moss' Jeff, on'y they don' th'ow um at ol' ign'rant niggah. They got mo' manners. You allus was a peart young 'un—too peart. When we wuz travelin' south from Kaintuck to Loosiane, an' Moss' Jeff wuz a baby and they was a whole passel o' other chillun, I felt lak th'owin' you to de wolves many's the time."

"Why, Miss Amanda!" Mary said. "Were you like that?"

"All right, Aunt Rhina, that will do. You've disgraced me now before my own young one. Brr! I can still hear those wolves howling around the camp. I'll not say another word. Go on and tell Miss Varina's fortune, then. Make it a nice one."

"I tell it true the way I reads it. Young Miss want to hear?"

"I don't know," Varina said doubtfully.

"No call to be afraid, Young Miss. Ol' Rhina know the good and the bad. They is good in yore readin', an' bad. Like allus. Will you listen, Missy?"

"Go on," Mary Bradford challenged, standing safely in the lee of her majestic mother. "Then Aunt Rhina can do me a new fortune. I didn't care especially for the one she did for me last."

Rhina peered at her.

"Same pusson, same fortune," she growled. "Signs don' lie, no matter how many times you read um. You goin' to ma'y 'way fum yere— a Nawthener, like I said. Aftah that, the signs ain' clear, an' good reason. That make trubble enough fo' ennybody. Pull up that stool, Young Miss, close to Rhina's cheer, so she kin figger out what she read in the signs this mawnin', knowin' you'd be comin' by—an' look at you whilst she speak the words."

With more curiosity than unwillingness, Varina did as she was told.

"That's a good chil'," Rhina said. "Are you a good chil', Young Miss?"

"Not especially," Varina confessed.

"You is and you ain'," Rhina corrected. "You is peart. It's all right to be peart, but not too peart. Trubble goin' to soften yore peartness. You goin' to know much trubble an' much joy an' gladness. You skeered, Young Miss?"

"Why, yes, a little."

"Don't be skeered, Young Miss. You goin' to ca'y yore haid high and proud in the glad years, but not half as high an' proud as when you lifts it 'bove sorrow. You goin' to make out all right. You goin' to ma'y—you wants to know about that, don' you?"

"Mercy, yes. Some people have said I wouldn't—ever."

"Sho!" Rhina snorted. "Why that?"

"The pertness, I suppose. And other things." Classic poets, willfulness, too much brain for a mere woman.

"Sho!" Rhina said again. "You goin' to ma'y high an' proud an' happy an' ve'ry soon. You goin' to ma'y befo' Miss Mary yere takes up with that Nawthener. You ain' goin' to ma'y a stranger. He goin' to come fum home. Right yere or yereabouts. You got to give the sign room to work in, but it's close in time an' distance. They's storm signs roun' this man's sign—wind and thunder and lightning and rain."

"Pshaw!" Miss Amanda said in her turn. "I could read storm signs this morning without poking in the ashes."

Rhina did not answer her directly.

"They's two kinds o' storm." Her voice began to take on a kind of drone. In spite of familiarity with such doings, Varina felt a stirring at the roots of her hair. Rhina was so old! Ancient, really. "They's a storm that come quick an' hard an' blow itself out soon. They's anurr storm that lay in wait and lastes longer. Both storm signs roun' this man's sign. Yore gladness an' yore sadness all mixed up with um. You goin' to be glad and sad 'count o' him, but mo' glad than sad— that's all I kin see.

"You goin' to ma'y this man an' make a jorney. A long jorney, but not as long as some beyon' that one. Lots o' trabel in yore sign, Young Miss. A wind sign seem to follow you roun'. You lights and lays still fo' a spell, then 'long come the wind an' off you puts agin. You goin' to trabel a far way, Young Miss. You goin' to trabel in style and then agin the jorney sign is set with trubble. But you goin' to come thu all right. You goin' to live high an' sometimes not so high, but you allus comes thu fine. You goin' to live a long, long time. That man you goin' to ma'y, he goin' to live out his days, too, come high, come low. An' you goin' to ca'y his heart in the hollow o' yore hands the whole way. Mebbe that's the reconcilemen'. You goin' to come thu all right. You skeered still, Young Miss?"

"Yes, and no," Varina said respectfully.

"Don't be skeered, Young Miss. You ain' goin' to be skeered when the time come. Oh, you'll screech and holler now an' agin but mos'ly you won' take time even fo' that. You'll pick up whatever load the Lawd sends and ca'y it and you'll come thu."

Rhina reached out suddenly and laid her hand lightly on Varina's forearm. It was a shriveled, brown hand, like a duck's foot, dried.

"Stren'th o' body," she said.

She peered up into Varina's face.

"Stren'th o' body and stren'th o' speerit. That will see you thu. With the Lawd's blessin'. That all, chil'. You got tears shinin' in yore eyes? Why that?"

"I don't know." Varina stood up. "Thank you, Aunt Rhina, for the long fortune. How . . . would you like cushions for your rocking chair? I'll make you some when I get home to Natchez and I'll send them to you—one to hang from the back and one to sit upon."

"You'll be sewin' weddin' ga'ments when you goes home, Young Miss, an' you'll forgit ol' Rhina."

"No, I won't, even if I am sewing wedding garments."

"Then I sho'll be thankful fo' what yore hands give out, Young Miss."

"Well!" Miss Amanda said, when they were outside again. "That was quite a fortune, Varina. Don't take it too seriously. Rhina lets her favor and animosities color her readings—like all seers, even in the Bible, I suppose. For some reason best known to her, you have Rhina's favor. I suppose you realize that."

"I realized and am thankful," Varina answered.

When the Hurricane wagonette drew up before Ben Montgomery's plantation store, James Pemberton, who had come to select early vegetable seeds for the Brierfield garden patch was on the point of leaving. He greeted the ladies from Hurricane respectfully, assisted them to alight, and then would have gone on; but Miss Amanda stopped him.

"Don't be in a hurry, James," she said, "I want to talk to you a minute. You run on in with Ben, Mary, and see about the groceries. Varina . . ."

"Keep Varina with you if you will," Mary said. "I want to talk to Ben on subjects personal."

"Now, Mary, if it's more plans for those charades," her mother said, "don't buy a lot of stuff, please. It does seem that with all we have lying around in trunks . . ."

"I'm not going to buy a thing," Mary promised. "I just want some information from Ben. That's all."

She whisked away with the storekeeper, leaving Varina with the usual signs of an idea blossoming in her brain. It was like soft bursts of light. She could almost see the illumination.

"I'll ask James for the uniform," she thought. "I'll ask him and swear him to secrecy."

She could hardly contain herself while Miss Amanda went on talking, though she had to smile at the tenor of the one-sided conversation.

"It's been some time since I've been down your way," Miss Amanda began.

"Yes, ma'am, it is. Mr. Jefferson has remarked on it."

"Has he? Well, not to me. How are things coming along at Brierfield?"

"About as always, ma'am."

He showed her the garden seeds.

"You did your usual good job on Jefferson's latest bout with neuralgia."

"Thank you, ma'am. I understands how to treat it by now, I reckon."

"Well, I hope we'll have no more alligator hunts."

"It ain't likely, ma'am. It's more politics now."

"Yes, and I don't see what he wants to mess around with those for."

James Pemberton did not commit himself on that issue, just waited, still respectfully, to hear what else Miss Amanda might have to say. Apparently she wondered about that herself and Varina spoke up.

"Please, I've a favor to ask of James, if you don't mind."

"You . . ." Miss Amanda was naturally surprised. So was James. He took a minute to show it before he bowed his head in subservience.

"I'll be pleased to oblige if I can," he said.

"With your approval, of course," Varina said to Miss Amanda, "and yours, James. We are having a big play-party at Hurricane Saturday evening, with charades; and it occurred to me that, since Mr. Jefferson is such a favorite with all the family, young and old, I might work up a tableau showing one of his early adventures. I thought," she spoke faster and faster, the idea seeming incredibly bold as she brought it out in words, "one of his nephews might impersonate him if we could borrow a uniform. Oh, do you think he'd be pleased? He wouldn't take offense, would he?"

"Why, he'd be flattered to death," Miss Amanda said promptly. "It's a charming idea, Varina." Then she added more doubtfully, "That is, if you stick to the purely military. What do you think, James?"

James did not say what he thought. There was a flash of pure malevolence in his eyes before he thought to hide it. He saw what Varina intended, if Miss Amanda did not.

"It might be well to ask Mr. Jefferson," he suggested.

Varina hated him for a second as much as he did her. Now, of course, she would have her way or die trying to get it.

"No," she said, backing up against Miss Amanda's support, "it won't mean a thing if it isn't a surprise."

"James," Miss Amanda said, "don't be absurd. The more I think of the idea, the more fun I think it will be. Jeff loves to be reminded that he was once a soldier. Brother Joe will be pleased and the children thrilled speechless. You have all his uniforms, I know, put away down there. You can send a complete outfit in a box."

"Yes'm, I could," James said, changing his mind about one thing, if not another. "If Miss Howell will specify what she prefers."

"A full dress army uniform with sword, sash and all," Varina said firmly. "And anything you please to go with it. An Indian war bonnet or something like that would help."

"Pack a box of stuff, I tell you," Miss Amanda said with authority. "You'll need to have it pretty promptly, won't you, Varina?"

"As soon as possible, please."

One more revelation of ill-will, then as sudden compliance.

"I'll send it over first thing tomorrow."

"And you won't breathe a word to Mr. Jefferson?"

"Not to anybody, Miss. Is that all, Miss Amanda?"

"Yes, thank you, James. Tell Maria I'll be down to see her one of these days, when the company's gone."

James Pemberton, then, was a broad back, slightly stooped, and a graying head moving toward the horse rack.

"That man," Miss Amanda said in exasperation under her breath, "is the most spoiled of all Jeff's people. He just about thinks he owns . . . Varina, I know I am as popular with him as a basket of snakes, but what on earth has he against you?"

By evening Varina was not feeling so pleased with herself. This play-party, with its tableaux, seemed a flimsy thing compared to the march of greater events.

"When it comes to accepting or declining your proffer of the Democratic candidacy in the imminent election of a representative from Warren County to the Legislature of the State of Mississippi, I think I should make myself clear on certain points. With regard to national issues, I adhere closely to the principles of government as laid down by the great leaders of the party, notably Thomas Jefferson and John Calhoun. I am opposed to a high protective tariff. I think the ideal thing would be free trade and worldwide, thus insuring a fair and natural exchange of imports and exports everywhere. . . .

"Miss Varina, this is what I'd call imposing on good nature. Surely you have something better to do with this hour."

"No, Mr. Davis, really I haven't."

"'Mr. Davis.' Am I the one member of the family toward whom you still feel so coldly formal?"

"What shall I say in place of Mr. Davis? 'Moss' Jeff'?"

"I like it better than the other. But I still think I am imposing on your kindness. If you had not proved yourself so able a scribe . . ."

"I wish I had paraded my abilities sooner. Please, go on."

It was pleasant, sitting in the dusty Hurricane office, writing from his dictation. There was a heady intimacy about the collaboration, Joseph having stepped outside to say good-bye to a departing caller while Jefferson composed his letter. The day being unseasonably warm, the latter stood near a window, his profile etched sharply against the light. It was very pleasant, if only he were aware of it.

"I believe in the annexation of Texas . . ."

Weary, weary—that she had ever longed to take part in politics!

"It is logically and historically and geographically an integral part of the nation. I do not believe that the Constitution of the United States gives the National Congress the right to interfere with the institution of slavery in the territories. I believe in every case that is a question to be decided by the economic necessities and consciences of the people resident in a locality. In short, I urge every state to defend jealously its guaranteed rights of local independence.

"So much for national issues. It is in purely local matters that I shall, no doubt, differ with many more established as leaders of the party. . . .

"Miss Varina, I warn you again. You are likely to be affected by our political heresies."

"How could I know that they were heresies, Mr. Jefferson? Politics is a subject in which I have had no education. Parrot-like, I have had to repeat the beliefs of those nearest and dearest to me."

"But that is what I mean. My beliefs are not likely to be those of the ones you call nearest and dearest. That is, I seem to remember your wearing the symbol of another party."

He remembered—there was a thing transcending all other issues.

"I am flattered that you noticed my silly ornaments, Mr. Jefferson. Please go on with the letter."

Because otherwise he might observe how excited she was over what might seem to him the merest trifle.

He went on for several paragraphs, which she wrote down mechanically; and then he stopped again. To cast her another crumb of comfort? No. his conscience was troubled, but solely on a point of politics.

"Miss Varina, you say you have not been educated in politics. As I make these high-sounding statements, I feel more and more the inadequacy of my own preparation. I think I should say something of that to this gentleman to whom we are addressing this letter. If you will indulge me, please . . .

"Sir, as you may perceive, I have mingled but little in active politics and have an arsenal poorly supplied for a campaign. Labour is expected of me and I am willing to render it. That is the most I can promise."

"Well, is the fateful epistle finished?" Joseph Davis asked from the door. "I've been out to the orchard. The peach blossoms are showing pink."

"We've composed a letter of a sort," Jefferson answered.

We, the word lay against Varina's anxious heart. When one has little to store, one must make much of that little.

"The peach blossoms pink?" Jefferson said.

"Yes, just. They are not too far along, I think, if the weather changes soon. Will you take your acceptance in person to Vicksburg, Jeff?"

Would he? How long would he be away? He turned to her, but with another question.

"What do you think?" he asked. "Will the letter be more or less potent if I present it in person?"

"Infinitely more potent," she said, "if that is what you wish."

"Ah, there's the point! If that is what I wish. I had almost rather stand guard over the peach blossoms."

CHAPTER IX

But he must have decided in the night against the peach blossoms, for in the morning he was gone and Varina walked—alone in spirit for all of Uncle Joe's now somewhat oppressive attentions, depressed, a victim of the melancholies—down the lines of trees, looking at the swelling, fuzzy buds with their precious glimpse of rose pink.

"Will they be nipped?" she asked.

"No," Joseph said. "My joints tell me that storm is on its way sure enough now. It will blow cold and we'll be safe enough until the next warm spell."

"I can't seem to think of you as having joints of that sort," Varina said.

"Can't you, my dear? Aunt Rhina and Uncle Rob can't do any better weather forecasting. If it were not for my joints and a few other things, I'd be riding where Jeff is riding now." Would he, sure enough? A man who liked to take his comfort? "I hope when the storm breaks that he will be close enough to reach home safely or far enough away to realize the folly of setting out."

And she committed to a tableau using his military gear and he not in the audience to witness the thing. What would those who did see, think?

"A Norther, do you suppose?" she asked, about the storm.

"Probably. Oh, we needn't run for the house just yet."

The sun was shining brightly. Frogs croaked in the marshes. The air was balmy, the wind light and uneasy. It blew up in little gusts, now from this direction, now from that. The horizon had a heavy, leaden look. They strolled back toward the house through the rose garden, where John O'Connor was cutting baskets of half-open buds.

"They'll blight when the rain comes," he explained, offering Varina a pink one. Would it be a Glory of France? She wouldn't ask.

When they were nearly to the house, Joseph excused himself and turned aside to the stables. If he was going to be shut up presently, he said, he should perhaps stir himself while he could. He invited Varina to ride with him, but she declined.

"Do ask me another day," she begged. "I see my maid on the gallery. She seems to be watching for me. She wants something, I am sure."

If Melissa had not been there, she would have found another excuse. Today of all days she would not have been able to hold the gait of any horse she mounted down to the easy amble of Old Speck. Once in the saddle, she would want to run. The uneasiness of the wind that didn't blow, as if it, too, were on a leash, fidgeted in her bones.

As it happened, Melissa was waiting for her.

"They's a box come from Brierfield," Melissa said. "Mr. James Pemberton, Mr. Jefferson's man, sent it."

"I was expecting it." Varina ignored the question behind Melissa's announcement. "Have it carried up to my room, Meliss'. Is it large?"

"Middlin'. It's a trunk like."

It might be better to seem to take Melissa into her confidence.

"Costumes for Saturday's charades. Sh!" she warned. "Have it taken upstairs and don't let anybody into it."

"It's got a padlock," Melissa informed her. "This yere's the key. Do you want I should keep the key for you?"

"No, indeed. Give it to me. Was there a message?"

"No'm." Melissa surrendered a small brass key. "Jes' the box an' Mr. Pemberton say it was fo' you, and this yere's the key."

The box, as Melissa had said, was a small trunk or chest, fashioned of rawhide over a wood frame, then reinforced by strips of hardwood, bound at the corners with more rawhide. It was not heavy. A house boy shouldered it and carried it up two flights of stairs without extraordinary panting.

"Well, I never!" Mary Bradford said when the boy set it down.

"No, you never; and you won't." Varina dangled the key before her, then put it away.

She made no move to open the box. She wouldn't, of course, while Mary was in the room.

She wouldn't right away when Mary had left, not even when she was sure that Melissa was the depth of the house away and she was quite alone. The arrival of the box had lifted her out of her melancholy mood. She was consumed with curiosity, but also a kind of awe. She studied the stout framework. She rubbed a finger over a scar on the wood, on the rawhide. Was it a trunk he—Jefferson—had made? It might be. Someone had said that up in the north woods, when the days were long and empty and a sawmill was handy, he had amused himself building furniture and the like. Some of the dark heavy pieces at Brierfield were of his fashioning.

What would she find inside the trunk? What would James Pemberton have sent, stiffly disapproving and unwilling?

It was evening before she set the small brass key into the padlock and turned it. Fun was at its height in the Annex. Mary Bradford was rehearsing her players in the music room. Varina's company had taken over the dining hall. She left them working out a pirate scene with young Joseph Davis in a costume plundered from Mrs. Eliza Davis's chests, while she went, she said, to look over some new stuff she had acquired. Young Joseph wanted to go with her, boots and all, to guard her through dark passageways and the darker the better; but she ordered him sternly to remain where he was—she would have special work for him later—and ran off.

The main house was deserted, except for a few of the older women, who sat with their sewing and their gossip in the small parlor, and for Joseph, again entertaining neighbors in his office. The stairs were dark and the halls; and the shadows in the large bedroom pressed close around Varina as she set a lighted candle on a table close by and knelt before the box. Her fingers did not fumble with the key. She was through with mooning and hesitating. She knew she would open the trunk some time. So she would do it now. This minute.

The key released the catch of the lock at once. Either fresh oil had been applied or the lock had never been allowed to rust. She drew the padlock out of the ring, laid back the hasp and raised the lid of the chest. A faint odor of old potpourri startled her. She did hesitate then, but shook aside her hesitancy and laid the lid back against the wall.

Old uniforms or Indian war bonnets are not laid away in dried rose leaves. Deep in the chest there might have been a coat with gold lace or a belt of wampum, but she did not penetrate that far. On top, as it happened, there was a piece of beadwork, but it was a lady's bag, for carrying a handkerchief, perhaps, and a mirror and other means of repair, in case one went out dancing where such things could be had only if one carried them. The bag was worked out in a design of flowers and drawn together with a gold cord, a little tarnished. It lay in the folds of a black silk cloak or mantle—a hooded cape, so far as Varina could see without unfolding it, which she never came near to doing. A cape with a hood and strings to tie under a fair, young chin. Beside the bag lay two slippers, made of what had been silver-gray satin, turned lavender with the years. Small, French kid gloves of the same shade had faded in the same manner. Both gloves and slippers had been worn.

Varina knew well whose garments these had been. She saw at a glance their significance. These bits of clothes might have been all a young girl's treasures of finery in the wilderness. They had been a girl's treasure and after that a man's. Rose petals, their color indistinguishable now, had been scattered over the bits of things when they were laid away. Only a loving woman or a man with a woman's tenderness of heart could have thought of doing that. A man with a touch of poetry in his loving—*A Ladies' Wreath*. Yes, and a man of everlasting devotion. Varina reached up blindly to lay hold of the trunk lid. It was the dry fragrance of roses she could not bear. It was the exquisite neatness and finality with which the mementoes had been laid away. It was the smallness of those gloves, those slippers, the rubbed spot across the toe of one as if a military boot had lost step on the dance floor. It had never been meant that she should see . . .

She brought the lid crashing down. A sob rose in her throat and stuck there. Blindly now she reached for the padlock, though her eyes were dry. She found it, slipped it into place and snapped it to, only to discover that she had not folded the hasp of the lock back into place.

"Ah!"

Exasperation made its way past the sob locked in her throat. Her movements were the fumbling of a person, racked with misery, who cannot let go and scream it out. Her teeth gritted over her pain as she unfastened the lock, freed it, then went through all the business of setting it correctly in place. She stood up, trembling. She took the candle from the table, but set it back. The dripping of the wax told her how her hand was shaking.

She shook with anger. Part of it was anger at the old servant, James Pemberton. His insolence, his presumption! How had he dared send her that chest? He would say it was a mistake. He had laid hold of the wrong trunk. There was another so much like this one that a person could hardly tell the difference.

He would tell her some such lie when she faced him with his insolence. He would speak softly, but he would be lying. He had made no mistake. He had sent her this chest with its sad, hateful contents for a purpose. What purpose? To tell her . . . what?

A thing she already knew. Most of her anger, then, was at herself for her own boldness—the willfulness that had exposed her to a servant's insolence. This end of things had been in preparation from the beginning. She had known the hopelessness of her quest from that day when she had turned red Sultan's head down the back lane to the Brierfield house and had first stood aghast before its stiff loneliness. She had known before that. In a garden path at Diamond Place, when this tall stranger had come around the hedge and had all but ridden her down, then apologized, still hardly seeing her. The signs had been there that day for anyone to read, but she would not heed them.

And now this.

She took up the candle again. The wax still spilled and again she set it down. She closed her eyes. A tear welled up in each, spilled over like the wax, and ran down her cheeks. She could feel the slow trickle. Poor Varina Howell! Poor Varina! The end had been in preparation from the very beginning, Granny Kempe would say. You take a girl, born headstrong and allowed to have her way about everything and determined to have her way, whether or no—horseback riding, tramping the woods and bayous with no proper feminine fear of snakes or other peril, wanting to lay her hand to anything she ever heard of anybody doing, just to say she could, cramming her head with learning as if she expected to take orders in the church or practice at the bar; you take a girl like that and let her reach the age when all girls, bright or dull, think of only one thing—marriage—and what could you expect? Not one man in a thousand would want such a girl for a wife. Men don't court women for their brains or their abilities. Not one in a thousand cares about such things.

Not one in a thousand, possibly. One man in ten thousand? Well, perhaps. How cruel, then, that their paths should cross when it was too late! What a life he and she might have shared had they met under other circumstance! They had so much to share. They could have known so much fun, so much richness of living. There was no telling to what they might not have risen together. Only, now it was too late.

Much, much too late. Where she was warm and reaching and wanting, there was only coldness on his side. All his loving, which she would have met so generously and fully and with such strength in the exchange, he had given to another. The ashes of his heart lay buried in a lonely grave in Louisiana. They were laid away in fading rose petals in a rawhide chest. They were locked away in an empty, lonely house. It was too late.

"It is too late. Let my master alone. He was all quiet before you came. Happy enough. Leave him to his quiet and to her. You . . . stranger!"

That was what James Pemberton meant to say. He had no right to say it; but someone would have said it if he had not, for there it was —the truth. Poor Varina Howell! Poor Sarah Knox Taylor and her *Ladies' Wreath*. Poor young, old Jefferson Davis!

Varina sighed. It was a fluttering sigh, but the sob in her throat subsided. She wiped the traces of tears from her eyes with her finger tips. She knew what she must do. She must finish with grace what she had so awkwardly brought about. She had no thought at the moment of sharing reproach with any other. The thing was of her doing, and she was contrite, and ashamed.

There was only one flaw in her repentance. There was one person to whom she could not, with dignity or pride, acknowledge her error of judgment. That was the servant, James Pemberton. If she sent the box back to Brierfield in the morning with no word, as it had come, James would understand that she had opened it and read the message of its pathetic contents. Then he would be the one who had set her straight about things. That she could not allow.

She would send the chest to Brierfield in the morning but she must ride over ahead of it, to say to James Pemberton before he could say it to her that he had made a mistake in the boxes. She must put him in the wrong, not permit him to impute wrong to her. She didn't know just what tone she would take with him, but she was sure instinct would tell her when the time came. It was not a good thing to do, or easy, to ride to Brierfield alone and bandy words with this too-privileged servant. It was the choice of two bad alternatives, but she was not Varina Anne Banks Howell if she could not carry it out successfully. She must do it that way.

So, that was settled. Why, then, did tears still pour down her cheeks? She knew. Overwrought, dismayed, defeated, she was not crying over Varina Howell. It was that other one. Poor Sarah Knox Taylor, who had held so briefly the happiness she had defied everyone to win! That was the potency of those things in the chest. As no words had ever done, they brought that girl, so long dead, alive.

Do not make yourself uneasy about me, dear mother. I am not afraid. . . .

But she would not weep for that girl. Given her choice, Varina Howell would have preferred three months of bliss to a lifetime of loneliness. Brushing at her tears again, she swallowed a final sob, turned her back on the chest and took up the candle. This time her hand was steadier. Still keeping her back to the trunk, and with her head high, she went out into the hall and down the stairs. On the first floor, young Joseph Davis waited, his face eloquent with devotion and pale with anxiety.

"Miss Varina," he said in relief, "in another minute I would have sent someone to make sure you were all right."

"I'm so sorry, and so disappointed," she sighed. "The things won't do—the things from Brierfield, I mean. I'll have to invent a tableau to take the place of that one."

He didn't know what she was talking about, but his sympathy was instant.

"You are disappointed," he said. "You are crying. Oh, Miss Varina, what can I do?"

"Nothing. That is—how silly of me to take it this way! You can help me think of something else."

She let him take the candle and guard her over the perilous passage to the Annex. Overhead the stars were shining, but dimly as through a curtain. The night was very warm.

As they opened the door into the dining hall, the burst of chatter made Varina wince; but she went on in bravely enough and the next minute was the center of the merriment. Her wits stood by her loyally all evening.

"Cousin V'rina, you're just wonderful. I wish I knew as much as you do. Nobody will ever guess. . . ."

"Sh! Small Lucy, you'll give it away sure."

Varina thought she was pretty wonderful. If a person invented and pretended and play-acted heartily enough, would there come a time finally when she wouldn't mind too much not having exactly what she wanted? Would something or someone else do? Young Joseph was sweet. How long would the process take? She felt as old as Miss Amanda right now—or almost.

In the middle of the night Mary Bradford shook Varina awake.

"Varina! Is that you moaning? What is the matter?"

Varina's hand went to the small brass key, which she had hung on a chain around her neck, when she undressed.

"As if I'd pry," Mary had sniffed.

"I didn't moan," Varina said now, pettishly. "It must have been the wind."

"There isn't a speck of wind. Everything is as still as still."

"Well, it wasn't me, I'm sure."

"Why, yes, dear, of course you can have the loan of a wagon. I'll get one of the older boys to drive, however—Thornton or Isaiah Montgomery. But, if it is only some more about those everlasting charades . . . must it be right off this morning?"

"There's only today and tomorrow," Varina said. "Miss Amanda, please, if it is possible?"

"To be sure it is possible. I was just thinking of the weather."

There was no sun this morning. The sky was gray and hung heavy and close to the land. From her bedroom window Varina had not been able to distinguish the river or its bars. The air was heavy, too, and still warm. The velvet riding costume was a burden.

"I can tell whoever goes," Miss Amanda said, frowning at the sky, "not to turn back if it has begun to rain or blow when he gets to Brierfield, but to stay right there."

Then she noticed Varina's dress.

"Riding this morning?" she asked. "Who's going with you?"

"Nobody. I don't feel exactly companionable. I've a sort of headache. Must I have someone?"

"Well, I'd prefer it. In view of the weather and all."

"I won't be long. I won't go far. I won't stir off the peninsula."

"My stars, the peninsula is four miles wide, straight across. Varina, are you sure you're not up to something?"

"I never felt less up to anything in my life, Miss Amanda. Please?"

Miss Amanda was deep in her household planning for the day.

"Well, see what Brother Joe says. He's in his office."

Reluctantly Varina turned back into the house. If Uncle Joe was in his office, all right. If he wasn't, she'd go right on out the back way and to the stables. Somehow, she hadn't counted on all this fuss.

Impulsively then, she turned again toward Miss Amanda and put out her hands in a plea for understanding. Miss Amanda, her mind on roasts and vegetables, hugged her warmly but absently.

"There!" she said. "There! Have it your own way, darling. Trot along. I'll not say another word."

"No, I'll ask Uncle Joe first," Varina insisted now.

But she didn't ask him. She didn't say a word to him about the ride. He wouldn't have heard. He, too, spoke of her costume, as he would have found something fine and flattering to say if she had appeared in sacking. He didn't really see her, being too entirely pleased with himself this morning.

"Come in, come in!" he said to her knock. "Oh! Varina! Lovely creature—just the one I wanted to see. I was about to send for you. Here's a thing you'll want to read. General Quitman brought it from Vicksburg with him yesterday evening. I think he took it off the press wet and dried it as he rode. Very thoughtful of him. Sit down, my dear. It's quite a piece."

The newspaper was the Vicksburg *Sentinel*. The passage that had put a haze over Joseph Davis's outlook was a marked editorial on page one.

"Elsewhere in this paper will be found the proceedings of the Democratic Convention, which met yesterday for the purpose of selecting a candidate to represent the city and county. It will be seen that JEFFERSON DAVIS, Esq., received the unanimous nomination of the party, a gentleman, who, should he be elected, will do honour to himself and his constituents. Mr. Davis is a sterling Democrat, a man of unsullied private character, talents of a superior order, extensive political information, and, judging from the structure of his remarks before the convention this morning, accepting the nomination, a fine public speaker. There may be some in the country to whom Mr. Davis, from the secluded privacy in which he has lived, is unknown. To those we repeat, Mr. Davis is what we have stated, *a man, every inch a man,* of whom Old Warren should be proud."

"And will be proud," Joseph said, wiping his eyes, but still not seeing clearly. "People will know him now. My dear, I hope you are pleased at your share in bringing this proud moment into being."

Whatever did he mean? Oh—helping Mr. Jefferson write his letter accepting the nomination. Uncle Joe was so expansively happy that he was willing to give generous credit to anyone just in on the surprise event. Varina returned to the editorial.

"Let us rally now around the man of our choice and the victory is ours. Let every Democrat walk up to the polls on election day and cast his vote . . ."

She looked at the date line on the paper.

"Why," she said, "this was ready to print before Mr. Jefferson arrived in Vicksburg yesterday. How did they know he would accept the nomination? Suppose he had said no?"

"Ah, but he did not, my dear. We—everyone thought his acceptance was more probable. A short while back, when the proposition was first put to him, he was not inclined to look on it favorably. Since then his views have changed."

Varina's head really began to throb.

"Do you think he will be elected?" she asked.

"My dear, you sound as if you hoped he would not."

"I don't believe he will get along very well with regular politicians," Varina murmured. "He seems to me too high-minded, too scholarly, too different. It's very hard to say."

"I know exactly what you would say, dear. You know him better than I realized. His thoughts and principles are on a lofty plane. That in itself lifts him above the common run and makes him a leader. And he has other qualifications, you will find—among them, devotion to principle. So, granted that he may lose this contest, his entry being an eleventh hour affair, the important result is inevitable. Men outside will have their first glimpse of the qualities you and I, and a very few others, know he possesses—qualities that make him a born leader for a cause that needs men gifted, as he is, with insight, devotion, and persuasive eloquence."

To Varina's numbed sensibilities Uncle Joe's effusions seemed pure sophistry. She put a hand to her now honestly aching head.

"But I'll not keep you, dear child," Joseph said. "I see you are prepared for an outing. It does seem close indoors."

That was all the heed he gave at the moment to the storm gathering in the sky. Varina mentioned to him neither the propriety nor safety of her contemplated ride.

Outside, the Hurricane wagonette was drawn up near the rear gallery. Betsy, the young maid-in-training, looked from it to Varina in mild inquiry. Rhina Number Two stood on her kitchen porch. Varina took off her plumed hat and handed it to the maid.

"It presses on my forehead," she complained. "Carry it upstairs for me, will you, Betsy? There's no sun and I'm only going for a short ride."

"You got a headache, Miss Varina?" the maid guessed. "I'll git you some headache vinegar."

"Don't bother. I have smelling salts in my bag," Varina fibbed. Melissa had some, no doubt, along with her witch hazel and other curatives; but Varina so far had seen the pretty elegancy only in hands older and more delicate than her own.

"Miss Melissa's upstairs," Betsy volunteered further, with a pout. "She sent me down yere."

Miss Melissa, Mr. Pemberton, Rhina Number Two, this wall-eyed young thing—what a hierarchy of supervision it all amounted to!

"For pity's sake, don't bother Melissa," Varina said, gathered up her long skirt, and hurried off to the stables.

Isaiah Montgomery would be taking the chest over to Brierfield. His brother, Thornton, met Varina at the stable door. To her request for Glory, the filly, he offered respectful excuse. Glory had a trace of lameness in her off foreleg. Mr. Jefferson had seen to the bandaging before he set out and wouldn't want her ridden until he came back, it was likely. Was there some other horse?

"I'll take Sultan, Miss Mary's horse," Varina said instantly; and, when Thornton racked his brain visibly for further obstacles, added, "Don't fuss about that now. I've ridden him. I know him. Gracious, I want to be back before dinner and at this rate I won't even get off."

Thornton moved away at once; but, of course, it took time to saddle the big chestnut. Varina heard the wheels of the wagonette rolling down the road. But that was all right. With all these eyes watching, she had no intention of setting out directly for Brierfield. She could take in several crossroads in a random pattern and bring up on the one she wanted ahead of the wagon, although Isaiah seemed to be starting off at a good gait.

"It's fixing to storm," Thornton said in final, cautious warning.

"I'll keep a weather eye open," Varina promised.

One thing happened now in her favor. Sultan accepted her as a rider with remarkable passivity.

"Good boy, good boy!" Out of earshot of the stables and, she hoped, fairly out of sight, Varina patted the colt's shoulder. "I need your help, Sultan. I need somebody's."

She set off down the main road toward the Quitman and Turner plantations and the isthmus; but, less than a mile farther along, discovering a lane between cleared fields which promised to lead back obliquely in the direction she desired, she turned Sultan into it. His passivity was more like stubbornness then, but presently he was pacing smoothly at a fair rate according to her hand's directing.

"Good boy!" she said again.

Just the same, perspiration started on her nose and upper lip. Sultan, too, showed some sweat, though she held him to an easy jog. She did not dare give him his head. She did not want him to break into a lather unnecessarily; and, in case the lane proved a blind lead, there was no telling where his stubbornness might carry them both. She was beginning to fear that the lane, which showed signs now of merging into wild land, really went nowhere in particular, when suddenly the road to Brierfield cut across it.

"Thank you, God," she whispered prayerfully and fervently. "Oh, thank you!"

Likely it was His help she needed most, though why He should bother to give it to her, neither she nor anyone else could have said.

"Willful," some cold, rebuking voice echoed inside her. "Pure, natural willfulness is what it is, Varina Howell. You just start for something and it seems like nothing will stop you."

She went on. She was on the main Brierfield road. She was pretty sure that the wagon was behind her. She would gain on it rapidly now. She would finish her business with James Pemberton and be gone down the lower road before it appeared.

But would she? The sky was more lowering by the minute. At least, it appeared that way as the canebrake closed around her, so that she had no wide view of the cloud masses. The light lessened steadily. When she entered the grove of oaks, the darkness was weird.

"Get along!" she said to Sultan. "It's only a small piece now. And we'll run all the way home."

A noise like thunder muttered in the distance. Thunder in January? It was not unheard of, though unusual, even ominous. There was a saying . . . no, that was about thunder in February. "Thunder in February, frost the same day in April." Perhaps it wasn't thunder, after all, though she knew it was. It had become an angry, fairly continuous growl as they emerged from the trees and the house of Brierfield appeared. James Pemberton hurried out of the door and down the steps. Was he wringing his hands or did she think of him afterward as doing that?

"Miss Varina," he said in tones of real anxiety. "Oh, Miss Varina!"

So, he hadn't rested well, either, during the night.

"Good morning, James," she said, and the thunder rumbled. "No, I can't stop. I just came to say that the chest you sent to Hurricane yesterday . . ." thunder stole her words for a long instant, "Isaiah Montgomery is bringing it in the wagon."

"Now? Oh, Miss Varina . . ."

"He's right behind me. He'll be here any minute."

"Miss Varina, I made a terrible mistake."

"No, James, I don't think you did." She was steadier now. "I think you sent those things to Hurricane on purpose."

"Miss Varina, I had no right."

"No," she said coldly, "you had no right, but you did. You wanted

me to know about her, didn't you? She was everything to Mr. Jefferson while she lived. Wasn't she?"

"Yes'm, she was, but . . ."

"She even took your place with him or threatened to. Then she died.
That left him yours again, all yours, to care for. You've taken very
good care of him, James—exceedingly good care. Be sure you do so
always. I don't know how he would manage without you. Oh! Here
is the key to the chest. I came over to bring it to you. And to say
good-bye. Good-bye, James."

"Miss Varina, you are going away?"

"Yes. As soon as a way of travel can be provided."

There was a crackle of lightning now along with the strange, unseasonable thunder.

"Miss Varina, you'd best 'light and wait out the storm."

"No, I can't do that. We'll run for it, Sultan and I. We'll make it."

"Miss Varina, Mr. Jefferson won't like it a bit . . ."

"Mr. Jefferson needn't know. Good-bye."

"Miss Varina . . ."

"Good-bye!" she called again.

As she turned Sultan and started him down the back road, out of
the tail of her eye she saw James running after her, surely enough
wringing his hands.

"Miss Varina, not that way . . ." she thought he called, but she didn't
stop to make sure. As she entered the grove of trees on the low road,
the horses and wagon from Hurricane emerged on the high one.

The first large drop of water splashed on her face a minute later.
Still she thought, with Sultan's strength and speed, she would reach
Hurricane before the storm broke in its full fury. The whole distance,
regardless of terrain and the road's meanderings, could not be much
over four or five miles. She would trot Sultan soberly until she had
forded the two sloughs, then give him his head and let him run for it.

This was a tale she made up for herself later, and told herself re-
peatedly, as if repetition would make her cause more just. She had
no real intention of trying to reach Hurricane. She was beside herself
with warring emotions. Renunciation was a thing so foreign to her
nature that she could not give it physical expression except in flight.
That had been in her mind when she had chosen Sultan back at the
Hurricane stables. She would give him his head, let him run and she

didn't care where the run ended, so that he ran hard and fast and far
—away from Brierfield, away from Hurricane, and most of all from
herself.

What she failed to reckon on was the swift approach of the storm.
The horse sensed it. She had trouble urging him forward. He was all
for turning back to the shelter of Brierfield. That was the one way
Varina would not turn. All the while the storm was drawing nearer.
Sound was now a mingling of thunder, wind and rain, a dull roaring.
The trees, she thought, multiplied and magnified it.

"Hurry, Sultan. We must get out from under the trees, if we're to
have lightning. Hurry!"

Madness did not include self-destruction—at least, not by lightning,
a horrid, searing death. Where was that slough? She couldn't have
taken the wrong road. There was only one in this direction. Then
she saw water ahead and breathed more easily. Sultan did not share
her pleasure. He stopped at the water's edge. He threw up his head
and snorted uneasily. Varina leaned over, picked up her long skirt
by the hem, and turned it back wrong side to above her knee, then
with a grim set to her lips, touched the horse lightly with her crop.

"Go on, Sultan, go on!" she urged.

Still snorting his unwillingness, Sultan forded the shallow ditch.
Relieved by so much, Varina thought again that the storm was still
more noise than anything else. The rain was only a spattering of big,
hard drops. She almost dropped her skirt, then thought that, as long
as she had it bunched up, she might as well keep it that way unless
she met somebody.

Sultan's reluctance to advance continued. By keeping at him constantly she persuaded him to a half-hearted jog. What in the world
ailed the brute? Never before had she felt so completely at a horse's
mercy.

And then it came. A streak of lightning, fearful to see, tore the sky
apart from end to end. Thunder crashed and the rain came down in
a torrent. If some power had picked up the Mississippi and turned
it upside down on the world the water could not have fallen in greater
concentration. The force of it all but threw Varina from the saddle.
It frightened the wits out of Sultan. He gave a peculiar, screeching
whinny, turned halfway around and bolted.

"Sultan!" Varina screamed and held the reins tight, but to no effect.

Sultan was taking direction from some other power than the bit in his mouth. A minute later Varina's gloves were pulp, and she felt the leather reins slipping. The horse plunged wildly on. She had no idea in what direction or toward what goal and was sure he had no idea, either. He was just running. He must have taken a course parallel to the sloughs because they plunged into no water. None, that is, except that which presently splashed up from the rapidly sodden ground.

Long before the wild run ended, Varina's impulse toward flight had given way before pure terror. Finally she could stand it no longer. She ripped one of her gloves off with her teeth and took a desperate hold with her bare hand on the reins. The leather oozed water. To tighten her grip, she wrapped it around her fingers. It cut, but she felt tension at last. So did Sultan, though his response might have been due to exhaustion. He slowed to a trot, to a walk. He stumbled and stood still.

"Oh, Sultan!" Varina sighed.

If he should fall, where would she be? Where was she now? The rain came down relentlessly. It made furrows and runlets down Sultan's shoulders and flanks. Her velvet looked like a piece of carpeting left out in the weather. Water ran out of the mass of her hair down her back, down inside the ruined ruching of her neckband. She thought of the plumed hat safe at Hurricane and laughed.

But not with joy. The vision of the hat was ludicrous but it did not better her present circumstance. She must not sit where she was and turn silly now. She must do something. When Sultan stopped heaving, she must try to get him back to the road. Which way would that be? She turned in the saddle to look over the way she and Sultan had come. She closed her eyes, bowed her head, and turned back.

She was in the center of trackless desolation. The rain had bent the tall cane halfway to the ground in windrows and hummocks without any plan or significant opening. Sultan had found a way through, but she had no idea how. She doubted that she could force him to retrace his course. She questioned whether it would be wise to try.

"We're lost," she thought. "We can't be more than a few miles from some place, but we're lost. We'll just sit here and drown, that's all."

But maybe not. Maybe the rain would lessen. At intervals the downpour seemed less violent, although it never stopped altogether. Sultan was not heaving as he had for a while, but he stood with bent neck and head turned—a wretched animal for one who could look so proud. Varina noticed the bunch of skirt in her hands and, thinking she had an inspiration, spread it quickly and flung it over her head. There was material enough to do that without exposing her body any more than it was already exposed. The makeshift shelter threatened to smother her and was heavy, but it did shut out the storm a little. If she could only help Sultan!

She couldn't, and was only a trifle less miserable than he. Her arms wearied of holding out the breadth of skirt. She dropped them and the velvet fell clammily over her face and around her neck. She threw it back angrily and the sky sent down a fresh deluge. She drew it up again and caught it together under her chin, holding it with alternate hands. When the fresh deluge was over, the world looked like a wide pond, with reeds and rushes and drowned trees standing up above the waters. Sultan shivered and blew his breath with an unhappy snort.

Varina's lips moved in soundless, wordless prayer. She couldn't imagine from what source or what direction help could come. How would anyone know where to find her? How could anyone look for her if the storm never abated?

"We'll die," she thought, despair taking hold again. "We'll just die right here."

Her head drooped pitifully. She shook herself in anger and flung it up again. She wouldn't lie down and die until she had to. This was her young vitality refusing to accept the inevitable or what looked to be inevitable. She held her head erect, her back straight, until that effort, too, exhausted her and she swayed suddenly in the saddle.

Fright brought her back sharply to consciousness. That would not do. She must not pitch off Sultan's back. He stood fetlock deep in mud and water, but his four legs held him and her above the slime. She must find a more restful way to sit. The rain must stop some time. It always did—finally. She sighed, and tried to shift her cramped hips, to ease her seat. Sultan raised his head and looked at her inquiringly.

"Poor Sultan!" she said gently. "Poor boy! I've got you into trouble sure enough, haven't I?"

She had no idea how long they cowered miserably under the lashing of the rain. It was probably not as long as it seemed, but that was near to eternity. She had no idea why Sultan had chosen this direction for bolting, if he had done any choosing, or why he had halted where he did except from exhaustion and in response to her frenzied pulling. He moved restlessly now for the first time, half-turned, drew a forefoot up out of the muck, made a half-hearted motion of pawing the ground, found there was none to paw, of course, then lifted his other feet in sequence and took a step forward, but cautiously. His head came up to stay. His sensitive ears pricked forward.

Why, the rain had stopped! Or nearly. Varina stretched her tired back. Her head and shoulders seemed a real weight. Naturally. The long riding skirt was almost saturated. She shook her head out of the clammy folds, but took care not to drop the improvised cape altogether for fear that she might not be able to draw it up again, and once more looked around.

Now that the rain had drawn off, she could see better. Sultan had followed instincts not entirely blind. He had run wildly but over ground that rose a little. Already hummocks of coarse wild grass were shaping up in pools of water and the pools were gathering into streamlets that flowed past them and away. A few paces farther on a sparse growth of willows grew up in a patch of brambles. They couldn't have entered it without a path being hacked out. It was no sort of breastwork for her, but perhaps it looked like something of a wall to the horse. He seemed to want to edge closer to it.

"Good boy!" Varina said, letting him have his way, without contrary pull. "Good boy, Sultan."

A current of air pushed suddenly at her cold wetness. She gasped and shivered and could hardly keep her voice steady. She started to lift the tiresome cape over her head again, then stopped to listen.

It was wind. She could hear, still in the distance, a kind of moaning.

It was wind. No two storms probably ever broke exactly in the same pattern. Usually, if there was to be wind, it came first in angry blasts or twists and the rain was behind it. This time the unseasonable warmth, the long brooding, which everyone had said presaged a storm, had broken first with rain. Rain and the phenomenon of midwinter thunder and lightning. Now that she gave the matter thought, she recalled that there had been no thunder since that awful crack which had set Sultan flying. Just torrents of rain, and now the wind would strike.

She tipped her head back to look at the sky. The solid darkness of rain clouds, the melting wet grayness of rain released, had changed to a curtain the color of slate overhead, merging, however, at the edges into an ominous smoky green. Rags and ravelings of clouds, like leakage from a cotton wagon, scurried across the curtain racing like mad to get away from the wind at their back.

A high wind. Not a twister. Not a cyclone. Not just here, at any rate. It might swoop down at any time, at any place farther on; but here it rode high—for the present. But it was wind and plenty of it. That was the moaning in the trees.

With her resources of reason and courage nearly gone, Varina fought against new terror. She must not be frightened. She and Sultan had come through the deluge safely enough. She must pretend to the horse that she was not afraid, that she was sure everything still would be all right.

"Good boy! Good boy, Sultan." She could muster, without shaking too much, the simple, habitual syllables as she urged Sultan closer to the bramble thicket.

But Sultan was not satisfied even there. He still made futile, pawing motions and his ears remained on the alert. He heard something that she did not.

When she did hear, she wouldn't believe. What sounded like a faint, far-off "Hal-loa!" could just be a variation of the wind's moaning.

But the sound came again. It was someone calling. In all the fury of the storm, people had set out in search of her. Probably from Hurricane and Brierfield, too. Neither household would take her safety for granted. There was no telling how many people had made her peril theirs, trying to find her.

But this was no time to think of that. She could repent later and would, she promised generally. Now she must make those who were nearest to her of the searchers hear her answer, if she could.

She tried; but the feeble, whimpering sound she made, as compared to the hail she meant to send out, revealed her exhaustion. Nobody would ever hear that. She tried again and made no sound at all. She had heard of people losing their voices in extremities of emotion, but she had never quite believed in such stupid paralysis. She would not believe it now. She would not have it. She swallowed several times fighting for calm and strength, and was about to try again; but Sultan forestalled her.

He raised his head and neighed with an abandon and a volume that must have carried from one end of the peninsula to the other. No inhibitions of emotion there, just pure need and rapturous welcome. A distinct whinny was his answer, then a hail that was nearer, followed by a vibrating call that Varina recognized.

It was that imitation of an Indian woods call familiar to all children who had ever played at being savages, made by opening one's mouth on sound and clapping the palm over the mouth to make the sound carry. It was easier than bursting one's lungs and always effective. She tried it now and laughed aloud at her success.

Sultan neighed again. The other horse whinnied in answer. There was further exchange of hails, ending finally in a triumphant, screeching war cry. Those fine, high-spirited young men, of Davis name and blood! Those blessed boys!

At long last she heard hoofs splashing. Surely there was more than one horse. Yes, of course. Those well-brought-up young men would know enough not to ride out into the storm alone. Only a silly girl, thinking of pride or such matters, tormented with sorrow and loss, would be so foolish and headstrong.

"Va-ree-na!"

They called her by name now. No cousin or Miss or other title.

"Here!" she called back, tugging at her skirt. How far must she drop it for modesty? The wind pushed and pushed at her. It cut through her wet bodice, her stays, her ribs. "Here we are!" Her teeth chattered. "Yeo-hoo! Here!"

"Stay where you are! Don't move!"

It was a command, sharp and incisive as the wind. It seemed to order the storm. Then he rode around the mass of brambles—he himself, Moss' Jeff, Mr. Jefferson. Varina could have died of shame. She was near as that to perishing of rapture. Not knowing which end to choose, for once in her life, if never again, she sat humbly still, docile as a new lamb.

He rode the big gray—Medley. As near an iron horse as there was in the stable. He had pulled his dark hat down over his head. A caped coat reached to his boots. Before him, across the saddle, was strapped a roll—a cape coat for her and a blanket wrapped in tenting canvas. He hadn't known how he would find her, just that he would, if it took him forever.

"Varina! My . . . poor girl!"

Varina could only stare at him and shake her head.

He loosened the straps that held the roll. He rode up beside her and laid the cape coat around her shoulders.

"I'm all wet," Varina said weakly. "I used my skirt for a tent."

"Hush!" he soothed. "This will keep the wind out until we reach the house. Girl, your hands are ice!"

"I lost my gloves. They got wet. I couldn't hold Sultan."

"Hush! I know."

He rubbed her hands between his. He slapped them, to restore circulation. From being numb, they tingled. She felt warmer through and through.

"If I could think how to wrap them," he said. "Whoa, Medley! Whoa!"

"Take my gloves, Jeff, please. I had an extra pair in my pockets. They are dry."

This was young Joseph Davis, riding the big, pale Comanche horse.

"Oh, Miss Varina, I am thankful," he said, as he gave Jefferson the gloves.

The gloves were large, clumsy, but warm from his hands.

"Are you all right, Varina?" Jefferson asked. "Can you ride now? You're sure?"

"I'm fine," Varina said. Why did her teeth still knock together?

"Brave girl! I'll fasten a lead strap to Sultan, then, so that you can have the reins to steady you. Joe . . ."

"Yes, sir?"

"I'll lead on—with Miss Varina. Drop back, but don't lose sight of us. When you're far enough behind, not to frighten Sultan, fire three shots, as we arranged, to tell the others."

In spite of her sodden misery—the more wraps that were piled on outside, the wetter she was below them—and through her hysterical relief at being rescued—she would be hysterical if she let herself go at all—Varina thrilled again to the clear, not-to-be-questioned tone of command. In all her life she had never heard anyone speak just so. She was included in the orders. Her obedience, too, was taken for granted. With good reason. She had no thought of refusing it.

"Yes, sir," young Joseph said crisply.

He drew an army revolver out from under the protection of his coat and held it ready as Jefferson and Varina rode past him. His eyes were hungry on Varina as if she were the most beautiful and precious creature in the world instead of a miserable drowned thing in grotesque wrappings. Jefferson added the blanket to the caped coat when he realized that her head was bare and her hair wetter than Sultan's mane. He folded it squaw-fashion and laid it over her head and pinned it under chin; and she looked like the old Witch of Endor, she was sure, but had neither the wish nor the will to oppose the quick, sure movements of his hands. Young Joe looked at her hungrily and with a strange, prescient melancholy as she rode by ignominiously on the end of a lead strap; and she saw, rather than heard the despair with which he sighed her name:

"Varina . . . oh, Varina!"

Muffled by the folds of the blanket, she heard presently the three signal shots and rather looked for Joe to join her and Jefferson then, but he chose to lag behind.

They must have made a strange picture, the three of them, picking their way across the gray waste. All the land was waste land now, all sodden wet, and still racked by the wind. She could not say that she felt the wind, wrapped against it, as she was; but she saw things bend before it and shrink from it. Jefferson lowered his head to the storm as he turned to speak to her.

"We must go as fast as we can," he said; but the firmness went in part out of his words as he realized Sultan's stumbling weariness.

He turned back to the business of holding his big gray to a pace that Sultan could follow and that was the last word he said the whole way to Hurricane. Varina saw that he and the gray were holding Sultan on his feet and tried to do what she could to help them. She would have liked to relieve the horse of the burden of carrying her; but, if there had been another for her to ride, she could not have dismounted to make the change. A dozen sloughs now ran between the cane of Brierfield and the Hurricane clearing. When they reached the home yard finally, everything was puddles and litter. Men and boys were coming in from looking for her. They dismounted at the gallery steps and stable boys rode off with strings of horses. Sultan carried her to the gallery, too.

Everybody seemed to be gathered there to receive her. She shrank from their greeting. What would they say to her? What could they say?

There was a minute of silence. Then someone led off with a cheer. Everybody talked at once, laughing, shouting, cheering. Strong hands reached up to help her from the saddle. Strong arms held her on her feet. Whose hands, whose arms, she couldn't say; but it was Joseph Davis, white-faced, who unpinned the grotesque blanket. Miss Amanda called from the house door.

"Bring her inside, you idiots. Out of that freezing wind!"

In the hall, halfway up the first flight of steps, Melissa stood, clasping and unclasping her hands, her face gone eighty years old in a few hours.

If just anybody had said a single word of the reproach that everyone must have felt! But nobody did. Instead, everybody seemed determined to conceal true feeling by extraordinary acts of kindness. Even young Joseph's mother, who had spent the hours while her son was out in the storm in terrorized prayer, brought Varina a herb pillow to coax up sleep.

"You want to sleep and sleep, darling!" she said, wan-faced, "and forget all about it, if you can. My, what you must have been through!"

In the end, however, Varina was Melissa's baby. Even Melissa didn't scold, except right at first. The hat with the blue plumes was lying out on the bed when Varina reached the third floor room. It was so lovely and untouched, exactly as Varina had pictured it, that she laughed and laughed.

"You stop that now!" Melissa said. "You stop that right this minute."

And then she went to work. She stripped off Varina's boots and wet clothing. She bathed her and rubbed her and lotioned her. She wrapped her in blankets and comforters and steamed her above a hot foot bath. She shook out Varina's hair and dried it, then brushed powdered orris root through it until it was sweet as a spring meadow, then brushed it again until it shone, and braided it. She put Varina to bed under every coverlet in the house that could be spared and poured down her everything hot that came up from the kitchen.

"I'll burst," Varina said. "I'll just burst—like a steamboat boiler."

"You ain' goin' to take a chill if I kin help it," Melissa told her.

A chill?

"If you'll take off just one comforter," Varina begged.

At last, she did go to sleep, for one reason or another, and knew nothing for several hours. She awoke feeling that she had put in a day and a night. She still felt a little boiled, but rested and very hungry. After all, many glasses of hot liquid are not food; and she had missed her dinner.

She sat up in bed and looked around. It was daylight. Not very good daylight, but still not the dark of night. The room had been set to rights. At first Varina thought it was empty except for herself; but then she saw Melissa rolled in the covers that she had tossed off to the floor, sleeping out another sort of exhaustion.

Varina thought, "I'll not wake her. I'll just get up and dress myself."

But she couldn't help laughing at the way Melissa looked, rolled up in the luxurious, surplus coverings; and Melissa awoke, after all. She sat up, rubbed her eyes and shook herself, then slowly crawled out of her nest and came to the bed, smoothing her skirt and her apron.

"How you feel now?" she asked.

"I feel all right," Varina said. "What time is it? Do you know?"

Melissa went over to a window and looked out.

"It's still daytime," she said. "It's raining again."

"Where is everybody?" Varina asked then.

"Restin'," Melissa said eloquently. "Just restin'."

"I'm hungry. I hope I haven't missed supper."

Melissa just looked at her.

"I'll get you a bite o' somethin'," she offered.

"A bite won't do. I'd better dress and go downstairs myself."

Melissa came back to her real character.

"You stay right there in that bed," she ordered. "How you think it's goin' to look—ev'ybody come tippy-toe up here, askin', 'How is she, Melissa? Ought we to try to get a doctor from the mainland?' An' you want to git up and dress and go downstairs! You ain' goin' to do it. They come clear from the Quitman and Turner places, thu the water an' storm, askin'. I don' know how they heard, but they did."

"Oh, Melissa, they didn't!"

"They did, too."

"Melissa, I'm sorry. I'm sorry I've disgraced you so!"

Melissa came back to the bed. She laid a hand on Varina's forehead, then her wrists.

"You don' feel like you got a fever, but you soun' like it," she said.

"I haven't any fever. Of course not. I just want to get up. I'm hungry and . . . Melissa, we'll have to go home now. Right away."

"Yes, baby, jes' as soon as we kin ketch a boat."

"Melissa, don't talk to me as if I were out of my head now. I'm hungry. I want to get up and dress. I want . . . I must see Uncle Joe and maybe Mr. Jefferson and Miss Amanda, and make my excuses."

"They restin' in their beds, ev'yone o' them, like you ought to."

"Well, I won't disturb them. I'll just dress and sit somewhere and wait until I can see them. I won't rest tonight if I don't see them."

Melissa was beside herself; but Varina was by now out of bed, tearing things to pieces, looking for her clothes. She meant what she said when she declared that she would not be able to rest, once her first exhaustion had been relieved, until she had lifted a load from her conscience. This was not willfulness. The load was real, a ponderable weight. From time to time as she dressed, she put a hand to her breast to ease the pressure.

But she dressed quickly. The room was chilly. She made no objection to a flannel petticoat under starched muslin and swiss embroidery. The skirt of the rose-colored merino accommodated all. Rain beat against the windows, lashed by the wind.

"It's fixin' to go on all night," Melissa said. "Nobody knows what'll come of it."

Varina listened to the dreary sound and beat down an involuntary and reminiscent shiver.

"Where is Mary Bradford?" she asked now. "Where are the children?"

"Their mammas took them in, so's you could rest better," Melissa said with plain sarcasm. "Will you have yore hair high or low, Madame?"

"Low," Varina said patiently. "It's not so heavy that way."

Melissa brushed it, smelled it, sprinkled cologne on the brush and dressed it.

"I'll say this," she concluded, "you look pale fo' yoreself and you got dark places under yore eyes that kinda save a person's pride. Where will you set, to wait on the ladies and gentlemen? In the pa'lor? They got fires goin' ev'ywhere against the cold and the wet."

"In the annex, too?"

"Upstairs an' down," Melissa said. "Mr. Davis, Mr. Joseph, that is, give orders that way. The gen'men that did the huntin' fo' you met with him there and took a bite to eat an' somethin' to drink an' their orders befo' they set out. The chil'ren was upstairs. Miss Mary an' Miss Floss take care o' them. Then, when word came you'd been foun' and was safe, Mr. Davis said to keep a bowl o' toddy ready and all the fires goin' for suppertime an' the usual social hour this evenin'—which I don' think anybody in this house is goin' to feel ve'y sociable tonight. Except maybe Mr. Joseph himself, who feels good about you bein' all right an' the storm bein' only rain and wind and not another hurricane."

"Yes." Varina sighed. She recalled Uncle Joe's white face when she had been set down on the Hurricane gallery. He had endured his own torment while she remained lost. If she had suffered any mishap, he could never have made atonement to her people. But Fortune had smiled on him again. She was back, safe and sound and—yes, he would be feeling very fine this evening, expansive, congratulatory. . . . She hoped she would not have to make her first explanations to him, though it would be hardly less difficult to explain to the others.

Dear Lord, what would she say to Jefferson Davis, if he asked to know?

"I think," she said, "I'll rest in the music room instead of the parlor. It will be more secluded there."

"You'll be jes' as lonesome one place as the other," Melissa assured her. "The ladies won't hardly gather today."

"They'll gather," Varina prophesied, "if they hear I am up and about. So, don't tell them, Meliss', if they inquire. Just say I'm doing all right and will be down to supper. It's just Uncle Joe or Mr. Jefferson or Miss 'Manda. I want to see them before I talk to the others. Um-m-m, a shawl feels good."

Out in the hall, at the head of the long stairway, she reached quickly for the balustrade, then, feeling Melissa's eyes boring into her, stiffened her back. She descended slowly, steadying herself at each step, her starched skirts whispering around her; but that was noise enough in the sleeping emptiness. At the foot of the stairs, Solomon, the major-domo, lolled wearily, slumped in a mahogany and damask chair. He awoke with a start and stumbled to his feet, eyes popping.

"Miss Varina," he said hoarsely, "is it you?"

"Sh!" Varina warned him. "Don't wake people. Melissa says the fires have been kept up in the Annex."

"Yes'm. You wish to go over there? I'll be pleased to light you."

The passage was dark, with every opening boarded over, but chilly and damp, from a seepage of water-soaked air. Varina drew her shawl tightly around her. She had not remembered that the distance between the buildings was so great, that there were so many steps to the second floor of the Annex.

But the fire in the music room burned brightly. A boy who had been set to watch it left at their coming, to fetch another log. The curtains had been drawn across the windows, shutting out the storm, except for an occasional noisy drive of sleet. A few candles burned in their sconces at the warm end of the room.

"Shall I light up fo' you, Young Miss?" Solomon offered.

"No, this is light aplenty." Varina let herself down at last on a cushioned chair. Solomon placed a stool for her feet.

"Kin I fetch you a glass of wine, Young Miss?"

"Thank you, Solomon. Melissa will get me anything I need. Go back to the house now, in case you are wanted there."

"Yes'm. Young Miss, ol' Solomon is mighty happy you didn't take mo' harm than you did from yore ride."

"Thank you, Solomon. I got off very lightly, I think. I hope everyone else fares as well."

"I pray the Lawd they does so, Young Miss."

But he wasn't at all sure that they would. Naturally not. Only the Lord knew how many people had been soaked to the skin and chilled to the bone this day, to save her worthless life. The Lord probably took count of them all, but she could pray earnestly only over one.

"Melissa, do you think you could find me a bit of something strengthening now?"

"Will you promise to set right here and not stir till I come back?"

"Melissa, don't be so troublesome. I couldn't move if I wanted to . . . and I don't want to."

"*Can't* lasts longer with you than *don' want*," Melissa said, and went off in search of food.

Varina sighed and leaned her head back against the tufted upholstery of the chair. The warmth of the fire stole across her insteps and ankles and rose comfortingly through her bones. She might have dozed off. She was aroused by a knocking at the door. She thought it would be the boy with the wood or Melissa, though why should the latter knock?

"Come in!" she called, without turning her head.

The door opened and closed. A firm, purposeful step sounded on the floor boards. Varina sat up.

"Please, don't disturb yourself."

Panic shook Varina's knees to jelly. She had said she wanted to see him, that she must see him and make her excuses or she could not rest; and now everything in the world depended, not on what she might say to him, but on what he would have to say to her. It seemed impossible that he would not have been told by now what business had taken her to Brierfield. Miss Amanda or Mary Bradford or even Young Joseph could have told him. It would seem a trivial thing as they put it.

"She wanted a costume for a tableau and asked James Pemberton to send some stuff over. What he sent she couldn't use and she rode over to set things straight. She did seem upset, now that I think of it."

Would he suspect the truth? His opening words indicated nothing of the sort.

"Solomon said I should find you here. I wouldn't believe him until I saw for myself. How are you now?"

Wild hope surged in Varina. Perhaps anyone of the three or all of them had tried to tell him what her errand had been and he had brushed them aside, unwilling to listen. Hope subsided. That left all the telling to her.

"I'm quite restored, or almost. But there are others, I am afraid . . ."

Only one other mattered. He was tired, very tired. He had ridden all the way from Vicksburg, racing to get in ahead of the storm; and, after that, she had no way of knowing how many miles he had ridden, looking for her. Dark patches of fatigue showed under his eyes; and then her attention wandered to the sweep of his hair, to the careless fastidiousness of his ingenious cravat, to the set of his shoulders, the immaculacy of his brushed broadcloth—was it things like these that made a man unforgettable or what was it? Had it been only a few hours or a day and a night since she had given him up forever?

"Believe me, nobody was in a moment's jeopardy except you. When I think what might have happened to you, everything turns black again."

He was not saying this to reassure her. He meant it. Sincerity vibrated in every word. Hope flared again, beyond all reason. Varina crossed her hands on her breast, as if so, she could hold it down.

"But you don't know . . ." she faltered.

He stood, in the familiar pose, his back to the fire, smiling down at her, waiting to hear what it was he didn't know. He was so tired, so tired; and yet, as always, he found a reserve of strength to make fatigue of no importance. Varina let her hands fall helplessly.

"As I see it," she sighed, "I've burned Kempton to the ground again."

"You've . . . what?" he asked, startled; and then Melissa appeared with the tray of food.

Melissa had had no idea he was in the room. When she saw him, she would have backed out and gone away, but he held her.

"Come in," he said cordially. "What have you there?"

"A little white m-meat of chicken and b-bread and butter and some p-port wine," Melissa stammered. Melissa!

"Fine! I suspect it is just what we need. Give it here . . . no, wait. I'll pull this table close to the fire."

Round-eyed, Melissa watched him place the table. Then she set the tray on it, swept her startled glance over Varina and fairly ran from the room. Jefferson looked after her, a whimsical smile touching his thin lips, then stood, seemingly lost in thought, listening to the storm. Rain, pointed with sleet, whipped against the windows. Now and again a spatter of it came down the chimney and hissed as it struck the fire. Wind moaned around the corner of the building. This time Varina did not think he had forgotten her. Time was her only respite. Almost any minute he would turn and ask her what she meant by burning Kempton to the ground again, and she must tell him.

However, when he brought himself out of his absorption, it was to turn to the table with an exclamation of self-reproach and pour her a glass of wine.

"Drink this," he said, not commandingly, persuasively, bringing it to her, "because, before you tell me anything, I have a confession to make to you; and you may need fortification against shock."

What sort of confession could that be? Drinking the wine obediently, for that, too, was respite, Varina tried to read his expression. Because his back was still to the fire, his face was in shadow. She thought only, "How like his mother, he is, really! How her heart must have bled when they bundled him off to school so young, and, for all she called him back to her, he never came back in reality!" Sorrow had set its mark on the lovely face in the portrait so long ago as that; and afterward, mere years of living had not mattered.

"I had the pleasure," Jefferson said, "of breakfasting with a friend of yours in Vicksburg this morning. Judge Winchester?"

The announcement had special significance. The Judge and Jefferson Davis had not met for breakfast by accident, she was sure.

"He was eager for news of you."

But how had he known Jefferson Davis was in Vicksburg? The paper, of course.

"Did you talk about me?"

"Of nothing else practically. I tried to persuade him to ride back with me, but he was otherwise engaged for the remainder of the week."

"I . . ." on the point of saying she was glad, Varina changed the subject. The wise old man would have seen through any flimsy decency of pretense she might put up and she would have found his understanding harder to bear than his compassion. "Don't lose your heart," he had said to her when they parted at Diamond Head. "Remember, you belong to us in Natchez." The very thought of it brought a threat of tears.

"Uncle Joe," she said to Jefferson, "showed me a piece in the Vicksburg paper, about your nomination. General Quitman brought it over."

"Oh, that!" He lifted his shoulders expressively and dropped them. "I don't think he—or anyone else—expected you home so soon."

"I couldn't stay away."

Then he must have seen the glitter of tears in her eyes, for he turned again to the table.

"I'll tell you why presently," he promised. "We'll see about this bread and butter and chicken first."

"No," Varina said. How could she have thought she was hungry?

"Yes," he insisted. "It frightens me to see you looking pale. It isn't your natural coloring."

"I'm afraid it is not."

The corner of his mouth—the one she could see—turned up in a smile, but he went on studying the platter of sliced chicken and a plate of bread.

"I probably won't do this as well as Melissa," he said, "but, if it were field mess . . ."

He spread a slice of bread abundantly with butter.

"You do better than Melissa," Varina told him. "Melissa scolds."

"Does she? Why?"

"She finds abundant reason."

"Mm!" He selected a slice of chicken, laid it on the bread and brought the plate to her. "Well, I can tell her one thing. She forgot to put any silver on her tray—for eating, that is. See now if you can bite through this."

Her hunger had vanished. The last thing she wanted to do was to eat. Just to oblige, she took the slice of bread into her two hands and bit into the edge of it. Bread, butter, and delicate roast fowl melted into a mouthful of deliciousness. She was utterly dismayed, and looked it.

Jefferson threw back his head and laughed. She couldn't take offense. The sharp outlines of his face, the brightness of his eyes melted into amusement, and a feeling that was much warmer.

"You are," he declared, with complete approval, "the most exhilarating combination of healthy child and sophisticated young woman I ever saw."

"Much nearer the one than the other," Varina sighed.

"You forget that I have talked with Judge Winchester."

"He is prejudiced in my favor."

"Very."

" 'Green young,' is how Melissa says it."

" 'Green young,' " he repeated. "It seems to me, Melissa is an overprivileged person. 'Green young.' It is an insolence on her part; and yet, it says everything . . . too well. Do have more chicken. You are looking much better."

Varina cleared the plate and consented to another taste of wine, but that was the end of docility. Excitement rising in her throat met the food descending. If that continued, she must strangle.

"No," she said. "You promised."

"What?"

"To tell me why you couldn't stay in Vicksburg."

"Don't you know? Because I wanted to be where you are."

"More than to strengthen your position politically?"

"Infinitely more."

"Why?" Every nerve in her body was jumping.

"Because my heart is where you are, and always will be. Because I love you."

"*I love you* . . ." the words filled her ears. It seemed to her that she must hold them there, unwilling to let them strike home to her mind and heart, fearful of their full meaning.

"Don't you know," he pleaded with her as he had pleaded hours on end with himself, "that you are the most beautiful thing that has ever happened to me? I knew it the first time I saw you—that day at Diamond Place. I was unprepared, I never dreamed . . . and there you were, directly in my path."

"Well, I must say!" Varina protested.

He didn't hear her.

"I rode on to Vicksburg. I didn't more than half believe I had seen what I had seen. But what I accomplished in Vicksburg on that journey, what was said to me and what I said, I couldn't tell you to this day. I came home all of a lather and there you were. A living reality. I saw you everywhere I turned at Hurricane. I saw you in my dark, ugly house at Brierfield. I heard you laughing among children at play. I met you in a rose garden. You sat in Brother Joe's dusty office; and your clear, young voice illuminated the dull stuff with which a man fills his days. I rode off to Vicksburg again. You were the reason for my going."

"Oh, no!" Varina protested. "No."

"You were all my reason. I seemed to myself such a shadow of a person, compared to you. I wanted to do something stirring and vital, to show real mettle; and the field of politics seemed my only opportunity. So, I rode off, filled with high purpose and intent, only to find when I arrived in Vicksburg that what I had engaged to do was most unreal, a shadow combat, and you were all that mattered. I had felt

compelled to enter the battle and now I was possessed of an even
greater urgency to hurry away from it all, to return here. I was consumed with impatience. I . . . it was as if I knew."

"Oh!" Varina wondered if she had moaned aloud. She wanted to
cover her face, to hide her chagrin. It had all been so unnecessary—
his becoming involved in those wretched politics and, even more, her
business with James Pemberton, ending in her wild ride to Brierfield
and its sad finish. At least, at the time, everything seemed unnecessary.
It was only much later that she saw how all points of difference must
have been worked out in some way at some time.

"I felt I must see you and talk with you, though all the while I knew
I had no right to speak to you of my desire, certainly not without the
consent of your parents, your natural guardians. There are many reasons why they might withhold that consent. I am nearly or fully
twice your age. Some people would say it doesn't matter."

Oh, it didn't matter. It had never mattered much.

"It matters heavily to me. I spent my youth a long while ago. I—
if you wish—shall try to tell you the whole story some day. I have
lived here the life of a near-hermit, with horses, books, Negroes and
the land for company—only this hurly-burly of political differences
linking me with outside affairs. It is not a life to tempt a young
woman, beautiful, gifted, merry-hearted . . ."

Wasn't it? How little he knew!

"But at the same time, there was this urgency in me to speak. I
thought of this elderly friend, who holds your and your parents' confidence. I looked him up and laid my case before him. In earnest
pledge of visiting Natchez at my earliest opportunity, if there seemed
any hope of success in my suit. Judge Winchester was most kind, most
generous, though he agreed with me fully that I should wait to speak
to you until I had seen your father and talked with him. I was satisfied, mentally, with his advice. I meant to act upon it. It was only my
heart that was still possessed by some urgency that would give me
no peace until I set out for Hurricane. So, I had my horse saddled and
set out, with the storm at my heels, only to arrive here and find you
missing."

Varina pushed the footstool out of her way and stood up. Did he
think he was making it any easier for her to declare what a fool she
had been? He would despise her properly when he knew.

"Who told you where I had gone?" she demanded.

"Nobody here knew. So I took a fresh horse and rode to Brierfield. James said you had been there and gone. He was in great distress. He said he had tried to hold you but you wouldn't stay. He told me you were riding Sultan. I thought, if Sultan bolted . . ."

Apparently it had not occurred to him to ask what had taken her to Brierfield in the first place.

"Sultan did bolt," Varina said, "but that was only part of it. I was the one who was running away."

"Varina!"

"My heart was breaking. All this you've been saying I didn't know. I had everything all mixed up in my head. I thought here was again a special punishment reserved for willfulness. The thing I would want more than anything else in the world, I could never, never have."

"Varina, what are you saying?"

He took a step or two toward her, uncertainly, but with light breaking over his face like sunrise.

"I don't know," she said. "Except that I am sure it's not what I should be saying, but I can't help it. I . . . oh, please!"

She flung her arms out blindly, in a gesture of surrender and appeal. He caught his breath and her hands in the same instant. A little shock ran through her. She had not meant . . . if this moment ever came to her, she had meant to meet it proudly; but now she clung to his hands as if she were drowning. She swayed as if she might fall. He caught her in his arms. She felt them close around her gently, still hesitatingly at first, then with strength and sureness and hunger—a hunger stored through years of want and self-denial. She thought, "If there is nothing beyond, still I will have had this," and her head found its home on his breast.

"My girl," he said brokenly, his lips against her cheek.

"My girl!" She would hear the simple words spoken by him in every tone imaginable—proudly, compassionately, admiringly, reproachfully, in hopeless anguish of the spirit, but always tenderly. *My girl . . . my brave girl . . . my poor girl . . . my girl!*

Two words that set a coronet on her dark hair that she would wear forever.

CHAPTER X

Many years before this, Andrew Jackson had said to a little boy, traveling over an Indian trace to school, that nothing precipitated trouble like the laying on of hands. How right he had been! To have held her in his arms was an experience Jefferson Davis was not likely to forget, a privilege he would not willingly forego. As for Varina, her heart was too full to hold abashment or chagrin. "Bring on your legions, O Caesar! Come in your ashen cerements, O Shade of another day, another joy. Try to wrest him from me now. You'll see."

"I didn't mean," Jefferson said, with brooding fondness, still holding her hands, "that just this should have happened now. I meant to declare myself and then, if the thought was not too repellent to you, to endeavor to persuade you . . ."

"I shall be very glad," Varina said shakily, "to be persuaded—now that I know."

He crushed her hands in his, kissed each one as he let it go, and, laughing with the release of pure joy, seated her again in the tufted chair.

"I will do everything in my power to persuade you," he promised, "because, I think, when you realize what dire consequences might come of your decision, you will require persuading. I shall devote every hour of every day . . ."

Varina shook her head at him.

"What of the political campaign?" she reminded him.

"That!" he said again. "Well, it is eminently possible that I shall make a disgracefully poor showing and be defeated for office."

"No," she said, not able at the moment to be bitter about the politics. "We can't have that."

"We can very easily have it," he assured her.

"Will there be a speaking?" Varina asked.

"Several, I am afraid."

"Then that will settle everything. I wish I might attend one."

"The good Lord forbid!" he said. "If I were to look out into the audience and meet your big eyes, I should forget everything I had pre- pared in the way of argument. No, I prefer my persuasion of you to be personal and private. How shall I begin? I know. But . . . you haven't finished your tea. That we must clear away, first of all. When did you last sit down to a meal?"

"Breakfast. And you?"

"Breakfast—with Judge Winchester in Vicksburg."

That seemed highly amusing now. The boy who had gone out after more wood a long time before this returned with his log then.

"Hello, Charley," Jefferson greeted him.

"Evenin', Moss' Jeff." Admiring devotion dripped from each syl- lable.

"Do you know where you can find somebody who waits on the table in the dining room?"

"I makes shift to help down there sometimes," the boy said wistfully.

"Do you? Then, bring another cup, if you will, and some knives and forks and spoons . . . yes, a plate or so. There's food enough, but we lack utensils."

"I'll fetch ev'ything, Moss' Jeff."

He ran out and came back this time in a hurry, with a linen cloth, besides the articles specified. He spread it over the table and set two places.

"Shall I serve the plates, Moss' Jeff?"

"Please do, Charley."

"Yassuh."

"Do you know, Miss Howell, I think Charley will make a good butler."

"Excellent, I am sure," Varina agreed.

"All this is very cozy and domestic, don't you think?"

"Very cozy, Mr. Davis."

And prophetic, it might be. "I'll never tell him now," Varina thought. "Perhaps he will forget to ask." She knew he would ask some time, but let it be deferred, O Lord, as long as possible!

"It's raining rivers again. That may be literal, you know. This could be the storm that, according to Sister Susanna, will surely wash us adrift some day."

"But hardly before tomorrow, do you think?"

"Certainly not before tomorrow."

Mention of Mrs. Susanna Davis, however, brought up before Varina a picture of the ladies' parlor.

"I have a favor to ask," she said.

"I'm sorry you need to ask it."

"It's this. Must everyone know . . . about you and me . . . right away?"

"When nothing is really settled?" he teased. "It would hardly seem proper." Then he added, more seriously. "There is one exception, of course. Brother Joe. I have no secrets from him."

If she had been asked to name an exception, Varina would have said she ought to tell young Joseph. Then she remembered his face out in the storm and thought, "Why, he knows. He knew before I did."

"I owe everything I have and am to Joe," Jefferson said.

Coldness blew across the table briefly, as if the storm had found a crack in one of the casements.

"It seems to me that you or someone else has said that to me before," Varina said. "I don't agree with you altogether. At the same time, I think he won't be pleased."

"Varina, you astonish me. Why in the world would he not be pleased?"

"I think he has plans for you that don't include me."

"What plans? I make my own. I always have."

"You see?" Varina said.

He was annoyed, not with her, not with any person, but with a situation, rather, to be exact, with the misconception of a situation. He left the table, perhaps to avoid her wide-eyed scrutiny, and paced restlessly back and forth across the firelit end of the long room.

"I will not deny Joe's influence," he said. "I have always been glad of his advice, or almost always. There has never been any compulsion."

No. Compulsion would have been a grave mistake. Jefferson stopped his pacing before the portrait of Samuel Davis, the Elder.

"Joe earned the right to advise me many years ago," he said. "Our father was a good, solid man and thrifty; but he never advanced beyond the ownership of one modest holding of land. When he died, if the inheritance had been broken up among all his children, it would have amounted only to a couple of horses and cows apiece and a hand or two, and no land, since our mother must still be cared for. Fortunately for us, there was no division. Instead, Joe, who was busy with his own projects credited each of us with our share, then built upon that credit until all had been provided for. He saw most of his brothers settled in professions or on land, he saw his sisters safely married, and me he kept at school."

He stopped here, to study a point, frowning slightly.

"He did not, however, secure my appointment to West Point, as is generally believed. Father did that, shortly before he died. I was in camp on the Hudson when I heard that he was gone. My appointment was endorsed—Father must have made that the main business of a journey East that he made about that time—by the great Calhoun himself. Naturally, I am proud of that."

Naturally. This would be the political influence, at work so long ago!

"It was due to Joe's advice," Jefferson went on to say, "that I remained at school. I was seventeen. I had already a fair classical education. I thought I could fend for myself. He thought otherwise. So, in perfect amity, we struck a bargain. I agreed to stay at West Point for one year. At the end of that time I meant to leave and finish my education elsewhere—at the University of Virginia, instead of Transylvania, since Joe thought my horizon wanted broadening; and then I meant to take up my study of law and be my own man. Well, you see how much better Joe knew me than I knew myself. It was of my own choice that I finished the course at West Point. I loved the school. I loved the associations I made there. I still do. I always will."

A man of deathless devotion, so she had been warned.

"It is a beautiful fortress site, rich in tradition—have you seen the place, perhaps, on your travels?"

"No," Varina said. "Philadelphia is as far as I've been."

"Oh, yes, the school. I remember. Well, I must show you West Point some day. I will."

But he never did. He might have, under the fairest circumstance; but events did not work out that way. When she saw the granite fortress finally, rising out of its forest of green, she was alone, her heart bruised and battered and . . . but that was of no consequence now.

What did matter was that he had abandoned reminiscence to come back to the table. He stood close enough to touch her. The electric thrill that always told her when he was near was there, but he did not put out a hand toward her. He studied her, instead, as if he had not seen her properly before.

"My child," he said sadly, "it has just occurred to me. All this must have happened before ever you were born."

"1826?" she said.

"1826 . . . I was halfway through West Point and you had just opened your eyes on the world. My dear, are you sure you have considered . . ."

"I have considered everything," she told him. "You've no idea."

In the next instant he had a very shrewd idea. She could see it taking shape behind his eloquent eyes.

"Varina . . ."

She was saved by a knock on the door. A knock with authority behind it, for the door immediately swung open.

"I beg your pardon. Do I intrude?"

"Joe!" Jefferson cried in welcome and, Varina could have sworn, in some relief on his own part. "Come in. We have been talking about you."

Varina was not willing to say then whether the master of Hurricane was pleased or displeased when Jefferson, without further consultation announced the great good fortune that had come to him, though, as he insisted and too truly, nothing could be considered as final. At least, he would not assume . . .

Of course, Uncle Joe pretended pleasure. He embraced Varina warmly before he held her at arm's length, to administer a deserved scolding.

"You sly minx!" he said. "Did you need to turn the world upside down to bring this about?"

He knew. At least, he had his suspicions. Varina would not have supposed she could experience unreasoning panic twice in the same hour, but her knees went to jelly again. She sank back into the tufted chair and put her hand to her eyes. It was the oldest and the weakest and the most transparent of feminine subterfuges, but it served. Jefferson, denying his own perplexities, stood between her and his brother.

"Shall we call a truce on questioning?" he said. "For this glad evening, at least?"

Pictures . . . two brothers standing in the glow of a fire. Alike and so unlike! The one the essence of everything fine and high, the other never his match in pure intellect or even nobility of intent, but wiser, for that very reason, in the ways of the world. Tell Joe? There was never any need to tell him anything. He knew. He was angry at Varina now only because for a few nightmarish hours she had threatened to overturn his chessboard.

That, of course, she did not know. Not yet. Time to her was still a respite, but only that. It did look as if, the more a person had, the more one might lose. She had breached the barrier that stood between her and her heart's desire. She was not safely entrenched on the other side of it. She did not know how, given time, she would strengthen her defenses. She only hoped that the tools would be placed in her hands.

Meanwhile every day brought its peculiar hazards. A truce had been called on questioning. Jefferson had said more to Brother Joe on the subject probably when they were alone, for the latter never opened the matter again. That would hardly quell the curiosity, spoken or unspoken, of others in the family.

"Varina . . ." Mary Bradford began the very day after the storm, and then, on the verge of forthright inquiry, hushed.

"Well?" Varina said, looking as innocent as she could, being by turns aglow with happiness and chilled to the bone with uncertainty.

"Varina, don't be an owl now!" Mary pouted. "What was in that Brierfield trunk?"

"Things," Varina answered. "Old things. I couldn't use them and

I wanted to get them back to Brierfield before Mr. Jefferson came
home. I got to thinking it wasn't polite to borrow his stuff without
his permission."

"Mercy!" Mary said. "Jeff isn't like that."

"I know he isn't. For that very reason it seemed impolite."

"And . . . I believe he'd give you anything you ask for."

This was again a rather direct probe.

"But I hadn't asked. That is the point," Varina said.

No use, with another woman, to put her hand over her eyes and
act vaporish.

"And you needn't have worried about James Pemberton making a
blunder. Anything James does is always all right with Jeff."

"Mary," Varina said, at her wits' end, "you will oblige me greatly if
you will never again mention any part of the hateful business."

"Mercy!" Mary said. "I won't, if that is how you take it."

Fortunately Mary's huffs were not lasting. Varina would find a way
to make peace with her. In the meantime, she might keep quiet and
there was one hazard turned aside. For the time being.

The day after the storm dawned bright and cold, the wind sweeping the clouds off to the south and east, the sun flashing on wet roofs
and ponds and runlets. Everything, if not afloat, had been thoroughly
drenched. In the very early morning bush and tree and ponds showed
a dressing of ice. John O'Connor mourned his camellias, brown and
blighted, and the roses he had not been able to save. He would have
no flowers to send to the house for days, he was sure. As for the pre-
cocious peach buds, they glittered like rosy prisms in their ice caps.

"That will teach them," Joseph Davis said, but ruefully.

By noon the ice had melted. The wind stayed high and it blew cold
for days, but the sun shone again as if its light had never been obscured. You could lift your eyes to the sky and almost forget the
desolation that had been wrought. But the desolation remained when
you brought your eyes back to earth again. It had been a bad storm.

Nobody ventured far from the house who had not business that
called him away. When Varina took her kitten down to the rear gallery for an outing, the little thing shivered and took on, and all but
forgot what he had come down for. He would put out a foot, feel the
cold wet of the ground, and draw back. Finally, when he did make up
his mind to leave the bottom step, he did so with a bound that landed

him in a clump of soaked grass. He humped his back, spat, then, finding himself wet all over, took everything more philosophically.

"Shoo!" Varina said, laughing at him from the gallery.

"Here, kitty, kitty!" Rhina Number Two called from the steps to her kitchen. "Rhina's got a saucer of warm milk when you are through there. Do you want me to mind him this morning for you, Young Miss? I ain't too busy."

That would be in exchange, of course, for a scrap of more or less revealing conversation.

"You're pretty busy, I know," Varina called back. "And he's been fed. Some other time, Rhina, thank you. Here, kitty. Come on now."

When she picked him up and turned back to the gallery it looked to her as if the whole household had gathered there. Expostulation flared up in her; and then she realized that they had not come out to watch her, but to receive Jefferson, riding in over the orchard road. As usual, some lookout in the house had spotted him and passed the word.

He wore boots that reached above his knees. Their splattered condition indicated that he had been where he had needed them. He flashed a smile over the gallery, managed to include a special one for Varina, then turned directly to Joseph.

"Everything's all right," he said, and repeated his news for emphasis. "Just all right."

"Thank God for that," Joseph replied. "You've been all around, I suppose."

"Yes. Some of the sloughs between here and Brierfield are running pretty full, but I think they will fall presently. The river was low; and, unless the ice melts in a rush up above and sends a flood, it will carry off our surplus."

"This time," Susanna Davis said.

Jefferson hardly noticed her remark.

"That will do on the boots, Mose," he said to the boy at his feet. "I'll only splash them again. I rode as far as the Quitman place early this morning," he announced to the gallery in general. "Mrs. Quitman wanted to know whether the charades would go on this evening as planned. If so, they will ride over. I can take or send them a message right after dinner."

"If you've been to the Quitman's," Susanna said at once, "you could see the isthmus. How was it?"

"*Mirabile dictu,* Sister, we are still attached to the mainland."

"That settles it. We'll pack and be off in the morning, Joe. If the Quitmans can drive over here, we can drive out."

"I said ride, Susanna, not drive. Nothing on wheels can go over the roads possibly for several days."

That meant that the light wagon from Hurricane would be held at Brierfield for an equal space of time. Jefferson saw the anxiety on Varina's face and tried to divert attention from her.

"The Turners will not come," he said. "Mrs. Turner does not feel equal to the ride, and they've had a couple of drownings there."

Attention was anything but diverted. Every face turned toward Varina. She shivered and buried hers in the kitten's soft fur.

"Ah-h-h!" Susanna Davis drew her shoulders up almost to her ears and hurried into the house. Her sisters followed, Miss Amanda last, stopping to pat Varina's shoulder consolingly, but at the same time reproachfully.

"Darling," Jefferson said, as she rustled away, "you didn't make the storm."

"I'm not too sure," Varina said. "Have you been to the stables?"

He took the kitten from her and fondled it.

"Yes, and Sultan's fine. Not a trace of stiffness or sign of cold."

She learned afterward that he had spent hours, while she slept, the afternoon of the storm, directing the work of the grooms on Sultan and the other horses, prescribing and administering tonic medicine then with his own hands. Had he been to the stables, indeed?

Pictures—tableaux in the music room. There was this silly business of charades to be got through with now. And, since they were part of her respite, she must carry them off with a flourish. She heard someone say at dinner, "Amazing! She doesn't show a sign. You wouldn't think, to look at her, that . . ." The rest trailed off into nothing, but she could finish the sentence in a dozen ways. It put her on her mettle. Nobody at the play party could have been gayer.

Her team of actors had for its prize offering a drama in two tableaux. In one she sat on a throne, a queen, beside her prince consort, young Joseph Davis. She wore a tinsel crown on her smoothly parted dark hair, and a daringly décolleté gown provided by Mrs. Eliza Davis, her modesty saved by a frill of lace around the décolletage and a broad sash of crimson ribbon that ran diagonally from one bare shoulder to the lower edge of the bodice. The sash was pinned to the bosom of the dress by an elaborate sunburst brooch that served very well as the emblem of a knightly order. Young Joe, for his part, had achieved royalty by way of a hunting coat, braided with yards of gold lace, and a pair of white trousers stuffed into highly polished boots. His sideburns did not match his hair; but he held his Davis nose high and looked quite regal—and foreign. The young queen was presenting him to a row of uncles.

"This is my Uncle Windsor, my Uncle Kent, my Uncle Gloucester . . ."

Varina tapped a play-sceptre haughtily against the arm of her throne and addressed the gaping audience.

"You," she said coldly, "are supposed to guess the significance, the meaning of this scene."

Well, they guessed that she might be Queen Victoria, in which case the foreign gentleman beside her would be Prince Albert, and the uncles were obviously dukes; but there conjecture, as had been intended, collapsed.

The second tableau presented Caroline Davis as another queen. She wore her tinsel crown on hair dressed high. Her chin was, with difficulty, kept above a ruff of lace, which had taxed the skill of every clear-starcher on the place and had precipitated more than one near murder in the laundry. Her stiff bodice and farthingale skirt were equally impressive. Elizabeth, beyond question; and the leggy knight in the slightly awry, close-trimmed beard was Drake, her admiral, because she called him Sir Francis. Otherwise identification might have been difficult. The action of this tableau also allowed the youngest members of the team opportunity to appear in costume. They made a row of sons and daughters to the admiral.

"Lud, Sir Francis," was the queen's line, "I had no idea there were so many of you!"

The line occasioned laughter at the time and had been a merry one all along, nobody having any idea, truly, of the great seaman's domestic affiliations, and it might have been a pity to make sure.

"Drakes!" someone in the audience hissed.

"Ah!" Queen Elizabeth sighed. "I just knew you'd guess this part."

Only the ruff and farthingale had persuaded her to take her role. There had to be a clue given somewhere, she had been told. But now the Queen Victoria scene had to be done over. Because no one had guessed the word play? No. Moss' Jeff asked to see it again. He suggested that now, given an opening, the answer might appear to someone. Then he stood back in the shadows, willing to look at the pretty picture the rest of the evening, if necessary.

"It has something to do with dukes," a fresh young voice said finally. The saying of the word aloud broke the spell.

"Ducks and drakes!" It was a kind of unanimous shout, followed by a burst of applause. Which was all very flattering, but it gave the prize for the evening's entertainment to Mary Bradford, whose top tableau was a homely piece, but downright unguessable.

Mary wore a gingham dress, a slat sunbonnet and a field hand's shoes. She led by a length of rope a fat, roly-poly boy on all fours. The rope was attached to a ring, which the boy tilted in his mouth to make it seem to be through his nose. In spite of this, he managed to grunt with gusto and realism. The strange pair sought passage through a toll gate.

"Well, I don't rightly know, ma'am," the gatekeeper said, "how to charge for a pig on a lead rope."

"Oink!" the pig protested, all but losing his ring.

"This yere's a hawg, man," Mary protested.

"Is it, sure enough? Well, that mought make a difference."

"Make up yore min', man. We's in a hurry to git along, ma hog an' I."

It was a too literate phrase at the end of the line; and everyone should have noticed that. Moreover, in the argument that followed the words were repeated; yet it was one of those conundrums that people miss by being too profound in their deductions. Only Varina knew the answer at once. Excitement always sharpened her wits, and she was on the point of crying out her conjecture, but did not. She thought, "If I keep still and nobody guesses the answer, this might make up to Mary for my snapping at her this morning. I hate not being friends with Mary."

She hated not being friends with everybody. She seemed to be endowed or afflicted with a host of new sensitivities. She regretted the new and thorny quality of her relationship with Joseph Davis. And there was no denying a sharpening of the questioning attitude of the other kinfolk. They suspected her hold on Jefferson. They did not enjoy being robbed of a tradition. Yesterday their unfriendliness—it came close to that now—had been masked by acts of kindness. That was while her health was still endangered. Today, with her up and about and in no way harmed that they could see, was another story. And Varina, knowing how insecure her position was, was sorry.

So she sat back quietly and with saintly forebearance saw the prize given to Mary. It was a crystal bottle of attar of roses. Mary, guessing Varina's concession, because she knew by now the sharpness of Varina's mind, insisted on her taking the pretty treasure; and then, in the fuss and flutter of protestations and laughter, it came.

"Varina," Miss Amanda said, perhaps no more loudly and briskly than was her usual manner, but it seemed so to her victim, "I thought you were planning something altogether different."

So? The attack was to be direct, and no quarter given. Varina put Mary Bradford aside and stood up to give her answer. She needed a queen's robes and a coronet and a crimson sash . . . no, perhaps not. She needed just to be Varina Howell, and remember.

"Why, no," she said, "I thought I told you. I had to abandon the idea."

"But I feel so cheated," Miss Amanda said. "Jefferson, do you know . . ."

It did seem pitiless. Perhaps Miss Amanda did not intend it that way, but the effect was the same.

"Please," Varina begged. "I'd rather tell Mr. Jefferson about it myself."

The truth was she didn't want to tell him at all, if she could help it. Again she was using subterfuge. She wouldn't tell him at another's prompting or at her own, only if he asked her outright what had happened. Would he do that?

"If you please," she repeated.

All the noise and fun seemed to have stopped. Everybody was listening for the next word. Jefferson gave it.

"I can't say what will be Amanda's pleasure," he said. "The idea pleases me very much. Miss Varina, will you honor me in the opening quadrille? I took the liberty, Joe, of bringing in some musicians."

They were a black man who sawed out tunes on a fiddle, setting the time with the patting of an enormous foot, and two boys with jew's harp and banjo. Under their magic a semblance of gayety was restored to the scene, but Varina's heart remained turbulent.

"I am an interloper here," she pouted at a turn of the dance.

"Dear interloper!" Jefferson said. "Chin up! You're a match for any and all of them."

His championship was balm, but it hardly improved the general situation. However, if he admired a fighting spirit . . .

"You lead a quadrille marvelously well, Mr. Davis."

"I am afraid I am clumsy on these smooth boards. I had most of my practice on puncheon floors, you know."

Puncheon floors . . . their splinters had scarred those small slippers. Varina would have withdrawn from the dancing after that set, but there was still young Joseph.

"Miss Varina, if it will not overtax your strength, will you dance a set with me? It may be the last time, you know."

A funeral march would have been appropriate accompaniment to that measure.

"I hope I am not being too bold, Miss Varina, in offering you my felicitations and best wishes. If I had known that Jeff was setting out to pay court to you, I would never have ventured to do the same. In the first place, I would have known the hopelessness of my efforts to please."

But it hadn't been that way. She had set her cap for Jefferson. Didn't he know?

"Dear Joe," she said, "I wish . . . but nothing is settled, nothing certain."

"I think," he answered, "you can leave that to Jeff."

She hoped that he was right. She hoped . . .

At last the evening was over, the musicians departing with their sacks of goodies from the white folks' feasting, the gayety breaking into bits and melting.

"Good-night, Varina . . . Cous'n Varina . . . good-night, Aunt 'Manda . . . good-night, all."

Beside a newel post at the foot of stairs reaching up, up through a hallway, a voice said softly into her ear,

"Good-night, my sweet, and happy dreaming!"

And happy dreaming . . .

Varina sat up on her side of the big bed, hugging her knees and the coverlet. Mary Bradford laid hold of the sleeve of her nightdress and pulled.

"What are you staring at, Varina Howell?"

"The moon," Varina sighed. "I believe a person could just walk out the window and right on up to it."

"Well, don't try that now, please."

"I won't," Varina promised, her smile as pure and unearthly as the moonlight.

Perhaps love was like that, a sort of purification, rough, worldly elements not being so important as one thought. With another sigh, she stretched out under the coverlet and went to sleep.

To walk a moonbeam in her dreaming. Joyously she followed the broad, bright path up and out into space. It did not need strength to support her weight, for she had none. The path ended, however, not at the moon, but suddenly in outer darkness. She fell then, like Lucifer, out of Heaven and awoke, clutching the counterpane. It took her seconds to realize her safety. She felt herself in the bed. She looked at the long hummock that was Mary Bradford, at the footboard, at the bedposts. Slowly, cautiously, her eyes moved over to the window. Everything outside was still silvery bright, but the moon was not looking in at her now. Mercy, what made a person have such dreams?

But an hour of communing with one's self and the moon in the solitude of night is a small part of living. Rough, worldly things mattered a good deal and all day long. Varina awoke the next day with her universe as teetery-tottery as before and herself as reluctant as ever to undertake the delicate task of giving it proper balance. Also she was as glad as ever for anything that put off the evil hour.

Respite was now seeing the various branches of the family off to their homes, then, as the house party dwindled, the political campaign. It was a thing not to be avoided now, Jefferson said. It would be soon over, one way or another; and then they could tell better what it all amounted to.

What it amounted to, first of all, was the almost continuous absence of Jefferson from Davis Bend while the issue remained in doubt. Perhaps it was only natural that Varina should feel again, and more strongly, a wish that she might attend one of the rallies where he spoke. Perhaps she would see right then what it all amounted to. Finally, wondering that Joseph Davis kept so carefully away from the actual scene of combat, she went to him and asked him to take her to Vicksburg for the final rally on the eve of the county election.

To her astonishment, she found this scheming, oversure gentleman as much a victim of unrest in his way as she was in hers. The political campaign was the paramount issue to him. Its outcome was so important that he dreaded knowing the results. He put up any number of excuses against escorting Varina or any other member of the family to the hall in Vicksburg.

"You won't enjoy the speaking," he said. "You know what he is going to say. Have you any idea whom the Whigs have brought up to run against him?"

"Yes. Seargent Prentiss. General Quitman told me. It shows the fear the Whigs have of him."

"Hm! It will probably spell his downfall. Why are you bent on witnessing his humiliation? He entered at the eleventh hour. Too slow to take fire . . . always was."

"I don't think he will feel humiliated," Varina said. "Because, no matter what happens, he will still believe what he believes."

"Hm!" Joseph said. And, after a moment's reflection. "Hah!"

Finally, perhaps, because he was too restless to bear inactivity any longer, he capitulated.

They drove to Vicksburg in the high-swung, swaying carriage—Joseph, Miss Amanda, Mary Bradford, and Varina. They set out in the gayest of spirits. Varina had persuaded them all that Jefferson would be much more tranquil, if he didn't know of their presence and that gave the adventure a delightful air of conspiracy. Varina wore her pretty traveling outfit of red and brown; and Mary was almost as fine in a costume of her favorite green.

The rigors of the journey occasioned their first dismay. The roads were in a worse condition than they had anticipated, so pitted with chuckholes that they made painfully slow progress. Sore in flesh and bone, they rested at Diamond Place overnight and set out again, a trifle subdued, after dinner of the second day. Only to find that the roads above Diamond Place were rougher than those below. They reached the hall in Vicksburg after dark and barely in time to secure places on a bench at the very rear of the room.

"Mercy, Varina," Miss Amanda said, "I do believe . . . no, there are other ladies present—a few. But it is just as well to be near the door. The air is stifling. Joe, don't leave us for a minute."

"Sh!" her brother said. "If you don't want our presence known, be quiet. I think the man at the door was a little suspicious, as it is."

"Well, unless somebody informs him, Jefferson couldn't possibly . . ."

"Miss Amanda, please," Varina begged.

"Oh! I keep forgetting."

"The crowd is quite orderly, really," Joseph said, meaning that he felt its potential disorder. "And it will be easier to hear the speakers in a hall like this than it ever is at an outdoor rally."

The hall was packed. Before the speakers took the platform, young men had pasted themselves to seats on the windowsills. Every now and again one would lose his balance and drop to the floor, creating a whirlpool of shouting confusion. All without bad feelings so far, but the roughness was disturbing. This was a gathering having very little in common with any Varina had witnessed, surrounded by the carriage aristocracy of Natchez.

But Miss Amanda was on her feet again, peering about.

"Varina, isn't that Mrs. Prentiss up front? Do you know her?"

"Yes," Varina said. "She was Mary Williams of Natchez. I can't see her; but maybe we can speak to her afterwards, if she is really here."

The hall was one that had been modeled to accommodate a local society of Thespians. It had a small, elevated stage, but few other advantages. The seats were on one level, not in graded tiers. This gave added excuse for what seemed to Varina a hungry restlessness on the part of the spectators. Up front, a few chairs with backs had been provided for special guests. The Davis party could have claimed places there, but secrecy condemned them to a backless bench.

On the platform a half-dozen chairs had been set in a row for the speakers and their sponsors. These were slightly in the background, but not too much so. Everyone would want a good view of the combatants. Near the edge of the stage was a small table with a pitcher of water and a glass.

The platform remained empty until an ominous movement of feet in the audience and a few outspoken complaints warned the principals of the affair that the crowd wanted what it had come to hear and see. Then out of some shed or dungeon or other secret shelter in the rear, the six men for the six chairs appeared, smiling and talking together in friendly fashion. They bowed to one another and they bowed to the stamping applause from the floor and took their chairs. It seemed to Varina that Jefferson Davis took his chair rather more quickly than the others. He had entered side by side with Seargent Prentiss; and the physical contrast between the two men was painfully apparent—the one tall and straight, with a superb carriage, the other shorter by the better part of a foot, with extra large head and broad shoulders, limping, carrying the weight of his lame side on a stout cane.

But this audience was not interested on the whole in niceties of behavior. After the first burst of applause, which was exactly like the roar of a lion as meat is thrown to it, there was a brief silence; and then again Varina felt that undercurrent of restless, greedy anticipation. Her earliest and worst fears were confirmed. To carry the banner of the Democratic Party in Mississippi, no matter with what high principles of belief of one's own, was to place one's self at the mercy of the mob. This hall held probably not more than two hundred people, but the two hundred had all the terrible aspects of a mob. Their stirring and impatience had demanded that the speakers come forth. Their whims and prejudices would have something to say about the conduct of the meeting. They might conceivably hoot or howl a speaker into silence if they took exception to his statements.

No! If that had been what Uncle Joe meant by humiliation, he had been right. She couldn't endure witnessing a thing like that. She would leave . . . she looked at the stage and found a measure of calm. She still could not see why Jefferson Davis had thought this a brave and doughty deed and one to please a lady—to mount that dusty platform in this suffocating little hall; but she recognized his superiority—Saul at his anointing could not have appeared more surely head and shoulders above the multitude. She thought that superiority must be evident to everyone else present.

He sat between fiery General Quitman and a small, wizen-faced, bright-eyed man, whom she recognized as Senator Robert J. Walker. Mrs. Walker was one of her mother's good friends, but generally she was pitied by the ladies of Natchez, though a senator's wife, because Mr. Walker was notoriously radical in his politics.

On the other side of the platform the great Prentiss sat between a quiet, unobtrusive gentleman whom Joseph Davis named as a Mr. Guion, Prentiss's law partner in Vicksburg, and a big, prosperous-looking man in flowered waistcoat and high stock collar, a power in the state, a blue-blood if ever one set foot in Mississippi—Judge Henry Foote of Natchez.

Varina opened her mouth on a sigh, then held it, resentment stealing her ruefulness, as this gentleman came forward pompously to introduce his friend. The resentment grew as his speech proceeded. It was a long one. His voice was full and rich—like his waistcoat. He played it like an organ, pulling out stops and pushing them in. He said he was not going to tax the patience of the audience with his periods and then, like Cicero, he went on for pages and paragraphs. Varina found herself trying to remember who it was at The Briers who disliked this man right properly. Probably not Granny Kempe, because the judge was another Virginian; but there was somebody.

"Why," she thought, "I could act like part of a mob myself, given sufficient reason."

Her ears at that point caught the import of strange words the Judge was saying. If you please, he was not introducing Seargent Prentiss. In a most unorthodox and backhanded fashion, he presumed to introduce Jefferson Davis. The Honorable Mr. Prentiss, he said, realizing his advantage of being known over the other candidate, a newcomer and a stranger, had graciously conceded the leading place on the program to his opponent. Perhaps the audience had really assembled for a first view of this other gentleman, who had been persuaded to leave a scholastic cell in order to champion the cause of what he and his friends were pleased to call Jacksonian Democracy.

Miss Amanda gave an indignant bounce that jarred the bench.

"Hah!" Joseph said, as the Judge made a magnificent final bow and retired. From the far end of the stage General Quitman sprang forward in best fighting attitude, but found himself politely, effectively blocked from advancing. Jefferson Davis, having been announced as a speaker, would carry on from that point. He came forward, pale, smiling a little. . . .

"Hah!" Joseph Davis said again.

Varina found that she could not bear his gloating anticipation. She could not bear anything else that went on. Her ears filled as if they had been plugged with cotton. Her throat filled with a bitter-tasting something or other. She pulled Miss Amanda's sleeve to command her attention.

"Hush!" Miss Amanda whispered. "Jeff's going to speak, don't you see? Why, Varina, what on earth?"

"I'm sick," Varina murmured, choking. "I will be in a minute."

It was the fumes from the oil lamps, hanging in brackets on the walls, most of them smoking. It was the fumes of the people, more than probably. It was the greenish light that the uncertain illumination threw over the speaker marching to the apron of the stage. It sharpened his pallor, the hollows of his cheeks. Then speaker, stage and audience began to swing in dizzying arcs.

"Joe," Miss Amanda hissed, "we've got to get out of here."

"No!" he said sharply and a few people turned, to glare and growl.

"Joe, I said now!"

Outside under the trees draughts of unpolluted air gave Varina back her equilibrium.

"Mercy!" she gasped.

"Well . . . pshaw!" Joseph Davis grumbled. "Now, how will we find the carriage in the dark? Where's that boy, Isaiah?"

"He's probably located a knothole somewhere," Miss Amanda suggested, "and is trying to hear what goes on."

Isaiah saw them, however, and came up, to show them where he had placed the carriage and team.

"You're sure of the road, Isaiah?" Joseph asked. "How far is it to Mr. Samuel's place?"

"Ain't mo'n a couple of miles, Mist' Joe. I been that way many a time."

"Then we'd as well be off. Miss Howell was taken ill inside; so we didn't get to hear Mister Jefferson speak."

"No, sir."

Master and man were upset, and the master displeased. The horses backed and plunged forward, the carriage creaked and swung. The air was cold and sharp, and remarkably pure.

"Watch out for chuckholes in the dark, Isaiah."

"Yes, sir. I'll hold the team in as much as I can. They're right sure-footed."

Varina put her hand on Joseph's arm.

"I'm sorry," she pleaded.

Joseph did not shake off her hand, but neither did he put his out to cover it, as he would have done in friendly fashion a week before this.

"I suppose you've hardly recovered from your exposure of last week," he conceded. "So, you didn't like what you saw? Well, politics is not a ladies' parlor game. Never was and never will be."

Varina received support then where she would not have thought to look for it.

"I didn't like it, either," Miss Amanda said from the seat opposite. "Jefferson's too fine for that sort of thing."

"Nonsense!" Joseph said, and Varina took her hand away. "He just looks that way. Somebody has to step to the front in a crisis."

Was there a crisis?

"Well, it needn't be Jeff," Miss Amanda said.

That came close to expressing Varina's sentiments. Involved argument and intricate reasoning might multiply words and phrases, but finally the protest resolved itself into that simple statement. "It needn't be Jefferson." Part of Varina's objection was selfless, part of it was not. Tonight's gathering, rough and appalling as it had been in some aspects, would be, as even Varina understood, superlatively elegant and orderly compared to some. Miss Amanda was right. Jefferson Davis was too fine for that sort of thing; but what loomed as more and more important in Varina's later study was his possible absorption in the thing he was too fine for. As, white-hot and determined, he had stepped to the front of the stage, he had forgotten there was a girl named Varina Howell.

Politics, then, might be a very solid part of that barrier from which, now it seemed to Varina, she had merely pulled a few brambles.

The party spent the night at Samuel Davis's plantation outside of Vicksburg, then early the next day set out on the return journey to Hurricane, by way of Diamond Place. This was the day of the election. In Vicksburg, as they drove through, people were already rallying at the polls. Isaiah rolled his eyes wistfully. The master of Hurricane, out of all patience with women, rode up front with his coachman, and bowed and spoke to acquaintances, then said a word to Isaiah that sent the carriage forward at a faster rate.

They ate an early dinner at Diamond Place, rested an hour, borrowed a team and drove on. Dwight McCaleb was absent at dinner. He was, Florida explained, out canvassing. They met him on the road an hour later, tired and spent.

"It's going to be close, sir," he forecast.

"Jeff entered too late," Joseph fumed.

"Yes, and not enough of the family located in Warren County," the younger man answered. "They'll hold the polls open for you, sir, at Palmyra."

"They'd better," Joseph said grimly.

Home then, by way of the Palmyra crossroads, home to a long night during which everybody tossed restlessly, too tired for sound sleep, too anxious. The result of the elections was not known until the next day, when Jefferson rode in with the word.

He rode almost to the veranda steps and sat on his tall gray horse, facing his brother.

"I lost," he announced.

"Well, I'm damned," Joseph said testily, "if you don't seem glad of it."

Jefferson smiled at him from some height more remote than that of his saddle, then dismounted, with perhaps a trace of weariness, and bowed to the ladies also waiting on the gallery.

"I can't honestly say I am sorry," he admitted.

I will devote every hour of every day . . .

So easily can a barrier seem to melt away. The defeat in the county elections left Jefferson Davis free to keep his promise to Varina. He did so with gayety, abandon and devotion. What wonder, then, if she forgot to be wary?

There was a stretch of road that followed the river embankment from Hurricane to the crossroads of Palmyra. When it drained and dried, it made a splendid race course. Jefferson would match his mount —Haidee, the Arabian mare—against Varina's brown filly. Down the road they sped almost every afternoon, neck and neck, with only a fraction of a minute finally in favor of the gray Arabian.

"Do you hold her in?" Varina demanded finally, the race being always that close.

"You know I don't. I wouldn't offer her that injury. She won't be beaten, that's all."

"Glory doesn't like to be outrun, either. Poor Glory!"

"I think she knows she has met her match. She is fast enough. I always suspected an Arabian strain in her. Now I feel certain of it."

"Poor Glory!" Varina said again. "Perhaps, if she didn't carry an uneven weight . . . the sidesaddle and this long skirt, sweeping and slapping."

"The new habit is very pretty," he judged. "More becoming, if possible, than the old one."

She had thought once he did not notice.

"It's practically the same," she informed him. "The new velvet was almost an exact match. Melissa made life miserable for the sewing girls who helped her, making sure that they set every stitch just so."

"Is Melissa your own girl?" he asked.

"No. She has always waited on me when I have been at home, but she is Mamma's maid, really. Why do you ask?"

"I feel a sort of jealousy of her."

"Oh!"

That he could experience jealousy and in her behalf! That should make it easier for him to understand . . . easier for her to speak; it did no such thing.

"I can't speak of her now," Varina thought. "I can't . . . unless he speaks first. This is too perfect."

"We must give you a girl of your own," he said the next minute.

"It isn't necessary," she said. "I'm sure Granny or Papa would find one for me. We have plenty of them."

"Wouldn't you like one of our girls?"

"Yes, of course."

But there was a slight rending in the admission. When she returned to Natchez presently, it would be only to make preparations for a long farewell. That is, if . . . resolutely she put all ifs aside for the present.

So it went, for another succession of bright afternoons. They would rest their mounts after a gallop, to talk of such matters as these and to look from the high embankment up the river. Some days they would talk of the river. With the water of the recent deluge draining off into it and some of the ice above melting, its level was rising.

"Were you ever flooded over?" Varina asked.

"Several times. But never cut adrift or drowned. And when the Old Man pulls back and goes on his way, he pays his toll, like the Nile, in silt; and we repair the damages and settle our accounts without too much complaining."

Once, as they sat there, Jefferson took her with him in reminiscence up to the sources of the river. He had been stationed at one time at the very portage which the early French explorers had used, crossing from Lake Michigan by way of the Fox River and the Wisconsin, to the Mississippi. She saw the trackless wilderness through his eyes— the small fort and garrison at the Portage, the trader's store. She was there the night a company of Dragoons arrived, detailed to break a cavalry trail through to the Indian village of Chicago at the tip of the lake. She went, under military escort, through the Winnebago towns. Jefferson had been adopted into the Winnebago tribe. He called one young chieftain brother. He had always got on with the Indians.

Another day he told her of the Sac Indians around Fort Crawford and Prairie du Chien. They had an evil name. They could be vengeful, he said; but they had cause for bitterness and implacable hostility. They were earth Indians, not nomads, as some people thought all Indians were. They had regular villages, around which they cultivated fields and, more important to them, near which they buried their dead. This land, holding the bones of their kinsmen and ancestors, was sacred. They did not want to give it up; but the white men, moving westward, insatiable, saw it only as sites for mill towns, for lead mines, for farms. Two different winters he had been stationed at Dubuque and Galena, towns farther down the Mississippi, trying to hold the settlers back from crossing the river ahead of treaty dates. But they wouldn't be held back. They had crossed unlawfully and the Indians had met them and there had been bloodshed and retribution; and so had come the Black Hawk War.

The Black Hawk War did not make a glorious tale as he told it. He had been sent down, when it began, into southern Illinois and Indiana, to swear in companies of militiamen. Farmers and farmers' sons, for the most part—big, raw-boned frontiersmen who didn't want to leave their fields or their families, but they had been border folk for several

generations and the fear of Indian raids was bred into them. They
weren't good soldiers. They didn't take to discipline. Some were good
marksmen and some were not. There was one long, lanky fellow
whose folks had come from Kentucky. He had been born near Hod-
genville, which was not far from the Green River valley where most
of the Davises, including Jefferson, had been born. Jefferson didn't
remember this black-haired backwoodsman's name. It seemed to him
that his mates called the man Abe, or something like that. He had
tremendous arms and was good chiefly for hewing wood for palisades.
He had a homely wit, too, and kept the spirits of his company up with
his drolleries, but he wasn't keen at all on killing Indians. Perhaps
that had called the young recruiting officer's attention to him. Lieutenant Davis, also, hated the butchery of Indians.

Because that was what it came to. The militiamen were no great
help in the fighting; but they swelled the numbers of Colonel Taylor's
command; and the Indians, who could never gather in much force
for a standing battle, were beaten from the start. The Battle of Bad
Axe had its spots of heroism and it went on record as a victory for the
white man, but the memory of it had always weighed on Jefferson
Davis's conscience. After it, there had been more Indian pow-wows.
Once he had marched out of a council lodge, unable to endure what
went on. The Indians were so much in the right and the white men,
however powerful, so much in the wrong. The upshot was always
the same. The Indians wrapped their blankets about them and moved
on; or they stayed and drowned their pride and sorrow in the white
man's firewater and died in degradation.

There was the sad story of Black Hawk, the Sac chieftain. Varina
smoldered in sympathy over his proud surrender to a force he could
not withstand. Jefferson told her how the white people all the way
down the river crowded on the packetboat, to gape at him, a prisoner,
to throw missiles and insults at him, until finally Jefferson had given
orders that they should not be allowed to board the boat. It was
strange, he brooded, how people who had trampled on every right of
one race could stir themselves to such indignation over the fancied
abuse of another.

Varina waited with some apprehension on the turn his talk might
take next. There was something half-angry in his final assertion,

something provoked and provocative. Naturally, being defeated at the polls had not taken all argument out of him.

Then her ready fears veered in another direction as he went on to speak of Jefferson Barracks, the post to which he had delivered Black Hawk a prisoner. It had been at that time and was still, he said, the command post of the Western Army of the United States. It had a proud location, high above the river. The officers stationed there were a gay lot. St. Louis, close by, was full of pretty girls to lend lustre to their parades and hops. He had, Varina gathered, visited St. Louis on occasions not purely military. It was a fine, thriving city, he said, with its interchange of trade between the East and the new West, between the North and the South. A busy city, settled, much like Natchez and New Orleans, with descendants of French and Spanish families and even more people from Virginia. He had friends there —dear, loyal friends. He mentioned one family by name—Christy.

He was on the point, Varina was sure, of telling her something significant of his social connections with St. Louis; but he changed his mind and merely held out his hand, begging for the privilege of carrying her plumed hat by its ribbon ties as they rode homeward. He liked to see her smooth, dark head bare, only a net holding its mass in order.

"Hoydenish?" Varina questioned.

"Never that." His eyes adored her.

"What, then?" she demanded.

"I must not say," he told her. "Not yet."

These were days of courtship, but also of reconnaissance, of exploration. Happiness had come too swiftly, too suddenly, for either to feel quite safe in its possession. They considered the miracle of their knowing each other, sometimes almost with awe. Some day there must be a reckoning, but each one said, "Not yet."

Every hour of every day . . .

Well, not every hour, of course. The new year was moving on. The weather was not warm as it had been those treacherous early days in January. It held some of the chill brought by the storm. Many a morning frost would show mud tracks hardened into ridges, and gullies and ponds and quiet backwaters glazed with ice; but all that would melt before noon and there was a feel now of advancing spring in the air. Rising sap colored the young outer growth of tree and shrub. Buds swelled on bare branches everywhere and the evergreens turned brighter and one could fancy the earth beginning to show a new carpet. It would be an early spring, after all.

And so, in the chilly mornings, the two brothers—the heavier, older one on his stolid, flea-bitten gray horse, and the lithe, erect, younger one on any animal in the stables that needed exercise—would ride out to look over the land. The rich, lazy "between-times" season was drawing to a close. Work lay ahead.

Varina, preferably from a third floor window, would watch them leave the stables and follow them as far as she could with her eyes; and she would recall, joyously, sometimes defiantly, the sudden decision she had made at The Briers the spring before:

"When I marry, it will be a planter."

Surely it was a life rich and full enough to satisfy any man, no matter what his gifts. Each year as the earth renewed itself, his life was renewed with it. There was a season of sowing which was all eager anticipation, then a season of growth and finally the harvest. When the harvest was gathered, it might be loss or gain that a man counted; but, whether it was loss or gain, he had to rest, with the earth, until spring came and it was all to be done again. Then, no matter what the past year had given or taken, hope surged again, with the new year beginning.

Surely it was a richer, fuller life than carrying a banner for a following mob. Why was she afraid of his doing that? Why? She could see as well as anyone what an inspired and inspiring leader he might make; but she never saw happiness or reward in the picture for him.

There was much happiness possible for him in the quieter life of a great plantation. In spite of his many activities, he had long hours of leisure; and he was a man to turn leisure to rich account. Even now, when he was busy paying his *devoirs* to her. Afternoons, if the weather was fine, he and she would have their run on the fleet horses. It was the only way, with propriety, that they could have much time alone. If it rained, he might join the diminished gathering in the ladies' parlor. He would sit on a fine, small chair, his long legs stretched out before him, fondling her fat kitten, watching her hands make a botch of a pattern of lace, until he could bear it no longer. Then he would take the tangled thread from her and give her in its place a book. That might be the latest number of *The Ladies' Repository;* and, for mischief, she would select a delicate, pearl-gray romance, which amused him mightily. Or, it might be that the spectacle of her—young, vital, high-spirited—reading such sentiment amused him.

This would end finally with his taking *The Ladies' Repository* from her and leading her off to Brother Joe's library and office, where the fare was richer. The ladies could follow if they would. Sometimes they did; sometimes by secret agreement, they remained behind. Slowly perception filtered through the household and the quarters that one of these days, nobody could say how soon, Jefferson would make a second marriage and the lonely house at Brierfield would have a living mistress. . . . If nothing intervened, of course. If and if and if . . .

The lonely house at Brierfield. Varina and Jefferson had not ridden even in that general direction since the day of the storm. The truce on politics and other troublesome matters was stretched to the breaking point, but it held.

I will devote every hour of every day . . .

The fare on the library shelves was rich and abundant. These days they passed by the more sombre volumes—Rawles' *Constitution,* Eliott's *Debates,* the ponderous bound copies of the *Congressional Globe* or the *National Intelligencer.* Sometimes hands and eyes would pause at the shelves devoted to history—Bancroft, Prescott, Gibbon, Hume; but nearly always the choice of book was one by a poet. Jefferson's favorite British poets were Byron; that Irish singer, Moore; and of the Americans, Longfellow.

"What?" Varina teased one day. "No Whittier?"

Joseph sputtered something inaudible and Jefferson shook his head at her. No Whittier, as much because he was a Puritan as because he was a hated Abolitionist. There was nothing by John Milton, either, in this library or the one at Brierfield. Both brothers hated Puritanism, but Jefferson the more intensely of the two. Dour, gloomy, chill, narrow were only the beginnings of his descriptive epithets, which ended always with his urging her gently toward Joe's office, his finger marking a place in a handsome volume by Sir Thomas More or one of the others.

There was an hour, at least, every afternoon or evening of reading in Joseph's study while that pleasant fortnight lasted. If it came in the evening, dusk overtook them. Dusk and Solomon with lights. Joseph sat back in the shadows, establishing and preserving the proprieties, hardly contributing anything else. He was a restless man these days. His mind was not on poetry. Jefferson might consider his defeat in Warren County conclusive. Joseph looked at it differently, and bided his time.

If they had only known! But that would have spoiled the fortnight, which, as it was, stretched out a chain of bright hours like gems trickling through Varina's fingers. And then, quite suddenly, the chain snapped.

To begin with, that afternoon as they turned their horses back toward Hurricane, Jefferson said, with an attempt at the casual, "If it is fine tomorrow, will you ride with me to Brierfield? There is no bad water between here and there now, and the roads have dried."

Varina discounted the matter-of-factness of his tone. His invitation had not been casual. He, as much as she, had put off the day of accounting, strengthening his vantage ground in the meantime. Now he thought, "I can't delay any more. I will be having an answer to my letter addressed to her father. If it is unfavorable, I must be ready to deal with any objections. If it is favorable, all the more reason why I must be sure of her. There is a thing between us."

But why did she pursue his thoughts? She had her own to deal with: "I don't want to go to Brierfield. It will bring everything to life again—the pain, the anguish—her. I don't want to be reminded of her. Brierfield is the house he built for her. She lives there still. I wish . . ."

"I can see you had rather not go," he said, against her silence. "I'm sorry. Perhaps if you told me what took you there the day of the storm. I've never asked, naturally, but naturally I've wondered."

She answered then, her lightness as thin a covering as his opening casualness, "I supposed James would have said."

"He would have, if I had asked him. Of course, I couldn't do that."

The clouds gathered fast now. There was a limit, then, to his confidences with James, the all-perfect?

"It's really nothing of much consequence," she said. "I will tell you, of course . . . tomorrow."

If she had only had the courage to say, "Now!" Between a day and the morrow there can be a fearful reach of time.

"Tomorrow," he said, much happier, with her promise. "At Brierfield?"

"At Brierfield, if you wish, or on the way."

She turned and put out her hand for her hat. The approach to Hurricane was just ahead through the trees. Usually at this point he gave her the hat and directed its adjustment. They were exceedingly careful on these rides. He touched her only to assist her in mounting or dismounting. There were so many eyes to see, so many to make talk. Today, however, he held the hat away, the expression of his face at once so warm and so hungry that she was both thrilled and frightened.

Confused, she turned again in the direction of the house and then spoke with quick imperiousness.

"You'll have to give me the hat, I.think. We're going to have company for supper. New company. In a minute Uncle Joe will be sending someone to look for us. Yes, there goes Moses to the stables now."

Two men were alighting from horses at the Hurricane veranda.

"Can you see who they are?" Jefferson asked.

"One is General Quitman. I don't know about the other . . . I can't be sure."

She was sure. He was a small man, slightly stooped. In riding clothes of loose English tweed. She had seen him many a time riding down Front Street in Natchez.

"It's Senator Walker," Jefferson said for her. "What's up now, I wonder?"

CHAPTER XI

Nobody at Hurricane remained in doubt long as to the purpose of the two gentlemen's visit. The committee of neighbors and friends who had urged Jefferson Davis to offer himself as a candidate for a seat in the state legislature was disappointed in his defeat, but not in his showing during the brief campaign. What Varna had seen in the few minutes before her hurried departure from the stuffy, odorous hall—that he stood head and shoulders above his following and his opponents, as well—they had seen, too. That only. So now the leader of the party for the state was interested in him. Senator Walker had not ridden to Hurricane to pay a social call.

"Melissa," Varina said, after she had passed the gantlet of presentations in the lower hall and hurried to her room to change for supper, "have you that witch hazel bottle handy? Company, and my head is swimming."

"When you going to learn to wear a hat out in the sun?" Melissa scolded.

"It's still January," Varina reminded her. "There's no heat in the sun."

"February's just 'round the bend," Melissa maintained. "Mebbe here ain' no heat in the sun, but somethin's sco'ched yore hair. Wind tangles again."

Wind tangles in her hair—Melissa could brush them smooth and laid, until the dark mass lay close to Varina's head like a shining cap; but who would straighten these other tangles? Who would help her?

Her father, when he wrote in reply to Jefferson's letter? Or came, perhaps, to give his answer in person and to fetch her home? No. Her father, if she consulted him, would say,

"Pshaw, Puss, the man's not worth bothering your head about. If you must have a husband, I'll find you one more suitable, easier to get on with."

That would be no solution.

When Melissa had finished dressing her, Varina stood before the mirror, studying her image. She took a mite of comfort from that. Shadows, which had appeared for the first time under her eyes after her adventure in the storm, had never gone away altogether. Fatigue or emotional stress brought them back, more faintly, to be sure, with each passing day; but they were eloquently visible now. They did not take from the luminous expressiveness of her eyes. Rather, they added depth to their brightness. The way his eyes were deep, she thought proudly. Feeling did that to a person's looks—just feeling. In the same way and for the same reason a new curve had come, she fancied, to the ripe redness of her mouth. It was sweetness, almost, but not quite, superseding willfulness. Sweet thoughts, tender aspirations, dreams . . . she opened a small box on her bureau and, with a flaring of defiance, fingered the Van Buren watchdog pin, but, sighing softly, chose a cameo brooch, instead. Melissa had set a ruching of white lace in the collar of the rose-colored, corded merino. Cameo, lace, wistfulness lent an illusion of delicacy.

"You filled out some," Melissa said grudgingly over her shoulder.

Then, she was no longer green young? Well, hardly. Her fingers hovered now over a bowl of red and pink and white camellia blossoms. With her usual sound instinct, she selected finally the most vivid of the flowers. Its color against her dark hair gave the lie charmingly to sleekness and the restrained prettiness of her dress. Melissa handed her a shawl. She held it around her with her elbows hooked, in a manner she had borrowed from Mrs. Eliza Davis, and, as fully armed as she would ever be, she thought, went on downstairs to supper

This was not the charming, informal meal that had come to be the practice as the household dwindled, served often in the ladies' parlor It was a state affair in the dining hall, complete with roast and game and wine and puddings, with Solomon and several assistants pouring at the sideboard, carving at side tables and handing dishes and bowl and glasses and plates around. Mrs. Eliza Davis, for reasons known only to herself, perhaps only on a whim, chose to be present. Jet sparkled on the rich black silk of her dress, in the lobes of her small ears, but not more brightly than malice sparkled in her eyes. Varina, who at the table kept her place on Joseph Davis's right, in spite of the growing tension between them, fancied that most of the malice was directed at her. This was so often the case that she had learned to derive satisfaction, rather than unrest, from the invalid's random shots.

However, they were not random shots this evening; and they were not aimed at Varina. Their venom was all intended for the master of Hurricane.

"Why, she hates him!" Varina thought. "She hates him murderously."

Did the family know? Jefferson? Miss Amanda? Mary? If they did know, they would not say. This was something other than the tragedy of loss. This, if anyone admitted it, was treason. Varina glanced sideways at Joseph. He knew. His manner and his shirt front were as expansive as usual, but he would have preferred that his wife should remain in her apartment and leave the honors of this occasion to him. He did not entertain a senator and a political power every day.

That was, of course, why Eliza Davis came to dinner.

"My husband," her jet, her silk, her manner seemed to say, "married me for my money and my position. Didn't you know? Yes; but how he hates to be reminded of it!"

So, while breath remained, she would remind him of it on telling occasions. This hurt nobody but her husband. General Quitman probably knew of the situation, if it existed. Senator Walker had his mind on other matters; but, if Joseph Davis squirmed, Eliza, his wife, had her recompense. He did squirm—imperceptibly, but a little. He could not defend himself without appearing boorish; and that, of course, he would not do.

Varina was shocked at her discovery, but also wary. Venom like this, no matter at whom it was directed, had a way of touching other objects close by. Mrs. Davis, while she remained at the table, dominated the conversation and there was never any telling what she would say next.

"Mr. Davis," she said to the Senator, for example, "tells me that you were kind enough to interest yourself in the, so far, rather forlorn political hopes of our Brother Jefferson."

The silence beside Varina was impressive. Mr. Davis had not mentioned the affair to her. Miss Amanda must have said something of the speaking at Vicksburg. Dear Lord, would Mrs. Davis know about that and would she tell? Inevitably she would, it seemed.

"I would not say that the future needs to be forlorn, if he really has hopes," the Senator retorted. "Everyone was favorably impressed by him."

"That is what brings me here," he might have added.

"Really?" Mrs. Davis said. "Well, of course, I only know what I am told. Mr. Davis took a carriage full of ladies to a rally at Vicksburg on the eve of the elections. I was not of the party. My health does not permit me to make such sorties; and, I understand, those younger and stronger found it all rather too much."

So, now! Jefferson, who had been amused by his sister-in-law's mention of his politics as forlorn, was startled in his turn. By itself the incident could have been passed off lightly. On top of her evasion about Brierfield, Varina could hardly say defensively, "Didn't Uncle Joe tell you?" From the far end of the table, Jefferson was looking at her in steady question, if not with reproach.

"Is this more deception, my girl?"

No, she would not have it so. Varina leaned forward. She would steal another page from Mrs. Davis's book. She, too, could dominate a table, if she chose, and more effectively than the other, being young and beautiful and wishing only to charm, not wound.

"Dear me, Miss Eliza," she said, "you've exposed a secret. Mr. Jefferson was not to know that we had gone to hear him. He asked not to know and we had agreed not to tell him."

Down the table her eyes now begged Jefferson to remember how he had said that, if she ever was part of his audience, not to let him know, he would find it too disconcerting. He must have remembered either the words or the occasion. His face warmed visibly and then Mary Bradford all but spoiled things again.

"Particularly V'ina insisted on not telling," she murmured.

Fortunately only those nearest to her heard her and General Quitman broke in as if she had not spoken.

"Did you enjoy the speaking, Miss Varina?" he asked. "It was rather a novel experience for a well-brought-up Whig, I should think."

"It was the first indoor event of the sort I ever attended," Varina said. And what, then? Be amusing? Yes, that would be the thing. "I must say the theater at Vicksburg seemed an improvement over ours at Natchez."

"Lord, yes," the General agreed. "At Natchez," he informed the Davises, "our hall crowds the town graveyard. You look right out of the windows on the tombstones; and, if we've had gully-washing rains, sometimes you look out on worse—the bones of the early settlers. But, go on, child. The Senator and I were on the stage. We thought things got right warm before the evening was over, but we'd like to have our opinion confirmed by someone out front."

Oh, dear!

"I'm afraid I can't help much," Varina said, ignoring Mary's poorly stifled mirth. "We didn't stay through everything. The audience was rather overpowering, to begin with."

"A little on the rough side," General Quitman allowed.

"Yes, and they wore such heavy shoes," Varina sighed. "They expressed most of their opinions with their feet and it made a terrific din. Not only that. They kept crowding one another off the high windowsills and I thought before the evening was done, somebody would surely be crushed." She was doing very well. Everybody was listening. "If I had been one of the speakers I should have been intimidated by all those boots; but, I suppose, you gentlemen are used to them. Judge Henry Foote was not disturbed, apparently. He's rather the master of the *praeteritio,* isn't he? 'I shall not steal time from the other speakers . . . I will not tax your patience . . .' "

She swelled out in front to the limit of bodice and stays and puffed her cheeks. The dining hall rang with laughter. Even Solomon's shoulders shook at the sideboard. Mrs. Eliza Davis's bright eyes were brighter. "Bravo!" she seemed to cheer. Only one person at the table was not amused. That was Senator Walker, the leader of Democracy in Mississippi.

"Very clever, my pretty," his sharp eyes commented. "Too damned clever, if you ask me. Who are you, anyhow? Oh, yes, I know. Varina Howell, of the Natchez Howells. The Dowager Kempe's granddaughter. But who are you in the life of this man, Jefferson Davis?

How much influence are you going to wield? How are you going to wield it?"

She felt his sharp eyes impaling her.

"I love him!" she wanted to cry. "I love him desperately. I know what you see in him. I can see that, too; and in the end he will probably go your way, not mine. But I'd so much rather he did not. I don't think his happiness lies in that direction—or mine. I am eighteen years old, my life beginning; and I want to be happy—with him."

But she couldn't say anything approaching that in depth or meaning. She could only sit forward and be beautiful and amusing.

"Which one of you turned giddy finally?" Mrs. Eliza Davis asked.

"I did," Varina said. "It was just as Mr. Jefferson was making ready to speak impromptu. The smell of those sperm oil lamps on the walls . . . or the people . . ."

"And you didn't hear Jefferson's speech? Not a word of it?" General Quitman asked.

"Not a word," Varina said, matching her rue with his horror; and the dining hall rang again, this time with Jefferson leading.

So that crisis passed. It was nothing, really. Foam on the crest of a wave. When the ladies left the table presently, Mrs. Davis asked for the support of Varina's arm. She leaned rather heavily upon it, Varina thought, though, of course, she was no featherweight.

"You handled your escapade at Vicksburg superbly, my dear," she said, as they went through the passage. "General Quitman and Jefferson were highly amused, Jefferson's brother, my husband, not so much so; and Senator Walker was not amused at all. I suppose you saw."

"Yes," Varina said, "I saw."

"Tell me, do you think that you, single-handed, can save Jefferson from his appointed destiny?"

"No, of course not."

"'No, of course not,'" the older woman mocked. "Then you had as well or better not try. And, if you want my real opinion, you would have done well to settle for the younger man. It is still not too late to call him back, you know."

This time Varina did not answer. In giving her heart, she had not consulted anyone—not even her own best judgment. Did one ever?

That Senator Walker and General Quitman had come to Hurricane to persuade Jefferson Davis to run another race or, at least, take up some political challenge was apparent to everyone that evening, though nobody but the men present at the discussion which followed supper could say just what the new business was or how important. The visitors did not spend the night at Hurricane. They rode away very late. Varina heard them go. A long time afterward another rider left the house, alone. Her heart beat thickly in unison with the fainter and fainter sound of his horse's hoofs. Having stayed so late, why did he not take a bed at Hurricane? What was it he thought he must ride off to face alone?

In the morning Jefferson did not return to the main house, as he had lately formed the habit of doing, dropping in sometimes for breakfast and always for a plantation conference with Joseph. At eleven o'clock someone called Varina and said that James Pemberton, Jefferson's man, was downstairs, asking for the privilege of a few words alone with her. Varina hurried down at once to the ladies' parlor to receive him.

Her first feeling when she faced James was shock. He had changed terribly since their last meeting. For the call at Hurricane he had spruced himself in the latest bequest of Jefferson's clothing, complete to the knotted silk handkerchief about the standing collar of a tucked white shirt. He carried in his hand a familiar, wide-brimmed, soft black hat, but Jefferson's black broadcloth coat drew pathetically across his bowed shoulders—pathetically because the shoulders were more bowed than ever. James looked a broken, old man.

"Why, James," Varina said, "this is a surprise. It's a long way from Brierfield here."

"Yes'm." The eyes he raised to her were humble, beseeching, with no trace of hate remaining. Whatever Varina's remorse had been in the past two weeks, the Negro's repentance had far surpassed it. His anxiety, too, had been greater.

"You ain' been down Brierfield way since the sto'm," he said, struggling to maintain his usual dignity; but it was a struggle. "I hope you took no harm from your soakin'."

"Why, no, James, as you see, I came off without a scar. But you . . . oh, James, were you out in all that downpour, looking for me?"

"No, Miss. I remained at Brierfield. I couldn't see what to do; so

I just remained. I waited for Mist' Jefferson—mostly on my knees, Miss."

"Oh, James!" Then, remembering Jefferson's way with him, she offered him a chair.

"You've come such a long way," she repeated.

"I had business at Ben Montgomery's store," he said. Then, determined to withstand her kindness, he was betrayed by his knees. They buckled and he sat, willy-nilly, though humbly, on the edge of the chair nearest him. "I'll just rest myself a minute," he said in excuse.

He sat there, turning the hat in his hands, his strong features working. What had he come to say to her? Was it to beg her not to betray him to his master? How could she reassure him, knowing so little assurance of her own?

"Miss," he blurted out finally, "I want to say I'm glad you changed your mind about goin' away so soon. I am glad because Mist' Jeff'son's so glad."

This was surrender. And it hurt.

"Thank you, James. Oh, I do thank you."

"Yes, Miss." Suddenly his eyes glazed over and with that the polish he had accumulated over so many years and had held so jealously deserted him. "Young Miss," he cried from his heart, "you ain' goin' to let Moss' Jeff go out politickin', is you?"

"Why, James, what do you mean?"

"I mean what I says . . . politickin' is a rascal business an' . . . you ain' want him to go, is you, Young Miss?"

"No . . . no, not especially."

"See, thar! Then you are the one who kin stop him."

"Oh, James, I am afraid not. Not if he wants . . ."

"But he don' wan', Miss. He walk the flo' most o' the night—what was left after he come home from yere—he walk the flo', arguin' with hisself 'bout it. He say to me when I try to coax him to lay down on the bed, 'James, this ain' how I planned it. I wish to my soul I'd never been so foolhardy as to tangle myself up this way. I thought I'd won free, by great good luck; but now see. I don't want anything to do with this business really. I want to stay right here at Brierfield, to work things out here. I want to be a farmin' gentleman like my father.' You ain' ever knowed Ol' Moss', Young Miss. He was a ve'y fine man. He an' Moss' Jeff had they little diffunces, but they set great sto' by each other.

"So, Moss' Jeff say to me, really talkin' it out to hisself like, 'I want to be a farmin' gentleman like my father. I want a home—not this gloomy cavern, a big, fine home, and a wife and a family, my own family growing up around me. It's my right. It's every man's right; and just when Heaven seemed to smile on me again, that this should happen! Why? Why does it have to be me?'"

The wily old Negro looked to Varina for the answer.

"Why do it have to happen to him, Young Miss, now?"

"It doesn't have to happen," Varina said. "He doesn't have to do what these others ask of him. If the things you mention are what he wants most, he will choose those things."

Brave words. As she said them she could hear Mrs. Eliza Davis's sly taunt: "Do you think that you, single-handed, can save Jefferson from his appointed destiny? ... No? Then you had as well, or better, not try."

"No, Miss," James said, "Scuse me, but he ain' boun' to choose 'em, bein' Moss' Jeff. He comes o' farmin' folk, but he comes o' preachin' folk, too. I knows. That time Ol' Moss' lef' me in Ma'yland, to wait for Moss' Jeff to finish school, I stayed with the preachin' kin. Good people, but ve'y sot. The fust o' them come over the ocean, leadin' a congregation. Moss' Jeff's got that strain in him, too—jes' strong enough to make trouble. When somethin' he wants runs up agin somethin' he thinks he ought to, that's when he walks the flo'. Like las' night. Talkin' to hisself an' pullin' out books an' groanin' an' carryin' on. He don' want, but he ought. He ought, but he don' want. Shall he or shan't he? It goes roun' and roun' like that an' finally ..."

"And finally," Varina finished, seeing, as perhaps she had all along, what the outcome would be, "he does what he thinks he ought."

"Yes'm, mos' usually. An' this time in spite o' hisself, he kinda wants what he ought as well as don' want, 'cause it look to him right; but what I aim to say, Miss, is this. He ain' able to do what those gen'lemen an' Moss' Joe keep eggin' him on to do. I know his stren'th and how he spends it. Some folks kin do a piece o' work an' quit an' laze aroun' when they feels tired. Moss' Jeff don' quit whiles the work is there. He'll keep at it, no matter what, till he draps. He'll break befo' he'll ben'. Young Miss, cain' you 'suade him?"

"How?" Varina asked herself as much as the old man, who still worried the hat brim. "How would I?"

"He sets sech sto' by you, Young Miss. Lately he jes' shine. He so full o' plans. Mo' so than any time I remember—even when he was a high-steppin' young sojer. He was ve'y high-steppin' them days, Young Miss—the high-steppin'es', the laughin'es', the braves', the singin'es', the dancin'es' . . . that's what his Cunnel have again him. The Cunnel don' see how sech a fella ever goin' to settle down. Young Miss, I got a thing to confess now."

Well, it was high time.

"Young Miss, I bin agin Moss' Jeff evah marryin' agin. With marryin' Moss' Jeff is jes' like he is about ev'ythin' else. He don' take it easy. The on'y thing he does easy is ridin' a horse. Ev'ythin' else goes hard with him. I didn' wan' him to ma'y Miss Sarah way back yondah. I was so proud speerited 'bout Moss' Jeff them days I didn' think any woman was good enough fo' him. I didn' hold the feelin' long, Miss. Nobody could hold out agin Miss Sarah; she was so gentle . . . well, she was like that. But she die so soon; an' when Moss' Jeff almos' died too on her 'count, I made up a prayer that it wouldn' evah happen again. No, ma'am! We went to Cuba an' to Washington, D. C., to try to git Moss' Jeff's health back; an' ev'y time a young lady look at him twice—mos' o' them did, too—I'd pray Moss' Jeff wouldn' notice.

"Natcherly he didn', not then. So we come back yere; an' when it took so long fo' him to git back his speerits and begin to be like hisself, I couldn' help prayin' harder than evah that he'd nevah set his heart on a woman again. I's a foolish ol' man, Young Miss. It stand to reason when he got real good an' well, he'd not be satisfied to live in that ol' house with jes' me an' a handful o' niggahs to wait on him.

"Then you come along, Young Miss; an', 'stead o' fightin' the idee, I shoulda gone down on my knees with thankfulness. 'Cause anybody could see you was jes' as high-spirited as he evah was—high-spirited, an' laughin' an' high-steppin'. Young Miss, I been on my knees mo'n once the past two weeks, seein' him so shinin' happy an' so full o' plans. 'This is where we'll plant corn,' he says to me, not noticin' hardly who's he's talkin' to, jes' talkin'. 'Here I think we can work these old fields into pasture. That's the way to keep the land from going poor, they tell me—trade back and forth between pasture and field. We aren't going to borrow everything from Hurricane after this,' he say. 'We'll raise what we need down here. We'll have our own stables, our own horses and mules. We'll have our own dairy and pigs and sheep. I heard of a new breed the other day. They make fine yarn from the wool—Saxony's the name.' That the way he ca'y on, Young Miss, jes' beside hisself with happiness. I feel so humble, so 'shamed, watchin' an' hearin' him. Young Miss, kin you fo'give an ol' man fo' bein' so wicked an' foolish?"

"Have you told me everything now?" Varina asked, refusing to let flattery plug her ears and other sensibilities.

The old man forgot his distress long enough to flash her a look of appreciation.

"No'm," he sighed. "I ain'. When we come home f'om our travels that time, Moss' Jeff stop off to see Ol' Miss, his mamma, down at Woodville. He sent me ahead o' him up yere an' give me my orders to make way with ev'ything he don' want to see again. He say to me, 'She's gone, James. She was never there. Do you understand? It was a dream.' I understood fine, Young Miss; but I ain' done like he said. It was the fust and the las' time I ain' ca'y out his orders exact as he spoke 'em. They wasn't much yere, come to find out. Mos' o' her things she packed and took away when they started for Loosiana an' I don' know what become o' them after that. They was jes' these few pieces o' clo'es an' some music. I put 'em all together in that trunk an' kep' 'em. I ain' a conjure man, Young Miss. I's been baptized in the faith an' I don' hold with charms an' spells; but I kep' those things agin a day when ary other woman would make him fo'get what happened to him an' Miss Sarah. Then I was goin' to 'mind him. I tried that, Young Miss. I put her music an' one or two other little bits out where his han' fell on 'em. He picked 'em up. He steddy a little ovah 'em; then he nod his head an' smile, like he knows where he's going and he goes right along. So, that lef' you. Young Miss, I knew what I was doin' when I sent you that box."

"I was sure all along of that," Varina said.

"Young Miss, I wouldn' do it now. I's sorry I was so brash. I had no right to be."

"No," Varina agreed. "Mr. Jefferson wouldn't like it if he knew."

"You ain' tol' him, Young Miss?"

"No, but several times he's been on the point of asking. What am I going to say to him when he does ask?"

The old man was shrewd. He didn't answer. He just shook his head and looked abject.

"I can't begin to tell him why I rode to Brierfield without getting you into trouble," Varina explained, perhaps unnecessarily.

"No'm." The old man worried his hat brim some more, then returned to flattery.

"You could kinda gloze it ovah," he suggested, "if you'd a min' to. Seein' he sets sech sto' by you. 'Bout all you'd need to do, I reckon, is look at him with yore eyes lit up. He ain' goin' to be too hard then on anybody."

"You or me, either," he might as well have said right out; and Varina thought the politics had been only a pretext the man had used for making his plea to her to save him or spare him in Jefferson's estimation when she made her confession; but there she did James an injustice.

"An' when you git him coaxed up an' on yore side, Young Miss, I hopes you will 'suade him agin the politickin'. I wants to tell you somethin' else now. When Moss' Jeff was a young man, befo' he knowed trouble, he was a right hearty person. You seen his picter in Moss' Joe's office? With roun' rosy cheeks? He look jes' that way. Rosy an' stout an' laughin' mos' o' the time. Then he went down with the sickness an' he ain' evah been nothin' but skinny-scrawny since. Till jes' lately. Lately he begin to fill out again. I knows, 'cause I tends him an' his clo'es. They tightenin' on him now. But you knows, Young Miss, nobody gits fat walkin' the flo' all night. I do hopes you finds somethin' you kin do or say. Nobody else would dast. An' I hopes you takes it all right that I come to you like this."

"Why, yes, James. I am proud to think you would." She was, too —the wily, old wheedler! "We are going to be friends now, aren't we?"

"Young Miss!" She had won him completely. He stood up, making a proud effort to straighten his back. He started for the hall, then turned. "Those bits o' things in that box," he said. "They's gone now."

"James?"

"I took an' buried them. It was the on'iest thing to do. Moss' Jeff wanted it that way and now it's done. I buried 'em good, Young Miss. Nobody will fin' them. Mornin', Miss. I thanks you fo' hearin' me out."

"You could kinda gloze things over," James had said; and that was how the first of her and Jefferson's last afternoon ride from Hurricane must have appeared to anyone privileged to observe and overhear and not knowing all that lay beneath the careful carelessness of their greeting and their conversation. Jefferson arrived at Hurricane just in time for dinner. No leeway was allowed for an office pow-wow beforehand and he arranged that there should be none after the meal.

"It is a wonderful day," he said at the table. "I am engaging Varina for the entire afternoon, if she has no objections."

She had none, of course, and excused herself early, to hurry upstairs and change to her riding clothes, so that not a minute should be wasted.

The afternoon was exceptionally fine—the best of all that golden fortnight. The ground had dried out just enough to be springy under the horses' feet. Riding had the ease of loafing in a rocking chair. A light wind—not enough to bend a sapling—tempered the rays of the sun. Pickaninnies rolled out of their path as they rode through the quarters. In the waste land frogs chanted of spring. They stopped to listen. They stopped for every little thing. A blue heron rose from its nest in the reeds. They checked their horses to watch its flight. Farther along buzzards circled over a marked spot; and they stopped to speculate, half-laughingly, half-seriously, over the black folks' superstition that, if they lit, the world would come to an end.

"They must light, of course," Varina said.

"Did you ever see them do so?" Jefferson asked. "I suppose that is the idea. It is best not to be too near when they do."

He showed her the slough where he had shot the alligator.

"I hear you are a good marksman," she said.

"Fair," he acknowledged; so she knew he was very good. "Are you thinking it is a good plan to choose a husband who can bring home the venison?"

"Mercy, no, Mr. Davis. Nothing so bold as that."

The air shimmered and tingled.

"Varina," he began, hesitated, then went on, "what is your full name?"

"Varina Anne Banks Howell," she recited.

"Varina Anne Banks Howell," he repeated. "It has a clarion sound. Varina . . . and so forth, and so forth, had you any idea when I asked for the entire afternoon, that I contemplated making a formal declaration today?"

"Mercy, no," she said again. "You find me entirely unprepared."

"You rascal, I am in earnest. Any day now I look for a reply from your father. Even if it is most favorable, he will have a number of questions that I must answer. The first will probably be as to my means. I am not a rich man, Varina. I shall never be rich, like Brother Joe, for example."

As if that were a thing that mattered!

"People talk about being rich," Varina said scornfully. "I never cared very much. I mean, this is rich—to live the way we do. To have land —not a little squared-off piece of land, as some folks have—but wide land, as far as you can see. To have land and plenty, to have work to do to keep one busy, but time to visit, too—time to know folks and books and flowers and trees and horses. To have people to do for us . . ." she hesitated. "Of course, up North some think that's wrong— to have people, as we do have them, to do for us."

"They don't know," he assured her. "They think they know, but they don't. We know. There has never been a time when people who lived in a degree of luxury, who were especially civilized, who enjoyed the culture that can go only with a certain amount of leisure, didn't have people to do for them. Time, the aging of the world, has divided men, willy-nilly, according to their gifts and abilities. It always will. Service is bad or wrong only when with it goes oppression. It is ridiculous, for example, for the Russians, who drive their serfs with knouts or whatever they call their goads . . . but here I am, making a speech . . ."

The word halted him. It might have recalled the misadventure at Vicksburg. If that had been all, they could have laughed again; but Vicksburg brought up the visit of the "politickin'" gentlemen. He hurried away from the subject.

"Our people are very happy, don't you think?"

"Happier than they would be anywhere else," Varina said quickly and might have added, "Happier than they are most other places," but did not. No arguments, if they could be avoided. Not today. "But you see what I mean about being rich. If I can live in Mississippi and have all those things, I am rich."

Her reasoning, which was, rather, the avoidance of any depth of reason, pleased Jefferson. He rode close to her and reached for her hand. She gave it to him, understanding his appeal. They rode so for several minutes, holding hands. It was a simple act of acknowledgment. Nothing that either might have in the future in his or her own right would have any value compared to what they might have in common. If nothing intervened. If . . . and if . . . and if.

"Then that is settled," he said, "or nearly. I just didn't want you to confuse my thousand acres with Joe's five thousand or more—my handful of slaves with his several hundred. As I said, I am not Joseph. I haven't his drive or his talent for gathering wealth."

"Shall I tell you something?" Varina challenged. "Once upon a time I said I never could like you as well as I did him. But now . . ."

"Now?"

The pressure of his hand over hers startled her and she pulled away.

"Now, I like you so much more that I dare not say how much."

She flicked her filly with the end of her riding crop; and that, as it happened, precipitated a near-quarrel. Oh, beautiful to seem to quarrel over a trifle and so, close one's mind and heart a while longer to real differences! Glory ran a few paces, then slowed to a walk, and Jefferson on Haidee caught up at once.

"Not today, young lady," he said. "You're not riding . . ." he stopped in consternation. "My dear, I'm sorry. I didn't mean . . ."

"It's all right," Varina said; but of course it wasn't. Her cheeks burned. "How is Sultan coming along? I mean, will he be all right again one of these days?"

Overcome by curiosity, she had visited him several times at the stable, carrying him a piece of apple or a lump of sugar, until he whickered now at her approach; but she knew that his exercise was still limited to slow walks around a paddock.

"He will be fit to ride soon," he said, "but not you—please."

"Is that a command, Mr. Davis?"

"I have no right to command you. If I had the right, I would say you must not ever ride that horse again. As it is, I ask you not to, please."

Unaccountably she was angry—as angry as she had been in their first encounters, when every instinct in her had only cried out a warning to her to be on her guard against this man, for, if she opened the way for it, he would some day shake her to the roots of her being, as she was shaken now. She rode ahead again, to conceal her anger.

"He is your horse, Mr. Davis."

"No, he is Joe's horse."

"Have you told him I am not to ride Sultan?"

"I have told no one but you."

She was beside herself purely with frustration.

"Please!" she begged. "Please, do not be so fair . . . so reasonable. A woman is not just a filly, to be gentled."

There was a long, awful silence. How could she? . . . How could she?

"I have not known many women," he said, "and none very well. Of those I have known a little, each was different from all the others; and you are the most different of all."

She turned Glory on the instant, showing him the tears in her eyes, the flush on her cheeks.

"Oh!" she said. "How you must despise me!"

No, he did not despise her. His expression was grave, somewhat puzzled; but, deep in his eyes, lights burned like chapel tapers.

"I do hate to be told I must not do this or that," she confessed. "I truly do. And yet, of course, there are things . . . well, riding Sultan is one of them now. I shall never take him out again. There . . . does that make everything all right?"

Oh, Varina! You were not going to bow down to this man the way others did. Remember? But surely it was worth the most abject surrender to bring those lights out of his eyes until his whole face was illuminated with adoration.

"Let's not talk of it any more," he said. "You may ride Sultan or any other horse in the stables. You may have Haidee for your own, if you wish."

"Don't be absurd," she said. "I think I understand. You were frightened for me. Was that it?"

"I would not want to think of you in such jeopardy again," he agreed.

"Then that does for Sultan forever."

He had all he could do not to sweep her off the filly into his arms. She saw that plainly and she was tempted to let him have his way, no matter how many loiterers might be watching them from the canebrake. She was so tempted that she was ashamed and so rode a few paces ahead again.

"And now you may proceed, Mr. Davis," she said shakily.

"Proceed?"

"You were making a declaration, I believe. I interrupted."

"Yes, a declaration." He was as unsteady as she was. Oh, heart, be still! "How far had I come? I remember. I had confessed that I was not a rich man and likely never would be. I have now demonstrated also that I have an unpleasant, dictatorial manner."

"I forgive you the dictatorial manner, Mr. Davis, as I do your poverty. Neither seems to me too formidable."

"Then, by your leave, I shall proceed, Miss Howell. And this is the hardest part of the declaration because I don't know how to make the approach. I suppose you know why. I am sure you understand why I wanted you to ride with me to Brierfield today."

"Yes," she said unhappily. "That was my unwillingness to come."

They had left the canebrake now and were riding through the final grove of trees. The chanting of the frogs was behind them. The light wind rustled and whispered in the leafless branches. Bright wings flashed against gray curtains of moss and were gone. Brierfield was just ahead.

"Why do you dislike my ugly house?" Jefferson asked.

"It does very well for a house," Varina said. "It is dark. Trees and shadows crowd it too closely. But it isn't the house I mind. It is an association . . . oh, if you find it hard to say in words, how can I say it?"

"Varina . . ."

"I knew it when I first saw the house. I came again to make sure. The silly business I pretended was my reason had nothing to do with it, really."

"You forget that I don't know what the silly business was."

"Oh! It was about costumes for the charades. I wanted something of yours. I asked James. He sent me a trunkful of stuff. He misunderstood what I wanted or he understood too well. I don't know."

"But what on earth could he have sent?"

"It doesn't matter. Please don't be vexed with him. He has worried enough about it, I am sure."

"Yes, he has had something on his mind. I've been concerned about him. And how can I forgive him if I don't know what he did?"

"You can forgive him if I do, can't you? I was the one he hurt—intentionally or innocently. Please try to think his motives were beyond reproach. He sent me, at my request, some old things from your military days. They belonged to the past. I knew they would when I asked for them. What hurt was that they made it too awfully clear that a part of you belonged to that past, too, and always would. That is what I see at Brierfield. I can forget it, or nearly, when I am away."

"Varina! I was afraid it was something like that. Now it is you who are absurd. Poor, gentle spirit! She would never have wanted it to be so."

Varina clenched her hands. How could he speak of her right out like that?

"Poor, gentle spirit!" he said again. "I should have talked of her to you long ago. I will today."

"At Brierfield?" Varina asked fearfully.

"Near by. Come, I'll show you."

The trees parted, revealing the house. James was waiting on the steps to receive them. He had recovered some of his tranquility since morning, but not all of it. His eyes were still watchful as he came to take the reins of the horses.

"Will you 'light and take some refreshments?" he asked, after the first greetings.

"Not just now," Jefferson answered. "I want to show Miss Varina about. Her visits here before this have been rather hurried."

The Negro made shift to smile, but weakly.

"Yes, sir. I hope good luck will attend her this time."

Varina thanked him. She could do still with a few interceding prayers, she thought.

"James is getting on," Jefferson said thoughtfully, as they rode away.

"Yes," Varina agreed. "We must take good care of him."

The *we* had slipped. If Jefferson noticed, he treasured his thoughts in silence.

"The place is dark," he said next.

"Could you spare a tree or two?" Varina suggested.

"I hate to take one down," he confessed. "I can clear a swamp or cane field with gusto, but a tree is another matter. I set too many in the beginning, I suppose. Someone told me trees between a house and cultivated ground held off the fever."

He had set up his ramparts too late.

"But they need not be so many or so close," Varina protested. "They smother a person. They make a house dark as a . . ."

She could think of no word but tomb. Buried hopes and buried joys. He considered her remark, omission and all, in another minute of silence.

"We'll not make the same mistake again," he promised. "Here, this is what I wanted you to see."

They had ridden slowly in an easterly direction from the house. Now they forded a drying runlet of water and climbed through cane and willows and scattered oaks to a knoll of ground that was, compared to the luxurious growth all about, practically bare of vegetation. Nevertheless, Jefferson would not let Varina dismount until he had tramped over every inch of the weed stubble; and, after that, he kept her in the saddle until she had looked about her in every direction.

"How would you like to build a house here?" he asked.

He was delighted when she was too surprised to answer.

"A house," he urged, "brand new and of your own designing?"

Varina struggled with words and with her emotions.

"I am very ashamed," she said, "that I should feel so about the other. You have been very comfortable there. It is home to you."

He covered her hands with his.

"We'll talk of that later," he said. "Now look."

From the saddle Varina could see a wide panorama of forest and swamp and field and canebrake, all slashed by river slough and bayou. From the upper windows of a house the view would be even more comprehensive. Jefferson, his hand still over hers, turned the filly and gave her the directions. This way was Hurricane, this way Palmyra Village, then the Quitman and the Turner plantations, and back of them, the mainland. The river had cut pretty sharply into the Turner lands, leaving part on the peninsula and part on the other shore of a small bay. He rather thought another bite had been taken away in the last storm. The Turners had suffered much more from the vagaries of the Old Man so far than had Brierfield or Hurricane. And now, if she would turn still more to the right, completing a great circle and would look past the chimneys of Brierfield, there was Hurricane again.

"Should we be able to see the house from here?"

"From a second story window, surely," he said. "The Turner and the Quitman houses, too, I think."

No more isolation, no more hiding in a hermit's cell. That was what he promised.

"I can make out the roof and chimneys of Brierfield from the top floor of Hurricane," she told him.

His hand over hers tightened.

"And the river?" she asked.

A quarter turn to the left, through a natural parting of the trees, she could just make out the glimmer of water, when she learned where to look. The view could be widened easily.

"A terraced garden," Varina said, the picture taking shape as, hardly of her own volition, she pronounced the words, "leading down to the water's edge. Would Mr. O'Connor . . ."

"John would be enchanted at the prospect of laying out such a garden, particularly if you asked it."

No, his pleasure would be in laying out a garden at last for Mr. Jefferson. She knew.

"What kind of house?" she asked now.

"I have a picture in my mind," Jefferson said. "See if you can match it."

She closed her eyes, opened them, and the house stood there on the rise of ground, complete. It was not a great tower of a house like Hurricane. It was a farmhouse, low and close to the earth, but with its own stateliness. It had a central structure, noble with pillared galleries, and lower, spreading wings. It would be a house with wide-open doors and deep hearths and laughter would echo through its halls. Yes, that was the house that he saw, too, or one very like it.

"When?" Varina demanded.

"We'll begin it today."

Then, for all their solemnity, she had to laugh. His idea of a beginning was to plant a tree. They rode back to the Brierfield quarters to
borrow a Bowie knife. With it Jefferson cut a switch or a scion from
an ancient, spreading oak; and they carried it back to the open knoll.

"Now, not too close to the house," Varina cautioned, "and don't
obscure the view."

They set the shoot finally at a turn where the drive would wind
down from the house toward what would be their river landing.
They would place a circular bench around the trunk of the tree and
be glad in their old age to rest under its cool shade. In face of that
picture, the switch in Jefferson's hands looked ludicrously small and
they laughed at it and themselves.

And yet, they went about the planting quite solemnly. It was a way
of pegging down the dream they shared. They cleared a small spot
of wild grass and weeds and briers as well as they could with their
hands. Jefferson said it reminded him of his first clearing, though that,
of course, had been on a grander, back-breaking scale. Varina laid her
smarting hands against her cheeks and wondered, then went to work
again for fear that he would notice her small discomfort. With a
sharpened stick he gouged a hole in the center of the cleared space;
and that, he said, was how they had plowed—he and a couple of boys
he borrowed from Hurricane. He set the live oak switch in the hole.
That was how he had put in seed—though not so deeply or with such
special care. After that, it was chop, chop, chop, until the young plants
could hold their own. It was easier to clear an old field, but cotton
did best on new land. So, after a flood, sometimes deliberately they
let land once cleared go wild again for a spell.

"There must be an easier way," Varina said.

"Perhaps we shall discover it," he agreed; and the air was all bright
and breathless again.

They tamped the warm, moist, root-packed earth about the live oak
switch, to hold it in its place. What, Varina asked, would keep the
weeds from choking it out? The nature of the tree and his own efforts, Jefferson answered. He would not let the weeds get a start. The
young tree would be wearing leaves when she saw it next.

When she saw it next . . . the tree was only a promise, a pledge.
The house which had seemed so clear that they could talk of views
and gardens and drives receded into the haze of unreality. He would

not build it yet a while. Other things had intervened. What things? Before she asked him that, she must hear from him about his marriage to Sarah Knox Taylor. She didn't want to hear. He didn't want to talk of it. But the hour could be put off no longer.

Varina gave the soil about the roots of the tree a last firm pat, stood up, dusted her hands and her skirt, shook it out and gathered it up over her left arm.

"Now," she commanded, "tell me about her. Can we walk the horses back to Brierfield?"

"It's farther than you think," Jefferson warned.

Even so, it would be better to be moving.

"I haven't had a tramp in a month," Varina insisted. "I like to walk."

They stood for a minute on the sunny knoll, for a last look all around.

"When was it?" Varina asked. "Tell me exactly when, so that I can see how much has happened since. How old were you?"

"I was twenty when I finished at West Point in 1828." Oh, yes, so Mrs. Eliza Davis had said. "After my graduation leave, I took my first training in company command at Jefferson Barracks in St. Louis. It is the Regular Infantry School of Practice."

"Did you know her then?"

"No. From Jefferson Barracks I was sent to Fort Crawford, Colonel Willoughby Morgan commanding. It was a frontier post."

"Just where?"

"On the upper Mississippi, at the mouth of the Wisconsin River. It posted the northern boundary in those days of the Illinois Indians and was a point of control if they went on the warpath against the Algonquin or Iroquois Indians or if the Sioux came down from the North and West."

"It was a lonely place?"

"Very. The only white society, outside of the officer circle at the fort, consisted of French traders and trappers and their families. Colonel Morgan died in 1831 and the next year Colonel Zachary Taylor came to take command, bringing his family with him—his wife, three daughters and a son, the latter just a boy."

1832 . . . Varina had been a child, exploring ravines and bayous, riding half-broken horses, showing a disturbing precocity for Greek and Latin verbs.

"Sarah Knox was the second daughter."

"Knox," Varina said, not without difficulty. "It's an odd name."

"She was born at Fort Knox, near Vincennes, Indiana. She was an army child. The whole family was army. Mrs. Taylor had lived with the Colonel all their married life—no matter where he was stationed. It was a hard life but neither she nor the girls would have it any other way. The Colonel hated it for them. That was why he didn't want his daughters to marry officers—one reason, at least."

"How old was she—Miss Taylor—when you met her?"

"Eighteen."

Mary Bradford's age—a little older than Varina, not much. And Jefferson—twenty-eight from thirty-two—he had been twenty-four, like young Joseph Davis.

"And beautiful?" Varina insisted.

"I thought she was."

Up there, in those rude surroundings. No, she was really beautiful. She danced—in satin slippers. She wore French kid gloves . . . eighteen—the Colonel's daughter.

"And you loved her very much?"

"I loved her with all my heart. I would be less than a man if I denied that love now. It was all so long ago that sometimes it seems to me another life; but it was a part of my life. I can offer you my heart—you have it, whether you accept it or not—whole and healed of all its scars; but it would not be a heart worth my giving or your taking, if I could say honestly that I had forgotten Knox Taylor or that I ever would forget. I tried. When it was all over and done, I sent James on to Hurricane to remove all her possessions before I returned. I didn't want to be reminded of her by old, lifeless relics. That is why you are so mistaken in thinking that Brierfield is haunted with memories of her. She was never there. There is nothing of hers about."

"Nothing? Are you sure?" Varina asked.

What about a *Ladies' Wreath?*

"Nothing of any consequence," Jefferson insisted. "James overlooked one or two things. Not long ago I found a stack of music in a drawer. I don't know how it got there. James cannot read, you know. He may not have known what it was or what it signified. I didn't know just what to do about it. It seemed unkind to destroy it then—and not very reasonable. Printed music, that has no life in itself. I carried it back to Hurricane and took it to the music room. I hope someone . . . do you play?"

"Very poorly," Varina said. "I should make a botch of it, I'm sure. If you wish, I could shift the pieces about, mingle them with the other music there—for Miss Amanda or Florida McCaleb to play when they come to them."

"See," Jefferson said, "you can be generous."

"But I'm not," Varina said, rather wildly. "I'm not generous at all. I thank you for talking to me this way of her. You honor me greatly, Mr. Davis; but nothing you say makes it any different. It still hurts."

"But, dear heart, why? It's a sad little story. We knew almost no real happiness. The courtship was clandestine, frowned upon by a father she loved dearly. She left home, defying him, to come to Louisville to be married. That was not easy for a girl as gentle as she was."

Yes, she had been gentle; but she had a will, too, Mr. Davis. And she had been brave beyond comparison, beyond the reach of ordinary mortals.

"The marriage was so brief," Jefferson went on, "that it hardly rewarded anyone for what had preceded it in the way of tears and trials. She began to droop almost at once; so that in the bitterest hours of grieving I often thought I had brought her to her death."

"No!" Varina could deny that. "It was her wish as much as yours."

"Yes, I came to the place where I could see it that way. So, why . . ."

"It amounts to this," Varina said. "I am a jealous, mean-spirited person."

"Varina Anne, you are neither one nor the other. You are not mean-spirited and you couldn't be jealous."

Oh, couldn't she? How, if she lived a thousand years, would she match a tale of courage and self-sacrificing devotion like that of Sarah Knox Taylor, who had become Mrs. Jefferson Davis, only to die? What could she ever do to make him, Jefferson, or anyone else speak of her with such awe and admiration? And how could she make clear to him that it was of this she was jealous?

"Varina."

A change in his tone startled her, and shook her, too.

"Varina, look at me."

"*. . . look at him, Miss, with yore eyes lit up . . .*"

They were swimming in tears. Her heart was torn to bits.

"Oh, my darling!"

Regardless of proprieties and any number of possible curious eyes —they were quite near the house again—he opened his arms and she ran to him like a hurt child. He held her fast and crooned over her as if she had been a child, truly.

"My proud, beautiful girl!" he murmured. "Do you know how lovely you are? And how proud? Proud to the marrow of your bones, I do believe. Maybe that is what hurts. It can hurt, I know. And you're so young, so incredibly, marvelously, beautifully young!"

"Green young," Varina sighed. "Will I ever be any older?"

"Not too soon, I hope."

So it happened that, when she saw the ugly house again, tears had softened its harsher lines. It was pleasant to rest a minute and enjoy a glass of sherry with a slice of Maria's pound cake. Dark faces peeped at them from the covert of bush and cabin. She made the acquaintance of a third slave—a boy named Stephen, who held their horses while they rested.

Varina thought, "The building of a house is slow. Time is more precious than some other things. I could content myself here a while if he were close by. I do not like the house. It is not mine. It is a lonely, dour place, really; but I could busy myself with this and that and be happy if he were within call. Rather than wait too long, I would do that."

James hovered on the margin of the gallery and her thoughts. Anxiously still. Oh, yes, the "politicking." She had done nothing about that. She would do nothing about it. James had exaggerated the importance of it. She had exaggerated its importance. Jefferson, whatever the visitors had asked of him and whatever his answer, had seemed quite carefree on that score for the present. He had not included a political career in his declaration. She rather thought he would not now.

He did not. They rode away from Brierfield in a mood of quiet that matched the waning afternoon, each a little weary and very full of heart. They said almost nothing until they rode out of the cane

into the open land between Jefferson's acres and the first bulidings
of Hurricane.

"Shall we run for it?" Varina challenged.

They had their gallop, pulling up short of the quarters, to spare
the oncoming crop of willing servitors. Jefferson's face, to Varina,
looked brighter than the western sky. Politicking, indeed!

This time Joseph waited for them at the Hurricane door alone.

"Well!" he said in greeting. "When you said you wanted the entire
afternoon, you meant just that, I see. Ben has been to Warrenton for
stores and returned, with a sack of mail. I hope you had nothing you
wanted posted. Ben said you had stopped at the store late this morning but had not inquired whether anyone was leaving the plantation,
to carry mail."

"Bless my soul!" Jefferson slapped his pockets in consternation. "I
did stop at the store. Ben had in some fresh peppermint candies. I
bought a packet . . ."

"And left them there," Joseph said dryly. "We were talking of mail,
I believe."

He kept his temper admirably, considering how he simmered underneath.

"No, I had no mail. I will write this evening. Perhaps Varina will
be good enough to be my scribe again."

"Then, you have decided?" Joe asked.

"Yes. I hate to disappoint John Quitman and I'm deeply apprecia-
tive of the compliment Senator Walker has paid me in coming here to
seek me out, but I think I shall decline to serve. It looks to me like a
full spring and summer of beating the political bush, with the reward
doubtful. The very busiest season on a plantation . . ."

"Other planters," Joseph began.

"Other planters employ overseers. We do not," Jefferson said—
clearly, decisively, not quite as arbitrarily as he sounded. Not in intent.
"Besides, I had another plan for this summer."

"Is a cotton crop," Joe asked, "or this other plan more important
than a national election?"

Varina, startled as she was by the unusual tension between the two
men—she had supposed they could never really disagree—found herself calculating years and dates. This was 1844—it was an election
year. The "Tippecanoe and Tyler, Too," campaign, with its torch-

light parades and log cabin banners and hard cider in barrels, had been in 1840.

"You'll not deny it is a critical year for the nation," Joseph pursued.

Perhaps it was. Within a month of his inauguration, General Harrison, the hero of Tippecanoe, had died of pneumonia or of his doctors' attentions, and had left the presidency in the hands of a Mr. John Tyler of Richmond, Virginia. Every bit as aristocratic and un-log-cabinish as Mr. Harrison himself, Mr. Tyler was expected to carry forward the principles of the Whig Party. It was common talk that he had done nothing of the sort. He favored the annexation of Texas, and territorial expansion was a byword with the Democrats. There were other points of difference. The result was that this own party distrusted him because of his actions and the Democrats did not like him for himself. He would go out of office. Who, then, would come in? Yes, a person with very limited outlook could see how the year might be an important one.

"Every national election is critical," Jefferson said, "this one no more so than another. The Democrats will nominate Van Buren again. I think there are other men far more able to lead the party. I should insist on being allowed to hold my own opinion. So we would begin with one disagreement and probably end with a dozen. No, Joe, I gave the matter serious thought and I have decided I am not qualified to perform the task Senator Walker mapped out yesterday evening, which amounts to a series of political revival meetings . . ."

"Ending," Joseph said, "with your being named elector on a winning national ticket."

"If it is a Van Buren ticket, I doubt that it will win. No, I've decided. If I thought I could contribute anything of real value . . . but I don't. I think I'll do better to rest at home. As I said, I've other plans."

It was Joseph Davis still who was agitated. Jefferson spoke in the best of humors; he was quietly sure and unperturbed. He ended with a warm, happy smile at Varina.

"Of course," Joe said, "if that is the depth of your feeling on the issues at stake . . ."

"The depth of my feeling is beside the point."

There was a ring to that statement.

"Uncle Joe," Varina said, "you spoke of mail. If there is some for me, could I have it, please?"

"Mail?" Joseph said. "Yes, of course. What are we standing out here for, anyhow? Yes, there's a letter for you from Natchez. There are letters for all of us from Natchez."

"Now, that's more like it," Jefferson said.

"Yes?" Joseph answered. "Well, come along. They're in the office."

The letters were on his desk. Only the one for Varina, addressed in her mother's round copy-book hand. There were two in William Howell's blacker, bolder script, one for Jefferson and one for his friend, Joseph Davis.

"Shall we read these as a family?" Joseph said. "I'll send for tea."

"No," Varina said. "If you'll excuse me, I'll run along and change. I . . ."

She hesitated. Jefferson had her father's letter in his hands, but he was looking at another on the desk, also for him, though the characters that spelled his name were shaky and uncertain, almost illegible. It was the unsteady writing of an old man—old or ill.

"Run along, then," Joseph said. "Come down when you've finished. There will still be tea."

While Melissa pulled off her boots and undressed her, Varina read her letter.

"My darling big girl," Margaret Howell wrote. . . .

My darling big girl,

You can imagine the excitement into which your letter, telling us that you had surrendered your heart so quickly and so suddenly, and Mr. Jefferson Davis's letter to your father, asking our permission to pay court to you, threw our quiet household. By the vagaries of mail service in these parts, both came down to Natchez on the same boat, Mr. Davis's letter in the hands of Judge Winchester and yours in care of the good captain.

You seem full young to me, my child, to take so momentous a step; yet, I know, by others' standards, you are quite old enough to know your mind and heart, and have always, for that matter, made up your own mind about everything. I must say also that I, at least, was not unprepared for this turn of events. It was indicated in your first letter from Hurricane.

Darling, you ask whether I knew that Mr. Joseph Davis had a younger brother. Yes, I knew that he had a number of brothers; but

I was not aware or I had forgotten that any of them lived with him at Hurricane. Mamma remembers several, but none named Jefferson, who, as you say, is much younger than the others. As it happens, Mr. Jefferson is the only one I ever knew.

I saw him just once and many years ago. It was the summer before you were born. Your papa and Baby Joe and I took a long tour East, to visit your papa's people. Mr. Davis went with us and insisted that we take a boat up the Hudson as far as West Point, where this young brother was attending school. I remember a cadet in gray trousers and short military jacket, very tall and handsome and well built, with ruddy cheeks and bright eyes, leaping over obstacles to reach the boat as it landed, and flinging his arms about his brother with unabashed and open affection. Their meeting was so touching that your papa and I presently strolled away, to give the brothers time to themselves. I assure you, had I dreamed that this young man would some day re-enter my life and in such a manner, I would have studied him more closely.

Darling, your papa is planning to take the next boat up the river to fetch you home. Not in displeasure. You seem, by every account, to have behaved most charmingly and in a manner to do us all credit; but we want you back with us and we want to see Mr. Jefferson Davis here. Also your papa wants to talk with him and your Uncle Joe about his prospects and several other matters. It is our duty and our right . . ."

What followed Varina had to get at another reading. She waved the double sheet of gray stationery like a flag.

"Melissa," she cried, "Papa's coming to Hurricane to fetch us home. He's on his way now, I shouldn't wonder. He . . ."

From the river on the instant came the hollow salute of a steamboat whistle.

"Melissa! You don't suppose . . ."

Melissa, having two shoes on her feet instead of one, reached the window looking out over the river first.

"They's a packet boat out there," she announced. "It cain't land, o' co'se. That's a thing about this island place. They's always too much water or too little."

"Melissa, do you suppose . . . Mamma said he'd take the next boat."

"Then, that's it," Melissa said. "That's yore papa goin' by right now."

"Oh, Melissa! He'll land at Diamond Head or Vicksburg this evening. He'll be here tomorrow. Melissa, where is my other shoe? Melissa, hurry. I want to be downstairs."

"Well, he ain' comin' tonight," Melissa objected.

"I know, but I want ... Melissa, don't be ornery. I want to tell .. Uncle Joe."

"He knows," Melissa said. "He got a letter, too. You said so."

"Melissa, will you hurry?"

In spite of haste, when Varina finally reached the Hurricane office Jefferson had left. Joseph rose to place a chair for her by the fire.

"Don't look so openly disappointed," he chided. "It isn't flattering to me. Jefferson took his mail off to digest it in solitude. Can you bear with me until he returns? Your tea is under a cosy—no, sit still I'll pour you a cup."

The tea was hot and lightly laced with rum. Varina nibbled a biscuit thoughtfully. Joseph's temper, for some reason, was improved.

"I hope Papa said nothing to offend," she said, feeling her way.

"To Jefferson? No. Your father wrote most agreeably to him, saving any unpleasantness he might feel for me."

"Really?"

"Yes. Jefferson makes light of it. He seems to think it quite comprehensible that your father should feel some umbrage at me on your account. In short, your father, my good friend, accuses me of all man ner of crime, including grand larceny—the theft, the deliberate theft of you, his eldest, and, it appears from his letter, his favorite daughter."

He turned his head just perceptibly, to listen to a sound outside Varina's sharp ears had caught it before his did. The sound was the rapid beat of a horse's hoofs—a heavy horse—Old Duke, the Comanche or Gray Medley. Jefferson riding at a gallop away into the winter twilight. Why? If her father had said nothing to disturb him, then it was that other letter, the one written with a cramped and shaking hand.

"Papa would say something like that," she said, with the piece of her mind that she could keep here in the office. "He grumbled over your very invitation last May."

"This was no grumble," Joseph said. "Your father's tone was quite severe. I might take umbrage in my turn at some of his accusation ... if I were not by honesty compelled to admit that they are just."

Varina put her teacup on the table, wiped her lips, and folded her hands in her lap—the approved posture for a lady showing composure, particularly if she felt she was beginning to lose it.

"You are speaking of young Mr. Joseph Davis, I am sure." She was not sure. She was still feeling her way. "I am so sorry. I found him most charming; and, perhaps, if I had never known Mr. Jefferson . . ."

"I am not speaking of my nephew," Joseph said abruptly. "I never for a minute thought he would be a match for you. It was Jefferson I had in mind all along. Now, what do you find vexatious about that?"

Varina did not answer. She couldn't. It wasn't only that Joseph's bald statement stole some of her delight. The reason went deeper. Joseph refilled his toddy glass and offered her more tea. When she refused, he set the pot in its cosy on table near her, saying she might change her mind.

"I can tell you now," he went on then, ignoring her unhappy speech-lessness, "this is something I've had in my heart for Jefferson for a long time. I loved him too much to think that one brief fling at happiness and the fullness of living were all he was to have. His habits of a recluse were hardly human. He has a gay and tender side to his nature, but you will have discovered that. But it's only part of the story. I admire my youngest brother, too, because I know him, perhaps better than anyone else, even himself. He has rare and special gifts that should not be wasted. I wanted him to waken out of his trance of contemplation. I knew the one answer would be a new love. Ah . . . but I knew, too, that the young woman who could rouse his heart again must be an exceptional person. She must have wit and spirit as well as beauty of a high order. Then I saw you and my very kin-ship with Jefferson told me that you were the one. Now, I repeat, what is so vexatious about that? My design included your happiness, did it not?"

"But was that all of it?" Varina asked. "Was happiness for either one your real reason?"

The sound of the horse's hoofs had been gone in reality for some time, but she still heard it in fancy. Joseph frowned at his toddy.

"The trouble with a woman having a brain," he said wryly, "is that she uses it with no discretion. You have touched, of course, upon a point of difference between you and me. I am disappointed in you in one particular. I credited you with more personal ambition than you seem to have. You are right in supposing that what I wanted for Jefferson was a complete awakening. He has, I repeat, rare and special talents. They are needed in our world, and now. As you and your father and every easy-going gentleman in our South, which you pretend to love so well, will see sooner than you think. Jefferson sees, when he is not too dazzled by other dreams. He can, as you know, stand here in this office and theorize till Kingdom Come; but what is that? He has no influence on events, he makes no converts here, where all agree with his views. Someone is needed to carry the light out over the hills, someone with exactly his ability."

"Oh, no!" Varina said. "No!"

"Yes," Joseph said relentlessly. "And I thought, when you two first met, the thing was done. Jefferson had been unwilling to enter the county campaign—the habit of not mingling with people, of course. But, after you came, he seemed to take fire. Of course, it was too late and he lost the election for that reason."

"And there was Seargent Prentiss," Varina reminded him.

"Yes, the great and only Prentiss," Joseph said impatiently. "The Whigs brought him in, to prove their extremity. What will they do without him presently, I wonder? For his days are numbered, you know. He is a sick man and a wastrel and presently the world will have forgotten him. To all the nation Jefferson will stand for Mississippi, for the South. He can, you know."

Varina clasped her hands more tightly in her lap, then threw them apart.

"Uncle Joe," she said desperately, "perhaps I ought to tell you now why I turned giddy that evening at Vicksburg. It wasn't the oil lamps or the close air. I had a sort of vision—Mr. Jefferson at the mercy of a mob . . ."

"Pah! A handful of rowdies affected you so?"

"It was not a handful. I saw thousands tearing at him, lifting him up, if you will, only to tear him down."

"Pah!" Joseph said again. "You are claiming powers of divination now?"

"No. I love him and I see so plainly . . ."

"You love him. Must a woman's love always be such a greedy, selfish thing? You saw, I suppose, he had another letter besides the one from your father?"

"I saw," Varina said, "I wasn't spying, but I saw."

"Yes. It was from one of Jefferson's particular heroes—General Jackson, written from The Hermitage, where Jefferson once visited."

"You wrote to him?"

Now Varina could understand the pounding hoofs going off into the distance. Of course, Jefferson would be influenced by a letter from The Hermitage. He would heed General Jackson's words, if only out of respect for the hero's years.

Joseph neither admitted the truth of her charge nor denied it.

"It was hardly necessary for me to write," he said. "Jefferson made deep impression during his brief campaign on people of far more prestige politically than I enjoy."

This was evasion. Varina stood up. She thought she might shake less on her feet, but she had to put a hand to the back of her chair, to hold herself steady. Joseph rose, too. She had never felt more green young than she did, facing him, more inadequate; but she had to speak her mind.

"What I shall never see," she said, "is how you can be so sure you are right in what you are doing. You speak of his gifts. Surely you know that one of them is his capacity, his willingness for self-sacrifice."

"That willingness is necessary to one who leads a crusade. The sacrifice is not inevitable."

"You speak of crusades. If you think one is needed, why do you not lead it in person?"

"I have not my brother's qualifications. I am a prosy old man. I don't inspire anybody."

No. He just sat here at his desk, plotting, using people.

"You see that, don't you?" he said.

"I see everything now," Varina said.

"Of course you do. You are a woman of rare perception. Your intelligence is not the least of your fascination, my dear, if you direct its use. For, though a woman may be as fair as Hebe . . ."

"Please," Varina begged.

"If she lacks wit to go with her beauty," Joseph continued, as if she had not spoken, "her charm soon palls. You are likely to be more and more fascinating as time goes on. Please take a sensible view of things, my dear. You can be of great help to Jefferson in the career of which he is about to make a beginning. That is . . . I don't suppose in your present outrage you are thinking of throwing him over? I wouldn't advise it. He will rise high."

Varina thought that any minute she might die of being angry. If she had not been so angry, she might have seen that this was a threat she could hold over Joseph, if she had a mind to. As to that, she would not know how to act until she saw Jefferson and talked with him.

"Yes," she said, inconsequentially, almost incoherently, not answering Joseph's innuendo, "he will rise high. No matter at what cost to himself, he will rise, because he is what he is. I hope then you will be satisfied, as you are now. He will go so far and rise so high that some day people will hardly remember anything you had to do with his success. He will be known to folks who won't know you, and he will be remembered when you are forgotten."

To that Joseph gave calm agreement. His quiet further infuriated Varina.

"You really think it is something good and great you are doing," she charged. "What if it is not? What if you don't find it even profitable?"

"Only time," he said, "will answer that. Like all ventures, this one will show profit and loss. I cannot predict the final balance. You may come to thank me some day for what I have done or you may come to hate me thoroughly."

"I hate you now."

"Once you hated him."

"Who told . . . I never did, really."

"Then I was misinformed."

"But I do hate you!"

How she hated him! Beyond all restraint of breeding or manners. He liked her rudeness, the fire of it. She hated him then for that.

"You don't hate me—really," he said. "You are frightened. Come have another cup of tea."

She would not. It would choke her. She begged to be excused. She would go to her room. When Jefferson returned, if he did return, she wanted to see him, please, no matter what the hour.

"I will send you word," Joseph promised.

Long after supper Jefferson came back to Hurricane, his mind clear and decided, his heart a little rueful, especially after he saw Varina

His decision was what she had known it would be. General Jackson had pleaded earnestly with him, insisting that he was needed in the work of rallying the Democratic forces of the state against the coming election. Respectfully he had heard the old man out, when he would not have listened to another, and finally had taken the appeal as a command.

"Varina," he held her by both hands, trying to make her feel by touch what he felt, "this is an obstruction. I try to tell myself it is only a delay but it makes impossible most of what we planned—at least, for the present. I don't know what will be asked of me. I have to confer with Senator Walker. I will take my orders from him, I presume."

The idea of that!

"I understand," Varina said. "Of course, building a new house . . ."

"What's that?" Joseph said.

"Nothing," Jefferson told him. "I'll explain some time. It's all out of the question now. Varina . . ."

Varina pulled at her hands, as if she wanted to be free.

"You spoke of letters this afternoon," she said. "I waited up to write them for you."

"My dear, at this hour? I wouldn't think of letting you."

"Nonsense!" Joseph said. "Of course, you'll let her. She wants to do it, don't you, Varina?"

"Yes," she said, "I want to. Please."

So presently she sat at the table before sheets of paper, pens and a well of ink. The first letter was to General Jackson.

"Dear Mr. President," Jefferson addressed him.

"Dear Mr. President,
"I appreciate deeply the honor . . .

"Varina, your father wrote to me most kindly. His chief stipulation is that he wishes me to address my suit from now on to you at home in Natchez. I had thought I would follow you there immediately, but now I can't . . . immediately."

"No," Varina said, "you must confer with Senator Walker first. Oh, forgive me, but I don't like that man."

"You needn't. I will not expect it of you. As to my coming to Natchez, it will be soon. And often. Wherever I go on this state busi-

ness, I mean to take a map, so that I may study the direction to you—
a map and an extra horse, so that I may visit you soon and often. If
you will receive me?"

"It will be most exciting," Varina sniffed, "to be visited by such an
important person. Shall we go on with the letter?"

"My darling, yes.

"I appreciate deeply the honor of your addressing a letter to me and
in your own hand . . .

"Varina, I can't dictate the letter tonight. It must wait for tomorrow."

"Tomorrow," Varina said, "I shall be leaving. Please continue, Mr
Davis."

CHAPTER XII

"**V**A-REE-NA!**"**

The call was thin and faraway—at least as far as the depth of the house. Perhaps she had only imagined it. If not, it would be repeated.

In any case nobody could want her for any very important reason at this hour of the morning. Jefferson would not have arrived yet. He was expected at The Briers today, but she would not begin to look for him a minute before noon. Back in the spring and summer and fall, when he had been riding up and down the state and to and fro in it, as if Satan were whipping his horse, she could never tell from what direction or when he might appear, for he had meticulously kept his promise to see her often.

"Jefferson, how far is *near* this time?"

It might be ten, twenty or more miles. Once it had been forty; and he had had to borrow a horse from The Briers' stable in order to return to a political rendezvous that same evening.

The suddenest, the most meager, the most delightful, the soonest-over of lovers' trysts; but this was different. The hateful, the wearing, the exciting business of these very critical national elections was now accomplished. Presumably all the great issues were settled, right or wrong, for another four years; and a man might travel to see his sweetheart for the pure purpose of setting a wedding date, without a cohort of busybodies pursuing him to the gates or waiting in ambush just outside the lauri mundi hedge. He had said he would arrive today, if

Mr. Howell would have the leisure and be disposed to receive him, there being certain legal formalities . . . Mr. Howell, indeed!

"He is coming! He is coming!"

Varina had wakened in the morning hardly able to keep from chanting her happiness aloud, and, for fear that she might sound as demented as she felt, had taken herself sternly in hand. This being a visit of ceremony and so announced, Mr. Davis would observe all the conventions, and she would do the same, if possible. She would not begin looking for him one minute before noon. Or listening. She would not think every time a door closed that he had stepped through the opening; and, every time anyone in the house called to someone else, she would not think the hail was for her. Goodness, she had enough to do to keep her busy, anyhow.

Busy? Was this possibly another January? Had a year really passed since that dark troubled evening at Hurricane? She could remember looking down the length of it from its beginning, wondering how she could ever endure the waiting. Would she not be shriveled and all beat out at the end of it? But, of course, regardless of circumstance, there had to be that year. A young lady of position could hardly marry respectably after a shorter betrothal, even if there had been no obstruction. There had been considerable obstruction, as she viewed things now—Jefferson's political engagements on his side and on hers a number of little peckish hindrances:

"Darling, you are very young. . . . Puss, are you sure? . . . I hope young Mr. Davis—" he was always young Mr. Davis to Granny Kempe —"realizes the honor . . . after all, who and what are the Davises? Good, honest farmer folk, while the Howells and the Grahams . . . Varina, he is older, isn't he? Quite a bit older, I should say. I don't suppose it matters, but . . . Cousin Varina, wasn't Mr. Davis married before this? A long time ago? Well, mercy, don't bite my head off. I was only asking."

It had taken most of a year to change these tunes.

"Darling, he is just right for you. I am so happy for you. . . . Puss, I like him. Can't help liking the man when you come to know him. . . . I don't mind telling you now, Miss, that, if the older Mr. Davis had had the younger one's charm, your name might not now be Howell. . . . Blood? Stuff! We all pioneered out here together, I reckon. . . . Well, I must say, Varina, luck seems to attend you. I doubt that we'll see much of you around here after you're married. So distinguished a man . . . Oh, Cousin Varina, I'd love to be your bridesmaid. I do think Mr. Davis is the most divinely romantic person. . . ."

"I don't suppose," Joseph Davis had challenged, "that in your present outrage you are thinking of throwing him over?"

Throw him over? No, indeed, nor loosen one finger's hold on him; nevertheless, there had to be that year. What with one thing and another, it had turned out to be a full one. She would not have supposed there would be so many things a young lady must learn or would want to learn in preparation for marriage. By comparison, the first seventeen years of her life had been sadly misspent.

She was in the kitchen now, pouring cake batter into a deep pan. This was to be a loaf cake, depending on God's will and her own deftness, a loaf cake being subject to more hazards than any other sort. By a special decree of banishment, she had the kitchen to herself except for one of her grandmother's maids, who waited to open the iron door of the chimney oven when she was ready—but not to close it.

"Now, Zenoby, now!" Varina commanded.

The wall-eyed girl lifted and pulled, and the door swung back. Varina slid the cake pan into the dark cavern.

"Now go away, Zenoby. Easy! If this falls, it will be strictly my own doing."

She closed the door softly, looked at its blank face prayerfully, then tiptoed out after the maid. Presently, when the cake was pretty well set, it would be time enough to see about cleaning up mixing bowls and having the kitchen put to rights before The Briers cook and her assistants moved in to get dinner.

Outside, the deceiving warmth of a bright midwinter day greeted her. Lovely, blue, unclouded weather—like that afternoon when she had ridden from Diamond Place to Hurricane, a stranger. Never dreaming—reminiscence died aborning as a half-dozen black children swarmed up the kitchen steps toward her.

"Miss V'rina, it's right warm in the sunshine. You goin' to give us nurr lesson today? Time's gittin' sho't, mebbe. Some of us ain' likely to git all the way from A to Izzard, like Ole Miss say. Miss V'rina . . ."

"Shoo!" Varina said. "Get down off these steps. Didn't Zenoby tell you I had a cake in the oven? Shoo! Get away this minute."

"Miss V'rina . . ."

"All right. I'll give you a lesson—I've just about got that much time
—but not right here. We can sit on the cistern platform, I reckon . . .
wait a minute till I feel the bricks. Umm! Yes, they're fine and
warm. You wait right here, then, while I get the primer from the
schoolhouse."

When Varina had first suggested teaching a few of the younger
children their letters, Granny Kempe's one stipulation had been that
the lessons be held out of doors.

"Don't smell up the schoolhouse, that's all I ask," she said. "That's
how these reforms usually end—the white folks get run out, to make
room for the black ones. What has come over you, anyhow, Varina,
that suddenly you must do good in all directions?"

Varina had given an evasive answer at the time. It was against the
Mississippi code of laws, she knew, to teach slaves to read and write;
but her urge had been strong. It had come over her one evening in
picking time, as she stood between her father and brother in the
scaffold-yard of one of her grandmother's plantations and watched a
field gang weigh in their cotton baskets. It was a scene as familiar to
her as sunrise and sunset; but, like everything else this year, it had
new meaning.

Down the dusty path from the field the pickers marched—men,
women and half-grown children, each head topped by a basket that
might hold anywhere from ten to two hundred pounds of cotton. By
day the baskets stood at the ends of the rows and the pickers filled
them from lighter, handier sacks. It was back-breaking work under
the hot September sun, snatching the full fresh bolls that burst low on
the stiff stalks. It was weary work, tramping the long rows to dump
the pick-sacks. They sang to make the work seem lighter. They sang
to forget aching backs, to set a rhythm for their fingers. They sang
because they were happy. They sang because they were sad. They
sang in the freshness of the morning because it was good to greet the
sun and they sang at evening because it was good to see that old sun
go down.

They sang now as dark fell, to hold lagging, stumbling feet on the
dusty path. They stepped in a line to the shed, set down their basket
and watched sheepishly, anxiously, or with carefree swagger while the

overseer chalked up the weight beside each name on the big slate in figures not a one of them could read.

Each time the overseer sang out the poundage and some could carry the numbers in their heads, but what did that prove? The amount of cotton he could pick on a work day was all a field hand's measure of worth. On Granny Kempe's or Howell or Davis land diligence and skill were rewarded—a few cents for a mouth harp or a bright ribbon or extra sweetening, or something laid by toward the price of ultimate freedom, if that was coveted; but, if a body could not read, how could he be sure? All right tonight, with Moss' Will and Young Mosser standing by; but suppose an overseer wasn't watched and wasn't honest . . .

The line stepped up to the weighing shed, set its burdens down, shuffled and danced away; and pain thrust itself at Varina's new sensitiveness. If only the brighter, more teachable ones could know enough to read and write their own names and simple sums! If some of the children growing up on the place could learn . . .

Hence these lessons in the house yard on a sunny morning, transgressing the law, but doing good in some direction, perhaps, if not in all.

In a minute Varina was back at the cistern platform, the lesson book in her hands, the children clustered around her.

" 'A' is for 'Apple,' for 'Abraham.' "

They made the sounds after her. They traced the outline of the letter on one of Maggie's alphabet blocks. They made it out of bits of sticks. One boy, nimbler than the others, scratched it on a Christmas slate.

" 'B' is for 'Boy,' for 'Ball.' "

Except in one or two instances, she made slow progress. She could not say honestly that the children thirsted after learning. They enjoyed the comparative idleness of the lessons. They reveled in her attention. She moved these days in the aura of her coming bridehood.

" 'C,' " she proceeded, glancing at Paladin, sunning himself on the porch rail, "is for 'Cat.' "

" 'K,' " the boy with the slate contributed, "is for 'Kitty.' "

The lesson, as it usually did somewhere, halted. The boy with the slate, delighted with his own precocity, dissolved into a kicking, giggling ball. The younger initiates looked in consternation at Varina. Could this be true?

" 'C,' " Varina repeated firmly, "is for 'Cat.' We will worry about Kitty when we get that far. Sollie, you are not to mix the little children up that way. You . . ."

"Va-ree-na!"

A door in the main house opened and her mother appeared on the south gallery. Varina stood up, shaking the black children like burrs from her skirts. It could be . . . it just could be . . .

But it was not.

"Varina, didn't you hear me call?" her mother fussed gently. "The dressmaker is here—the one from New Orleans. In Mamma's room. I must say her fashion plates and samples are extravagantly beautiful."

The whole business was an extravagance. There was not a more skilled or gifted seamstress in the South than Melissa. Given the material and the plates and the help of a couple of sewing girls, she could turn out a trousseau fit for a queen. She was well along now on the wedding dress—muslin sheer as a cobweb, traced with exquisite embroidery—a dress to set any girl to dreaming; but Granny Kempe dreamed after other patterns.

The New Orleans dressmaker was Granny's idea. She sat securely entrenched in the latter's room, with Granny herself mounting guard in her armchair. On the counterpane of the huge poster bed, under the heavy tester, were spread picture plates of costumes for every hour of the day from morning until night, most of them so extremely fashionable as to seem fairly outlandish. Interspersed among these were sheaves of samples—velvet, worsted, silk, satin—and trays of buttons and tinsel trimmings. A mulatto boy stood by the center table in charge of more trays and books of samples and a folio containing more picture plates.

Varina took exception to the boy in his blue silk cutaway coat and fancy white vest and pantaloons and his buckled shoes. He would be impudent if he dared. She took exception to the dressmaker. She was so ultra-ultra in her austere black silk and her bonnet, lined with white ruching, suggesting a nun's hood but too modish for anything beyond the suggestion. She wore besides that such an air, as if it pained her really to represent the most fashionable and expensive *couturière* in

New Orleans, whereas it did not pain her at all. She thought she was honoring The Briers with her presence. A hired hack stood in the drive out front. Varina had no use today for any vehicle that did not carry one certain person. If she had heard the wheels in the drive, her heart would have been in her throat.

"My granddaughter, Madame," Granny said in presentation.

"Darling," Margaret Howell pleaded, "do feel the texture of this corded silk."

"Mamma," Varina began.

"My granddaughter," Granny continued, "is making what we are pleased to believe is a distinguished marriage."

"Mr. Jefferson Davis," the *couturière's* representative murmured. "Aside from his excellent connections, one hears great things of him."

Sharp ears, but naturally one heard. A year ago a Vicksburg paper had called him little known, owing to a secluded life. Now there was not a one-bale farmer in the remotest back country who hadn't seen him or heard him speak at least once. Joseph Davis had triumphed in this particular, at least. Varina had kept fast hold of Jefferson Davis's affections, but he belonged now to thousands of other people as well as to her. That Mississippi had voted heavily in favor of a Democratic candidate for the presidency in November had been due as much to his persuasiveness and indefatigable efforts as to the popular demand for annexing Texas.

Jefferson himself made light of his successes.

"I am a good shot with the rifle," he would declare, after electrifying a back-country rally. "That seems to have more weight than argument. With argument I make little or no headway. It is no secret, I believe, that I have my favorite candidate and have insisted from the first on being allowed to speak in his behalf. I always open with a plea in favor of Mr. Calhoun; but, just as I get really warmed up, a gentleman out front will rise up from a crackerbox and demand, 'What you got agin Mr. Van Buren, Mister?' Naturally I have nothing against Mr. Van Buren, but I prefer Mr. Calhoun. I sweat and I strive for another hour and the man out front sits down finally, saying, 'Well, be that as it may, I'm still adding my tally to Mr. Van Buren's count!' "

His reproduction of the sandhill drawl was perfect. Gentlemen on crackerboxes, indeed! Piney-woods rednecks, most of them!

Later, when General Jackson from The Hermitage picked a candi-

date for the presidency that nobody in a deadlocked national convention could object to, because nobody knew much about him, Jefferson was even funnier.

"I understand that this Mr. Polk," he drawled, "was born in South
Carolina and that is as near as I came to naming my man. Well, I've
got a new rifle, loaded and oiled. I still think I can draw more votes
at a shooting match than at a speaking."

He could laugh, but after November and the Democratic victory
nobody in Mississippi called Jefferson Davis little known. Well, that
was over now.

"Mr. Davis," Varina maintained on this bright January morning,
"is a planter."

"There will be a honeymoon in New Orleans," Granny said inexorably. "That much at least."

Varina looked at her in sharp inquiry. How did she know? Had
she special information? No, she was just divining, like old Aunt
Rhina.

"Goin' to trabel a far way . . . goin' to live high . . ."

Granny, Varina often thought, was Joseph Davis's best ally at The
Briers. She had not been too surprised at discovering that Uncle Joe
had been Granny Kempe's choice of husbands for her favorite
daughter. Granny had foreseen his rise to wealth and position. Disappointed then, she was enjoying or meant to enjoy some vindication of
her judgment now.

"Ah!" the dressmaker was already measuring Varina with her eyes.
"A suite at the St. Charles, no doubt. Seats at the opera . . . the pre-
Lenten balls. The young Madame will require one or more elaborate
evening costumes, and street attire in keeping."

"Darling," Margaret coaxed, "you will indulge me and your grand-
mamma?"

Varina sighed and gave in. Once, smothering in a sea of cashmere
and silk velvet, she made a slight murmur.

"Mr. Davis will be overwhelmed, I know."

"But that is as it should be," the dressmaker said, her la-dee-dah
gentility melting as she perceived the likely richness of her order.

"Skirts," she said in the next breath, "will be fuller than ever this
season. There is talk now of reviving the use of hoops. Beyond question, a wide skirt, thus supported, does much to render a small waist

infinitesimal and also to obscure the . . . ah . . . more generous proportions."

The thing had advanced now to tapelines and a chart of measurements. Varina knew well that she was not infinitesimal. In fact, she
had lost quite lately all desire for fragility; but that, too, was past.
The next instant she was racked with laughter.

"Some consider hoops awkward and impractical," Madame was saying, "but they can be of use. Lately a fashionable young lady of Paris
was involved in a boating accident on the River Seine. The boilers
exploded, throwing all passengers into the water. Many were drowned
but Mademoiselle's hoops held her skirts out and made a very effectual
life-preserver."

The spectacle of the modish young lady afloat by reason of her skirts,
the spectacle of herself riding the Mississippi in such a framework, was
too much for Varina's control. Her laughing shook a pickaninny out
of a tree near the house and set off a yelping of dogs and a variety of
other shrieks.

"Varina!" Granny Kempe said sharply.

"Mademoiselle is very young?" the seamstress suggested.

"My daughter has a wicked sense of the ridiculous," Margaret apologized. "She gives offense sometimes where none is intended."

"I'm sorry," Varina said at once. "I . . . I was just thinking, if the
River Seine is anything like our old monster, the French young lady's
dress must have been ruined. And that would be a pity, if the material was anything like as lovely as this, for example."

They went on to plan a ball gown of silk the color of blush rose
petals. It would be made in an extreme mode, as a concession to the
bride's newly acquired status of a matron, but trimmed with falls of
delicate lace, in tribute to her youth and modesty. Madame went back
to work with her tapeline, slightly mollified; but Varina had to picture
herself in the ballroom of the St. Charles Hotel instead of afloat on
the river, to insure a continuance of pleasant relations.

It was a bright picture. She could see it clearly enough—herself in
the exquisite gown, a jeweled comb or pin in her hair, perhaps, instead
of the girlish camellia. No, she would always prefer the flower. Anyhow, there she would be, shimmering and shining, with long, white,
French kid gloves past her elbows, meeting the falls of lace and the
bracelets Granny Kempe was keeping for the first bride of this gener-

ation. What would she be doing? Why, bowing and talking to this stranger and to that—about her husband presumably, since in this new life she would be well-informed on no other subject.

Fright, such as had not visited her in a long while, swept over her suddenly. Where was this husband, for whom these elaborate preparations were being made? She could not fit him into the picture, she could not vision him there at all. She came out of her fantasy abruptly.

"There!" she said. "I knew. There won't be time to finish these dresses. The wedding will be very soon."

"Varina!" her mother was shocked at this frankness of impatience. The dressmaker was even more shocked. Granny Kempe alone maintained her calm.

"There will be fully a month," she stated. "That should allow time."

A month? Why didn't Jefferson come? Zenobia, the little maid, came instead. The minute she stepped through the door, Varina remembered.

"My cake!" she cried. "My beautiful cake! Zenoby . . ."

"It's all right, Miss V'rina," the girl said. "Sinai took it out."

"Did it . . ."

"No'm, it didn't fall one bit. It's fine."

But Varina raced out to see for herself.

Noon. Dinnertime passed and no Jefferson.

The long afternoon wore away. Varina iced her cake. She consumed an hour in her father's office, helping him with his accounts, studying this and that. It seemed to her that her father had not picked up as fast this between-season as he usually did. The longer the real cold weather held off, the more trouble a planter had getting his cotton in before a killing frost ruined the staple. Good masters—William Howell was too easy, most people said—did not like to work their hands in chill winter rains. And here he sat, consuming a good day in idleness.

He saw the concern on her face and turned it aside.

"You're good at the books, Puss. You've caught on fine."

Varina smiled at him fondly. A better business man than he was, no doubt.

"It's complicated," she said. "I had no idea."

Hardly anyone did have. Her Aunt Sally had gone back North in the thick of the planting season, deeply impressed.

"I'm going to tell everybody I see," she said. "What looks so easy isn't easy at all. A planter has everything to do. He is supposed to be a doctor, a carpenter, a priest, a brick mason, a millwright, a judge advocate, a ditch digger, a financial wizard—the Lord himself couldn't know it all."

"You could take hold and run a plantation as well as the next one," William said now. That was Varina's reward for earnest application. She had felt that she must learn this thing, too. "Naturally, I hope you never need to."

He was thinking that she just might.

"Papa . . ."

"He's only delayed, Puss. Something came up and he had to take a later boat. Or, the one he caught had trouble getting away from a landing. The rivers are running full right now and every downstream packet is loading to its chimney stacks."

Varina knew. Beginning in October, cotton wagons rolled and lurched over every rutted and pitted road in the state, making the first stage of the long journey to the Gulf and the "market." Cotton squares and warehouses were soon jammed. Bales were piled high on every wharf of every stream that was navigable, if only for a few months out of the year, waiting for deep water. When the water level rose, the steamboats appeared. They tied up and stevedores hooked and slid the bales aboard, stacking them to the top deck. Style and glitter and accommodation to passengers gave way to the priority of the precious freight. Varina knew, but . . .

"Puss, you're not troubled over something?"

"I'm troubled," Varina said thoughtfully, "over whether I should be troubled."

"Ah!" her father said. "I reckon that's true of most of us right now. It's a strange thing, Puss. When I came out here a matter of twenty-five years ago, hard and long as the journey was, this was still the far edge of the same country as my home back in Jersey. All the uneasiness, the growing sense of separation has come about since. Nobody knows when it began or why."

"Papa . . ."

"Puss, a year ago, when your Uncle Joe set all this confusion afoot, and I thought he was trying to snare you for that nephew of his, I was all against the idea. I had no notion of letting him adopt you into his family, just because he had taken a fancy to you. Now I don't know but what I'd be easier in my mind if you had taken the nephew. I don't suppose you gave him really a good looking over?"

See! He, too, believed that the delay was something more significant than a slow cotton boat.

"No, Papa. I chose Jefferson."

Her father creaked up out of his chair, shook himself and laughed his pleasant, booming laugh.

"I'll wager you did just that," he declared. "Well, if we're not to have a visitor right away, I should be riding out. You wouldn't chance accompanying me, would you?"

"No, Papa, I'll wait here. Thank you."

The balance of the afternoon she fretted away in the gardens near the house—both vegetable and flower gardens. Up to the preceding summer she had hardly known peas from beans in their growing state. Now she was pleased to note that they could have garden peas for dinner almost any day. As for a flower garden, its ultimate purpose was, to be sure, to provide posies a maid might pluck and thrust into her braids or fragrant, moonlit paths when she might stroll with her lover—too seldom, by past record—but there was a deal of work needed to maintain both possibilities. That she had mastered at least the work program was evidenced today by the increased activity of hoe and rake and shears wherever she moved. John O'Connor, she thought, would be surprised when the time came to lay out flowerbeds at Brierfield. What a garden that would be if . . .

And there her world hung, impaled on a condition.

At suppertime Varina would not have the cake cut. She had all but abandoned hope, still would not make the final admission. Others of the family felt that Jefferson would not come now. It would be to-morrow or they would hear. Still they pretended to humor her in her dwindling expectations. A fire of fragrant cedar logs was laid on the polished andirons under the marble mantel in the best parlor and lighted. Early in the evening Varina in a dress of warm, red cashmere cloth and a granny shawl about her shoulders against the increasing chill of the January night took up her vigil at a mahogany desk close by. She spread a sheet of writing paper, prepared a pen, and then sat motionless.

This was extraordinary for her, usually as glib at writing as at speaking. Her purpose was, of course, a letter to Jefferson. If he did not come, if he should send word, instead, she meant to have an answer ready to go back by the same messenger. Her exercises in patience and forbearance had been the most trying of all the year's experience, but she had mastered those virtues, too. Or so she thought.

Why, then, could she not get on with this letter? She couldn't seem even to begin. She was at a loss over the mere problem of a fitting salutation.

Dear Mr. Davis . . .

No. It was fun sometimes to address him so, the mock formality having the force of endearment. Tonight the words seemed stiff and forbidding.

Dear Mr. Jefferson . . .

No, again. Neither one thing nor the other. Obsequious, rather.

With a sigh that gave the lie to her drilling in patience, she tossed the pen aside, stood up and walked over to the mantel. She stood before the bright fire, fighting for a calm that would not come. Instead, presently she began to strike her fists, one against the other, in a frenzy of despair.

She was more than ever sure that Jefferson's non-arrival was not due to boats. It was Brother Joe. After a period of quiet, pretending to allow her and Jefferson to plan their lives afresh, he, or someone directed by him, had moved into the fight again. The war for possession was not over. He had only granted a truce. That was the most of peace she might enjoy for years to come, perhaps forever.

"I hate you," she had told him at Hurricane.

And she did. Fundamentally and deeply and, of course, in secret. There was no one at The Briers to whom she could confide her animosity and distrust. Nobody would have believed her if she had called him openly a sly, scheming old man, except possibly her father. For Jefferson's sake, she did not want to widen the slight breach which she felt existed already between the two outward-seeming friends. She and Uncle Joe had parted at Hurricane with an adequate show of affection and she had not seen the man since.

For a while, then, after her return to Natchez, distance and other occupation had softened her animosity, at least to the point of her being able to reason things out. It hurt, for one thing, to give up an idolatry she had cherished since childhood. It was quite possible, she thought, that she had, in her outrage at Joseph's making of her and Jefferson pawns on his private chessboard, condemned him too completely. A man of his peculiar abilities would more or less treat all people that way. His fault was not that he lacked softer impulses or failed to understand them. He understood them so well that he made good use of them—in shaping the lives of others to do his will.

As summer progressed, however, and Jefferson on his fleeting visits seemed lean and hollow-eyed with weariness—sometimes, sitting outside, with his head tipped back against a pillar, he would seem to drift into unconsciousness and Varina, frightened, would speak to him softly to call him back—as bitterness crept even into his laughter, her anger was renewed. She did not question then the cold, ruthless calculation with which Joseph had taken advantage of his younger brother's unhappiness to serve certain purposes he had had in mind from the beginning. All those eight years during which Jefferson Davis had led the life of a scholar and a recluse on Davis Bend, Joseph had been subtly at work on him.

This did not necessarily imply any weakness on Jefferson's part. He had, to be strictly honest, a number of radical and independent beliefs of his own. These he had brought home with him. The thing was that another sort of life, more happily directed, with more worldly contacts, might have mellowed and broadened these views. Seclusion, amounting to isolation, too much communion with books instead of men, except family and neighbors, a feudal patrimony on which to work out his theories, enough money gain to make him believe that his way of living, if not interfered with, was not only pleasant but practical, had turned him into a bright-eyed zealot, Joseph's part being hardly more, after the initial groundwork, than that of counselor and benevolent patron. If Jefferson had not been the kind of man who could formulate his own beliefs and build on them, until they had the power of fanaticism, he would not have been of any use to Joseph, who, as he himself said, was quite content to be outstripped finally by his disciple.

All this then, by patience and a manipulation that was only a touch here and a touch there, Joseph Davis had achieved, only to find, when the time was ripe for his gifted younger brother to enter the turmoil of a nation's unrest, that the world had lost its tempting flavor for Jefferson. But for that, too, Joseph had been able to prescribe. Varina, young, intelligent but innocent, lively and, as he had supposed, ambitious, had been the formula he tried. He had never gambled more shrewdly or, for that matter, more ruthlessly. He had risked his brother's peace of mind and the girl's happiness . . .

It was at this point always that Varina's anger passed the bounds of control. She was ready then to believe the man guilty of the darkest crimes. His wife's invalidism—might that not be a reflection on certain infidelities? The thought sickened and shamed her, but it would not subside. What of Knox Taylor? Had he disliked her and so given her and Jefferson the most noisome end of the peninsula for a home, thereby all but destroying Jefferson as well as his bride? Anything seemed possible when she realized that she owed her happiness, the most wonderful thing that had ever happened to her, to this man's whim. And now, how sure he was of her!

"I don't suppose . . ." she could hear him taunting.

She unclenched her fists, ran back to the desk, snatched up the pen and dipped it in the ink.

"Dear Moss' Jeff," she wrote furiously, and stopped again, thinking she heard a horse galloping. Dear Lord, all her life would she wait for that sound?

But her imagination had not tricked her this time. A few seconds of silence gave her time for doubt; then quick, sure steps that she would have been able to identify in a multitude of echoes crossed the boards of the gallery and the knocker clattered.

"Jefferson!"

Others must have waited nearer the outer door. Whoever admitted him was brushed aside by his entrance; and on the next instant he was in the parlor, gripping Varina's hands hard, as if he, too, had needed to be sure of her.

"Varina!"

He took her into his arms then and held her just as tightly.

"My girl . . . my girl! You are well?" he asked. "You are sure?"

"Jefferson, I am always well."

"You are not always well," he contradicted. "In November . . ."

"Oh, that!" she said deprecatingly. "My one adventure in fragility. It was nothing."

He would not agree that anything that befell her was nothing.

"Your mother—all of us were alarmed," he said. "Brother Joe . . ."

Yes, Brother Joe probably had taken fright again. She could smile readily at that.

"I was not allowed to come," Jefferson charged.

"You were busy electing a President," she reminded him.

"Oh, that!" he said in his turn. "I didn't elect him single-handed, you know. Anyhow, I would have dropped everything to come, if . . ."

"Would you, truly?" she parried. "Then I should have got right up and been well immediately."

"They would not have let me set foot in the house," he said, so plaintively that her heart was enriched with laughter. "I wasn't even informed until afterwards."

"That," she said gaily, "was the incredibly silly old doctor."

"But . . . what happened?"

"I fainted," she confessed. "If you can believe it, for no reason at all I fainted dead away."

"You're making light of a serious matter," he accused again. "I won't permit it. You're to tell me, Varina—everything."

That was how they were whenever they met in this year of constrained separation. "Tell me all that has happened while I've been away," their eyes, their lips, their hearts demanded. "Every little thing, mind. It's all vital because it happened to you."

He placed her now solicitously in a chair near the fire and he took another. He had to double his long length to accommodate it to the pretty rosewood piece, but he was not awkward in the act as he might have been. He had a grace, she thought, as if she had just made the discovery, that could suit itself to every circumstance.

And then she thought, with the turn of a knife in her heart, "Something has happened. It was not the slowness of boats that delayed him. Something important has happened and he is putting off the telling of it. He looks too grave. I wish he would smile. He would like to smile, too, to reassure me."

"What did the doctor give as a reason?" he demanded, going back to the trifle of this illness she had had in the fall.

"Why, the incredibly silly doctor," she said, "declared I'd had too much excitement, following the long, hot summer. He said, at my age . . . now, the idea of that! I'm full eighteen now."

"I know," he agreed, still too gravely. "You had a birthday in May. Another May you'll be nineteen. A tremendous age, but that's what time does to us. Now be serious. Where were you when you fainted?"

"In Granny's room, of all places," Varina said ruefully. "When I came to, they had put me in her big bed and there she stood at the foot of it, watching me; and I'll have you know, from that time forward she hardly took her eyes off of me. Every time I woke up, there she was, either at the foot of the bed or sitting in her chair beside it."

"Tell me," Jefferson prompted again, his lips twitching a little. He admired Granny Kempe a lot and . . . well, it was a right funny tale.

"There she stood," Varina continued.

" 'How are you feeling?' she asked, as frightened as anybody but determined she wouldn't show it.

" 'All right, I think,' I answered in a kind of dying cat squeak. I was some scared myself, as it happened. Even in the big bed, things kept slipping away.

" 'Likely you'd as well begin on the medicine then,' Granny said; and out she came with a big black bottle the doctor had left.

"It was the bitterest brew! I couldn't swallow a dose. I had to spit it out.

" 'Hm!' Granny said. 'You're a long way from dead or dying.' "

Was the twitching of Jefferson's lips going to be a smile? Presently, maybe, but not just yet. Varina smothered a sigh.

"And with that Granny pulled up her chair and sat down, and there she stayed."

"A week—your mother said you were in bed that long," Jefferson reminded her.

"Yes, indeed. The doctor said I must stay in bed a week and no company. So, a week it was. Then, seeing that I wasn't making much progress that way, Granny thought we should try something else.

"It was late in the afternoon of the seventh day. There had been a number of callers at the house. Granny, who had stepped out to say good-bye to the last of them, returned to her room and directed Flora-

bel and Zenobia, her maids, to fetch in a couple of hampers she'd left
in the hall. The girls did as they were told and came back with their
eyes rolling—the baskets were that heavy.

" 'Set out the stuff on the stand,' Granny ordered.

"But the table by the bed wouldn't hold one tenth of what was in
the hampers. There were bottles of all sizes and shapes. There were
covered bowls. There were boxes. Stiff paper pinched into envelopes
—for powders. There were bunches of dried herbs. There were bags,
sewed and attached to cords, for me to wear around my neck. The
litter covered the stand, a second table, and the dresser.

" 'The doctor said no visitors,' Granny explained, 'but everybody
from here to Memphis in one direction and New Orleans in the other
has called or sent or written. We didn't like to offend anyone by not
following the recommendations. So, there you are!' "

Hurrah! There was the smile at last.

"I never saw anything like it in my life," Varina declared joyfully,
"and the smell was indescribable—asafoetida, camphor, turpentine—it
was awful! And there was no getting away from any of it while I
remained in bed. So I got well immediately; and that's the whole story
—truly."

The smile burgeoned into laughter. Jefferson's eyes shone with the
delight she had stirred in him. In the adjacent rooms Varina could
hear a rustle of movement, where duennas in unknown numbers were
not exactly eavesdropping but could hear laughter well enough. She
could fancy the nods, smiles and raised eyebrows.

Then Jefferson's face was grave again.

"You are older," he said now.

"A long year," she agreed.

And was it then that he told her? It must have been then, for afterward, when the family gathered in the dining room and Varina cut
her cake, everyone knew and murmured and generally took on.

It seemed there was a vacant place in Congress. No, the vacancy
was impending. The choice of a new member from Mississippi would
not be made until much later in the year.

The National Congress this was—at Washington, the Capital.

"Goin' to trabel a far way, Young Miss ... goin' to live high ..."

All this talk of boats!

"Jefferson, are you glad?"

"I am both glad and sorry," he said. "There is no question that this is likely to alter all our plans for living. Life will not be the simple idyll I promised you—or myself."

"You won't build the new house at Brierfield now, will you?" she asked, knowing the answer.

"We will build it together presently—perhaps not right away."

Not right away. Not soon. The live oak shoot they had planted would grow to be a tree.

"But you wouldn't think of refusing the honor," she said.

"I couldn't." He left her side then and paced the floor here before the pretty white mantel and its fragrant fire. "I suppose I made my decision a year ago. It was a small gesture, I thought then, of no great importance; but the thing has grown and now to turn away would be to play the coward."

"I cannot imagine you a coward," she said.

"Varina, would you prefer that this had not happened?"

"I am a woman," she told him. "A woman is a creature of many fears."

"Not you."

"My share in you dwindles as this other thing grows."

"Varina . . ."

"That, of course, is my selfishness speaking."

"But you are not selfish. You . . . are an angel."

"The idea of that!" she scoffed, her heart torn a dozen ways. "It is high time, I think, that we join the family. They are waiting. They will want to hear."

To stand at a side table then, cutting her lovely cake with its sugar icing, while the others made much of her lover and his gifts of remembrance and his new distinction, was to try in a small way this business of sharing him. These people, however, were close to her. The multitudes—she had no doubt now that there would be multitudes—were strangers.

She kept her eyes on the broad, sharp knife and the pieces of cake that fell away, but she heard all that went on. Her father, who this year had forsaken the tenets of a lifetime to vote, with most other Mississippians, the Democratic way, would still tease Jefferson about his party.

"I understand that at the Convention this summer," he said, "they elected one chairman and eighteen vice-chairmen. One for each state represented. They had to do this, to keep peace."

"The sovereignty of the individual is the essence of the Democratic principle," Jefferson answered in the same tone of jest.

"Yes. Well, somebody has to speak for us, but I hope you are good at dodging missiles. It's rough road you're likely to travel and small thanks . . ."

"What if it is rough?" Granny Kempe demanded. "Sounds exciting to me. Reminds me the least bit of life when I was young. Sometimes I think I've grown old in a very dull way. I like a good fight."

By now, having cut enough cake to serve everyone twice, Varina laid down her knife and looked up—to find the eyes of everyone in the room on her—Jefferson's, tender, solicitous, fond, her father's fond in another way, but anxious, Granny's keen and searching, her mother's wondering.

"I declare," Varina said, "this is the first really secure minute I've enjoyed since I stirred this cake together this morning."

And the door knocker clattered again. Everyone jumped. Jefferson exclaimed in dismay.

"It's Purnell," he said. "I forgot to mention that I was expecting him. I forgot him, to be truthful."

Purnell was the name of friends in Natchez with whom Jefferson lodged whenever he could extend his visits over more than one day. They were also friends of the Howells, and Mr. Eli Purnell, Jefferson's particular friend, had been a frequent caller at The Briers. He was received cordially now and given his piece of cake and a glass of wine. He complimented Varina on the cake.

"Am I being premature and presumptuous," he added, "to offer more significant felicitations and good. wishes?"

But that, Varina knew, was not the purpose of his call. He had come to escort Jefferson in safety back to Natchez. Jefferson had traveled many a mile of lonesomer road alone before this, but now those who would further his career of service felt a responsibility. And that was how it would be—more and more. So little time for himself, for her . . .

"You'll be here for breakfast?" William Howell said when he was ready to leave. "We can settle our business then."

"I'll be here early," he promised, and found a moment, after all, to murmur his special good-bye to Varina.

"Your eyes are dark pools of trouble," he chided. "Are you really so distressed?"

"I care so much more than all these others," she said, "but they . . ."

"My dear! I know. Shall we look at it all again by daylight tomorrow?"

No, she would not spoil tomorrow, too!

"You must think I'm a silly," she said.

"I love you," he answered. "Good-night."

But it was not a good night. For much of it her sleep was troubled and fitful. That in itself provoked her. Since she had plainly lost half the battle, she might, at least, make sure of victory on the other flank. She did want to greet the next day and Jefferson serenely, with bright, clear eyes. A person who tosses instead of sleeping is never clear-eyed in the morning.

And yet, it is in the dark of night that fears become monsters. She did not know whether it was better to lie awake and reason with hers or go to sleep and have bad dreams. In one of these she was lost in a swamp. It was a dark and dreadful place—more dark and dreadful than any waste land she had ever seen, because its terrors were combined of shapes she had known and the fantastic hobgoblins of all the tales she had ever read or heard. Growth was dark and rank and thick. Curtains of moss and of snaky vines hung from every tree branch. The moss was clammy to the touch and she must not put her hand on a vine unless she was sure it was not a writhing serpent. In the poor light she could not rest body or hand against a tree trunk. What looked like the bole of a tree might not be that at all. At certain seasons of the year, always when the water was high, young snakes liked to roll themselves together in a ball, maybe a hundred at a time, and rest on a cypress knee or just hang on somewhere in that shape.

The water all about her feet was high and rising and there was no bottom. If she chunked a rock into it . . . there were no rocks, only herself and things that crept and crawled. Alligators boomed at her and the frogs never stopped. There was nobody to shoot the alligators and she had no gun or long pole to thrust down the throat of any that might crawl out of the water and come at her. She dared not step in any direction. The ground under her feet quaked and quivered horridly. The water waited to suck her down and swallow her.

She could only stand and shiver and quake and tremble and that did no good. Nobody ever got out of a swamp or a jungle or a bad dream that way. She knew that. The strange part was that she didn't seem to be herself. She was a white, thin, wraithy sort of being, with no stiffening in her spine and no real sense in her head. She couldn't be Varina Howell. Varina was not afraid of swamps. She knew about swamps. That was all nonsense about ponds having no bottom. Alligators and frogs wouldn't live in water with no bottom. Alligators didn't crawl out of the mud after people, and frogs never hurt anybody.

She wasn't Varina Howell. Varina wore stout shoes when she went woods-walking and she tried the ground with her foot before she put her weight upon it. She carried a stout stick and she kept her eyes open and alert for signs. She knew that if she found her way into a place there was a way out. There was a way out of this dark place, too. Varina could have found it. If she could just be Varina again!

Wishing helped. No stout stick materialized in her hands, but her spine stiffened. The ground seemed not quite so quaky. The frogs sort of hushed . . . and then she heard someone calling. It was a thin cry, far-off; but she heard it.

"Va-ree-na!"

Simultaneously she saw a pin prick of light in the darkness. She reached for the light and it disappeared. She tried to answer the call, but her throat closed. Frustration swept over her again. Of course. Because she was still that thin, wraithy creature, the call was not for her.

But it had to be for her or she was lost. There was something she could say or do that would make the beautiful name her name once more and bring back the light. With bursting heart she struggled for repossession of her world.

And the call came again: "Va-ree-na!"

Not for her? Of course it was for her. It was her mother calling. She must answer her mother. And she did. The words were put on her lips much as Granny Kempe had held the cup of herb tea.

Do not make yourself uneasy about me, dear mother. I am not afraid.

The words were magic. *I am not afraid.* The pin prick of light became a green path, laid down by sun shining through trees. She followed it out into the open and safety.

She awoke, sitting up in bed, the soft words still beating on her consciousness. But they were not her words. They belonged to another. She remembered distinctly now. That was what Knox Taylor had written to her mother as she left for Brierfield, a bride.

She clenched her fists. She would not be helped out of any morass by Knox Taylor. The help smacked of correction and reproof.

She clenched her fists, then slowly opened them. Who had a better right to show her the way than one who had gone to her death to prove her love? She lay back on her pillows relaxed and at peace. A couple of tears crept to the edges of her eyelids but did not fall. "Why, thank you, gentle spirit," she thought. "Thank you. I am sure you are most kind."

In seconds she was sound asleep.

In the morning her eyes were as bright as if they had been washed with dew. To see the anxiety of Jefferson's first look clear before this brightness gave her all the extra strength she needed. Demurely she took her place at the breakfast table and this rapturous business of setting a wedding date.

"Now," Jefferson said. "I am here and if Varina is ready . . ."

"Soon," Varina added, meaning, "Before I must climb another hard mile to reach some new eminence."

But her mother really decided.

"Not a minute before February," she declared. "After all there are certain preparations to be made."

Varina, about to speak up, held her peace. Her mother referred, she was certain, to the lovely dresses ordered from New Orleans. Well, they very likely would be needed now. Chiefly, of course, she wanted to see whether Jefferson, unaided, could cope in argument with her mother and Granny Kempe.

As she suspected, he could not. The date was set for February.

After breakfast Jefferson had an hour with William Howell in the latter's office. What they discussed Varina, for once in her life, did not ask to know. It seemed to her that new issues in her life and Jefferson's made property settlements, ownership of slaves and chattels, and contracts in general fairly insignificant.

She waited, with what patience she could summon, until Jefferson emerged. Her horse and his were ready at the steps. They mounted and rode until nearly noon.

"It is the last time," Varina thought, "the very last time that I, Varina Howell, free and a maid, shall ride so over these roads with him, my lord and my love. There will be other rides on other roads, in other places; and I shall be as happy—no doubt, much happier, if that is possible; but it will not be the same. Never the same again. Good-bye, dear Natchez country. Good-bye, Varina Howell. Good-bye!"

Part of the ride was a wild, free running. Part of the ride was sweet with joy borrowed of the future, the trees and vines of the old Trace arching over them, guaranteeing a minute or two of aloneness.

"Since we must add another month to the long waiting," Jefferson said in one of those quiet interludes, "I can be making a few preparations of my own. Shall we do the thing in the best style, with a honeymoon in New Orleans?"

"I am sure that will please everybody," Varina said demurely. "It is only fitting, I suppose, for a gentleman about to enter Congress."

"My darling," he said quickly, "is your aversion to a life of public service still so great?"

She pondered how she should answer that and finally she said on a whim,

"Jefferson, suppose I were to say that you must choose between that and me . . ."

"Varina, you wouldn't!"

"I am not saying what I would or would not. How would you choose? Answer me truthfully. It is very important."

"But I don't know just how to answer. It is important to me, too. It is a thing that has grown in importance all this past year. It is as I told you last night. I made my decision that long ago and now there is no turning back."

"Thank you, Mr. Davis. You have answered me very clearly. If it should come to a choice between me and serving your country, you would choose to serve the country."

"Varina . . ."

"You make me inexpressibly happy," she said. "If you had answered me in any other way, I think I could not have borne it—this morning. I, too, have had time to be ashamed of the timorous creature I have been. No, no, please, I mean every word. And so . . . a honeymoon in New Orleans, by all means. I shall be very happy contemplating it. And . . . will there be the usual round of family visits?"

She knew there would be.

"One, at least," he said. "Woodville, to see my mother. Our Ole Miss. I am afraid her time on earth is growing short now and she would want to see you before she goes."

"I shall be most proud to be presented to your mother. And what of Bayou Sara?"

"Varina, I wouldn't ask it of you."

"But you would like it, and so would I. Please. For I must tell you this, too. Your gentle spirit is not a haunt any more. She never will be again, I think."

Beyond this, however, she would do no explaining. Jefferson would find her dream childish, perhaps. She was afraid he might.

As a matter of fact, he was so deeply moved by her mere statement that he could hardly answer. He thanked her unsteadily, then went on to lead the conversation away by the first path that offered.

"It so happens," he said, "that General Taylor boarded my steamer last evening at Rodney. He is on his way to take command of a new Army Department based in Louisiana, in preparation against any trouble that may come of Texas."

"Did you have a pleasant meeting?" Varina asked.

"Very. I told him I hoped to marry soon. He offered me his felicitations and sent you his heartfelt best wishes. He is a fine old soldier —a fine old man."

They had another gallop then, to shake sorrow out of their happiness; and finally they walked their horses soberly toward home. When the spreading, friendly house was just visible among the trees, they made their last halt.

"Have you any idea," Jefferson asked, "how plainly The Briers can be seen from the river? As you approach from downstream, I mean? A landmark and a lodestar to me." He stepped his horse close to Varina's and laid his hand over hers tense on the leather. "Some day, my own girl, we will build our house at Brierfield. I've not forgotten.

I've even taken the first steps. I have cut down a few trees to open the view and John O'Connor has your rose cuttings laid by."

"Jefferson . . ."

"Some day," he repeated solemnly, "that house; and under its protecting roof a life of simple plenty and content—God grant that much to us some day!"

"Why, perhaps He will," Varina responded.

February . . . A year, almost to the day, after he had brought Varina home to The Briers from her visit to Hurricane, William Howell met Jefferson Davis at the Adams County Courthouse and gave his bond as her guardian, attesting her fitness to enter into a marriage contract; and Jefferson Davis gave his, attesting his fitness to take on the responsibilities of a husband; and a license was issued.

February . . . the grass was green at The Briers and daffodils and hyacinths were in bloom. White hyacinths filled the house with their waxen beauty and earthy fragrance. The camellias had passed their best blooming; but enough flowers remained for Varina to choose a white, half-open bud for her hair and a pink one for her bridesmaid, Cousin Margaret Sprague.

"I never saw such a change in anybody," Aunt Jenny said approvingly.

"She's still of this earth," Granny Kempe retorted.

In her room under the eaves, with the light coming through the green branches of the bay trees, Melissa dressed Varina for her wedding. The dress was a cloud of white on the bed. On the bolster lay a prayerbook bound in white kid, with a real lace handkerchief and a brief veil. Varina had fussed a little about the veil, wanting only the flower in her hair; but she had retreated before a scandalized outburst of dissension, and Melissa had achieved a simple mantilla arrangement that could be removed after the ceremony.

Melissa was brushing Varina's hair. Near by, in order to see, but far enough away to be respectful, stood Betsy, the pert young maid from Hurricane, Rhina Number Two's daughter, who had finished her training now and had been given to Varina for her own, a peace offering from Joseph Davis. For the preceding month he had showered her with attention—delicacies by every boat, a priceless shawl for her trousseau, jewelry, and now this sweet brown young thing to serve her always. Betsy had been at The Briers a week, taking final instruction from Margaret Howell and Melissa, bearing with the latter's acid temper marvelously. Melissa's day was passing. Hers was at the dawn.

"You watch real close how I do," Melissa said now. "It's heavy hair and it twists in yore hands."

"A horse's tail," Varina said softly.

Tears popped from Melissa's eyes and rolled down her cheeks.

"Miss V'rina, don'," she begged. "Don' say that evah again. It's the mos' beautiful black hair in Natchez or New O'leans or Washin'ton, either one. Ain' I keered fo' it ev'y day since you was bo'n almos'?"

Outside on the lawn there was soft, muted singing, with now and then a rich tenor or a high, true soprano raised in a sudden ecstatic line. The Negroes from every Kempe and Howell plantation were assembled there, waiting to see Ole Miss's granddaughter leave in her bridal "kerridge." It would be a day to remember.

"Let them sing," Varina said. "It's the only music I want."

So they sang. The house servants, of course, behaved more decorously. They had begun to gather early in the morning on the south gallery. They would watch the ceremony in the parlor through the windows.

Margaret Sprague knocked now on Varina's door. Melissa was in the act of settling the fragile white bodice into its exact position above the cloudy fullness of Varina's skirt. Margaret with her pink ribbons and pink flower looked like a rosebud herself, but she gasped when she saw Varina.

"Oh, Cousin!" she said.

So Varina knew she looked lovely for her wedding.

The ceremony was, as always, fleeting as a dream. The black and brown faces at the windows were a blur, the white ones in the pretty parlor only a shade more clear. Afterward she could remember Judge Winchester and her mother and Granny and Miss Amanda and Mary Bradford. Once she heard small Jane Howell speak out in childish wonder and heard young Maggie hush her. Joseph Davis stood on Jefferson's left; and young Joseph, pale and stiff, stood just behind them. The minister in his best surplice and stole waited before the marble mantel.

Everybody, somehow, looked pale and almost cold, it seemed to her, except Jefferson Davis. He was tensely alive to the moment and its significance. His voice was solemn as an organ note on the responses. She thought, "What is all this talk of birth and breeding? He is absolutely the noblest gentleman that I have ever known, that I shall ever know. Nobility shines from his eyes, rings through his words. Nobility is a thing one has or has not, regardless of lineage, for one may draw everything fine or everything gross from those who went before. He is more noble than I could be . . ."

The minister waited now for her to repeat her vows. A minute more and she was Jefferson Davis's wife, bell, book and candle; and the house servants were being marshalled toward the kitchen and then to the stairs to serve the wedding breakfast.

It was still too cold to serve the breakfast on the south gallery. The dining room would not accommodate the "few chosen guests." Only the double parlors upstairs would do. Afterward, Varina learned that half the people in Natchez were offended because they had not been invited to the wedding, but it seemed to her that everyone was there. An hour, another, passed in bright confusion—greetings, embraces, jests and tears; and, in the end, she went down to the boat hungry.

An odd sensation surely for a bride, dressed in fur-trimmed velvet coat of the latest pinched-waist and full skirt, with plumed bonnet and a muff to match, waiting on the steps to be handed into the carriage. It swung up the drive, and there sat her father on the high seat beside the grinning coachman. Nobody else should drive his child down to the boat. And Joe Howell and young Joe Davis had mounted horses to ride beside her down the river road. How lovely, how sweet! Was it time to go?

She looked at Jefferson. The petals of the camellia in his buttonhole were turning brown. The day was passing. He held out his hand, smiling. As she placed hers in it, from the river came the deep, imperative summons of a steamboat whistle.

"Oh!"

Nobody understood her hesitation or why she turned for a last look at the house, bright in the sunshine. She was only listening to an echo, remembering, as she would always remember. Nobody understood, that is, except possibly Jefferson Davis, who drew her with gentle urgency to the carriage and seated her there, then took his place beside her.

"Good-bye, darling!" Margaret Howell called. Granny stood on the top step, stiff and proud.

"Good-bye!" Varina's answering cry was lost in another shattering sound—the blast of cannon fire. What on earth . . .

"Quitman's Fencibles," William Howell said, pulling the reins tight on the team. "He was bound to send you off with a salute and the Captain probably gave him the word early, not knowing how many rounds he would think fitting."

The carriage rocked down the road to repeated cannon fire. Varina laid her hand on her husband's arm.

"Yes?" He bent his head to hear what she had to say.

"Nothing. It's a proud way to go, isn't it?"

"Do not make yourself uneasy about me. . . . I am not afraid."

Author's Note

This is the portrait of a young lady. In later years she became, I think, one of the great women of our national chronicle—the brilliant wife of one who was in turn Congressman, Cabinet Member, and Senator in the ante-bellum circle of the National Capital, later still a lovely, capable and distinguished First Lady of the Confederacy, and a heroic figure through long years of bitter defeat and loss. With all who know her story, I offer homage to those accomplishments; but my interest as a novelist is not so much in the years of momentous events as in the earlier ones when those traits of character were developing which made heroism the inevitable answer later to the demands of time and circumstance. I have limited the period of my story to the two years covered by Varina Howell's courtship and marriage, hoping that, when the last word has been said and the reader has stepped with her over the threshold into history, he will agree that here is one who might be expected many years afterward to walk five miles through deep mud and storm, carrying a year-old baby all the way, and offer in simple explanation these words: "my nurse being ill and my maid unwilling."

In working up the background of fact I read the usual yard-long list of books—history, personal correspondence and diaries, newspaper files and geography, cotton reports, politics and debate. More valuable to me than all this was my personal contact with Mississippi and Mississippians. I had visited the state before in connection with another story. I returned this time, to attempt the reconstruction of a picture when cotton was king. I traveled with notebook, camera, and interested and *observing companions down the river road through the plantation country during cotton harvest, bringing up finally at Natchez, where we had the privilege of being guests at "The Briers," Varina Howell's girlhood home, now the property of Mrs. William Winans Wall. I walked the bluff path, looking down on crumbling earth walls into bayou and river. I dreamed by noonday sunlight and evening moonlight on the long north gallery. I sat in the schoolhouse, under the moss hung trees, on the cistern platforms.*

We made our special pilgrimage of Natchez. It was not the season of formal entertainment; but the hospitality of the South is never below par, if it is offered at all. My deepest gratitude, of course, must go to Mrs. Wall for rebuilding "The Briers" from a state of post-war ruin. Next in line I owe thanks to her fellow members of the local chapter of the D.A.R. and the Garden Club of Natchez, all of whom opened their homes and their memories to us with equal generosity. I treasure and I used many of the anecdotes I heard those bright autumn days; but the most precious part of the experience was being allowed to sit by and listen to those ladies—with now and then a host as well as a hostess—"go on." They gave life and body to my picture. Then, the tour of the day over, we would come back to angel cake and Coke or sherry at "The Briers"; and Mrs. Wall would each evening unearth a new scrapbook or memento or record just as surely as Mabel, her ineffable and inexpressible cook, would turn out hot biscuit and grilled ham and café au lait the next morning for breakfast. If there is color and warmth in the story, I owe it to Mrs. Wall, her friends, and her servants.

The liberties I have taken in shaping the story are chiefly the shifting of minor dates—never by more than a few weeks—the enlargement of incident from the bare statistics of record, and the supplementing of the list of main characters by the invention of needed secondary people. In the interweaving of fact and fiction I strove hard to capture and establish an elusive but genuine truth of interpretation rather than to add anything to the already formidable list of annotated biographies. If I have done this and the story pleases, I am satisfied.

SHIRLEY SEIFERT